SILVER AND TIME

Merle King

Rudling House

Rudling House

Rudling House Publishing Limited
Suite 11480 145-157 St John Street London EC1V 4PY

www.rudlinghouse.com

Published in the UK in 2010 by Rudling House

A CIP catalogue record for this book is available from the
British Library

ISBN 978 0 9562760 1 8

Printed and bound in Great Britain by CPI Antony Rowe
Chippenham and Eastbourne

ABOUT THE AUTHOR

Merle King was born in Manchester. Her work includes features for newspapers, magazines and radio and her plays have been performed in England and Spain. She travelled Europe in a camper van with her partner, Peter, and has written *This Gypsy Life*, a book about their adventures. *Silver and Time* is her first novel. Merle now divides her time between visiting family and friends in England and life in Spain where she writes and enjoys walking the *paseo*.

THANKS

Thanks to Ole Dammegård for the cover design, Marc Anderson for the cover photograph and to Nuria Fernández and Rosa María Fernández for being in the picture. To Robina Lowry for her editing and Haim Tsur for his advice in historical research. To Liz for all her practical help, advice and encouragement.

TO PETER

Without whom this book would not have been written.

PROLOGUE

Smoke fills my nostrils, clogging up my throat. Flames are flickering along the wooden floor. I pull open the bedroom door but the landing is full of smoke blocking my way. Slamming closed the door, I run to the window and grab at the black grille but it won't budge. I'm trapped in my bedroom at the top of the burning house. The din of shouting and running footsteps rises from the street far below.

I hear a crashing up the stairs and – "*Venga venga!*" shouts from outside. "*Venga!* Come on now, quick!" A hand is reaching out for me. Putting my head down, I run towards the door – but no – wait. Fighting against the pulling arm, I lurch back into the room. I clasp the precious object to me as flames engulf the doorway.

PART ONE

CHAPTER ONE

ESTEPONA – PRESENT DAY

Wide-awake, Kate stared wildly around. The bedroom reeked of smoke with a hint of saffron. Was that a shadow in a long skirt hovering by the door? She pushed her head under the bedclothes, knuckles pressed tight together.

Stop imagining, Kate, be rational. There is no fire in the room, nobody is waiting to get you. It's the end of the bad dream. Calm down, lift your head out and look round. See, there's nothing and no-one there.

The door swung closed … but it was only a draught and the room was empty. Stop shaking.

But it didn't work. The fear and sadness was deep in her, along with the smoke. Kate wanted that precious object so much, whatever it was. It had to be connected with her coming here to Spain – wasn't there something in the nightmare in Spanish? There would be no peace until it was found. She staggered into the bathroom and stared in the mirror at her white face, two frown lines etched deep into her forehead. Pulling on her dressing gown, she crept down the long corridor and slumped onto one of the sofas in the living room, next to a chipped black and white spotted elephant. He gazed back at her with enormous eyes framed with painted eyelashes.

The fourth floor apartment of this six-storey block didn't help. It screamed cheap holiday rental with its artificial flowers and orange curtains. The lock on the French windows was broken. Rows of glasses were stacked in the kitchen cupboards awaiting wild drinking sprees, but there were only two sensible mugs and one was chipped. Unpleasant chemical smells wafted from the bathroom, and from the small bedroom window Kate counted fourteen working cranes. The Costa del Sol coastline was a vast building site. Her new life was an anti-climax.

When the college caretaker took early retirement and set off for a new life in Southern Spain, Kate had thought, typically, why not me? She'd missed promotion to Head of Department and the latest man in her life had left abruptly for another – younger – woman. She was alone again, a thirty-eight year old English and Drama teacher, the odd one out of the old gang. They were all cosily married except her. She knew her ex wasn't right, he didn't like dancing, walking in the hills and he loathed Abba and Chuck Berry. But the chemistry had been good between them and she couldn't bear to stay in Manchester where she might bump into him in all the old usual haunts – Café Rouge, Waterstone's, cinemas, the Trafford Centre.

She was looking for a meaning to life and love that continued to evade her. Kate's mates had rolled their eyes and called her unstable for years. On various push/pull whims she'd moved to St. Ives and back, the Lake District and back, Hebden Bridge and back. Even the West Coast of Ireland for two and a half non-stop rainy months and back. She'd had six teaching jobs in ten years ... so what now? Move to Spain? She went to a Spanish class two nights a week and was up to the subjunctive. The pull was strong.

Uncle Roger, retired builder and elder statesman of the family, helped her do it on a Sunday afternoon. He had two sensible children and umpteen grandchildren, but he was fond of Kate and tended to indulge her impulsive waywardness. While Aunt Susan prepared lunch, he poured himself a medicinal whiskey and gave his advice.

"Have a good time, Kate, get it out of your system. But don't burn your boats. Take a leave of absence from your job and let your house – don't sell it. Give it a try for six months and then come back. And don't just sunbathe."

"Yeah, yeah. I won't."

"And see a bit of the country. Get yourself to Cordoba."

Kate looked up, intrigued. "Why there?"

"When my mother lay dying," he continued, his eyes almost shut in concentration, "she gripped my hand and told me I must go back to Cordoba."

"Why did she say that?"

"Can't really remember now, my dear."

"Back to Cordoba," Kate mused.

Uncle Roger sighed. "It was your mother who was the restless spirit like you, but all she did was buy a caravan in the Lake District." They were silent, thinking of her parents.

Kate looked like her Mum. She had her big brown eyes, wide forehead and high cheekbones. Her hair was thick, brown and curly and she went for nipped-in waists and long full skirts. That was a tactful way of saying she was deeply bosomy and heading steadily past a size fourteen. Too much liking for pastries flavoured with the hint of saffron.

Both her parents had died early; Dad from lung cancer and Mum with a heart attack in her fifties. There was nothing to stop her.

Before she sold the house, deeply against Uncle's advice, Kate checked out her latest impulse with *The Book of Help* – a small book with a picture of a deserted beach, blue sky and one cloud on the cover. She'd found it in Waterstones Self-Help section on a lonely between-men-Sunday and which, in place of organised religion, she treated as a bible.

"Should I change my life again and go to Spain?" She stared at the cloud and opened the book at random. The reply was swift: 'GO FOR IT, GIRL.'

That was all Kate needed. She resigned her teaching post and sold up. Rented an apartment found on the Internet for six months minimum in a quaint sounding town called Estepona on the Costa del Sol. The money invested from the sale, plus the savings from her parents' estate, would help support her until she looked for a job, or came back. She took the ferry from Portsmouth to Bilbao, drove down through the plains and over the mountains in ten hours flat … cue the guitar plunking.

And this was it! Another mistake?

"No!" Ana gasps at the sight of them. She feels a draught of cold air and shivers in the low-necked wedding dress that Grandmother has made for her. She clutches Pedro's arm as the music stops abruptly, leaving Felipe's chords hanging in the air. Papa should not have done it. Do we all think the same? Ana jerks her head round the room to Mama, María, and Grandmother. They have stopped celebrating, eyes and thoughts now on the two candlesticks, radiant in the lamp light – and on the forbidden inscriptions. The sweet baked pastries, the lemonades and wines all are forgotten.

Papa, a well-established silversmith by trade, had been planning a secret. It was obvious by the way he'd been running off to the workshop early every morning for the last few weeks, even on Sundays after church. Sometimes he forgot to put his warm coat on, he was in such a hurry. And this was the result of his work, a beautiful gift for her to treasure all her married life.

"I do love them," Ana sighs to herself, "but how they frighten me."

Mama's face is pinched, her cheeks two scarlet spots, the way she looks when she is infuriated yet again with Papa. Her eyes flash angry signals at him. They are saying clearly: 'You wait until later, you foolish man.

You mean well, but you do not think of the danger in exposing yourself and all of us in this way.'

Above the sweet aroma of rosewater that pervades the room, Ana senses it. Another unseen presence nearby is looking over her shoulder, dancing beside her on her wedding day. Trying to warn her.

CHAPTER TWO

ESTEPONA – PRESENT DAY

The white and blue apartment block was enormous, a cross between an ocean liner and a hospital. A small patch of cultivated park stood to one side, with a fountain containing a collection of beer cans and coke tins but no water. Across the level crossing and round the corner was a pharmacy and a handy supermarket. Beyond was the hulk of a monstrous half-finished deserted development, accompanied by scaffolding and four motionless giant cranes. It towered over the little roundabout. Goodbye vision of quaint Estepona.

Kate wandered inside a nearby café where coffee machines gurgled and hassled girls shouted orders and then scurried, laden, to the tables. These were crammed with gangs of Spanish from the local offices, deep into their second breakfast of coffee, talk and smoke. Welcome to 'Real Spain.'

In her best, careful Spanish she asked for a fresh baguette. The little man with a goatee beard pushed the bread, crunchy hot, into a long paper bag. The heat of it warmed her hands and she hurried out of the café, away from the smoke.

Back on the balcony, munching and gazing out to sea, life seemed better. The lighthouse, with its dark honey-stone stem in front of her, was a welcome symbol of stability in her changed life. Beyond, a stupendous view stretched over the harbour and on to Gibraltar, and that mass beyond was Africa. How thrilling to look at two continents and know that she was sitting on the edge of one of them. Fishermen chugged out with their boats and a dog in one of the huts below started howling in Spanish. Hundreds of seagulls set off together from the beach, circling away over the sea. Hammering filled the air. A man working on a boat sang lustily as he went about his business.

Kate tripped upstairs to the roof. Eastwards stood the old town of Estepona with its church spire and medieval tower rising above the huddle of houses and red roofs. The long sandy bay curved round towards the large supermarket and a further cluster of building cranes. Behind town rose the mountains, waiting for her. She embraced her new life, amidst the seagulls, satellite dishes and washing lines.

"I need to find a man tra la ..." she sang as she pegged out clothes. Then she recalled the advice in her Self-Help books on combating insecurity, expectation and low self- esteem and changed the mantra to "I wonder if I'll find a man ... I could join a walking group. Maybe I'll find someone there."

It took sixteen minutes along the *paseo* – the promenade – to get into town. The locals eyed her up and down, mostly the pensioners in their caps and cardigans. A little old Spaniard crept by and whispered '*guapa*' as she swung past, which she knew meant 'beautiful.' An elderly man waved his stick from his position on the third bench along.

"*Eres de Estepona?*" he shouted and Kate smiled back and nodded '*Sí.*' Yes, she was from Estepona now. She wandered the narrow streets, found the English bookshop, stopped for a coffee and *tostadas* in a delightful leafy plaza and beamed at the world.

In the supermarket, the butcher with melting brown eyes cut up chicken fillets and pork cutlets to stow in the freezer compartment.

"*Algo más?*" he asked, knife dripping with blood at the ready. 'Anything else?'

"*No, nada más hoy.*" 'Nothing more today.' The days were a living Spanish lesson and Kate was on a high. As she approached the apartment block, a skinny man banged out of the front door and walked towards her. He had a blue cap stuck on his head, below which burst an eruption of untamed black frizzy hair; he wore crumpled baggy jeans and a stained grey anorak. He came right up to Kate, shouted loudly in her face and then pushed away violently. The danger and menace emanating from him set her heart racing.

I'm swirling down into a well of fear. People are staring at me, mouths drawn back into hideous grimaces; a man kicks out, pointing an accusing finger, the whole procession has stopped. Why are they all looking at me?

And it was gone. The street was back, the bus-stop where it should be on the right, with its broken glass panel. A stout dark woman sat on the bench, waiting for the bus as the man strode off, muttering to himself.

Kate's head was spinning, her hands shaking so much she could barely get her key into the front door lock of the building. What was that all about, those images she'd conjured up? Her chest was tight, she was left with a deep fear that yammered in her head and asked questions she couldn't answer. Who was that man? Why did he do that? What if he lived in her building and she bumped into him in that creepy car-park basement with its tortuous winding route round the columns, and lights that switched off after ten seconds? And most frightening – what was that memory he'd triggered? A sick feeling of loneliness and loss lay heavy on her stomach. She wished her Mum were still alive. Part of her wanted to catch the next flight straight back to Manchester.

Trembling, she let herself into the apartment and poured a large whiskey that Uncle Roger would be proud of. She sank back onto the creaky couch and allowed herself to remember. Okay: she'd always had a vivid imagination. When she was eight a little boy threw a lighted sparkler at her face on Bonfire Night. Her woolly scarf caught fire and burnt her throat. She'd had bad dreams for weeks after that and refused to go up to bed alone because she could see hot coals burning and swirling in the patterned red and black stair carpet. After a panic attack one night Mum finally took her to the doctor who did some tests, pronounced the little girl normal and consoled them by saying she wasn't a cabbage and should one day look for a career where she could put those creative talents to good use – hence, the English and Drama.

Kate touched the spot where she still had the scar. So the visions were her imagination again, working overtime – part of the settling-in process. She calmed down by preparing her favourite comfort supper of chicken and saffron. Took half a teaspoon of saffron threads, crushed them with a pestle and mortar and put them in a quarter cup of warm water. The spice went a deep golden colour that warmed her heart. She fried onion and garlic and added the chicken pieces and red pepper; poured the saffron infusion in with the chicken, a little stock, wine and bay leaf. The aroma was the main thing.

Loud shouting broke out below and she ran onto the balcony to see what was going on. An elderly woman was feeding the wild cats that occupied the patch of waste ground adjoining the back of the building. Three young boys had parked their bikes and were out there taunting the cats and throwing stones at them. The woman yelled at them and as Kate watched, the fear surged through her again. The boys continued to jeer while the cats sat like frozen rocks of feral fur. This had to be stopped and right now.

"You lot down there," she bellowed. Summoning up all of sixteen years' teaching experience with teenage lads who didn't want to do English and certainly not Drama, Kate could sound as powerful as was necessary. "Just stop that!" The noise reverberated round the port, taking in the ice factory, fishing boats, marina, shops and restaurants. Even the howling dog stopped momentarily to register the competition. Despite their lack of English, the boys got the point. They looked up, grabbed their bikes and cycled away and she felt a gleam of triumph. Covering the chicken to simmer, Kate nipped down to join the woman who was still furious, the pom-pom on her red and green beret bobbing in rhythm to her anger.

"I tell you, they are so ignorant," she grumbled.

Kate stood on the rough ground where cats roamed, black bin liners gathered and the occasional vagrant settled on his jacket for a swig of beer. They introduced themselves. The woman was Gertrude, from Austria.

"And I'm Kate, from England." She pointed upwards. "That's my apartment up there, fourth floor on the left."

"Ah, then we are neighbours, so it is you who is next door to me. I thought I heard you through the wall. You are new in the block, yes?"

"I've been here about a week."

"I tell you, Kate, the cats they are so funny and you know what? When I speak to them in German, they know what I am saying. The black and white one is so cute, I call her Nina. But they won't let me touch them." She bent down and lovingly ladled more of the brown stuff into plastic containers. The cats shrank away, tails straight up, when she tried to stroke them.

"Here, *schatzi*, darling, look," she crooned.

Gertrude was small with a firm body and thin brown hair sticking out from under her beret. She reminded Kate of somebody but she couldn't think who it was.

21

"You're so strong, I do admire you," she said. "Those boys are a nuisance."

"You have to be strong to live in Spain. You know what, I found a dead cat in the fountain last week? It was horrible."

"No! What did you do with it?"

"I put her in the bin, what else could I do?"

"How awful," Kate muttered in sympathy. As Gertrude scraped more food out of the tray, her beret slipped over one eye.

"I like your hat, it's so unusual."

Gertrude beamed. "I have this hat you know, all my life. My mother made me wear it when I went horse riding. Now all the girls look at it and they admire me." She peered close into Kate's face.

"I tell you, you trust nobody out here. And you don't put your washing on the roof, they come and steal it." Now Gertrude was going too far.

"I won't," Kate promised, patting her hand. She didn't dare tell Gertrude that she'd already done so and that her knickers were perfectly safe.

Kate smiled at her reflection in the mirror as the lift carried her upwards. Gertrude was still crooning to the cats when she reached her apartment. The sound made her feel more grounded, the contact with Gertrude giving her a much-needed feeling of safety, to counteract the lurking danger, imagined or real, emanating from that wild man in the street.

I'm running down the narrow street towards a closed door at the end. I know I'm going home but when I get there, I can't open the door. I hammer on it, please let me in … give it back to me. A girl laughs inside. How I hate that girl!

Kate woke again in the middle of the night. Cars bump bumped over the slow-down humps on the road far below, and music pounded over from the nearby port. The beat poured out from the clubs and bars nearby and the wind brought the noise of wild laughter and voices to the windows of her apartment.

CHAPTER THREE

CORDOBA – 1463

Rosita, the white kitten, stalks along the edge of the fountain and licks Ana's fingers.

"She's tickling me," she whispers, giggling at the soft wet touch. Rosita is like a little white rosebud and although she is Felipe's kitten, she follows Ana everywhere. Felipe doesn't mind. He is more concerned about his little stringed vihuela, a guitar-like instrument, that he received from Mama and Papa for his fifth birthday. He is trying so hard to play it properly and Grandmother is helping him to pluck the strings into a melody. When he practises, Ana loves to sing and dance round the living room, pointing her toes and moving to the rhythm – until María drowns out the music with her powerful, pure voice.

María pushes Rosita away. "She's a stupid cat!"

Although they are sisters, they do not look alike. María is tall for her eight and a half years, slim, with long straw-coloured hair and bright blue eyes that miss nothing. Seven-year-old Ana is a plump little dumpling with round rosy cheeks and two tight curly braids of hair caught back with red ribbons. Grandmother says she's the living image of herself as a child.

It is a warm Cordoban evening and pigeons flap lazily round the small plaza. The kitten balances with dainty paws on the stone edge of the fountain, her sharp eyes following the sparkling sprays of water spouting out of the carved cherub in the centre. Two women walk through the plaza, deep in discussion as Grandmother draws water from the well in a corner. María and Ana are playing with eight-year-old Pedro, their friend who lives nearby, across the wide main *calle* – the street. They throw small pebbles into the air and try to catch them on the back of their hands before they hit the ground – and before Rosita pounces on them. Ana hums as she tosses the stones. She is determined to beat María and for once she's winning.

As Ana collects the stones for her turn, a bunch of boys run loudly into the plaza and straight through the middle of their game. They knock Ana over and she falls, hitting her head against the side of the fountain wall. A large lad in torn grey trousers runs round kicking and scattering the stones and then he deliberately bumps into Grandmother. She is thrown off balance as she heaves up the creaking bucket. The water spills over and Grandmother is furious.

"How dare you! You stop this, do you hear!" She scolds the boys loudly and the kitten shrinks into a blob of fluff, hiding beneath Ana's long apron. The big boy sneers at Ana who stares at him fearfully. The bump on her head is beginning to throb.

"What are you goggling at?" he taunts her. "Is the old lady going to poison this well next?" The other boys titter. One of them crouches down close to Ana. He

25

puts his fingers up to the sides of his head and wiggles his hands at her derisively.

The leader picks up a stone and swings round, pretending to throw it at her. "Where are your horns, eh? And your furry tail?" he shouts. He twists and aims the sharp stone at Grandmother. Pedro springs between them and the stone hits him hard on the shoulder. The two boys grapple and Ana starts to cry. Her head is so painful.

"María!" she wails, clutching the kitten for comfort.

"Ana!" sings back her sister, mocking her tone exactly. María, who enjoys dramatic conflict and isn't frightened of anyone, relishes this encounter. She strides up to the ringleader and shouts right back at him.

"I know you. You leave us alone, do you hear or I'll tell the priest about you." Her hands are on her hips and her head is high. The boy pauses his attack and looks confused. A horse with a rider clatters down the street and into the plaza, and the boys run away with Pedro chasing after them. Grandmother is muttering as she lowers the bucket again. She draws up more water and marches off, grumbling down the alley to their house. The horse drinks noisily at the fountain and then is led away by his rider. Rubbing at his sore shoulder, Pedro returns, breathless. He is not afraid of bullies and won't be intimidated by lads he's known all his life.

Ana sits huddled, knees clutched up to her chest. "Why did they do that?" she whispers, rubbing away her tears.

"Don't cry." He kneels down, pushes his face up close to her and tickles her neck. Rosita picks her way

26

between them and walks off to inspect the fountain again.

"Ana, see this!" Pedro picks up a tiny stone and throws it lightly into the air. Leaning forward, his arms outstretched, head raised upwards, he catches the stone on the tip of his nose where it balances for a few seconds until he jerks his head down and traps it in his hand. Pedro enjoys playing the clown to make his friends laugh, but this time it doesn't work.

"My head hurts." Ana clings to María, who inspects the wound with older sister experience.

"It'll heal," she declares. She dips her handkerchief into the fountain water, squeezes it out and applies it firmly to the grazed area, wiping away the fine trail of blood. "I've seen that big boy at church, you know. His name is Luis."

"He's horrible."

"Pooh, he thinks he can do anything because he knows that once our family were Jews. They say Jews put bad things in the wells and caused the Black Death to come to Spain. So they say we're like devils, but they can say what they like."

Ana looks blankly at her. "But that has nothing to do with us." Why should they pick on me, she thinks. I'm a good Catholic girl, my name is Ramírez, my family have been Christian for many years. We are not Jewish now and it isn't right for that horrid boy to taunt me.

"Do stop fussing, they're just lads, that's all." With a toss of her long hair, María returns to playing with the stones.

This was no nightmare waking Kate up, this was the real thing. The high-pitched sound started in the middle of the night, shrilling into the apartment. It could have been a power drill, a baby crying or a puppy whining. She went out onto the balcony and looked round. Yellow lamps lit up the ground below, temporarily empty of cats. The port was deathly quiet so it wasn't coming from there. The fishing boats had long since chugged away from their moorings and were distant beams of light, far out at sea. Kate leant over the edge of the railing as far as she could, trying to see down to the balcony of the apartment below. A light shone out and the noise was coming from there.

At four-thirty Kate couldn't stand it any longer.

"Why can't you shut up!" she shouted loudly and knocked heavily on the floor with a long brush from the kitchen cupboard. The din stopped abruptly and silence fell for half an hour until the yapping, fretting, whining started up again. She'd been praying that the wild man wouldn't be her neighbour, and this is what she had instead – a menagerie. *The Book of Help* was useless.

"What shall I do now?" she asked it.

'JUMP INTO THE MOMENT,' it proclaimed. Which meant what, pray? Kate threw the book across the room in a petty rage and it fell open at 'YOU'LL BE SORRY FOR THAT.'

"I tell you what to do, you wear ear plugs, the wax ones are the best, you have to press and mould them." Kate was in Gertrude's apartment complaining about last night's din. Gertrude had heard nothing. Her place was the same design as Kate's but her bedroom faced eastwards over Estepona and the half-finished monstrosity next door. When the wind blew in, Gertrude got the full frontal whiff from the tip next to the lighthouse land. The cleaning machines were busy depositing rubbish there, where it fermented in smelly mountains until more big trucks with flashing lights bleeped their way past the fishermen's huts and toted it away. All the cranes and diggers were working.

"Do you think this'll be finished one day?" Kate asked, momentarily distracted by the throbbing activity outside.

"Hah! I have been here twenty-five years, since I retired from my work as a secretary and they have never stopped. You should have seen it then, a little village – but now!" Gertrude pointed at the lighthouse in front of them. "You know, a young man once lived there with his family. He used to do t'ai chi on the top balustrade. And he was so good-looking, the local girls gathered on the beach to watch him. They were all in love with him."

Seagulls and starlings jostled for space on the lighthouse railings and the stocky lighthouse man stomped around far below tending his vegetables, followed by his two little dogs who barked after the cats lazing on the corrugated roof. Kate watched the man and wished she could be as centred in her daily life as he appeared to be.

"I'd love to learn t'ai chi."

"I tell you, Kate, there will always be something – if not this, then something else. You don't live in Spain and expect peace and quiet. You have to accept. It could be worse."

The vast Mediterranean sea spread out to the south and behind town rose the Sierra Bermeja mountain range, glowing pink in the morning sun. The summit appeared so close and clear with its two transmitters on top. The clashing of these powerful forces of energy facing each other in close proximity could cause huge ripple effects on the environment and its inhabitants. The Spain of the Costa del Sol was a highly-charged mix of heaven and hideous.

"Maybe I'll get out, find somewhere quieter to live, more peaceful, perhaps in the mountains, away from all this. And grow vegetables."

Gertrude sighed and clicked her teeth. "Kate, you listen to me. This is what you do, you look the other way, you find other things."

"I was planning to start Spanish classes next week."

"Good. And you know, there is a very good *sevillana* dance class near the bus station. And now I go out early to my Flower Arranging." Gertrude swayed into her bedroom to put on lipstick and collect her red hat.

Kate's mother had passed her negative genes on to her daughter. She'd revelled in them.

"That's me and I can't change it," she'd announce with blithe unconcern when Kate was inwardly screeching her head off at her. So the cup was more than a little half empty. But Kate could bounce back. She liked making plans and writing them down, they helped to bring a semblance of order and control over her life. Back in her apartment she made a list of possible activities to help her look the other way: dance, Spanish, sports centre, swimming … and then she remembered something. Rummaging in the waste paper bin she retrieved the crumpled leaflet picked up at the bookshop in town. 'WALKING GROUP' it said. 'We meet the third Saturday in the month at Carrefour supermarket car park. 10 a.m. and bring sandwiches. Phone Jayne.' The timing and date was right for this weekend. *Sevillana* dance next week. Right now, Kate was getting out and going.

Luis, the ringleader, stands at the top of the street as Ana trots back from the bazaar, carrying a live chicken in her apron. Was he waiting for her? He knows where she lives. He moves towards her and she turns down their alley in order to avoid him. As she nears home, he runs and catches up with her, grabs her skirt and pulls her forward.

"What do you want of me!" Ana tries to wriggle out of his grasp.

"Squeak squeak little *marrana*, piglet poisoner!"

"Please stop," she begs. "Leave me alone!" Luis sneers and yanks hard at her pigtail. As Ana struggles, she drops the chicken which runs away, fussing and squawking. Then he releases her and walks off, whistling, towards the plaza. Ana stumbles the last few steps home and Mama has to chase the chicken up and down the street. When the bird is safely caught, Mama gathers the sobbing Ana in her arms.

"Analita, do not cry." Mama strokes her daughter's hair back from her forehead and twists her fingers round the long curly pigtails while Grandmother tuts quietly. She has been observing the chicken chase from the doorway.

"He called me a *marrana* piglet. What is that?" Ana whispers from the safe haven of Mama's lap. She is happy to have her undivided attention for once. Mama

32

is so occupied with them all, especially father, the biggest child in the family she says. Mama tends the family spice booth in the bazaar and organises the regular delivery of spices from the Port of Almería. Mama can do anything.

"They were nasty words, forget them, don't think of it now."

"And did the Jews really cause the Black Death?"

"That was a long time ago, little one, when many died from an illness that spread through the country." Mama's voice lifted. "They always try to blame the Jews but they forget that many Jews died then also." She pauses. "And as you know, our family once was Jewish but that was also long ago when we converted to Catholicism. Now we are *conversos*, good Christians. And you have your confirmation coming soon. Of course we are not Jews now. Do not forget that."

Mama's words help to comfort Ana but she is not stupid. Although their religion is Catholic, she knows their ways are different to the boys outside and to many of their neighbours. Even in the cold winter months they often have no fire burning on Friday nights and Saturdays.

On Fridays, Grandmother prepares the Catholic fish meal. When Elvira, their young servant goes home early, Grandmother often stops cooking the fish and makes a special supper of meat or chicken instead. Ana has seen her burn wool at the same time, so that nobody outside can smell the meat cooking. These rituals are part of their family life, but she doesn't know why they are done or what they signify. Grandmother tells her that

33

when she is older, she will understand. She always says that.

When the children are in bed, Papa takes Mama into the quiet inner courtyard.

"I want to talk to you about Ana," he says with a serious face. He sits on the chair beneath the orange tree in the centre of the patio while Mama collects the fallen oranges scattered on the ground.

"Beatriz, I am disturbed about Ana and I would like her to come to the synagogue with me. I have not been for a long while."

Mama looks up at Papa with a worried frown. "No! She is far too young."

"There is no law that forbids me to visit the old synagogue and take my daughter with me. As you well know, many of our *converso* friends continue to go, and I am not going to tell the whole world."

"But look at the trouble she is already having."

"She sees how we live here. And she has never been to the *Judería*, perhaps it will help her. I want to show her that the Jews are not monsters. And she will have to know where she comes from one day."

"Not yet, Antonio, it will confuse her more."

"I am sorry but I believe it is necessary now."

Mama is angry. She throws the oranges back onto the patio floor and walks away from Papa twisting her hands in her apron. Antonio is wrong. They must move away from the past, sever their links with the old religion once and for all. Why can he not see that?

CHAPTER FOUR

ESTEPONA – PRESENT DAY

A woman stood by the gate dangling a rucksack. Kate sidled towards her and risked a hesitant raised eyebrow.

"Here for the walk?" she asked before Kate did.

"Yes. Are you?"

"What do you think?" she retorted with a grin, indicating the rucksack. She was wearing laced-up boots, smart green combat trousers and a woolly jerkin in toning beige and green. She was tall and skinny, with slightly protruding teeth, blonde streaked hair shaped in a neat bob and lots of make-up – a strong tan foundation, shiny pink lipstick and thick brown eyeliner circling large enquiring eyes. They waited and chatted. She wasn't Jayne, she was Rosemary and she rambled regularly.

"It's great fun," she said in a husky deep voice, "especially if we're doing a long haul up. Not so good if the old ones come, dragging their dogs. Takes them hours, they've got to stop every other minute." Her large eyes peered into Kate's and she laughed a hoarse laugh, started to cough, took out a screwed-up tissue and blew her nose. Rosemary – call me Rosie, everyone does – was sporting large binoculars hanging from a strap round her neck.

"Where do you come from?" Kate asked.

"Outside Preston." Rosie stuffed the used tissue back in her pocket.

"I thought I recognised the accent. I'm from Manchester."

"That's nice, not far from where I was. Are you new out here?"

"It's been a couple of weeks now."

"It's fantastic isn't it," said Rosie, smiling.

"Wonderful."

A sort of affinity sprang up between them. Cars drew into the car park and men and women in walking boots and binoculars formed a group. They were now six dedicated walkers headed by tall, hefty Steve, a man in his mid-forties judging by the level and depth of the lines on his tanned forehead. He was a dominant looking alpha male with a loud voice obviously used to shouting commands. His body was sturdy and upright, enhanced by a broad face and a shaven head. A bright blue anorak and neck scarf matched his eyes. In manner if not in looks, he reminded Kate of her last boyfriend, and she couldn't help being attracted. The rest of the group introduced themselves. Val n' Pete, and little Christina from Sweden. There was no sign of Jayne.

"I nearly didn't come today," whispered Christina in a soft little voice. "Did you hear about the puma?"

"What puma?" chorused the rest of them.

"It's been on Spanish television. There is a puma roaming in the mountains between Gaucín and Ronda. Walkers have been warned."

Steve sighed heavily and tapped his fingers. "Okay now listen gang, don't be silly. It's a puma, it won't harm you, it's more frightened of you."

"What do we do if we see it?" Kate queried. She wasn't that keen on meeting a puma.

"We'll ring the Guardia Civil, I've got their number. Now, can we possibly make a move please? We're already late."

Steve rattled off in an old blue Saab and the group followed in a swift convoy of shared cars westwards down the N340 towards Sabinillas and then inland down a rough road that slunk under the motorway. They parked by an old farmhouse and commenced the walk down into the valley. A gaggle of scraggy, light brown goats greeted them as they crossed the river.

"*Cuántas cabras!*" called Rosie in a thick Spanish/Lancashire accent to the smoking, crooked peasant standing at the door of his shack. How many goats?

He raised three fingers and rasped "*Trescientas.*" Three hundred! Kate marvelled over the number as they squeezed through and continued up the opposite hillside, towards a *pueblo* – a small village shining in the distance.

The bushes of gorse grew heavier as the path narrowed and the hill turned into a sheer cliff with the Bermeja mountain range ahead to the right. They were climbing upwards, northwards scrabbling through the gorse in single file and Kate was getting cut and slashed to heaven. Had Steve brought first aid? What if a mist came down and they met the puma? Steve heard her mutterings and snorted loudly. He led them round a bend of the hill and they were out of the gorse line. A rough, high plateau stretched ahead with the white houses of the *pueblo* looming closer, its castle standing out on a rugged outcrop against the sky. The sea, Gibraltar, the African mountains, all were behind them.

Kate felt better as she strode out in the clear fresh air and chatted to Rosie who had the stamina to walk vigorously and talk non-stop at the same time. All Kate needed to do was nod, smile and say 'okay' and 'really?' at appropriate moments and with the right upward inflections. Rosie was about her age, thirty-eight, a house agent and enjoyed fun, friends and a good night out.

"Where do you go?"

"Anywhere, up and down the coast. And then there's this walking and the bird-watching, it's really fantastic, wouldn't miss it. I'm not saying I don't love the Costa, but it does do you good to get away into the mountains, see the wildlife in its own habitat. Reminds me of the Ribble estuary when I was a kid – but better."

"And have you been married?"

"Yeah, and divorced. He was bad news. Lives in London now. No children, no thanks Kate, couldn't be doing with them." Kate warmed to Rosie's honesty. They had their love of walking and their thirties singles life in common, plus they both came from the northwest. Rosie lived in a one bedroom, rented apartment along the coast past Sabinillas.

"And where are you staying?" she asked Kate.

"I'm renting by the port."

"Good lord, must be bloody noisy there."

"It is at the weekends. And a new problem has started with some nuisance below. But on the positive side, the views are extraordinary and it's so central. Right next to the *paseo*."

"The *paseo* is fantastic, tell me about it!" Rosie paused. "And are you looking to buy?"

Kate hesitated. "Well I could be. One minute I think it's what I want, living out here, then something goes wrong and I want to run back to England and be with everyone I've always known." She didn't mention the nightmares to this pleasant woman she'd only just met. She didn't want to appear too emotionally needy, it might put her off and she needed all the friends she could get.

"First things first, have you got a house to sell?" Rosie enquired. "It's no use looking if you're not ready. Owners tend not to like time-wasters. They're only interested if you're a ready buyer."

"My house in England is sold."

"So you've got the cash?"

"Yes. It's there if I want it but I couldn't think of buying until I'd got myself a job – oops!" Kate clutched Rosie's sleeve and almost lost her balance, stumbling over a large stone. Rosie heaved her up, arresting Kate's downward plunge towards the river.

"You daft thing," she shrieked. "Nearly had us both in!" She blew her nose again with the same grubby tissue. "Well, if you are looking, you've got to come to me," she continued. "We've a terrific selection and I can get you a fantastic price on anything you want."

"I'll think about it."

"Don't wait too long, the market's on your side at the moment. Hello, what's that?" With a long lolloping gait Rosie pushed ahead up the narrow track. "See that down there?" She called to Steve and directed his attention towards a large white bird with spindly legs standing in the river.

"Stop, everyone!" commanded Steve. The group whipped out their binoculars and they all froze in concentration. "What is it?" he asked challengingly.

"Yep, a cattle egret," stated Rosie.

"No, look again," said Steve. "It's got a black bill."

The group gazed on and Kate screwed up her eyes, feigning interest to be part of the gang. She made a mental note – must buy some binoculars on Monday.

"It's a little egret," chorused two or three voices.

"Correct." Steve fidgeted with his rucksack and pulled out a bottle of water.

"Okay, whatever," said Rosie.

Kate couldn't understand what all the fuss was about. It was just a big white bird.

They descended the hillside and re-crossed the river, stepping over large stones. An old ruined house stood deep in the valley.

"Hey, you guys, you know this place was probably destroyed and left abandoned in the Civil War," shouted Steve, demonstrating his knowledge of local history. He strode off to check the route and the group were allowed an eight minutes' food break, close by the

Roman aqueduct. Steve was far too macho to stop for lunch.

Kate devoured her egg and tomato sandwiches. Rosie perched next to her on an inflatable cushion produced from her rucksack and noisily ate her way through a packet of low-fat crisps followed by Werther's Original sweets.

"Substitute for ciggies," she said, coughing into a tissue and passing the bag around. "I never get fat."

She replenished the gloss on her pink lips as Val took photos through the arches of the valley, with the *pueblo* beyond.

Their approach led past the cemetery, sited next to the rubbish dump. A main street led up to the heart of the place. Kate withdrew from the chatter and let the others walk on ahead. The terraced houses with their flowery windowsills were all so familiar in this beautiful white village she'd never visited before. The sign for an artisan's shop dangled down a quiet alley on the right, and she was drawn to it. She had to go down to it, something was scratching and picking at her navy fleece and her soul.

Inside the shop it was musty cool with an abundance of goodies. Gold-framed paintings covered the walls and stood in piles on the floor. The top of an ivory painted chest of drawers was crammed with ornaments; plates painted in blue and yellow patterns filled the corners; linen hankies with frilled edges spilled out of the open drawers. A flamenco dress, red with white spots, dangled on its hanger. Rows of gold and silver ornaments adorned the far shelves and Kate's eyes wouldn't, couldn't leave them. Classical music played in the background, the sound of the violin haunting in its beauty and sadness.

"What is that music?" she asked the man reading behind a desk by the entrance. He had a pleasant, melancholy face, a longish nose, sad dark eyes and thick dark hair interspersed with streaks of silver grey. He reminded her slightly of a basset hound.

"It's Paganini."

"Do you have the CD?"

"No no, I am sorry." He smiled and closed his book. "It is not for sale."

She was trembling with cold on this warm day and Rosie stood at the door of the shop, hands sharp on hips.

"Kate, what are you doing? We've all been looking for you."

"Could you wait a minute, please?"

"Sorry, but we're moving on."

Kate had to stay here. She ran to the shelves and searched along, sniffing and shifting ornaments around, hoping she'd find the something that should be, had to be there for her. The man in his grey wool sweater and tartan scarf knotted neatly round his neck, looked at her with an enquiring expression.

"Do come on." Rosie was impatient. She pulled her away from the man, the sadness, the music, the silver ornaments. And from the subtle smell of smoke and spice in the air. And Kate knew what it reminded her of – the shop had the same smoky aura as her nightmare. And yet the association here was benign rather than terrifying. She reversed reluctantly out of the doorway and the smiling man returned to his book.

In the central plaza a chorus line of elderly men in caps and jackets filled the benches, walking sticks between their legs. A smattering of tourists sat outside a café drinking in the sun and the local life.

"Ah, she's here at last, let's get moving, you guys," commanded Steve from the café entrance. He shepherded them inside and up to an open terrace on the top floor where he ordered coffee in spot-on Spanish, his arm round the shoulder of the owner.

"Anyone have any problems if I smoke?" he shouted, waving his cigar.

"Yes, me, if you don't mind," Kate called, putting her hand up. Steve shrugged and put the cigar away.

This was the best part of the day, breezy and clear, with views of the surrounding mountains and distant sea. The group relaxed in after-walk satisfaction and spread round the table to chat about themselves. Jayne used to lead the walks until she went off to Portugal. Scottish Val n' Pete had a large villa with a heated pool where she swam naked day and night, all year long. Christina, the Swedish lady with the puma story, came from the other side of Marbella where she lived on the eleventh floor of a tower block and climbed the stairs twice a day for exercise. Even with her shopping

"So, do you like it? Will you come again?" Rosie whispered into Kate's ear while the others argued with Steve over the bill. He wanted to pay it all.

"Yes I will, the mountains are marvellous, this *pueblo* and the plaza, it's all so spiritual and invigorating, so different from the coast …" Kate burbled on. She could live up here.

"That's an impressive list," said Rosie. And Kate hadn't even mentioned the little shop.

"What about us lot?" Rosie continued. She indicated Steve with a discreet nod of the head. "He's so knowledgeable about the area but he can drive people mad. I know. He even does my head in sometimes."

"No, he's a character, you're all lovely as well," Kate hedged, giving nothing away. Rosie coughed and blew her nose again.

"Listen, I'm off to Madrid for a week on business. I'll get in touch with you soon as I get back and we'll meet up. There's some fantastic properties to show you." They exchanged mobile numbers. Val insisted on taking a group picture and as they huddled together Steve put his arm round Kate and their heads moved closer, almost like a couple. This was the first time she'd been at peace since arriving in Spain. There were no clashing forces of nature up in the mountains. Large birds circled the castle and the crags.

"Those are griffon vultures," said Rosie. "They nest on the rocks of the Crestallina, we did that last time." She pointed to the distinctive ridge of jagged peaks behind us. "Great walk. We normally do seven hours."

"This was enough for me."

"It's not over yet, we've got to get down."

"You're joking?"

"How did you think we'd get back then?"

"Of course, I hadn't thought of that!"

Going back was easier, steadily downhill with the wind blowing towards Africa. Steve zipped up his jacket, stuck his hands in his pockets and walked with Kate. Rosie was chatting with Val n' Pete behind.

"So what are you doing out here?" he demanded loudly as they marched along at a cracking pace. "You're far too young to be wasting your time playing. Or can you afford to play?"

Kate tried not to resent his tone. "I will get myself some work eventually," she replied in a firm, gentle voice in an attempt to counteract his arrogant condescension. "Probably teaching, but no, I don't need to, not yet."

"You're lucky."

"Well I sold my house, so I'm giving myself a little break. Living it up, throwing myself into Spanish life and culture. To see what sticks. It's a gut reaction that I should be out here. But it's difficult."

"What's difficult in this paradise?"

"Well, the language for a start."

"I've lived here for fifteen years, haven't had a Spanish lesson in my life and I can get by." Kate wittered on about the headache of using the subjunctive.

"They don't mind if you get it a bit wrong." Wrong was *equivocado*. Or was it *un error*? Needed to check. She knew *pinza* was a peg.

"The Spanish are wonderful," he declared, pulling out to avoid six gorse bushes. "I don't go along with those people who bury themselves in poxy little ghettoes and say they hate the Spanish. I say this: if they hate the Spanish, then don't come here."

45

"They come for the sun, the *sol*, the golf, the fun, the eating out, the Costa glitz." Steve nodded in agreement and she was relieved that they'd managed to find some common ground. "And the relaxed life-style," she continued. Though so far she'd found it anything but relaxing.

"The Spanish are hard-working," declared Steve, "because they're lazy."

"That sounds like a paradox."

"Yeah, whatever that is. They're like happy children. All they want to do is have fun in the sun. They work hard so it will be finished and then they can enjoy themselves."

"And what do you do out here?" It was about time she took command of this man and showed him she could be feisty.

"Was in the navy, then came out here to run a boat accessory business."

"And now?"

He shrugged. "This and that. I do some work down at the port on one or two of the yachts. Mostly that big one by the tower."

"Yes, I've noticed it. Think I can see it from my balcony."

"Matter of fact I'm writing a book about the wild-life of the area, coast and inland."

"Gosh, are you? How interesting." He shrugged again.

"And do you live in Estepona?"

"Here and there," he said and and stopped talking. He stared straight ahead as they marched on in silence.

46

"Hey," he said, from nowhere. "Why don't we meet up one morning for a coffee? I'm at the café on the right corner of the main plaza in town most mornings from twelve-thirty. It's closed on Wednesdays."

"Sure. Why not." She was flustered by the old surge of adrenalin. She knew, because Rosie had informed her in the toilets, that Steve was presently partner-less.

"I'll call you. Full name?" He produced a small pad and pen from his trouser pocket.

"Kate Mason."

"And numbers please, landline, mobile and email. And your address, plus postcode."

She stammered out her details, mesmerised by his force and blue eyes.

"And this is me." Steve thrust a small card at her containing his mobile number, and his name, Steven R. Hickson – nothing else.

"Hey you guys, all up for it next month?" barked Steve to the group. The group barked back in agreement.

Kate joined Gertrude on the waste ground along with the dog dirt, broken glass and empty beer cans. The six cats stalked the territory as if they owned it. She was aching but aglow with exercise, mountain air and more than a little bit of Steve.

"Here, *schatzi*, little one, come here …" Gertrude crooned to her cat family. "Will you look at Nina. She is so cute." Nina rubbed sensuously round Gertrude's legs. Gertrude stretched out a questing hand to stroke her and Nina grudgingly permitted it for a moment.

"I met some rather interesting people today," Kate said, begging for attention. Her life was at least as interesting as Nina's. "Steve and Rosie. Do you know them?" Gertrude looked up sharply from the cats.

"The one with the shaved head who works on the boats? Yes, I know him. And her."

"They seem very interesting."

"I tell you Kate, you trust nobody out here."

"Not even Steve?"

Gertrude continued to feed the cats, pretending she hadn't heard.

"Do you mean Steve?" Kate persisted, following Gertrude round as she rinsed the pan and poured milk mixture into it.

"Gertrude?"

Her head bobbed up. "You know what, Kate. You be careful."

On Saturday, they slip out of the house early. Mama is wearing a shawl that covers her head and shoulders, and she holds Ana firmly by the hand. Papa hurries them along the *calles* – the streets, through the *Judería* Gate and into the walled Jewish Quarter. María has refused to go with them. Secretly, she has peeped inside the *Judería* once or twice, to see what it is like. She hates the old Jews, the noisy chatter and the overpowering stink of onion and garlic.

Behind the walls of the *Judería* sprawls a different world of noisy, cramped streets full of men with long cloaks and straggly beards. To Ana it seems that they all know each other, talking and calling across the street as if they were cousins, uncles, aunts who have grown up in the same neighbourhood.

Ana and Mama join the women upstairs in the gallery of the small synagogue and Ana watches Papa below, sitting with the men. They are wearing long shawls with tassels and praying in an unfamiliar language she has never heard before. After the service a man puts his hand on Papa's shoulder and embraces him, as if he is an old friend who worships regularly with them.

"*Shalom!*"

"*Shalom!*" Papa is beaming at everyone, obviously delighted to be part of the Jewish prayer and the comradeship of the synagogue. Mama taps her feet and

49

sighs. She is ill at ease in the old Jewish community, anxious to get out of the Quarter. Yet despite her mother's restlessness, Ana loves the ancient building and feels at home amongst these alien people talking in a foreign language that Papa says is Hebrew. She walks home beside him and smiles at the people in the street who stop to acknowledge her father. But what are they doing there if they are Christian? She cannot be both.

The next day at Mass, the priest reads from the Bible in Latin and then explains his text to the congregation. As they line up to take the Holy Wafer, Ana senses an atmosphere in the church, an uneasiness emanating from the stone walls and cold floor. For the first time, she feels uncomfortable there. I liked it better in the other place, she thinks. She shivers and clutches Grandmother's hand.

María is happy. She prays and sings the hymns in her powerful clear voice and takes the Sacrament with fervour. She wants everyone to see what a good Christian girl she is, eager to embrace the processions, the ceremonies, the worshipping of the Christ figure. But María is sly. When Mama's eyes are cast down onto her prayer book, she exchanges glances with Luis, the boy who attacked them by the fountain.

CHAPTER FIVE

ESTEPONA – PRESENT DAY

Loud door bangings erupted from below, waking her up. Two men were leaning over the balcony, smoking and shouting at each other, a dog fussing at their heels. Then the music started. It was the heaviest, most powerful music, with that throbbing, tortuous beat so beloved of the Port bars between two and five on a weekend morning. But now it was all coming from the apartment beneath her. Despite every shutter flung down, every window closed, every blanket over her head, the din went on all night long. Kate was deeply devastated and this time it was much worse than before. The earplugs made not a wax blob of difference.

At first light she was back in Gertrude's apartment again, almost weeping. Even hard-of-hearing Gertrude had been disturbed by the noise. It shouldn't be allowed. It was against the rules of the Community, which stated clearly 'No Animals' and that the hours of rest must be respected.

"I tell you Kate, this is what you do. You put on your own loud music at six o'clock in the morning when they go to bed and you stomp around in your high heels. That will teach them." But Kate wasn't made like that and she didn't wear high heels.

The mobile rang as she was getting dressed. It wasn't Steve.

"Hi Kate, Rosie here, where are you?"

"At home, I slept badly."

"I'm back from Madrid, and down at the Estepona office. Do you fancy coffee and a *paseo* walk?"

"Yes!" Kate's spirit lifted at the prospect of a walk into town. And she'd buy that pair of cheap binoculars from the supermarket on the way in.

The hot early December sun beat down on the terrace of the café. Holidaymakers strolled by in shorts, T-shirts and sunglasses. All the Spanish shuffled past in dark clothes, thick jackets and boots because it was now their winter. Kate and Rosie were somewhere in between, not tourists but not authentic locals. Kate was cosy in a long black skirt, little lace-up boots and cream anorak. Tight elegant jeans encased Rosie's legs, topped by a bronze leather jacket. She wore huge gold earrings with a gold necklace and bangles to match. Her teeth were a trifle too large, her lipstick too shiny, and her face too thin and gaunt for beauty, but she was striking. And in sharp work mode, in contrast to Kate's wilting, drooping self. Rosie ordered an *americano*.

"*Un café descafeinado de máquina con leche para mí,*" Kate requested in her best *español*. A mouthful to say but it was good practice and necessary. She loved the frothy coffee from the machine but Spanish real coffee was too strong for her. And if she didn't stipulate the machine, it was a glass of hot milk and a little packet of decaff to sprinkle over it, with no Spanish atmosphere at all.

Rosie produced the usual torn tissue from her pocket and blew her nose. "Not got rid of that cold yet and Madrid didn't help, bloody freezing up there. Now, have you decided – are you serious about looking for a place out here."

"I can't stand what's going on much longer."

"Yeah, well shall we get started." She pulled out piles of papers from her case and spread them out. "What are you looking for and how much can you go to?"

"It's difficult to say just like that. There are lots of factors to be considered."

"Honestly Kate, you want to get out of that place and quick if you've got problems. They won't get any better. And like I said, the market is pretty favourable to buyers at the moment." She leant back, put her arms behind her head and grinned winningly. "I can so see you in a town-house. Your own little patio, oodles of bougainvillea, fantastic, yeah? You want to get on with it."

Rosie's picture sounded like heaven: a peaceful home, her own space ... maybe an orange tree. The adrenalin was stirring again, the urge growing to up and go to the next place which had to be better – and she did have a weakness for houses and looking at them. It was a genetic link straight to Uncle Roger who loved building them.

"It sounds so tempting. But I can't think straight today."

"Don't want to pressure you," murmured Rosie. "You do sound a bit down."

"When things go wrong and you're out here on your own, it's not like home is it? That's when I get homesick."

"You're so right. That's when you miss your good friends, family, people you've known all your life, who you can trust. You know where you are with them."

"Exactly. That's just how it is."

"You've always got me, you know. Don't forget that."

"Thanks, Rosie." Kate leant forward and pressed her hand. She was moved by Rosie's unaccustomed sympathy. "You're making me feel so much better."

Rosie pulled a face. "Let's not get soppy. How about that *paseo* walk?"

"Come on, let's go."

Rosie pushed all the stuff back in again as Kate paid the bill for them both – Rosie's turn next time.

"How long have you been out here?" Kate asked as they strolled along in step, walking westward towards the Port. She was learning it was the first question the ex-pats asked each other.

"On the Costa del Sol about four years now." Rosie linked Kate's arm. "I wanted to travel as soon as I left school, took a diploma in travel and tourism at college, that's what got me here in the first place. You name it, I've done it: house-sitting, direct selling, private tutoring. Even did some bar-work and that, believe me, is the pits. So I've been working at this estate agency for eighteen months, last six in the Estepona office. It's not bad, hard work though, I don't like doing weekends. What about you?"

"I've been an English and Drama teacher for years. That can be hard too."

"Do you like teaching?"

"It has got worse lately, no doubt. But yes, I suppose I do. It's a challenge and it's great when you get through to the students with *Macbeth* or *Brave New World* and they can relate it to their own lives."

"I bet you're a good teacher. Do you miss it?"

"Not yet I don't." They walked on. "What's your apartment like?"

"Kate – don't even go there. Grotty in miniature is a kind description. They said there was a view of the sea, what a laugh! If you lean off the balcony you can just about see it through the gaps between the buildings. I'd give the world to be in a decent place, with a bit of land so I could have a garden at least. But I don't mind." Rosie's voice became deliberately upbeat. "I'd want to stay in this area for the birds and the walks. Though I wish there was more going on."

There seemed plenty to Kate. "We could start a cultural centre here if we had the money," she remarked casually. Rosie stopped walking and faced Kate, her eyes bright with interest.

"That's a really great idea. We'd have quiz nights, jazz, bingo, rock bands, Karaoke …"

"Wait a minute," Kate said, laughing. "Not much culture in all that."

"What do you suggest then?"

"Well – a book club, discussion forum, writing groups, even a choir, perhaps."

Rosie frowned. "Sounds a bit grim, I'm not sure if we'd get the punters."

"We could have a mixture of high and lowbrow," Kate said, playing along with her. "But there's a lot of hard work in it."

"Don't kid yourself, all we need are the premises, we could put on shows, make some money, it'd pay for itself, you leave it to me. I'll have a good look round."

"And we could run it together." Kate was swept along with Rosie's enthusiasm. What had she started?

"Hello! What are those?" Rosie exclaimed, peering at a cluster of black flapping things crossing the Mediterranean. Kate produced her new binoculars from their bag and Rosie grabbed them and focussed. "I think they're cormorants, yeah, flying low over the water. They're looking for fish."

Kate followed their heavy flapping flight across the bay. It was a magical moment with anything possible on this bright Costa weekend morning, even a cultural centre. And the *paseo* was the queen of it all, the best anti-depressant there was. They should manufacture it in pill-form and who cared if it was addictive. And she was part of it, part of this glorious Andalusian day with its plump holiday pensioners sitting on benches holding hands and raising their starved-of-the-sun faces up to the sky. Teenagers performed handstands on the beach. Young, dark-haired husbands were on the weekend pram push with their babies. Tiny dogs pattered importantly by, children shouted on the swings and roller-bladed up and down the pink and grey tiles. Babies, old men, dogs, mamas, all strolling the *paseo*.

Oranges danced in the trees of the plazas. To the left lay the sea, to the right the Sierra Bermeja mountain, both accepting each other's proximity without any clashing forces this morning. The church spire, surrounded by scaffolding, stuck out of the maze of the old town. Building cranes and magic combined.

This is why I'm here, thought Kate. She stopped to watch a child playing with some pebbles on the edge of the *paseo*. Deep in concentration, the little girl lifted the stones into the air, clutched them tightly and then let them trickle and clatter onto the ground. A woman with a shawl round her head was sitting on the low wall nearby. She stared at Kate with huge eyes. Kate gasped at the sight of her.

A memory was trying to grab her and it wasn't a good one. Was it connected to Gertrude and those boys throwing stones at the cats? No, it was further back than that and surrounded by a child's fear. She could see the creamy colour of her linen apron, sense the heavy texture of dark hair against her neck. Feel her terror – no – stop!

Kate closed her eyes and yanked the memory out of some corner of her subconscious, tore it into tatters and threw it in the nearest rubbish bin.

Rosie was still intent on the birds. She was moving the binoculars around, trying to adjust them. "Honestly, these are lousy! Why did you get such cheap ones?"

"Rosie – please tell me, can you see that child on the *paseo*, by the wall?"

"No. What child?"

"Can you see that woman with the shawl?" Please let this woman be real, not imaginary.

Rosie moved her binoculars. "Yes, course. She's over there." She pointed to a woman walking away from them, holding a small child by the hand. The shawl covered the woman's back. The child turned round to look at Kate, her startled brown eyes meeting hers. As Kate stared back, the child flung a pebble onto the beach, pulled away from the woman and ran ahead of her, down the *paseo*.

"Why the fuss?" said Rosie. "Do you know her?"

"No." Kate felt foolish and she couldn't explain it.

"So shall we walk to my car and go now?" asked Rosie, stuffing Kate's binoculars back into their cheap case.

"What?" She'd been so involved with the child and the pebbles, she hadn't been paying attention to Rosie.

"For heaven's sake, stop dreaming, Kate."

"Yes, right." They were off, apparently at her urgent request which she didn't recall making, to view a fantastic development of beautiful town houses just on the market that were absolutely perfect. The image of the woman with the shawl and the child faded further away.

Rosie's sleek surface elegance didn't extend to her car, an old noisy Seat garnished with a few rusty dents and littered inside with Werther Original toffee wrappers. She handed over a sweet and they rattled off. Their destination was five minutes' drive out of town and up a newly constructed road with shiny lamp posts at regular intervals and little else. To the right lay the half-finished development. To the left, land was being mercilessly cleared for a golf course complex, clubhouse and luxurious townhouses. It was a hideous sight.

Beyond the row of joyous flags proclaiming the 'Latest Development For Your Dream Life In The Sun' Kate counted six cranes, four bulldozers, and armies of men in helmets hard at work, although it was a Saturday. Some of the Phase Two properties further along were completed, displaying their newly glazed windows. The phase that Rosie led her to would be finished in six months, a year behind schedule.

"But this is so ugly." Kate was shocked at the blatant devastation of natural beauty, all in the cause of dream houses being constructed above, behind, below them. Rosie seethed at her lack of appreciation.

"Why don't you use that imagination and think what it'll be like when it's finished. Two bedrooms, both with fully tiled en suite bathrooms, two large terraces, twenty-five square metre patio, air-con, split-level dining-room, real fireplace, private parking, landscaped gardens, two communal pools, tennis courts, gated community and it'll have a fantastic view of Gibraltar. And it's all off-plan which means it's a bloody good investment if you should want to sell."

Kate managed to break into Rosie's pitch. "And all I have to do is pay for it before it's finished?"

"At a vastly reduced price."

"Well …" Kate tried to be diplomatic, "it isn't that I'm not grateful. But I would want an established area,

59

pretty and green, not too far out of town and the local life. I do like to be able to walk to the shops."

"Right, no problem, why didn't you say, I know what you mean, leave it to me." They drove down to Sabinillas for yet another beachfront coffee that Kate paid for. "And I've got some old binoculars I'll let you have," Rosie promised airily, turning on the charm again. "Anything's better than that pair."

I'm lucky to have a friend like Rosie, Kate told herself, as off they dashed back through Estepona and San Pedro to the cinema at Banus in time to catch the film that was showing, just two days behind England. And then on to an Italian restaurant on the Golden Mile for a noisy pasta surrounded by a bevy of Rosie's lively women friends, followed by a pop-in to a smart hotel for the dinner jazz. Rosie introduced Kate to the musicians, the disc jockey, the crowd and the waiters.

"There's a really good concert and dinner there, first Tuesday of the month," she said as she drove back to Estepona. Kate was dizzy with caffeine, booze, Werther's Originals and the socialising Costa life. Rosie was great company and managed to give the impression that it was all happening round her and she'd be a fool to miss out on the action. So they marked the concert evening down in their diaries. Along with dining clubs, film nights, pub quiz nights on the first Friday, second Saturday or third Thursday of the month. They weren't lacking anything except some peace and quiet – and a cultural centre.

"How about a night-cap at the port?" shouted Rosie above the engine rattle of her car.

"Rosie! I'm exhausted." The morning's coffee had lasted over twelve hours.

"Come on!" Rosie hooted and accelerated in impatience to pass the dawdling car in front. "Really Kate, You have to put yourself about, establish yourself."

"Excuse me, what have we been doing all day?"

"You can still widen your circle of comfort."

Kate dug the nail of one thumb into the flesh of the other to release her frustration.

"Please don't tell me what to do." Rosie's non-stop energy, warmth and zest for life inspired her. But she was beginning to resent and even dread her swift impatience and rough, controlling behaviour.

"Listen Rosie: I'm coming to the music with you, I'll probably buy a house from you and who knows, we may even start a cultural centre – but no more for tonight!"

Was this what she'd changed her life for, to follow this woman and do her bidding?

The morning seemed a century ago. Kate sank into the balcony chair and let her mind stop racing. She thought again of the child she'd seen on the *paseo*. There wasn't a sound from below. The moon was up, the sea silent and unruffled except for a mass of round humps that rose and fell out of the water. The grey shapes, lit up by the moonlight, could possibly be a school of dolphins. How incredible it would be to see them! As she turned to nip back into the apartment for the despised binoculars, she looked down once more.

A girl was hurrying along the path, lit up by the yellow glow of the street lamp. She wore a long skirt with a dark cloak over it and she was carrying a bundle in her arms. As Kate watched, the girl stopped and looked up at her. Kate could see her set face, her intensity, the fair hair hanging to her shoulders. Then she hurried away. The quick clatter of her shoes on the ground echoed up to the balcony as she rounded the corner and was gone.

Kate knew that girl with the long soft hair and the sway of the long skirt. She'd heard her laughter before. And what was that object she was holding?

CHAPTER SIX

ESTEPONA – PRESENT DAY

Kate joined a *sevillana* dance class on Tuesdays and Thursdays at a gymnasium near the bus station. She also enrolled at a Spanish class on Tuesdays (before *sevillana*) and Fridays at an academy in a pretty square in town. Tutor Lali was round and cheerful with a loud voice, tight brown trousers, a bulging sweater and thin-heeled boots. She conducted the class totally in Spanish and although Kate had taken lessons for two years, she found it difficult. The others students, a mix of German, Irish, Dutch and English were friendly but they all seemed sharp and fluent, laughing at Lali's jokes which Kate didn't quite understand. Because she was a new girl, she was put in the teacher's chair and the rest of the class asked her questions like: "Why did you choose Estepona?"

She replied in halting *español* that she believed it was like a real Spanish town. Lali praised her attempt at converstion, all she needed was practice, and said that of all the Costa resorts, Estepona was indeed considered an authentic Spanish village. The group smiled at her and Kate glowed, her brain bursting with Spanish immersion.

Today the class finished early. The streets were full of cafés with their packed outside tables; women were

63

gossiping, babies gazing and the old men on benches sat watching it all. The village heart of Estepona was an antidote of movement, life and light and its bustling activity helped to push the dark night into its place. Forget fair-haired girls in cloaks – Kate had bounced back. Plump with the Spanish subjunctive tense, she perched on a bench doing a spot of lively foot-tapping and hand-jiving to the busker's rendition of Chuck Berry's *C'est La Vie* when she saw Steve at a nearby bar. He was talking to a man with a silver-grey ponytail.

"Hi, Steve," she called over to him. He turned, stubbed out his cigar and came over to her. He surveyed her with disapproval.

"You shouldn't do things in the street that draw attention to yourself," he admonished, standing squarely in front of her. "It reflects badly on you and those who know you."

"Piss off Steve," Kate retorted, high on rhythm and blues. "Come and dance with me." Steve joined her on the bench.

"I believe you're considering starting a cultural centre," he remarked. She noticed his feet tapping slightly to the rhythm.

"Who told you that? Was it Rosie?" So Estepona was a village and did she want to live where everyone knew her business and thought her eccentric? "Find me a millionaire and I will."

Steve laughed. "I was expecting to meet up with you at the café."

"I was expecting you to ring."

"Where are you off to now?"

"*Sevillana* dance until this music seduced me. I can't resist Chuck Berry."

"Yeah, well … I'll come with you."

"You?"

"You asked me to dance with you," he said, rising from the bench and hauling her up beside him. "So put your money where your mouth is."

"But you can't do it."

"Stop fussing, woman and let's go!"

Kate led Steve into the class expecting him to stand against the wall and look scornful. But he danced the *sevillana* like a native. He was the *hombre*, the male equivalent of the Spanish *señora* with her frilly skirts tucked up at the side and black short-heeled shoes with elastic straps across. He stamped, twirled and swayed his body round hers as the rest of the class cheered him on. They finished the final stamp of the first section on the *olé*, on the flourish of the hand together and Kate was breathless with the thrill of living in the dancing moment with Steve. Gertrude was also there, dancing sedately at the end of the line. She wore a frilly mauve skirt with pink lipstick to match, and a crimson rose in her hair. She was twirling the wrong way round and her grim face in the background soured the session. Her eyes were cold as she acknowledged Steve with a curt nod.

"Time for a coffee?" he asked Kate at the end.

"I never say no to a coffee, as long as it's decaff."

The bar across the road was very Spanish with its chipped half-tiled walls, blue checked plastic tablecloths, a noisy TV on the wall and the customary row of men in checked shirts, smoking at the bar. They all embraced Steve like a brother, arms clasped to shoulders. Kate didn't need this.

"Steve, I'd like to sit outside."

"Because of the smoke, no problem." As they settled at a table, Steve pointed to a poster stuck on the door advertising a dance for the following Saturday.

"You see what it says?"

She translated it slowly. "It's about finding a *media naranja*. That means ... half an orange! What have half-oranges got to do with dancing?"

"In Spain they call a *media naranja* your soul-mate. The advert is saying come to the dance and meet your soul mate." Kate liked that. She looked deliberately deeply at Steve so that he'd get the message and request her to accompany him in white tie and tails.

"You going to the party on Friday?" he asked instead. Val n' Pete from the walking group were having a pre-Christmas do at their posh San Pedro villa before going back to Scotland for the holidays. The walking group were invited.

"Yes, are you?"

"Yep. See you there, then?"

"Great!" Steve and Kate had a date – *media naranja* style?

Later, at the wine-drinking hour, Kate sat on the balcony and thought of Steve. An interesting man with those blue eyes she always went for, tough physique, big personality. His challenging manner gave her something to hit back against. She was attracted to Steve, despite Gertrude's hostility. She stretched and sipped a *tinto*, her glass of red wine. *The Book of Help* might answer her question:

"Have you any comment on Steve?"

'LET TIME TAKE CARE OF IT.'

Kate went to bed thinking about Steve and slept all night long without earplugs. There was no disturbance from below.

The rooms are swept, the oil lamps cleaned and young Elvira has gone home.

"Now lay that table well," Grandmother instructs Ana as the afternoon turns into evening. "And don't forget, we have no fire tonight."

Ana adores her Grandmother Ysabel who teaches the children their letters, sings and plays with them. A tiny lady, she is top-heavy with a large bosom and a neat waist accentuated by the full grey skirts she wears. Her cheeks are soft, pink and unlined, and her fine silvery hair is pulled into a bun with stray wisps framing her face. Ana strokes the soft nest until the old lady loses patience and pushes her away.

"What do you look like with your hair down?" she asks, but Grandmother only smiles, checks her hairpins are in place, and shakes her head.

"You know," says Ana, "Papa told me he's never ever seen you with your hair loose, even when he was young."

"Get on with you, child," retorts Grandmother with a twinkle. She is busy in the kitchen. With its pans on the stove, the meat hanging on hooks from the ceiling, she is in her domain. Rich aromas of wine, chicken juices, saffron and ginger are filling the hot room. As she works, Ana can smell the tang of spice from her chubby, perpetually orange-stained fingers.

Grandmother is a superb cook who relishes the unique musty aroma of the saffron flavouring she sneaks into every dish. Even, Papa says with a grimace, into their breakfast gruel

"I would love to be able to cook like you."

"I promise that one day soon I will pass on to you my culinary secrets, Analita, especially the mutton stew with chickpeas, rice and onions."

Ana sings as she lays a white linen cloth over the table in the living room and sets out the bottle of wine and freshly baked bread for their Friday night dinner. As it becomes dark, Mama whisks round the living room, lighting the lamps.

"Ana, come here." She sighs over her daughter's brown skirt and stained apron. "Go and have a good wash and change into a clean dress before we eat."

"Is this a special Friday night?"

Mama ignores her question. "Hurry up now, child. And don't forget to put a clean kerchief on your head."

Ana scampers up the stairs to the attic bedroom, smiling at Rosita curled up and blinking sleepily on her side of the bed. She loves Friday nights.

Humming softly, she pours water from the pitcher into the bowl, cleans her face and hands and tidies her hair. She laces herself into the brown woollen dress with long sleeves. The fine wool feels soft against her body. There's something different about tonight, Ana decides. She puts on a fresh white petticoat, pins a dark kerchief onto her hair and pulls on her boots. What are culinary secrets, she wonders.

"My, don't we look pretty," says María from the doorway.

"Are you not getting changed? Mama will be displeased if you're late."

María sniffs and twirls into the room. "I don't wish to. Mama says I may stay as I am. And I know what it's all about. I've already seen it."

"Seen what?" Ana pauses. "I know anyway, it's to do with culinary secrets."

But María merely smirks, flicks some water onto Ana's gown and saunters downstairs. Ana follows, her cheerfulness somewhat dampened. Why does María always have to know everything because she's older than me? Why does she try to spoil things?

Papa's face is clean-shaven, his hair neatly trimmed, and he has changed into a freshly laundered linen shirt. Mama and Grandmother are dressed in clean clothes, their hair neatly arranged with no wisps escaping. As soon as dinner is over and the plates cleared away, Felipe is sent off to bed.

Papa lays his hand on Ana's head. "You are ten years old now, my Analita, and ready to learn a family secret. Move back now."

What is happening? Ana stands close to Grandmother as Papa and Mama pull the long wooden table in the living room to one side and roll away the patterned rug. On the bare stone floor is a black iron ring with a heavy lock. This is new to Ana, she's never seen it before. How could she have lived her whole life in her own home and not been aware of what was under the carpet!

Papa bends down and undoes the lock. He hoists up the ring which lifts up a plank of wood. Tucking her skirts in, Ana tiptoes to the edge of the black hole below. She peers into the chasm of darkness while María yawns and looks away.

"Come, let us go down," says Papa. "Be careful where you put your feet." Taking his hand, Ana climbs down the steep wooden steps after him and Mama follows, carrying a lamp. When they are all safely in the cellar, Papa pushes the door closed above them, reaching up to lock it again. There is a musty damp smell, it is so eerie and dark down there and Ana is frightened. She clings to Grandmother, hiding her face in the folds of her heavy dress. Papa goes straight to the far end of the cellar where a cupboard stands in the dusty dim light. Mama is behind him, holding the lamp high to illuminate the space as Papa beckons to Grandmother to come over with the two girls.

All of Papa's actions now become slow and deliberate, as if he is performing a ritual he has carried out many times before. He opens the door and brings out a worn old book wrapped in a cloth which he places on top of the cupboard. Then he draws out a folded shawl and shakes it open with tremendous care. Ana can see that the shawl has frayed fringes hanging from the edge. Papa kisses a corner of the shawl and drapes it round his shoulders, and now he looks like the Jewish men worshipping in the synagogue. Mama lifts a pair of oil lamps out of the cupboard and places them next to the book.

Papa sings a short blessing in the Hebrew words that Ana recognises from the Saturday service. Mama produces a white piece of cloth from her pocket and covers her head with it. She lights the oil lamps, turns her two palms towards the lamps and then towards her face. She kisses her hands three times as she blesses the lamps and welcomes in the Sabbath. Unlike her usual brisk movements, Mama performs this ritual with care and slow precision and then she is silent, eyes closed for a moment. When she has finished she opens her eyes, lifts her head and beams round at them all. A warm glow of peace and family unity lights up the cellar.

Papa smiles at Ana. "This is what we call welcoming in the Sabbath. Strictly speaking, it should be done at dusk, but we have to make allowances." He lays his hands on her head and says another short blessing in Hebrew over her.

But María turns her head away. "Not me, Papa." She screws up her face when he tries to bless her.

The ceremony is done. "We should by tradition allow the lamps to burn themselves out, but it is not safe to leave them here," Papa explains. Mama blows the lamps out and Grandmother damps down the wicks while Papa places his shawl and book back in the cupboard. He locks the door and they all climb back up the narrow stairs.

"Mama, Papa, where have you been?" Felipe is standing in the living room, his face wet with tears as they emerge from the cellar. He has woken from a bad dream, come downstairs and doesn't know where his family has gone. At eight years old he is a serious little boy, excellent at his music and he thinks his ideas through with great clarity. Why is everyone rising, one by one, as if out of the floor? It does not make sense to him and he is terrified.

"Hush now, Felipe," soothes Mama. She swings him into her arms, cuddles him close and carries him back up to bed. Papa carefully replaces the wooden panel and locks the trapdoor. With Grandmother's help, he rolls the rug back and together they place the table in its usual position. Ana looks round the living room at the oil lamps and the silver ornaments fashioned by Papa on the sideboard. The chairs, the flowers, the pictures framed with dark wood are all so safe and familiar. But everything is different now. Grandmother settles into a comfortable armchair and beckons her over.

"It is strange the first time I know, but you will get used to it. And Ana, you speak to nobody about this Friday night practice. Do not even talk about it with María."

"Yes I know, Grandmother. Culinary secrets," she whispers – though Ana is puzzled. María is part of the family and knows full well what they are doing.

"You remember what we have told you," Grandmother continues. "We are not Jews, we are good New Christians, good Catholics. Never ever forget that."

CHAPTER SEVEN

ESTEPONA – PRESENT DAY

Val n' Pete's villa was a symphony of luxury bathrooms, palatial living spaces and soft leather couches. It boasted real fireplaces with fir cones and logs, two two-hundred square metre terraces with views to Gibraltar and all decked out in purples, softened with beiges and cream. Even the original oil paintings toned with the purple decor.

Kate wore a long, black suede skirt with nipped-in waist and sexy side slits bought from a cheap shop in Estepona. Pointed-toe black boots and a thin, silvery, low-necked silk top completed the ensemble. Rosie was a long streak in tight gold velvet trousers and a see-through shirt with ruffles at the deep-cut V-shaped neck. She sparkled with necklaces, earrings and a heavy gold belt. Kate was the quietly elegant one, Rosie the bit of brash flash.

Kate was cautiously optimistic and determined to enjoy the moment, but already weary of it before they were through the door. Steve must be there but she couldn't see him in the crowd. She recognised a lot of the gang from her outings with Rosie the other week. Two women from the dinner jazz mouthed greetings. A Dutchman from the Spanish class gave her the regulation kiss kiss on both cheeks. It was a small, limited world out here. Sooner or later, wherever one went, everybody knew everyone or knew someone who knew someone. The connections were circular and grew smaller which led to an intensity of social life and expectation. They swarmed from one glitzy event to the next like a cluster of tadpoles in pointed toe boots, smart tops and jollity. But nobody seemed particularly happy, or was it just her?

Kate stood with a glass of red wine, nibbling at purple delicacies, talking endlessly and vivaciously, blowing away smoke and keeping up her superficial corner. She bonded with a size sixteen blonde woman from Sheffield until Rosie, clutching a glass of champagne, lured her away. Rosie's eyes were glittering and slightly blood-shot.

"Don't even go there," she chortled. "Do you know that woman does nude cleaning." Kate was aghast, curious and even a little envious. How, where, who paid, her or them? And should she have a go? She'd have to think of getting a job soon.

"And that's her partner over there." She indicated a middle-aged man in a grey suit and silk tie chatting inoffensively in a corner. He caught Rosie's eye and blew her a kiss.

"Don't even ask what he does!" She wandered off, waving her glass at another acquaintance.

They played charades in two teams, shrieking with wild laughter. Everyone glittered in a buzz of bonhomie of looking, hunting, not daring to miss the next swarm that could be The One. Kate's feet were pinching. She loathed the smoke and the pretence. But she'd come with Rosie and would have to wait until she was ready to go. And where the hell was Steve?

She left the din round the food and moved into the empty room next door. Sat on the pale fawn couch and pulled out a newspaper from behind the designer cushion. Now she was happy, doing the crossword. Nobody bothered her until about midnight when Steve materialised, holding a goblet of chocolate mousse topped with a purple berry.

"You look very sweet and contained," he said, handing Kate the mousse and crouching beside her.

"Where have you been?" she asked.

"Hunting for you all evening." She didn't believe him for a second, but she was intrigued.

"Do you fancy a ramble up in the *campo* tomorrow? I need to check out the next walk."

"Love to. Shall we ask Rosie to join us?"

"How about just the two of us going?"

Her insides did a little *sevillana* twirl. In her confusion, she knocked over the glass of mousse and stained the couch with the lone purple berry.

"Look what I've done!" Kate searched for a damp cloth in the kitchen and rubbed it over the spot, spreading the stain and making it worse. She had to confess to Hostess Val who was amused. She had a part-time business sewing and repairing luxury cushions when she wasn't sunbathing nude and buying purple accessories. So she was indifferent to the lone stain which was purple anyway.

"Kate, I've got a surprise for you. I've been meaning to give it to you for ages." Val ran into the purple bedroom and returned with a print of the photo she'd taken of the walking group on her first ramble in the mountains and the white village.

"There you are, it's for you. Don't you and Steve look great together."

"Gosh, yes! Thanks." Kate noted her face shining with pleasure and Steve with his arm around her waist. She pushed the print into the secret back pouch of her purse, along with the scruffy bits of paper containing all her pin numbers. Val hesitated as if she wanted to say something significant, but didn't.

Kate's spirit was uplifted but it wasn't from the party. Not even from Steve. And it wasn't from the photo, or not directly. Behind the smiling group, she could see the mountain crags. The thrill was coming from the mountains and what they held. A secret was up there, calling her back, waiting for her to find it. The mountains led the way.

María is fast asleep, sprawled over the bed. Ana sits on the velvet window seat, running her fingers back and forth over the soft purple fabric. The shutters are open and Ana can smell the blossom heavy in the night air. Rosita pushes the door open, stalks into the room and curls up beside her.

"Hello little rosebud." Ana strokes Rosita and tries to figure out her mixed emotions to the Jewish service in the cellar. Although she warms to the old religion, Mama and Papa have brought her up to be a good Catholic. For years they have been taught by nuns and priests, the catholic prayers and catechisms. They are a religious family and observe the laws of the church. Mama will never touch pork but she makes it clear that this is purely because she has a bad stomach reaction to it. On most Sundays they attend regular Mass at the nearby Iglesia San Francisco; they take communion with their neighbours and together they worship Our Lord Jesus. They all wear their crucifixes although Papa often pulls his off as soon as they are home. And if he has many orders, he will go to his workshop on Sunday afternoons. At *Semana Santa*, Easter time, they cross themselves when the statues of Christ and the Virgin Mother are carried through the streets. As their good neighbours do.

78

With a shiver, Ana remembers last Easter. How she had stood with Papa among the crowd of people watching the Holy Processions pass by. One of the penitents stopped moving forward and Ana saw his eyes clearly through the slits. He seemed to be looking directly at her and she stared back at him, stiff with fear, unable to look away. Onlookers in the crowd noticed. They turned towards her, murmuring amongst themselves until Papa ran forward, kissed the good man's gown and crossed himself fervently. Papa's crucifix against his waistcoat was there for all to see.

The unrest subsided, the man moved on, but the incident had lingered in Ana's mind.

And now? After the ceremony in the cellar tonight? Young and innocent as she is, Ana knows their ancient ways are different. Which religion does she wish to belong to?

CHAPTER EIGHT

There was no Costa buzz in the mountains behind Estepona, no devastation of the environment. Instead there was nature, the white *pueblo*, and the two of them climbing the zigzag trail to a distant pylon on top of the hill. Steve pointed out griffon vultures and white and grey wagtails, all of which Kate pretended to see through her rubbish binoculars. On balance she preferred the big birds with their dramatic swoops rather than the twittery little ones.

"Hey, take a look at that." Steve stopped to admire a lesser kestrel hovering above them and it was beautiful. Kate knew she could live up here, away from the roller coaster buffeting below – amid the hushed spirituality of mountains, goat bells and circling vultures.

They achieved the pylon with high-up-in-the-hills elation and scrambled down to the other side to the river. It was pure pastoral bliss until they met a brown beast with grass in its mouth, barring their way. Horned cattle reared up from rocks and crannies in and out of the river, and they were all glaring at her.

"I'm not going past that lot!" she shrieked. Steve strode up to them, shouting commands in gravy-brown Spanish. The animals showed deep respect. They threw up the symbolic equivalent of their hands, performed the Spanish shrug, backed off and scattered over the stream.

"Hurray!" Kate cheered. Steve chased her as she ran ahead up the stone steps back to the *pueblo*.

"You shouldn't be frightened of animals," he shouted at her uncaring back. "They're more frightened of you." She collapsed in a heap at the top, gasping with laughter and he fell beside her. They rolled over, breathing heavily, looking at the blue sky and each other.

Lunch was at a marble table on the roof of a charming rural hotel. It was hot in the December sun and they discarded their jackets, piling them in a heap with the rucksacks. The terrace was decorated with green potted plants bearing bright orange berries. Wooden beams formed a canopy against the stone walls, and to the left the turret of the castle rose from the hillside. It was guitar-plunkingly romantic and delicious. As were the *tapas* dishes of red and green peppers, avocado and prawns, and hot meatballs in curry sauce with a hint of saffron. Kate buttered her crusty roll.

"You should use oil on your bread like the Spanish do. It's much healthier for you." Steve rubbed a piece of garlic into his bread and then poured oil onto it from a little jug with a narrow spout.

"I will next time. Now stop telling me what I should and shouldn't do. I don't like it." The friction was strong between them and it wasn't all to do with physical attraction.

"Sorry," he said, raising his shoulders and opening his hands out in exaggerated apology. "It's a bad habit of mine. Forgiven?"

"I suppose so." Kate pretended to be stern. He fixed his blue eyes on her face until they both started laughing again.

"Now you listen to me for a change." She proceeded to lecture him with long words about theatre, literature and cooking with eastern spices. Baffled him with her superior intellect, bossed him artlessly, cut into his long-winded bombasts about birds and chattered on about things she thought she knew about and he didn't. And all the time, Kate was on a high, her energy rising to meet his.

After lunch they strolled the deserted streets, their bodies close. His hand could have touched hers if he'd extended it three and a half inches to the right, but she had stopped focusing on Steve. Kate knew what she was looking for and eventually found it – the artisan shop.

It wasn't closed, even though it was siesta time. The flame-coloured polka-dotted flamenco dress dangled invitingly on its hanger and the kindly man with sad eyes continued to read his book to violin music on his CD that wasn't for sale. As Steve rifled through the pictures and cards displayed outside, Kate fingered the pillow of frothy flamenco frills. She could wear this dress at fiesta time in the summer when the dance class took to the floor. She should be doing the *sevillana* properly by then.

"It is your colour," twinkled the man from behind his book. Kate longed for it, but the time wasn't right and it wasn't what she'd come for. What she'd been drawn back to. Her heart was thumping as she approached the shelf where sat the row of gold and silver ornaments. The thumping increased as she searched again for what should be there but wasn't. There was nothing that she wanted. Sick with disappointment, Kate bought a little silver teapot to compensate.

Steve chose an old picture postcard of bulls charging through the streets of a *pueblo* and the kindly man wrapped their purchases in two separate parcels.

"Are you local?" asked Steve in firm Spanish and the man answered politely in English.

"I come from here but I have been based in Malaga for many years. Now I have returned to live here for a quieter life."

"What is your name?" He was so friendly and easy to talk to, Kate wanted to know more about him.

"My name is Juan."

"Thank you, Juan, for this pretty teapot."

Juan's mouth was full and wide and his eyes spoke to her. His thick brush of dark brown and silver hair edged the neck of his blue wool sweater.

"The article is made locally," he told her. "You have chosen well."

"I know." Her teapot might not be the answer but it was the beginning of her quest.

María and Ana stand huddled together among the crowds of waiting people as the steady drumbeat grows louder. The drums are sounding by order of the Bishop of Cordoba. The procession is leading a man through the city streets. He is an old friend of Papa's, a stocking maker by trade and a *converso*. His family converted from Judaism to Christianity long ago and, like the Ramírez family, he attends church regularly. But he has been denounced for secretly practising his Judaism and is now facing his punishment.

"Look, here he comes!" María jumps up and down, clapping her hands. "You are a traitor to Christianity!" she shouts, pushing forward to shake her fist at the shamed *converso* as he trudges past. A large man in a long gown and grey curling beard marches close behind, brandishing a stick, shouting and goading him on. The procession passes slowly up the main street and María runs along with the crowd, following it. Ana scuttles beside her, hating it all.

"We shouldn't be here!" She grabs hold of María's skirts to try and stop her.

"Don't be such a baby!" cries María pulling away from her.

"I can't watch, it's horrible."

"You go then. I'm staying."

"You know Papa would not want us here." Bending down, Ana dodges between the legs of the spectators until she is safely in a side street with few people and she can make her way home. But María stays with the crowd as the procession moves slowly into the main plaza.

"Halt!" bellows the leader. María watches avidly as he forces the stocking maker onto a wooden platform in the centre of the plaza. The terrified man stands there, his lips pale and pressed together. The crowd gathers round, jeering and throwing rubbish at the shamed man. He doesn't speak but remains defiant to the catcalls of hatred and derision. Dribbles of rotten egg and tomato trickle down his face and tunic.

"Now hear me!" The leader grabs the stocking maker by the arm and shakes him roughly. Going close up to him, he spits into his face. "I order you to swear a public oath in this place that you sin no more. That you cease now your evil practice of Judaism."

"Never!" The man is quaking with fear but he stands firm. "Behold! I must die one death!" he shouts above the tumult. "And I declare that the law of Moses is the best, and that by it shall men be saved!"

These words are a trigger for the mob. The front men push and storm up the steps and seize the stocking maker. María screams with excitement as others in the crowd jostle past her and go wild. First one and then another pick up large stones and hurl them at the pathetic figure. He is stoned to death in the plaza.

That evening Ana and Pedro sit on the stone edge of the fountain. María is before them, full of self-importance, her face flushed red and alive. The words spill out of her and she screeches with laughter. "You have never seen such a stupid man! He should have known that no person can be saved unless they abide in the bosom and unity of the Catholic Church. Our Virgin Mary and Our Saviour Jesus Christ, they are the ones who can save you. The mob went wild and killed him. It was so thrilling!" María finishes her tale with a flourish and sits down, twirling her long hair. She laughs loudly again. Her delight, almost intoxication in the hideous spectacle makes Ana shrink from her.

Pedro's eyes meet Ana's. Although they do not speak, Ana knows he shares the horror that she feels at María's behaviour. Ever alert, María sees them exchange glances. Her hand dives for her crucifix, she crosses herself and bursts into tears.

"To tell the truth it was all so horrible. I hated it so much, it was so cruel," she cries, and then they have to pet and comfort her as her eyes brim and tears roll down her face. María is a sensitive soul, or a polished liar. Or both.

Papa is horrified by the savage killing of his old friend. He shuts the workroom early and refuses to eat supper. Still wearing his long coarse work apron, he sits at the table weeping silently, his shoulders shaking, head in his hands. Ana hates to see her father so disturbed. She lays an arm on his sleeve but he pushes her off.

"You know, we shared a secret *bar mitzvah* service together," he mutters to Mama.

"Please Antonio." Mama shoots a warning look at the children. But Papa carries on.

"It started with the massacres in Sevilla way back in thirteen hundred and ninety-one and it has not ceased since. All over Spain, they hate us. And it is getting worse."

Felipe looks up at Papa with puzzled eyes. "What is a *bar mitzvah* Papa?" He struggles over the words. "And who hates us?"

"Now look what you've done!" Mama is angry with Papa but he will not stop.

"And there was that terrible time in Toledo."

"Antonio, enough! You don't want to upset the children any further."

"About fifteen years ago it was. Your cousin told us about the riots. And that wealthy *converso*, the tax collector, who was tortured into confessing he'd lived as a Jew. They hung them all from their feet! And other *conversos*, they were sentenced to be burnt at the stake. Even the well-off ones are not protected any more."

"There is nothing to be gained from talking about it now."

"Face the truth, Beatriz. We *converso*s are in danger all over Spain. You know that many in Valencia have already left Spain and sailed to the Orient. They plan to revert to Judaism. Perhaps we should consider going also."

Felipe's round little face crumples and he starts to cry.

"Enough, husband!" shouts Mama. "We have work to do."

Papa closes his mouth tight and remains motionless at the table. When the women have finished clearing away, he pushes the table to one side, rolls aside the carpet and stomps down the stairs into the cellar.

"Come, María," says Mama crisply. They go to unpack a new spice delivery in the cool windowless room next to the kitchen where the stock is stored. Grandmother takes Felipe upstairs to practise his music and Ana is left alone in the living room.

If she crouches right down under the table and twists her head sideways through the hole, she can see Papa through the open flap on the floor. He is standing by the lamp at the far end of the cellar wearing the special shawl draped over his shoulders. He holds his book and rocks back and forwards, facing the wall and chanting in Hebrew. But Papa must have sensed somebody watching him. He turns round, strides over to the opening and shouts to Ana, above him.

"You leave me alone now, do you hear me?" He reaches up and slams closed the flap.

Ana sits brooding and fearful on her window seat in the bedroom. I hate Papa being angry. And I wish I wasn't so timid. Would their secrets in the cellar be found out? The slaying of the stocking maker and the earlier attacks in Toledo related to their lives also. They are *conversos*, and are they not guilty of the same sin of Judaising? Are they not in danger of similar attacks upon themselves?

Her mother is terrified of their hidden practices being discovered.

The death of the stocking-maker causes repercussions throughout Cordoba and in the Ramírez household. Mama makes Papa take his precious Hebrew book and burn it. He no longer visits the synagogue in the *Judería* on special days and he stops going to the workshop on Sunday afternoons. From that day on, they do not miss a single church service. They all wear their crucifixes on top of their clothes. Inside the house and out.

CHAPTER NINE

ESTEPONA – PRESENT DAY

"Hi, Kate. It's Rosie. I hear you've been having a really good time lately. Do call me when you get round to it."

News travelled quickly down here. Steve and Kate have defied Rosie and the iciness of her displeasure was hitting via her peeved phone message. Yes, Kate thought, I suppose I should have insisted that Rosie came to the mountains with us. She hated to miss anything. But I've got my own life and mind, they aren't owned by Rosie. Kate said this a few different ways to practise being assertive. Assertiveness was so tricky. She could role-play a situation but it rarely worked out the way she intended it. She loathed assertiveness even though she used to go to classes and teach them. She hated it when Customer Services were assertive and kept repeating that they're sorry, please bear with them but there's nothing to be done. She wanted to hit them. Assertiveness was a con. Bring back straightforward aggression.

So Kate rang Rosie who was a little cool and Kate was a little apologetic. Feeling guilty, she agreed to view another fantastic property.

This time Rosie had got the message. They weren't on a building site but at an established development off the main road past Manilva, crane city. This area used to contain farmland, vineyards and seventeen thousand inhabitants. The forecast for the next ten years was that the vines would decrease, tourist development increase and the number of inhabitants quadruple to seventy thousand. How would the infrastructure cope?

There was nothing wrong with the two-bedroom town house. Furnished with Andalusian dark furniture, the rooms were square and spacious. A charming little terrace blossomed with pots of flowering plants. The sea was a mere eight minutes' walk away across a bridge spanning the road and Rosie could get the property at a good price. As she continually pointed out, Kate would be much safer from noise pollution in a town house within a gated community than in an apartment at the port.

But the property didn't sing to Kate. She could see the road, hear its traffic noise and the deserted development depressed her. It wasn't the real mountain thing, it was cutely manufactured as a pretend *pueblo* for the residential tourist market. A hint of dankness lurked in the downstairs rooms and it wasn't near to the life of anywhere, stuck between Estepona and Sabinillas.

"Do stop looking so sulky, you can always walk along the beach or get the bus in if you don't want to take the car." Rosie's impatience burst out of her like a popping balloon. Kate pointed to the bus stop below, garnished with a line of patiently waiting women who had been there at least as long as they had. It wasn't for her.

"You are so negative and difficult to please," Rosie sighed as they drove home. It was becoming her mantra.

"And you're always trying to sell me a house!" Kate flung back at her. "Will you stop being so negative and saying I'm negative. I'm not. I know what I don't like, that's all." So much for assertiveness.

"Want a Werther's?"

"No thanks."

Rosie delved into her seat pocket and extracted a sweet. She tore off the gold wrapping with her teeth as she drove. "What do you like then?"

Kate sulked for a few minutes, counting the cranes and building sites as they passed them. What was the point of being angry with Rosie? Kate needed her. So she confided her dream of mountain views and villages, a simple life of alley-like streets and charming crooked houses with beaded curtain doorways where they sold lentils in large sacks. She didn't mention the artisan shop.

"Humph!" Rosie made a right turn into the port without signalling, neatly avoiding a motorbike that was going straight on. "Those *pueblos* can be so claustrophobic. All the old houses that haven't been converted are very dark, they can have termites, the whole village knows your business and you can't get away from it – boiling hot in summer, damp in winter. Honestly, you could be sitting in a rain cloud up there with all those warped windows getting stuck, when it's nice and sunny down here. And don't think it's quiet because it's the country. A cock crows, dogs bark, the kids play in the streets, they've all got motorbikes, you can hear them zooming and echoing all over the valley. Plus you can be so isolated, it can drive you crazy. It takes ages to come down to a decent supermarket. And you'll miss your life down here, your new friends; there are a lot of odd folk up there – a very mixed bag." She stopped the car outside the building, keeping the engine running. "Look, Katie …"

"Please don't call me that."

"Sorry. Kate." She turned to her, forced a smile and touched Kate's hand with sisterly compassion. "I know you're seriously looking, and trust me, I know what you want. I can show you many more houses on new developments closer to town, even a converted town house in the heart of Estepona could suit you."

"Thanks, Rosie."

"Don't mention it." She paused and then banged the wheel with the side of her hand and smiled broadly. "I've just had a smashing thought about mountain properties. You wait – leave it to me."

Kate waved goodbye and trudged back to the apartment. The cup was half empty and she was weary. Rosie's force and determination unsettled her, making her doubt her own ideas. But I suppose she is right, Kate thought. I would love a little house, but on the other hand, do I want to disappear up to a *pueblo*? And leave Steve, now that a relationship is possibly developing between us?

Kate wanted a man and Steve excited her. She couldn't stop thinking about him when she wasn't with him – always a sure sign. But she didn't want to rush it. Should she confide in Rosie? Her instinct said don't. Say nothing. Stay safe. Go nowhere until you're ready for it.

If she wasn't going to move to the mountains, what about the property Rosie showed her today? Kate stared beseechingly at the cloud on the cover of *The Book of Help* and opened the book at random to help resolve the dithery indecision. 'ALL THINGS CAN BE RESOLVED IF YOU FLOW WITH THEM,' it declared, loftily. Now what on earth did that mean? As she was pondering and re-flicking, Steve called.

"Hi, fancy meeting up for a Chinese at the port?"

"Why not, I'd love to." Yes!

"Eight-thirty then, at the top corner on the right?"

"See you then." Heart pounding, sweaty hands. 'Who knows, could be'… she sang from *West Side Story*, choosing and flinging clothes on the bed as she got ready.

The lift took her down to the ground floor and clattered to a stop. The door slid open and Kate leapt back in terror. The man was standing there, filling the space – that same man who had shouted as he collided into her on the street weeks ago. He was reeking of smoke and booze, his hair a wild, tangled bush, his face swarthy. With an angry snarl of yellow teeth, bad breath and bloodshot eyes, he pushed past as Kate wriggled out of the lift, out of the building and away from him. With fumbling fingers she unlocked the blue back door that led to the waste ground.

Steve was coming up the slope to the top level of the port. His sleeves were rolled up over brown hairy arms, white shirt open to the waist, jeans neatly pressed. He oozed sexy, rugged, A-Class virility. Kate ran up to him, flung her arms round his neck and burrowed against his tanned chest.

"Hey! What's all this?" He pulled away to look at her.

"I'm – so glad to see you," she stammered.

"You're looking pale, anything up?"

"I... er... nearly crashed the car in the garage."

"I'm not surprised. Never seen anything like that basement, bloody columns everywhere." She couldn't tell him about the man in the lift. He'd say it was her fault for being there in the first place and she should get out this minute and buy a place from Rosie.

They devoured spring rolls and Peking Duck with egg fried rice, and Kate tried to relax with two large glasses of white wine that Steve insisted were therapeutic. Next to the table stood a large aquarium where lobsters and large crabs stretched out their claws and crawled over each other in slow motion. Erotic in a seafood way. Steve's foot touched Kate's below the table. She slipped her shoes off and rubbed her toes up and down his leg.

As they said goodnight on the corner of the building, Steve kissed her cheek and pressed his lips to her mouth. The cats observed them silently. Kate swayed drunkenly off-balance and he thrust his body up against hers. She clung to him.

"Kate!" he moaned into her hair. "Shall I come up with you?"

"Oh yes." She was aroused by him and she didn't want to go into that building on her own. He followed her in. His hands caressed her hips as they stood in the lift together. She knew what would happen and it did.

Trembling, she led Steve into the dark room and pulled him onto the bed. His intensity and desire had awoken hers. It was quickly done.

Afterwards, they lay crumpled together and held each other. Kate stroked his stubbly shaven head. He kissed her shoulder, sat up, pulled on his clothes, laid a finger on her lips, and went, promising to ring. He closed the front door softly behind him. Oh what a night! They'd reached a new place in their relationship. Now it was richer, more deeply intimate. It was pure sex, no cosy cuddling, no meaningful staying the night. Love wasn't mentioned but it was in the air.

Kate stretched out on the bed, hands behind her head, and breathed deeply. Not a sound came from below and her urge to be elsewhere was waning. Contentment streamed out of her like a golden streak of honey.

Kate remembered Gertrude and her warnings. She pattered down the corridor and found the book. It was time for one more go with *The Book of Help*.

"Am I safe with Steve?"

'WHO KNOWS WHAT MAY HAPPEN.' So obscure, annoying and yet so relevant.

Eleven year old Ana wishes she could be anywhere other than in Papa's cramped and airless workroom. She feels grumpy and trapped and it isn't fair. She does not like being the middle one, always caught between María's will and Felipe's kind, gentle nature.

And how she dislikes the work. She has to help Papa every day. He has been a master craftsman for years and fashions small silver pieces to order – spoons, buttons, shoe buckles, and larger articles such as bowls, teapots, candlesticks and inkstands. The silver pieces are kept in a cool, dry place at the back where his work tools are stored, with a range of hammers, anvil heads and bellows. Under his workbench stands a vat with a strong acid solution that is used to clean the silver that tarnishes so rapidly. It is Ana's responsibility to rub the pieces down regularly with a polishing cloth. It is dirty work and she has to scrub the black grime out of her nails afterwards.

She is relieved when Felipe is allowed to join them in the cellar on their occasional Friday night service. This means Felipe is growing up. Papa starts to teach him a special blessing in Hebrew preparing him for manhood.

"Please Mama and Papa," Ana asks that night at supper, "now Felipe is old enough, I was wondering – could he help at the workshop instead of me?" There is a silence as her parents look at each other. Ana holds her breath and counts from one to five in her head and then Papa puts down his knife and fork.

"I do not see why not? What do you say Beatriz?"

"I agree." For once both Papa and Mama agree. And it makes sense. Felipe is destined to become a silversmith like his father, and he will soon be starting his seven years' apprenticeship. Ana conceals her delight with dutiful, downcast eyes but she doesn't miss María's knowing wink.

"What would I have to do?" asks Felipe. His forehead is furrowed and he does not look overjoyed.

"Well, son, to be a good silversmith," Papa begins, "you have to be able to clean the silver, follow the procedures closely, and practise, practise."

"Yes, Papa."

"You also need a creative mind, to be adept with your hands and excel at mathematics." All this is not to Ana's taste, but suits Felipe to perfection.

Felipe agrees, although he is not convinced. He does have his own dreams. Grandmother has given him another new wooden vihuela for his birthday and he longs to be a troubadour when he grows up and travel through Al Andalus playing the instrument with his two sisters as a singing, dancing accompaniment. But Mama and Papa laugh at him. What a dream! Felipe knows that he will have to stay and work in the family business.

* * * *

From the first day on the family spice booth, Ana feels free. Now she is allowed to help with María and Mama, and this suits her far more. She loves being in the open air amidst the bustle of the bazaar. Every weekday morning the girls help Mama carry the brown sacks to the large plaza a few minutes' walk away. It is primarily a horse-trading bazaar and the animals are brought in regularly from the surrounding countryside to be sold. The bazaar is full of stalls and booths selling a range of goods, including the family spices. Ana and María lay out their products in colourful rows at the front of their booth. Ginger, cumin, coriander, cinnamon, pepper, nutmeg and saffron are the most popular with the wealthy upper classes of Cordoba. They are willing to pay high prices for the fine flavours they bring to food and drink.

"This stall has been in my family for generations," Mama explains to Ana. "The spices are expensive because of the cost of bringing them here. They come to us in a regular delivery from the East by ship, and then by camel train to Egypt, on to Venice and from there to the port at Almería. They are picked up by your uncle José who lives nearby on the coast and brought by horse and cart to Cordoba."

Ana enjoys handling the fragrant spices, particularly the scooping out, ladling and weighing of the ground saffron with its deep rich colour, fine texture and pungent aroma. She takes pleasure in serving their regular customers who are always courteous to her. And she likes knowing that Pedro is nearby, with his father at the leather stall next to theirs.

After they close up the stall, Ana and María push through the bazaar which is still busy with traders and horses. The passages are full of loaded donkeys, litter, half-empty booths and stallholders calling, arguing and packing up. Customers rush to make last minute purchases.

The two girls walk home along the cobblestone streets, singing and telling each other stories as they swing the spice sacks between them. They tease each other about Pedro. María can imitate Pedro's husky tones so wickedly. Neither will admit how they feel about him, of course he is only a friend and it is not proper to think of him in any other way. But they both admire him. As for Pedro – he must surely prefer María with her vibrant personality. When she is in a good mood, María dominates the space around her, talking, laughing and tossing her long fair hair. Then Ana correspondingly becomes more subdued, unable to think of anything bright and clever to say to Pedro.

"It's hard to believe you two are sisters," Grandmother declares and it is true. They are growing up so differently both in looks and temperament. Ana loves their Friday nights and the old traditions whereas María has no time for Jewish practices. She prefers to worship the prayers and ceremonies of Catholicism with an unnatural fervour, muttering her rosary which she carries with her everywhere. María is always running to the church or to sing at the convent and she insists on keeping a small image of Our Lord Jesus Christ in their bedroom. She prays to Him every night and tries to push the rest of the family to follow her actions. Papa is driven to distraction with her religious obsession, as he calls it.

"That piece of wood is not sacred, it is nothing but wood and paint!" he announces one Sunday after Mass when they are safely home from church.

"That is not true, Papa!" María stares at her father with cold, blank, blue eyes. She has passions that will not be shifted.

Back in their bedroom after the morning's work at the bazaar, María kneels down again and prays loudly to the little religious image until Ana pushes her fingers into her ears to drown out the words.

"For pity's sake, please stop doing that!"

María is furious. She marches over to Ana, shouting in her ear. "You are so stupid. Why can't you ever see that we are the true followers of Jesus."

She runs downstairs and Ana follows, anxious not to quarrel but fearful of her sister's temper and what she might do next. When María is in a good mood, there is nobody like her – she is strong, cheerful, capable. She adores cleaning and can tidy the kitchen faster and better than their maid Elvira. But even as a young child, María was unpredictable and possessed a violent streak. She had broken toys in a rage, and once she dug a little knife into Ana's foot and drew blood. If María was storming round the house, it was prudent to keep well away from her.

Now she prowls the living room, drumming her fingers as Felipe practises scales on his new vihuela.

"Will you stop that scraping grating noise!" she shouts, snatching the vihuela out of his hands. "I will smash it if you go on."

"No you must not!" Ana tries to take the instrument off her. They fight over it until María pulls hard, hits Felipe on the head with it and breaks the strings. Was it an accident or deliberate?

"My music is broken!" Felipe sobs.

Papa takes the vihuela to a musician friend who promises to mend it for him by the end of the week. All that evening María lies in a chair, huddled and wretched under a blanket. She is too upset to eat and everyone is so sorry for her, they forget to comfort the little boy.

"It's such a shame it got broken," she cries to Ana. And they are best friends again.

"That girl reminds me of my husband's Aunt, *Tía* Madelena," says Grandmother when she and Ana are in the kitchen after supper, washing the dishes. "Although I never knew her, I heard what they used to say about her when she was young." Grandmother leans forward and whispers in Ana's ear. "You have to be careful with María. A very good actress. Good at twisting the truth. Watch yourself."

"But she is my sister."

Grandmother sniffs as she always does, her lips thin and pressed together. She will say no more.

CHAPTER TEN

ESTEPONA – PRESENT DAY

"You know what? Such a bad thing has happened. You know the black cat, the one with the damaged leg?" Gertrude was at Kate's door, her head bobbing in agitation. "He is so wicked! He is at all the cats. And I am sure that Nina is pregnant. We have to stop it right now, we must take her to a vet and get her seen to." Suppressing a sigh, Kate put down her Spanish homework and prepared to help out.

Gertrude had borrowed an animal cage from an English couple renting on the top floor. It had a cunning spring system with enough wires and pulley systems to catch a puma. Would Gertrude be able to lure Nina into it?

On the waste ground there wasn't a cat in sight. The cage door dangled open and Gertrude's warm brown stew waited inside. They stood in a state of high tension broken by the stares of curious men strolling past, toothpicks jammed between their teeth. Nina and the black cat arrived and hovered. Nina was cautious, the black cat less so. She approached the cage, sniffed and edged her body half inside. Nina copied her. Both the black cat and Nina were half in half out of the cage.

"I close it now," muttered Gertrude.

"But the black cat's in there as well."

"It doesn't matter, we get them both." Gertrude pushed both cats and their tails fully inside and snapped closed the cage door. Kate drove them all to the vet.

As they carried the cage in, some of the stew fell out. Kate picked up a meat globule and pushed it back through the bars. One of the cats stretched its paw out and scratched her on the left index finger and thumb. She was in pain and blood dripped from her.

She threw the cat cage at the vet and took off to the local health centre. Fortunately Kate kept the international medical card in her bag and was treated like a queen. They pushed her ahead of the rows of waiting Spanish, gave her an anti-tetanus shot, sloshed the wound with brown disinfectant and supplied antibiotics for five days. She should go to the doctor in one month for a further shot. They were in and out in five minutes while all the Spanish sat stolidly on. Kate went straight to bed with mega-strong painkillers from the chemist.

After a night of throbbing pain, she looked up rabies on the Internet and found that one can only get it if one has been bitten. The bleeding stopped and there didn't appear to be any sign of infection. A lucky escape for Kate and the cats. If rabies was diagnosed, all the wild cats in Spain would have to be destroyed and what would Gertrude do then?

Noise and smoke from below filled the apartment. The gang were home for the Christmas holidays and smoking non-stop. If she opened the windows for fresh air, smoke poured in. If she closed them, it got in through all the vents and communal tunnels and ducts and what have-yous, filling the wardrobes and her clothes.

Steve had rung twice: "Hey – why did you miss the last walk, what are you playing at, and when can I see you?" Not yet. Kate looked a wreck, spotty face, lank hair and she felt worse. She couldn't face him and his energy until hers was up again.

Rosie rang. "Do you want to go to a fantastic Christmas Pop/Flamenco concert in Malaga with me this weekend?" No she didn't.

Kate used her scratched hand as an excuse and sank back onto the lumpy couch cuddling the black and white spotted pot elephant and carefully avoiding the scratched area. Again she thought, this wasn't why she'd come to Spain. She was homesick, missing old friends who were all busy for Christmas. Should she stay, fly back to England or go up to the mountains? It was the story of her restless life yet again and she was no closer to achieving peace of mind. She jumped up, got *The Book of Help,* stared at the cloud and flicked the pages.

"Please, please tell me what I should do?"

'YOU DON'T NEED TO ATTACH MUCH IMPORTANCE TO THIS,' it said smugly. But she did – desperately. She made a list of Good Things in My Life:

1: a) Steve? b) Sex? c) Question marks??

2: Gertrude who mysteriously remained a profound emotional influence although she'd no idea that she was.

3: The little silver teapot on the sideboard.

Kate's mood lifted. Through its shining round shape, she thought she could see something, perhaps a glow and the glimmer of a reflection of what looked like a round face and long brown hair … and then there was nothing except a blank silver teapot. Perhaps it was a fantasy brought on by the side-effects of the medicine. Like the Spanish coffee, the antibiotic came stronger here.

* * * *

"My word, don't you look terrible."

Rosie, who went to the New Year celebrations and fantastic fireworks in Estepona centre and then on to six parties, was here on an official visit. She was worried about Kate's pale face, dark circles under the eyes and the blotchy purple scratch which, Kate assured her, wasn't infectious or developing into rabies. She made tea for them both in the little teapot and sank beside her on the couch.

"So sorry you had to miss all the fun. Poor you." Sharp, impatient Rosie had evaporated. Even the shiny pink lipstick was toned tactfully down and this was her friend at her very best, kind, thoughtful and what a Good Samaritan. She'd brought with her a bag of Werther's Originals, a bunch of green grapes and a magazine on Best Apartment Buys in Andalucía.

"It's got some really good articles about financial investments and advisers," she said, curling her legs up and playing with the spotted elephant. "Kate, I'm concerned for you."

"I'll be fine, I'm practically better."

106

"You need some help to counteract the effects of those antibiotics."

"Please do be careful with that elephant."

Rosie got up and took a sweet from the bag. She unwrapped it, dropped the wrapper over the balcony and stared down at the dredger that was busy removing mud and sludge from the harbour bottom with a giant prehistoric-looking black claw.

"You could really do with getting away for a change," she said over her shoulder.

"Oh please!"

"Don't 'oh please' me like that. And don't you worry, Kate, you'll like what I'm going to suggest." Rosie approached, knelt down close, and took Kate's good hand in hers. Kate shrank back from her intensity.

"I'm house-sitting next weekend up in the mountains. Do you fancy joining me?"

"No way – too much effort and I can't be bothered."

"It'll do you the world of good. It's a fantastic house, Casa Sueños, right in the country." Rosie waved her arms to illustrate her point and in so doing, she knocked over the elephant that shattered into three pieces. They both looked at it with horror.

"Now see what you've done!"

"For heavens sake!" Rosie bent down to reach for the scattered pieces. "It was an accident. It's a cheap pot elephant. Why are you such a drama queen!"

"Look who's calling who a drama queen. And leave them alone, I'll do it." Rosie sat back as Kate crawled over the floor to collect the pieces of elephant, tears sliding down her nose. "I think you'd better go, Rosie."

"What about the weekend?"

"Just go!"

Rosie heaved a huge exasperated sigh, marched to the door and then turned round. She looked at Kate and Kate looked at her. Kate raised her eyebrows. Rosie raised hers.

"We're fighting over an elephant," she said. And they both began to laugh. As if on cue, loud music and shrieking voices started up below and the smell of cigarettes edged its way into the apartment. Kate threw herself down flat on the floor and pressed her ear against the cold marble. The sounds below were amplified a million fold. Guitars and drums crashed, heels click-clacked on the floor, a woman shouted. Kate caught some of her Spanish words … *mira* … *venti seis* … Dogs were barking.

"What are you doing? Who are these people?" demanded Rosie. Kate sat up on the floor and it poured out of her.

"Gertrude says and she should know, they're new tenants on a long-term let and they're multiple occupancy. They leave smelly bags of litter in the basement and drive the wrong way up the one-way street. They come and go all day and night and who knows what they're working at. And they smoke and shout and have the television on loud and wake me up every other bloody night. I've been down to the supermarket and bought a screwdriver, unscrewed all the ventilation vents in the apartment, yes, with my bad hand, stretched cling-film over all the apertures, screwed the vents back on but the smoke continues to pour in. At least I've learnt the Spanish for screwdriver. It's '*destornillador*' which I thought meant a zipper. I want to die or murder them. Or both."

Rosie came over and helped her up. She unwrapped a sweet and handed it over.

"Thanks." Kate sucked at it furiously. It was like a baby's dummy.

"What about the Community, can't they help? That's what they're there for."

"The Community Office know all about it but nothing's happened. Gertrude says everyone in the block is complaining. But it makes no difference. They don't care!"

"You don't need this. Come up on Friday and stay there with me for the weekend."

Deep in the middle of the night Kate sat on the stairs between floors in her candlewick dressing gown as music poured out from under their door. What was she afraid of? Why didn't she knock and ask them to be quiet? Because it wouldn't make any difference. When she shared a lift with these tough, tattooed, shaven-headed smoking men, these brilliantly made-up women in tight jeans, with orange lip-liner outlining their pouting mouths, they all acknowledged each other with neighbourly decorum. They smoked on and Kate was busy holding her breath so she wouldn't inhale and retch. Timidity stopped her from speaking. They got out at their floor below and she got out at hers, let out the held-in breath and kicked the wall in frustration. Inside, she tore her clothes off and hung them out to de-fumigate. She couldn't bear it and yet she did nothing. Her neighbours could easily retaliate with slashed tyres in the basement car park, or worse. Kate didn't want to get into a vendetta game.

"I don't like that game."

"You never want to do anything!" María and Ana are in their bedroom on a hot afternoon. Twelve year-old Ana would far rather sing, laugh and then fall asleep curled round her sister. But María is bored and she wants to play. Her favourite game is to change clothes with Ana and pretend that one sister is the other. María can imitate Ana's soft tones and her solid walk to perfection. Quite often she will take Ana's cloak or her skirt, wear it without her permission and forget to put it back in Ana's cupboard.

The last time they played, Maria padded out her slim body with an old garment in order to look a little plumper. She slipped on Ana's gown and covered her fair hair with a large shawl. "Come on Ana, now you put my clothes on."

By holding her stomach in tight, Ana managed to squeeze into them. Then they had gone downstairs to find Mama in the kitchen. Ana, uncomfortable in different clothes, hung back by the door.

"*Hola*, Mama, can I do anything for you?" María called out, imitating Ana's soft voice. Mama turned round and smiled at her.

"Ana, I'm glad you are here, please help me sort these spices." She was convinced it was her youngest daughter.

María had nudged Ana and giggled into her ear and Ana had pretended to giggle back.

But Ana now rejects María's more deceitful games.

"Please do play for just a few moments," insists María, pushing at Ana's shoulder.

Why not give in to her? It is so much easier and then she will be my friend again. But the afternoon is hot and Ana is sleepy. She rolls over. "I'm sorry but I'm not playing."

When Ana wakes, the room is empty. She doesn't see the slim figure in the shadows outside her half-open bedroom door. As she reaches for her apron lying on the bed, a black spider the size of her hand, crawls out of the pocket and over her arm. Ana screams, clenching her fists together in a frenzy of fear. She sees the creature scuttle jerkily off the bed, across the floor and disappear around the door. But she doesn't see her sister gather up the realistic toy she has made from dark wool and a length of invisible thread.

She finds María downstairs in the kitchen, singing softly as she dries and stacks the plates next to Grandmother who is chopping eggplant.

"You did that!" Ana screams. "You put a spider in my apron pocket!"

"What spider?"

"Don't pretend you don't know."

"If there was a spider, it must have crept up from the cellar," insists María, her huge eyes wide with innocence.

"It did not! I don't believe you. Grandmother, she put a spider in my apron."

"No I did not, you are lying."

"She did, it was the size of a kitten. I hate her!"

"I did not. Anyway, Mama knows I'm far too frightened of spiders myself to ever touch one." She raises an eyebrow at Ana and flounces out of the kitchen. Grandmother sighs, looks over at Ana, says nothing and gets on with the eggplant.

Nobody can control María when she is like this. Not even Grandmother.

CHAPTER ELEVEN

ESTEPONA – PRESENT DAY

Driving up into the mountains in the clear January air towards the *pueblo* and beyond was invigorating and straightforward. Casa Sueños was past an old mill on the right, then left and down a dirt track for three kilometres. At a junction with a building on the corner Kate took the right-hand fork up along a further track. 'Track' was a kind word for it. The car struggled with the rough terrain, bouncing and weaving over rocks and stones.

Two wildly-barking alsatians leapt out from the open yard of a large, tumbledown farmhouse with sagging walls and a crooked roof. Set against the sharp rocks of the hillside, it stood on a dusty corner plot of overgrown orange groves and weeds. The river ran below. Kate was deeply glad she didn't live in the up-down-around-here in the middle of nowhere even with the tremendous views of the Crestallina, Sierra Bermeja, *pueblos* folded into the distance and the sea reaching away towards Africa in the distance. Plus the fantastic view of Gib. She wouldn't be able to get away from it. Never get past those dogs.

The track did a final somersault and deposited her at a gate with 'Casa Sueños' outlined on it in black wrought iron. She pressed a bell on the side wall, the

114

gates slowly opened and Kate followed the winding drive to the house entrance where a King Charles spaniel greeted her, woofing politely.

Rosie stood in the doorway. She'd discarded her customary sharp Costa style and gone for a laid-back country/ethnic look with a long-sleeved, gently-flowing cream linen dress. African necklaces, and clunky carved bracelets tinkled on her arms and ankles. The varnish on her toenails was silver, her blonde bob adorned with painted butterfly combs; open brown sandals with silver studs completed the ensemble. She embraced Kate and dragged her inside.

"Can't wait to show you round. It's so fantastically rustic, you wouldn't believe."

An old wooden table and sturdy chairs stood in the middle of the square open kitchen. Copper pots and a row of utensils dangled from a large wire arch suspended over the sink area and beyond were terracotta terraces. There were beamed ceilings and four bedrooms with views across the valley towards the *pueblo*. The tour finished at Kate's guest bedroom with its own en suite plus a kitchen area, furnished with a fridge, two electric hobs, coffee, milk, water, Weetabix and a bowl of sugar.

A stream ran through grounds that were burgeoning with *andaluz* nature – trees laden with dangling oranges, olive trees, lemons and limes. Gorse bushes framed a lower stoned area where a large oval-shaped pool shimmered.

At twilight they wrapped up warm in thick quilts and sat in basket chairs on the terrace facing the evening sky. The dog lay on the floor beside them.

"I'm house-sitting for him, basically," drawled Rosie. She stretched and raised her jewelled feet onto the stone wall. All her movements had slowed to a lower gear, including the way she spoke.

"Colin who runs the Sotogrande office rents here with James, his partner. They're due to leave in about six weeks, so they've gone off to Cadiz for a weekend fling. They asked if I'd keep an eye on Chester for them." Chester raised his head obligingly at the sound of his name, yawned and subsided back into a heap beside Rosie.

"He looks very sweet-natured."

"He's a little darling, aren't you?" Taking her time, she poured a glass of red wine for them both, settled back and ran a finger slowly round the top of her wineglass. "Great place this ... isn't it?" Dots of light flickered on in the distant *pueblo* across the valley.

"It's very peaceful."

"You like?"

"It's magical."

Rosie put her glass down. She leant over and pushed her head close up to Kate's, so close she could smell Rosie's winy breath.

"It's this house that could be available." She leant back again in her lounger, her eyes glinting, her cheeks flushed. "We could have all this!" She flung her arms out to embrace the night.

"What are you talking about?" Kate surreptitiously wiped Rosie's spit off her cheek as Rosie went coy, sheepish, cunning and triumphant all at the same time; tricky but Rosie could do it. She twisted round, brought her knees up and faced Kate again.

"We're thinking of buying it."

"Who is we?"

"Kate, this is such an amazing investment," she intoned in a low, hypnotic tone. "Fantastic position, views to die for and what a bargain. The owner is desperate to sell, he's had it on the market for over eighteen months now."

"Why do you want a huge place like this up here? It's miles away from anywhere."

Rosie threw her a triumphant grin. "De-dah! You suggested it."

"Me? Where do I come into this?"

"A centre – you fancied a cultural centre."

"Yes, but …"

"Hush and listen, okay? I told you I had an idea about a mountain property. Well, this is it! And we could get it at such a good price with the help of a mortgage and I know the people to go to. It'd be a crime to let this one go."

Kate was laughing, she couldn't help it. "But just because I mentioned a cultural centre down in Estepona, I didn't mean for you to go out next day and buy one."

"Excuse me, but you shouldn't say things you don't mean," Rosie snapped.

"We were only talking for fun, you can't blame me." Kate sank back onto the lounger, dabbing at her eyes.

"Okay, I get where you're coming from. But listen Kate." Rosie raised her voice an octave in her eagerness to convince. "It would be so ideal for you, and so therapeutic away from those noisy neighbours."

"Rosie!" Kate turned to her, full on. "You have to be joking! No way am I going to leap into some wild scheme I've just heard about, especially a cultural centre – in this wilderness!"

"You're always going on about how you don't like the buzz down there. Think, open your mind a little. We could run the centre up here together. Listen to nothing more noisy than blackbirds in the morning, goat bells tinkling."

"Rosie, what can I do with you!"

"I'm asking you to hear me out – and don't start laughing again." She refilled the glasses and stretched out her legs. "Just have another drink and relax."

"Rosie!" Kate repeated, shaking her head in disbelief. But she succumbed to her will and the beauty of the evening, and drank deeply. Stretched her legs out until her feet rested on the stone wall alongside Rosie's. They wiggled toes in unison. In silence they drank their wine.

"Ready now?" Rosie asked.

"Suppose so. If I have to be."

"Good." She put down her drink. "Now take a look around you." The garden lay below them, with dark trees at the bottom of the hill and the silent valley beyond.

118

"Honestly, Kate, isn't this all absolute magic? Everyone wants to come to Andalucía and not only to the coast. Inland is opening up all the time, it's turning into a hot spot of alternative life-styles. We'd be in on the crest of the wave. We could market this place as a cultural centre, holistic retreat, whatever. It sleeps about eight people as it stands and we could put up little cottages in the grounds, or even tents. You could run it, set up a web-site, organise courses in painting, art, drama, writing, you name it. And we could offer bird-watching courses." She paused to take a breath. "And get Steve to lead them."

So Steve's in it as well, Kate thought. Mmm. Not so bad. We could be up here, a good team, swimming in that pool together. His dynamics and my flair ... and I'm really ready to start working again ...

"Don't you think it's a marvellous idea?" Rosie pressed on.

Kate dragged her thoughts away from Steve. "But what about your work on the Costa?"

"I'd go down to half-time until it was established."

"How could you give up the Costa life for this? It's so remote. I thought you loved it down there."

"Don't you think I want a decent place for myself one day? It's my dream. I can have dreams too, you know."

"You said they were a funny lot in the mountains."

"Not everywhere, love. And here, it's just us."

The sky was clear, with more stars than Kate had ever seen in a Manchester night. Rosie was doing a good pitch and yes, Kate had to admit she was more than slightly hooked. How she'd love to be settled, at peace and in a place like this. But there was a question hanging in the air between them, unmentioned. The finance.

Rosie dished up an onion and ginger soup for supper followed by breast of chicken with rice, champagne and a melting pear and orange pie with thick whipped cream for dessert.

"I didn't know you could cook like this. It's all delicious."

"More pie?"

"Yes please."

"I love housework. This is how I'll cook for our guests, when we get them, you wait." She hummed round the kitchen, slicing and pouring. Money was still not mentioned and Kate was too replete to care.

Saturday morning brought condensation on the windows and chilly rural bliss. A blackbird sang his song on a tree outside the window. Rosie dashed into the bedroom to say goodbye. She was already dressed in her tight work trousers and carrying a briefcase.

"Got to show a client round a property nearby. Help yourself to breakfast and why don't you have a swim in the pool, I'll be back in under an hour or so."

"It'll be freezing cold and I haven't brought my costume."

"Don't be such a baby, it's fantastic once you're in. Borrow one of mine, go into the bedroom, bottom drawer of the chest under the window. Or why don't you swim in the nude. I often do when I come up here. There's nobody around and who cares anyway." Rosie unwrapped a sweet and popped it in her mouth.

"See you later."

Kate tiptoed down the path wrapped in the towel, followed by Chester pattering behind her. The sun was up but the water was icy cold and she plunged in and swam round with frantic little breaststrokes until she got used to it. Then it was exhilarating, swimming up and down, revelling in the sensual contact between her naked body and the water. She could do this every day if she lived up here. As she clung against the side doing leg exercises for the ever-hovering flab, the sound of a car droned up the drive. It must be Rosie returning early from her meeting. She backstroked up the pool, eyes closed against the bright sun.

"You look very beautiful." Kate's eyes jerked open to see Steve standing by the edge of the pool, his blue sweater casually thrown over his shoulders. He smiled down at her, making her heart pound.

"What are you doing up here?" She stood up in the water, attempting to cover her breasts with her arms, covered in goose pimples from the cold. She was trembling at the sight of him.

"Didn't Rosie tell you?"

"Rosie said nothing about you coming this morning. And please look away while I get out."

"You want me to throw you the towel?" Steve was playing with her and she knew it was deliberate. She swam to the pool steps trying in vain to hide her bare buttocks. He laid the towel on the ground by the steps and turned away, whistling to himself. Kate climbed out shivering and wrapped the towel round her nakedness. But she was aroused again by Steve.

"Are you decent now?" he threw over his shoulder.

"Sort of."

"Want me to rub you dry?" Steve presented her with a blossom he'd plucked from a nearby bush. He stuck the flower into her hair. Then he opened the towel and wrapped it round both of them.

And they kissed and kissed again. Kate was shaking with cold and desire as he led her inside.

"Down this corridor." She directed him to her room and closed the door on Chester who woofed in protest and then subsided. Steve pulled the blind down, stroked her body and kissed her delightfully all over. They fell onto the bed. And it was good again.

By the time Rosie returned, they were sitting on the terrace with Chester between them; snugly-smugly, nice and tidy, drinking coffee.

"Hi Steve, glad you made it in time. Mind if I join you both?" Rosie's smile was slightly forced as she poured coffee from the cafetière and plonked her briefcase down. Did she sense what they'd been doing?

"Time for talking," she announced. "Steve – shall I?" She looked from him to Kate enquiringly. Steve frowned and Kate decided to take over.

"It's about buying this place, isn't it? You want me to invest in it?" A silence descended. Nobody moved or spoke until Steve carefully put his cup down.

"Well?" Kate asked again. Rosie and Steve exchanged quick glances.

"Yes," said Rosie. "Interested?" But before Kate could speak, Steve did.

"You ought to be. You'd be a fool not to come in with us. It's sitting on a goldmine, this place is." He smiled into her eyes and Kate's cheeks flared hot and red. She felt seventeen years old again. This was idiotic. Get back to business.

"So you are both in on this?"

Steve drummed his fingers on the table. "It was my idea."

Rosie threw him a warning glance and he muttered and swigged his coffee.

"What is the situation exactly?" Kate pressed on.

Again they looked at each other over her head and with all this body language, she began to feel like Alice Through The Looking Glass trapped between the Red and White Queen. And she was picking up the hint of a sense of danger emanating from these two. Perhaps Gertrude was right after all? They could be up to something and even Rosie's absence this morning and Steve's seduction, delicious as it was, might be a deliberate part of it.

"Now Kate," he continued in a measured tone, spelling out the words syllable by syllable. "This property is up for sale and we're very keen to put in an offer on it. I can raise a sizeable amount up front and we wondered if you'd like to be involved as well."

"That's the house and the business we're thinking of," Rosie broke in.

"How much do they want for it?"

"Well," said Rosie. "It started at a million and a half euros."

"What?" Kate couldn't believe this. "Even if I wanted to, I haven't got that sort of money!"

"Don't you worry," soothed Rosie. "We'll get a mortgage for most of it. The asking price is now down to around nine hundred and seventy-five thousand. The market's very flat at the moment and in this instance, that suits us. And the price includes all the land, the fantastic fixtures and fittings. As it stands, basically – the contents we can negotiate on. I'm convinced we can get the whole thing for less."

"And don't forget," added Steve, "that price includes the old house as well."

"What old house?"

"You passed it on the way in," Rosie said, her tone a tad impatient.

"That ruin on the corner with the barking dogs?" Kate was astounded.

"Those dogs are going. The owner left them there to guard the place until it's sold. That house is included in the deal."

"But it's hideous!"

"Unlimited possibilities," said Steve. "There's a lot of land that goes with it, right down to the river, with a view to further development. It could be seen as an extension of our operation here."

"Not an operation, Steve, a cultural centre," snapped Rosie.

"The details are unimportant at this stage, Rosie," he barked back.

"Not to Kate they're not." Deadlock seethed between them. With an obvious effort, they both turned to her and smiled.

"We may have a little trouble getting all the finance," Rosie continued. "That's where you might like to come in with a bit of capital to boost ours. We thought we'd approach you first, give you first refusal."

"That's very kind of you."

In her eagerness to win her over, Rosie missed, as usual, Kate's attempt at irony. She swept on with her pitch.

"Now, you could either invest some money in the project, or we could borrow it from you. You'd get it back easily by the summer. Goes without saying, it'd all be done legally. I've got a fantastic lawyer. And you'd be in with us right from the beginning." She pushed her chest forward over the table. "You're going to have to buy eventually, so why not into this. You'd have it all: your own house in the mountains and a fantastic money-making career opportunity."

Rosie sat back. Steve took out a cigar. Rosie looked meaningfully at him and he thrust it back into his shirt pocket and drummed his fingers again. While Kate thought about it all.

Of course she wasn't going to commit to anything yet, of course she wasn't. She'd have to do a lot of research about it first and know much more about the whole set-up. And what about those dogs? But it was tempting. She was already three-quarters in love with this house, the grounds, the views, the swimming pool. She loved the idea of running it as a business and being close to Steve, working with him. It was the impulsive house-hunting oh-why-not old Kate back again, preparing to plunge into another new adventure that would get her neatly out of the one she was in.

"As a matter of interest, how much investment exactly are you looking for?" she asked, forcing down the cautious side, schooled by Uncle Roger and latterly Gertrude. She refused to focus on the image of her uncle's pink worried face and Gertrude's pursed lips and disapproving comments. Rosie and Steve snapped to attention.

"Don't worry about that now, let's first see what we can beat him down to," sang Rosie. "And we'll have a drink before he comes." She looked at her watch. "He's due this afternoon. Quick lunch everybody." She gathered up the coffee cups and went into the kitchen. Steve looked at Kate and winked at her. He leant forward and touched her shoulder with a gentle pressure and desire rose in her. She wanted him again.

The vendor arrived at five. He parked his car and walked up the drive. They stood at the front door and watched him.

"Look who it is!" Kate recognised him instantly. It was Juan from the artisan shop in the *pueblo*. He was dressed formally in a dark suit and tie and carried a briefcase.

"*Hola Juan.*" She recalled his friendly manner and the way his thick neat hair brushed the back of his neck. And the little silver teapot she'd bought in his shop.

126

"Hola, *señora, buenas tardes.*" He was clearly surprised to see Kate there. He bowed, kissed her on both cheeks but there was no twinkle today. The pleasant, laid-back manner had gone, it was strictly business as he shook hands with Rosie and Steve and they all sat down. He took coffee strong and black, no sugar. Negotiations started. But before Rosie could launch in, he stopped her.

"I have to tell you, *Señora* Rosa, I will not back down from the price we are asking."

"And I have to say that nine hundred thousand is our highest offer," retorted Rosie. "We all know the tenants are due to leave in six weeks. We can come in and take it over from that date. Save you any more hassle." She looked at Juan, head on one side, and raised her eyebrows at him winningly. Kate found that she semi-resented Rosie's flirty manner and her strategy wasn't working anyway. Juan remained unimpressed.

"I have already dropped the price far below its true value," he pointed out.

"If you want to sell the place, you have to be realistic. And with respect I must point out, *señor*, that there is work to be done. The roof needs attention, the kitchen needs reforming."

Kate listened as Rosie turned a potentially fantastic cultural centre into a dilapidated pile at the twist of a phrase. Juan clasped his hands, twitched and sighed. He was no match for Rosie.

"I cannot accept lower than nine hundred and fifty thousand," he declared.

"Nine hundred and twenty-five," she insisted swiftly.

"Not including fixtures and fittings."

"We can negotiate over those."

"I don't know." Juan sighed again. "It is worth much more but … well, I suppose I have to accept."

"So we have a deal at nine hundred thousand euros?"

"Nine hundred and twenty-five thousand, I think we said – and extra for the contents."

"A little, they're not in the best condition." Rosie made an effort to hide the triumph in her voice. She rose, ready to shake hands and embrace him to seal the deal. Juan was reaching for his briefcase when Steve butted in.

"That price of course includes the old house on the corner," he said. It wasn't a question, it was a statement.

"What are you talking about?" Juan glared at him. "That property is no part of the deal."

"It's already been discussed."

Juan sprang to his feet and so did Steve. "The other house is not for sale and is not negotiable, you know that!" shouted Juan.

"There's no point in this place without that one," snarled back Steve. They were like two angry lions facing each other head-on. Chester crawled beneath the basket chair, growling and whimpering.

"Steve!" Rosie tried to shush him. She could see her deal was sliding down the hill into the swimming pool. "Please, I'm sure we can work this out, don't you think, Kate?"

But Juan snapped his briefcase closed, zipped it up and straightened his jacket. His face was set and grim, his movements quick and decisive.

"I don't know who you have been discussing with. I have told you before that the other property is not included."

Kate couldn't stop, she had to say it. "Why do you want to keep that dreadful old place?"

Juan looked at her with pity in his eyes. "As for you, I thought you knew better. You are with these two. You are like them." He swung his briefcase round as if he was going to hit somebody with it and they all backed away.

"Goodbye," he said with a formal little bow. "There is no deal here." He marched away down the drive towards his car.

"No, stop." Kate ran after him, clutched his arm. She wanted to tell him she wasn't with them yet. She wasn't like them and she didn't want to lose him, let him go like that.

"Leave me alone." Juan pulled her hand away. "You get back to your friends."

They stood in a silent group and watched him leave. Chester barked after him.

Steve was livid. "You didn't handle him right," he blazed at Rosie.

"You mean you didn't, typical of you, so bloody tactless." With an effort she managed to breathe deeply and tone down her voice. She turned to Kate and tried to smile. "But don't you worry, Juan will come round.

He's full of bluster and then he caves in, that's the way he negotiates. He's done it before with another property. In the end we got it for way under the price. And this place, lovely as it is, is worth less than it's going for. The local council have got plans to build a sewage farm at the bottom of the garden. It's always been the land that goes with the old ruined house we've been interested in. Now that's got huge potential."

"You didn't mention a sewage farm."

"You're very naïve. It won't happen, I can guarantee. We'll get it. We'll have it all. There'll be a cultural centre here by the summer."

"And how are you going to get that?" sneered Steve.

"And you can shut up!"

The blissful weekend was truncated on Saturday afternoon. Steve drove off in a cloud of gravel and dust, with Rosie screaming after him. Kate followed in her car, slowing down to look again at the hideous old ruin of a house on the corner. What was all that fuss about? Why would anyone want to keep that? And what was she doing getting involved in all this?

Lost in fretful musing, Kate narrowly missed crashing the car at the busy Sabinillas roundabout and pulled a face at the woman driver trying to snake past her. The woman lowered her passenger window and shouted back, throwing her cigarette butt towards her with an aggressive gesture.

The traffic blanks out and Kate can't see anything but smoke swirling round her.

"Look where you're bloody going, can't you!" The English driver of the car behind was shouting and trying to get past. She had stalled on the edge of the roundabout with an orchestra of hooting cars behind. With trembling fingers, shoulders hunched in apology, she jerked the car forward and moved on. At the next available turning, she pulled off the main road, stopped the car and waited for the sweat and shakes to abate. What was happening to her? Where was she? She hadn't lost control of the car before like that. It must have been the stress of the weekend that had brought it on. She had to get home.

The burning house is here again, smoke, flames, terror, whirling, taking me over. This time I'm outside on the cold ground, choking, gasping, the sound of horses' hooves galloping off into the distance. A silver candlestick lies on the ground, rolling away ...

She woke with the taste of smoke and sadness in her throat. The room looked different. She was lost in a no-man's land and wanted desperately to go home but didn't know where home was. Down the long corridor? Where was that candlestick? There would be no peace until it was found. She knew she was on the wrong path with the wrong people.

CHAPTER TWELVE

The Sunday morning market beckoned, beneath blue Costa skies. Shadowy grey fish swam in the oily waters of the harbour, performing acrobatics for the children who crouched down to throw them morsels of food. Music swayed out of the stalls selling CDs. Gertrude sat on the terrace of the corner cafe, a pearly queen in a beige satin waistcoat, leather skirt and wide scarlet hat. She raised a glass of wine to Kate who waved back. As usual, the bright Costa del Sol morning was therapeutic. She felt better.

The mime artist stood on a plinth by the market entrance. He was poised as an airman in grey battledress uniform with a made-up shiny-grey face. He remained frozen in gaunt metal-grey position, clutching a red rose on a long green stem, until a passer-by dropped money into his box whereupon he eased into life, waved his rose at the donor in thanks and blew kisses to the crowd. And then froze into his next position. Kate felt in her pockets for some loose change to give to him. As the airman's eyes returned to statue-blank, her mind clouded over.

The image of the mime artist dissolves and standing in his space is a clearly defined young girl. She wears a long brown dress, held in at the waist with a leather belt. A fine scarf catches back her long dark hair. She looks straight at Kate, an arm outstretched. She is alien and yet so familiar, as if Kate has always known her. The port bustle retreats and all that Kate is conscious of is the young girl, her sad eyes pleading.

"*Ayúdame* ... help me," she begs.

Kate feels the girl's sickness and fear, she can smell the smoke of last night's dream and a thousand dreams going back hundreds of years. She needs to stop, sit, fall down.

The market swirls dizzily round her and Kate stumbles. She is aware of somebody far away tugging at her arm.

Slowly the vision of the young girl faded and the morning spun back to normal. The stall that sold tops and ties settled back into its slot on the right. The airman was back on his stand, blowing kisses and waving his rose.

And Gertrude was there beside her. "Get up my dear, you must have slipped." Her matter-of-fact tones helped Kate regain her reason and let go of what must have been a minor form of hallucination. She found she was holding a fifty *céntimos* coin in her hand and walked unsteadily forward to drop it into the airman's black cloth spread out on the ground. He sprang into mimed life, waved his rose and blew her a kiss. Kate was confused, her head half-full of that young woman in the long brown dress. She wished she could have kept hold of her. Helped her.

Gertrude twittered on. "I'm so glad I find you, Kate, come see what has arrived at the back door." She took her hand and they pushed through the crowds, the market smells and stalls, the cafés bustling with holidaymakers, their tables in front line market positions. Kate had done this before. She'd smiled through a market, acknowledging friends and acquaintances, with someone she loved at her side. But this half-forgotten recollection wasn't sinister and full of smoke. It was a cheerful memory that only made her sad because she was no longer sharing the moment with whoever it was. She missed that person although she didn't trust her either.

She was thinking like Gertrude, she must be taking on her suspicious nature. Quick girl, back to here and now. Where tourists in shorts hunted for bargains, ordered lunch and read the Sunday papers while people-watching fellow punters at the stalls. All such harmless but grounding activities that she was so grateful to be part of. Gertrude chivvied her like a mother hen up the chipped staircase of the port and past the kiosk on the corner which was surrounded by men in red checked shirts. She'd seen those men before.

"Ah, he is here, will you look, he is so sweet." A tiny scrap of vulnerable kitten crouched by the blue door. Gertrude picked up the handful of scruffy wool by the neck. "*Schatzi*, you will come with me, yes?" The kitten had milky moon-like pearls where his eyes should have been. He was blind but he had enough sense to meow pathetically at Gertrude.

"Gertrude, I saw the oddest thing at the market," Kate began. Gertrude gave her a look. Her eyes had known Kate for centuries and they perceived a truth far beyond her and her present sphere. She said nothing.

Kate lay on the bed, facing the wall splashed with splodges of squashed mosquito. Had she imagined that young girl on the aviator's plinth or did she exist; was she trying to send her a message from another time, and if so, why pick on her? There were no psychics in the family. Kate's paternal great-grandfather did predict the Second World War but that was on September first, nineteen thirty-nine, three days before war broke out and therefore not that incredible. *The Book of Help* was no help at all.

'THE ANSWER LIES IN ANOTHER PLACE,' it infuriatingly informed her. She could have told it that.

CHAPTER THIRTEEN

CORDOBA – 1469

When Ana takes a deep breath, the cloth buttons on her dress pop open. The hem of her skirt barely reaches the top of her ankles.

"You will soon need a whole new set of clothes," Mama notes. Ana sighs as she listens to Felipe playing his music and she cries and laughs for no reason.

Three weeks before her fourteenth birthday Ana has her first bleeding and becomes a woman. Her eyes are shining and she has developed a bloom on her cheeks. Her figure has changed from little-girl plump to curving and rounded. She stands tall in front of her bedroom mirror, throws her head back and swings her hair which falls in thick glossy waves. She likes what she sees.

It is Friday afternoon and Elvira has gone home early as usual. María is out singing in the choir at a nearby convent, or so she says. She will be back in time for supper. María keeps her life a secret, known only to herself.

Ana chops peppers and onions for the rice and chicken stew while Grandmother stirs the sauce and mixes in the herbs, saffron and vegetables. When the dish is simmering in the large pot over the stove Grandmother washes and dries her hands.

"Analita, finish what you are doing and come to the patio." This is an odd request for late afternoon when women's work has yet to be done. What could Grandmother want? She follows her into the flowery inner courtyard and Rosita patters after them.

Mama joins them, even more unusual. She busies herself watering hyacinths and picking dead heads off the flowers that blossom in earthenware pots fringing the patio. Ana can smell the orange scent and the heaviness of the damp earth.

"Please, Beatriz," says Grandmother, and Mama stops her work. Even Rosita ceases her purring and peers into Ana's face from a distance of two inches. "Come, Ana." Grandmother indicates the little chair and Ana pulls it close to her and Mama. "We have some things to tell you." Rosita settles on her lap as Grandmother starts to explain.

"In our family, as in many others, it is common sense to wait until the children are old enough to be told the complete truth about their heritage, when they are able to deal with it." Grandmother's lively face is solemn, and Ana is nervous, sensing that this is an important occasion relating to their religion.

"What do I have to know?" She clenches her fingers tight, staring at the petals scattered on the tiled floor. Rosita jumps off her lap with a meow of protest. Why can't our lives be clear and straightforward, she thinks. Why do we have to be *conversos*? Ana is well aware of the brooding hostility she frequently encounters in the streets. She has never forgotten those boys shouting and jeering at them at the fountain when she was a child.

She hates living in fear of what might happen outside her own door.

"Hush, Analita, there is nothing to fear," Mama reassures her. "We are good, observant Catholics, but you do realise that we also hold to the old Jewish ways. You know about our Friday nights in the cellar. And when Papa took you to the synagogue when you were a little girl? Because it was only seventy, eighty years ago that we were Jews and we do have the Jewish roots. Some of the customs we observe are from our Sephardic traditions and they are important to us. Especially to your father. He was taught to follow the law of Moses, and he learnt the Hebrew from his father who learnt it from his father before him." When Mama explains like this, Ana understands the mixed emotions she has felt in church and in the synagogue.

"It is our heritage," Mama continues. "You were born of parents both descended from Jewish blood, however Catholic your life is. And you should be proud of it."

Grandmother leans forward and tucks a stray brown curl behind Ana's ear. She squeezes her cheek, as she used to do when Ana was a little girl. "You know, my love, you are so like I was at your age." She sighs. "Then my hair was thick, not like this silver grey bush I have now."

Mama frowns. "Mother please, can we return to Ana?" Grandmother smiles at her strong-willed, sometimes impatient daughter-in-law, and nods.

"You even have a secret Jewish name," Mama continues. "It is Irena."

"Irena." Ana repeats the name. Yes, she likes it.

"And mine is Leah," says Grandmother. "I was named after my grandmother, to keep her memory alive."

"But your name is Ysabel! This is so confusing." Ana can't help smiling at all their secrets.

"Analita, we must not let go of our Jewish roots." says Grandmother. "Although many do, *conversos* should not visit the synagogue. And so it is up to the women of the family to keep the Sephardic traditions alive in the household. It is time for you to learn the ways of a good Jewish woman so you can pass our knowledge on to the next generation."

"Culinary secrets," says Ana with a knowing smile.

Grandmother smiles back. "And a little more."

After supper they sit under the orange tree in the patio, drinking camomile tea. The evening smell of jasmine fills the air. Papa, in his clean shirt, has looked in approvingly and taken Felipe away upstairs. Rosita, as an honoured female of the house, is between them, heavy and purring. María is not. She has eaten supper, cleared away the plates in a few minutes, sighed heavily at the solemn gathering in the patio and gone out to look for life by the fountain. Ana is glad she isn't with them, and she senses that Mama and Grandmother are relieved also. The house is at peace, the front door closed. They are safe from the outside world.

"Now Analita," her mother begins. "We will teach you what you need to know for when you have a husband, and your own home and family." Ana giggles and

139

blushes, Rosita yawns and blinks. Grandmother brings out her embroidery cushion and sews little pink stitches as Mama stands to show Ana the traditional blessing performed over the lamps to welcome in the Sabbath, the blessing Ana has seen her perform many times in the cellar. With Mama's guidance, Ana memorises the words and actions. She practises turning her palms outwards as if towards the candles, and then inwards towards her face. She kisses her hands three times as she speaks the blessing.

"*Boruch atah Adonai Alohiynu melech haaolom asher kidishanu bemitsvotav vetsivanu lehadlique nerot shel Shabbat ... Amen.*"

Ana stumbles over the unfamiliar Hebrew cadence and Mama embraces her proudly when she manages to complete it correctly.

"Good girl! It means 'Blessed are you, Lord, our God, sovereign of the universe, who has sanctified us with His commandments and commanded us to light the lights of Shabbat'. And after the blessing you can then pray to God for a moment and wish for your own private desires." Ana wonders what she would wish for. Maybe not to be frightened of who she is?

"You can perform the blessing with me next time we celebrate Sabbath in the cellar and soon it will become easy, you will do it without thinking. And this blessing you will pass down to your own daughters one day, God willing."

"God willing," repeats Grandmother.

"Now, do you have any questions you want to ask?"

"Mama, I've always wondered why we do not have a fire sometimes on Friday nights and Saturdays? Is this also part of our tradition?"

"Yes, Ana, it is. We do our best to observe those times as special. Orthodox Jews are not supposed to light fires or cook on the Sabbath. That is why we often make a big dinner for the Friday so there is enough for us to eat the next day as well and no cooking needs to be done on the Saturday. But people are watching us, ready to denounce *conversos*. You never really know who your friends are. Very often we will light a fire on the Sabbath so the smoke can be seen coming out of the chimney and this shows everyone that we are as Catholic as our Christian neighbours. And you will try to do the same, as best as you can and when you can. At the very least you will try to preserve our traditions." Mama takes hold of Ana's hands firmly. "But do not forget, Ana, that even within our close family circle, different family members can have different beliefs. I am warning you seriously, Analita, to perform this blessing in the secrecy of your immediate family, and even then, keep it with those you know you can trust. Say nothing about it. Not even to Felipe. Not until he is thirteen."

"What about María?"

"No. Not with her either." Mama's tone is sharp, and Grandma stops her sewing to listen intently, her needle poised.

"But she has learnt, has she not? She is older than me. Why has she not performed the blessing with you?" Silence floats round the plants encircling them.

"I repeat, you do not discuss anything we have done tonight with María."

"If she shares our heritage, why have you not shown her?"

"We have decided not to teach her the old customs, at least for the moment."

But Ana is persistent. "I am a woman now, you have to tell me. We do everything together."

Mama sips her tea and does not speak. Grandmother sets down her embroidery on her lap.

"María has been so devout in her church-going," she says, her round cheeks pinker than usual. "We think she is not receptive to the old teaching."

María's religious devotion to Christ is apparent to them all, although Ana does wonder if it is artificially imposed because it suits her purpose. Beneath her impassioned protestations of faith, María remains totally self-motivated and will do exactly what is best for herself at that moment, albeit with the utmost charm and plausibility. Yet despite their quarrels, they have been playmates as well as sisters, sharing all their activities. They studied their Catholic lessons, sang, worked together, sat in the cool evening by the fountain and bathed secretly in the river in the baking hot summer months when there was no rain and the ground was dry and dusty.

María is her confidante but Ana has to admit that she has behaved oddly, even violently at times and does not always tell the truth. She remembers the many deceits, the mystery of the spider in her apron. They all need to protect themselves. These are dangerous times.

142

Mama breaks in with a firm voice. "It is happening to *conversos* all over Spain, and here in Cordoba. You will have to take our word." Grandmother nods her agreement. Best to say nothing.

Their warnings succeed. Ana vows that she will never speak of their secret history. But she worries over the deceit. She has never been good at dissembling and she knows that María is capable of digging out the truth if she suspects a secret, and using it for her own needs.

"What about Pedro?" she asks, suddenly thinking of him. Grandmother returns to her embroidery and picks at the lace edging she is working on. Rosita yawns and closes her eyes.

"Pedro is fine. We know the family well. They are like us."

Ana feels a huge sense of relief that Pedro shares the same history. And does he have a secret name?"

"He has another name. It is Jacobiquo."

"Jacobiquo!" Ana laughs until her eyes are wet. She can't help it.

María pushes Ana into the fountain and holds her down in the shallow water, pressing hard on the back of her head as she wriggles and tries to squirm free.

"Aren't we having fun," she whispers. Ana splutters to the surface, coughing and spitting out water. Her hair straggles over her cheeks and water drips down her neck.

"Why did you do that?" she chokes out. "I could have drowned."

"Nonsense, you can swim and I am always here to save you. I'm giving you a Jewish ritual bathing, now you are a woman." María flicks her hair back and laughs wildly.

Gertrude and Kate watched Nina and the black cat as they licked each other on a mound of newly mown grass by the lighthouse and curled up together. The two cats had bonded through their adventure at the vet, and were now inseparable. They appeared at teatime and allowed Gertrude to stroke them so they had the best of both worlds. Freedom and food. There was a lesson for Kate here: know what you want, be single-minded and go for it. Did that include Casa Sueños? Gertrude-Wise-Woman was horrified at Rosie and Steve's offer on the house.

"You know what, Kate, you say nothing and you don't trust nobody.

"But it's a lovely house."

"You don't get involved with anything to do with your own money. Especially with those two. And him!"

"What is it about Steve? Please tell me."

"Don't ask me." They watched the cats in silence. "You know what," continued Gertrude, head bobbing. "You should travel. See some of the real Spain, that's what you have come for. Get away from here for a bit. Get those two out of your mind."

"Real Spain." Kate repeated the words and started to think.

"And you know, it's not that difficult, you don't need to drive yourself. There are plenty of coach trips

145

going to Granada, Sevilla, Cordoba. You should see the culture of the country, give yourself a break. You deserve it."

"Cordoba!" Kate breathed. How could she have forgotten about Cordoba and Uncle Roger's advice to go there.

"Or I tell you what, Kate, there is the regular bus, you could go on that, it's much cheaper. Get a move on and do it now."

"Should I go to Cordoba?" Back in the apartment she stared and fluttered *The Book of Help* and waited. It came up with an identical response in capitals. 'GET A MOVE ON AND DO IT NOW.'

Those were Gertrude's words! Gertrude could be a guru after all, or at least the witch Kate had suspected she was. She had to get going on this. At best she'd be doing a good thing for Uncle Roger and all the family. At worst it would get her away from the din below. From Steve and Rosie coming at her with news about Casa Sueños, that Juan was persuaded/wasn't persuaded to change his mind and then she'd have to make a huge decision she wasn't ready to make.

"Should I escape and spend all my money on Casa Sueños/Rosie and Steve with or without the ruined old house?" *The Book of Help* was pissed off with her as she pestered it again. 'IT COULD BE SOMETHING QUITE SPECIAL' was what it continued to declare in vague, petty fashion. Kate apologised. She'd been nagging it a lot lately. She'd try positive thinking.

Mmmm ... breathe in, breathe out ... let thoughts of noise, smoke and ruined houses wrap themselves into

146

parcels with frilly ribbons and evaporate over the sea to be replaced with loving thoughts … of what?

She could escape and go anywhere, but it had to be Cordoba. Kate prayed that Cordoba would provide new possibilities and answers. Correction, Kate. Chant the self-help mantra: I *wonder* if Cordoba will open any doors for me. Yes, she knew it would. She didn't need to ask *The Book of Help*.

The regular service to Cordoba departed at nine-fifteen from the bus station and arrived at four o'clock, not on Sundays or holidays, and that would do. That gave her two days there, and back in time for Spanish class. She splurged on a good hotel near Plaza Maimonides, in the heart of the old town, the Jewish Quarter.

Her bag was packed and she was off, feeling that she'd escaped. She switched off the mobile so Rosie and Steve couldn't get her. Throughout the journey she remained hunched against the window and spoke to nobody except the bus driver when she paid him. The other passengers were mostly backpacking youngsters and sturdy Spanish women and nobody was interested in Kate. Beneath her calm exterior simmered a bubbly belief that she was going back home. Back to Cordoba.

PART TWO

CHAPTER FOURTEEN

CORDOBA – PRESENT DAY

Kate found her hotel in the old town. A teenage youth sat on the ground playing a flute, his back resting against the wall. The hotel interior was expensively serene in soft beiges, with a large light atrium to the right. A canvas awning was pulled over its open ceiling. The material had little round holes set at regular intervals causing the light to shine through and form blue dots of patterned sky on the floor tiles. Music from *The Hebrew Slaves* played discreetly in the background. Black and white pictures of wise men wearing turbans in ancient Cordoba adorned the walls of her cream and brown room. It overlooked an inner courtyard with no sound of traffic.

Kate unpacked and sallied forth for the late afternoon stroll, waiting for the magic to start. But she had to confess to feeling no ancestral pull as she walked the crowded lanes of the old town, the *Judería*. It was easy to get lost in the winding maze of closely packed houses and souvenir shops, crammed with tourists. She was frustrated because she couldn't respond to being there in the meaningful way she'd planned. Yet when she saw the *'CUERO'* sign above Cordoba's Leather Workshop, it nudged her memory. Unbidden, there came into her mind the vision of a young man in a long

151

apron, diligently sewing beautiful slippers of the finest leather. She longed to touch him and be near him.

A car bleeped its horn and Kate jumped to one side of the narrow street to let it pass. The image of the young man vanished but she was left with an even deeper determination to explore properly and seek an answer to these memories or imaginings. This was what she'd come for.

Her spirits lifted as the gentle breeze blew, cool and fresh. A large dog with a ribbon round his neck lapped at a puddle of water in the street. In her own happy little time, Kate tracked down the Information Office by the side of the Mosque, near a line of tourist carriages and horses. The assistant provided a map of the Old Quarter with which to do her own tourist trail. The grandeur of the Mosque could wait. For the moment she merely wandered.

Close to the old Jewish Quarter, she found the small, rectangular-shaped Plaza del Potro. Cervantes had stayed at the old inn opposite, now a museum. Kate had written a sixty-page thesis on Don Quixote for her English degree when the other students were doing Jane Austen. There must have been a subliminal connection even then. She drifted on with growing confidence. She knew these streets.

She located the *Judería* Gate beyond the Mosque and went through to find her way back into the old town. The lanes and close-packed, white terraced houses embraced her now with their leafy patios glimpsed behind half-closed gates. Indoor patios suited her nature

– an introverted extrovert, true nature half-hidden and safe, all the goodies tucked away.

A wooden door stood enticingly open to reveal a courtyard with a blossoming tree in the centre. A nun in a brown habit was busy sweeping the yard with a long brush. The streets were similar to how they must have been in the fifteenth century: dark, narrow blind alleys, birds calling, spitting men, sewage smells. A notice on a shop-front declared 'The most Beautiful Patio in Cordoba – Step in and Browse' as Kiss FM radio played in the background. She was besotted and hyperventilating with Cordoba and had to stop for a decaff.

A fountain sparkled in the little plaza and nearby was a café in a courtyard ringed on three sides with townhouses. A baby wailed from an upstairs window and far away in the outside world, the taxis cruised by. Kate spread her map out and planned her next foray into the Jewish Quarter: up the streets of Blanco Belmonte including Calle de las Flores; then Calle Barroso, down Levi Aguilar, to Plaza Angel Torres and back, right along Buen Pastor. This was the inner core of the *Judería*.

By the time she was ready to start again it was early evening and the Quarter was revealing a hidden quality – as if it had secrets it was now letting her into. Although it was more than a little eerie in this mysterious setting of shuttered houses and hushed streets, she felt at home. Streets were emptying, doors softly closing, the tourist buses and sightseers long since gone. Just the odd person remained, flitting round corners and away.

She passed the statue of Maimonides sitting on a plinth in his plaza. His wise eagle eyes stopped her. Had she been here before? Was Uncle Roger right about Cordoba?

The waiter served her evening meal with a dour sulk on his face. Kate called him over and advised him to smile at the table.

"I think," said the waiter, pink with embarrassment, "it look more professional to behave formal."

"No, believe me," she said firmly, "it's much better to be friendly." So the waiter smiled at her whenever their eyes met. And she smiled back. Soon the whole dining room was smiling. The waiter bowed as she left and she almost kissed him on both cheeks.

In the cold February night air Kate sat on a bench opposite Maimonides, huddled into a camel scarf.

"Hail Maimonides," she called softly upwards. He was ensconced on his brownish stone plinth, wearing his turban and long gown. He held his stone book on his lap and looked knowing. The Cordoba Information Guide stated that Maimonides left Cordoba when he was thirteen years old and ended up in Egypt. He was a great Jewish philosopher and surgeon who performed cataract operations in the twelfth century. Kate watched him as dogs and stars emerged into the night.

"I'm here, Maimonides." She urged him to communicate. "Give me a sign." His eyes radiated wisdom but he said nothing.

154

"He's my Monides!" She threw her head back to look at the sky and tasted the first drops of rain.

* * * *

"*Venga!*" Smoke fills my nostrils and throat. Flames are shooting, growing, starting to spread down to the wooden floor.

"*Venga!!*" Come on! I hear the call again. This time I've woken up in the heart of the nightmare, I'm trapped in it, yet I know what is going on, what will happen next. I know it's a bad dream although it's impossible to control. It can destroy me if I let it, if I do not get out and quick. Heat is growing, smoke, burning … as I clasp the candlestick. I must save it …

Kate sat bolt upright, gasping for breath. Sweat poured down her face, between her breasts; her cheeks and forehead were clammy. She managed to put the bedside light on and look at the time. Ten past four in the morning. Smoke was in the air and in her sinuses, and she had again an overwhelming sense of loss and foreboding, a grief coming from deep within her soul.

She fell back against the pillow and let the dark Cordoban night comfort her. The smoke receded, she breathed heavily and slowly calmed down.

Her face was stark white, the pupils of her eyes dilated. She made a cup of coffee and sat up in bed, sipping it slowly. Half of it slurped into the saucer. There was no question of rational thought or returning to sleep. She lay down and breathed, using her

155

abdomen, in and out. And thought of a quiet haven …
where she was doing t'ai chi on pine needles under trees
in a space unfamiliar to her. But it was working,
soothing. The trauma trickled away, the strong sense of
something lost was subsiding.

She dressed in her black tracksuit, pulled the hood
up and left the room. Down the corridor she crept, past
bedroom doors with empty wine bottles lying outside.
The cleaners were already in the foyer and the front
door was locked. A woman came forward with the key
and let her out, rattling away in a thick *andaluz* she
couldn't take in. Her mind was on other things than
excuse me, *por favor*, slower please.

The silent chilly streets looked different from
yesterday. The alleys that had become her friends were
alien to her now and a left and a right turn led to yet
another dead end. Kate had lost the conviction and
sense of direction she had the evening before. But by
following the line of street lamps, she managed to reach
the Mosque, a clear landmark against the sky. She
continued past it and along a straight empty street that
took her out of the old Jewish Quarter and beyond, into
a small plaza with a fountain. Like a yo-yo retracting its
string, she was drawn straight to an alley off the plaza,
with its two narrow rows of silent sleeping houses. She
stopped there because she had to. A tingling sensation
ran through her body, from the back of her head down
to the edge of her toes. She knew this alley of shuttered
windows so well although she hadn't been there before
in her life. She kept repeating 'not in this life.'

156

Kate stood next to a high, three-storey terraced house, narrow with black grilles in front of its wooden framed windows. As she stared up at the top window, the door opened abruptly and a stout, elderly woman bustled out. She was dressed in a long brown cloak, and wore an angular shaped hat tied at the chin. Kate pressed into the shadows as the woman closed the door and set off down the alley towards the plaza. She hadn't seen Kate; was she invisible? Kate had to follow her. Determination took over from fear.

The woman made her way through the plaza and Kate continued to trail her as she rounded a corner and joined the hum of activity in a wider lane. And in an instant they were in the middle of a clear morning, the sun bright on the buildings opposite.

It had to be a film set with a cast of medieval extras galvanised into life by the director's call of action. Women in long skirted clothes stood in groups, scarves covering their heads. The young men were clothed in shortish tunics, their legs covered with coloured woollen leggings. They wore leather belts at the waist and some carried swords. Older men were wearing long cloaks and turbans, similar to the Maimonides statue and the pictures in Kate's bedroom. She saw olive skins, thick beards, dark eyes, long hooked noses. The streets had to be the same shape and size as yesterday, yet they appeared different. Smells of sweat, food and sewage were circulating, but they were more pungent and heavy. No taxis cruised past. Men were riding by on donkeys and mules and squeezing through the throng on horses and carts. And she was in the middle in her black tracksuit. Nobody seemed aware of her presence. She looked at the gold watch that had belonged to her mother and which she wore all the time. Her watch existed, therefore she did too. But how, where and when?

Her quarry, the elderly woman, disappeared around another corner and Kate ran forward to catch her up. She must not lose her. She entered the small plaza that she'd seen before, but then everything here she'd seen before, either from yesterday or perhaps from another time, another life. This plaza had the rectangular shape of yesterday's Plaza del Potro. Over there could be the same inn where Cervantes had stayed but now a circle of men were thronging the entrance, talking and jostling each other. They reminded her of the swarthy gang clustered round the kiosk at the Sunday market in Estepona.

It was market day here. A gang of lively horses were tethered, watched over by boys with long sticks. The plaza was alive with stalls, crowded with yet more men and women wearing what had to be medieval attire. The tunics, leggings and long cloaks reminded Kate of Chaucer's *The Canterbury Tales* and she should know, she'd produced it with final year Theatre Studies' students two years ago. A brilliant thought struck her. This had to be a Spanish TV reality show! Or was Cordoba staging a medieval market? Estepona had one in the summer.

Although she was bewildered by the activity around her, Kate couldn't help enjoying the vibrant, sensuous scene. A noisy horse auction was taking place in the corner. The open booths were laden with a variety of products. Luscious fruits were piled next to plants, tiles, baskets, perfumes. Food stalls were heavy with roughly made breads and cakes, and succulent hams, chickens and lamb joints dangled from meat stalls. Fresh fish gaped in a row and a group of musicians played a whining melody. It was very different from the Wednesday market in Estepona. There were no vans filled with rails of jeans and cotton drawstring trousers, no stallholders busy with mobile phones, cigarettes drooping from the side of their mouths. No middle-aged tourists in baggy shorts with digital cameras; no signs of modern life. As she surveyed the scene, Kate realised that she'd lost the woman she was following. Frantically she scoured the market. Nobody took any notice of her because nobody saw her.

There she was! Kate caught sight of the woman at a stall, down the far end of the plaza. She made her way towards her, pushing past the donkeys and clucking chickens in wooden cages. Nearby, a boy was singing a plaintive song, pure, clear and sad.

A stall on the left was selling leatherwear. Brown and black shoes and soft blue slippers, purses with fine stitching and beading were spread out on display. A young man wearing a long apron sat on a high stool at the back of the booth, working away at a pair of leather boots. He was intent upon his craft but Kate realised that he could see her because he put the boot down and looked enquiringly in her direction. Or was he looking at someone behind her?

No, he smiled and gestured at Kate. He was slim, with a round face, wide full mouth, curly black hair and an olive skin. Was he the young man she thought she remembered yesterday? She wanted to stop and talk to him, look at his work, buy a pair of blue slippers, but how could she? She didn't belong there.

Kate moved on to the next stall, still looking for the woman. Herbs and spices were laid out in rows at the front of the stall. The aromas of basil, ginger and thyme were pungent and the smell of saffron was overpowering. A girl was working behind the counter. She was clad in a long dress, narrow to the waist, and her rich dark hair rippled in waves down her back. Her eyes were large and brown, her cheeks full. She was beautiful, like Snow White, the classic Disney version. Kate's mouth dropped open at the sight of her. She was dizzy again with the clash of centuries, of knowing. Kate recognised her. She was the young woman who had been standing on the aviator's plinth at the Sunday market.

The girl finished weighing the brittle red strands of saffron and wrapped them in thick greased paper. With a smile, she handed the parcel to her customer, an old lined man with gnarled hands and a turban. But when she turned to Kate, her body stiffened, her eyes widened in shock.

Kate's astonishment was greater. She realised she was looking at herself, but a good few years younger and more beautiful. The girl had Kate's lips, her wide hips, round brown eyes but hers were larger, more doe-like. Her hair was curly like Kate's, but darker and longer.

Without taking her eyes off Kate, the girl stretched out her hand. She was speaking to her.

"*Ayúdame*," she begged again. "Please help me. Only you can."

And then Kate saw somebody else in that frame, another girl with long fair hair, her back towards her. She was laughing with a large young man whose face was obscured. If she turned round, Kate would know who she was. Perhaps this other girl could see her too! Kate sensed danger, had to get away. She pushed through the crowd and out of the market.

The prickling sensation in her body had returned. She was in front of the house again. She knocked on the heavy wooden door because she believed there was a person within needing help and someone who might help her. The door opened and a young girl with long fair hair stood there, identical to the girl she had half-glimpsed at the market. But how could she be there, when she was at the spice stall a few moments ago? The girl's mouth fell open at the sight of Kate, her face turned ashen. She screamed and slammed the door shut. Her footsteps echoed on stone tiles inside the house.

Run run away Kate, run down the alley. Down the long street ...

When she opened her eyes, she was half-lying in the street with the dank Cordoban morning rising around her and her face throbbing. She must have fallen on the cobbles. A car was hooting, a voice shouting. A taxi was stationary in front of her, the driver blaring his horn.

Gone were the market sounds, the sights, the smells. Kate struggled to her feet and moved to the side of the street to allow the taxi to pass. She walked carefully into the little plaza as another taxi navigated the fountain roundabout and out. A siren wailed in the distance. But where were the carts, the caged chickens, the horses? The people she knew? Where was she?

Kate sat down on a stone wall circling the fountain. The water rippled in front of her. A group of young men headed towards a nearby university building, laughing and joking. How she envied them. How easy to be a student and study here and wear long narrow dresses with these chickens squawking round her. She wanted to live here. Does she live here? The street swayed and settled into a green blur which materialised into a stout woman wearing green shorts, a striped green blouson jacket and green and white trainers.

"Are you okay, honey?" She had an American accent and she jogged Kate's shoulder gently. She repeated her question and Kate looked up and leaned back against the stone. She pushed the hood of the tracksuit off her head. Cordoba stopped moving round her. She must have had a mini black-out.

"My, what have you done to your face?" Kate touched her cheek, and felt the wet blood and the bruise.

"You sure have taken a fall." The woman was kind. She sat with Kate on the edge of the fountain as she re-orientated. Now the taxis driving past made sense. That

162

was good. At least there was no time or space ambiguity about *them* – they were here in present time and therefore so must she be. Kate found a tissue from this century in her tracksuit pocket and dabbed at the cut.

"You need to get that washed and put some disinfectant on it."

"I will, as soon as I'm back at the hotel."

"Where are you staying?"

"Not far from here, I think." Kate wished she could remember the name of the place.

"Let me take you to the nearest medical centre – or at least for a strong coffee."

"No no, thank you, you are very kind, but I'm fine now. Do you happen to know the square where the statue of Maimonides is? My hotel's nearby."

"Sure, it's quite a way, back in the old town." She directed Kate to a lane off to the left and with more thanks for her kindness, Kate set off.

She could see the landmark of the Hostal Bagdad – and now she'd got her bearings – she was on Calle Sánchez de la Feria and close to Maimonides and the hotel. It was a Thursday. Kate was back in the twenty-first century, with a bleeding cheek and a memory that was vanishing fast, like a dream she couldn't keep hold of. Her watch told her it was gone ten o'clock in the morning. But she'd left the hotel before dawn. She'd lost a lot of hours.

163

CHAPTER FIFTEEN

CORDOBA – PRESENT DAY

A sign for the *Sinagoga* hung on the right. Beyond the brown entrance door, half-open, lay a paved courtyard leading to the synagogue. An elderly man with a walking stick beckoned her through – please come in, it's free to visit.

A group of female tourists filled the small square room. They stood together, arms on sturdy middle-aged hips, in an attentive circle. The long lean guide addressed them in thickly accented English. He wore black trousers, a white shirt and a black cape, and he had a thick pointed black beard with a shock of black and silver hair to match. A little round cap balanced on his head, held on by a large clip. Dark-rimmed glasses perched on the end of his long nose.

Kate hovered at the edge of the group, until one of the women called her over to join them.

"We're all from Utah," she confided in a drawling aside. "We're a mix of Jews, Christians and Muslims, and we've come in a special united group to see the Golden Age of Cordoba."

"Thank you, I would like to hear what he's saying."

"You can stand here with us and listen in if you like." This must have been Kate's lucky day for kind

164

American ladies, so she did, at first half-heartedly and then avidly as the guide went through his routine.

"The Golden Period of Cordoba was around the tenth to twelfth century," he proclaimed in emphatic tones, "when communities of Jews, Arabs, Christians, all lived together in harmony. Cordoba was the cultural, scientific and philosophical centre of Spain in the tenth century. The first synagogue here was built before the Mosque, or *Mezquita*, it stood where the Mosque stands now. It was here before the Roman church, before anything. This one was built in 1316." He swivelled and pointed and they all followed his direction. "Here, you can see the raised platform – the *bimah* – facing east and above this room is the women's gallery. It was a private family place of worship back in the fourteen hundreds. After the Inquisition and the Jewish expulsion of 1492, it stopped being a synagogue and was used for other purposes, such as a business centre and a refuge for sick children. That is why it was not destroyed with the rest of the synagogues in Cordoba."

The guide's words were resonating in her head. She had to speak to him.

"Thank you ladies, that is all." He concluded his presentation. "Any questions before we move on?" One brassy-blonde lady with a blue Alice band requested that they sang a religious song to commemorate the visit and she started up with *This Little Light of Mine*. While they warbled and swayed, arms lovingly round each other's waists, Kate sidled up to the guide.

165

"That information was so fascinating. I'm very interested in what you're saying, about the past in Cordoba, and Jewish history."

"Then you should come on the next tour," he replied, head down, busy checking his notes.

"Are you Jewish?" Kate blurted out. She had to ask him although it was impertinent, the personal kind of question she used to tell the kids at school not to ask.

"Are you?" he boomed back at her.

"No. Well, I don't think so."

"You don't think so. What kind of answer is that?" This man was as hectoring as Steve. Being over six foot tall didn't give him the right to be so overbearing.

"Look, I'm not a regular tourist," Kate explained. "But I'd like to find out more about the Jewish past, to see if I've any connection with it."

"Okay now, my name is Josef Gómez. And I live in Toledo." Perhaps he'd sensed her desperation or taken pity on the upturned, wounded face.

From his leather rucksack, he pulled out a stubby pencil and a scrap of lined paper on which he wrote down his address in Toledo and his telephone numbers, landline and mobile. "You want to know anything, you get in touch with me."

"I apologise for taking up your time."

"It's no bother, they are happy," he replied, waving a dismissive hand at his swaying, harmonising group. He took another look at Kate's face, which must have been showing at least a hint of what she'd been through.

"Pardon me, but you seem troubled, and you have a bad scratch on your face."

166

Kate's hand flew to her cheek, shielding it. "Yes. Something has happened which I can't explain. To do with the past. But it's gone, it's all a blank now."

"You have to respect the past," he said briskly, packing his pencil, notes and information leaflets back into the rucksack.

"Excuse me, you didn't tell me, if you are Jewish."

"What do you think?" He shrugged. "Half of Cordoba is Jewish, don't you know that?"

"How can that be?"

He sighed impatiently. "You must learn about the Sephardim, the *conversos*. The Crypto-Jews, the *marranos*, whatever you want to call them. Do some homework."

"Are they all Jewish?" They sounded an odd bunch to her.

"Of course, but it's far too long a story to start now." And he surprised her again by stooping forward and down, and kissing her on the good cheek.

"You should clean up that scratch, it could be infectious. I will be home in two weeks, I'll help you as much as I can. Please give me back the paper." He added his email address. "So, you can email me if you wish."

The women finished their song and Josef returned to being the guide. "Ladies!" He clicked his fingers to attract their attention. "Okay, now we are going to look at the Roman Bridge and the Torre de la Calahorra Museum." Kate's Utah confidante mouthed a goodbye and the group departed. She felt bereft without them, but she'd met Josef Gómez. In the few minutes she'd been with him, she had discerned that although Josef

167

lacked patience, he did have passion, integrity and knowledge. He knew the history of Spanish Jews and he could be a link that would help her to uncover the mystery of her past.

Kate walked the streets in turmoil, desperate for some base to bring her back to normal life. On impulse she rang Steve but his mobile was switched off so she tried Rosie on hers. It rang and after a while Steve answered. He was out with Rosie, they were having a drink. She was paying the bill. A massive shaft of jealousy hit her. How come, thought Kate, they were together when he was supposed to be my boyfriend, having a thing with me? And when had Rosie ever paid the bill when I'd been with her?

As she sprinted back to the hotel, she gave Maimonides a swift salute and received his customary non-response which carried a hint of reproof. Very clever, Maimonides. He could make his enigmatic blankness convey anything he wanted.

It was now gone eleven, breakfast finished at eleven-fifteen and the bus left at one. Kate had been up half the night and she was starving. She washed the scratch and dabbed the blood away, it was only a surface graze and cleaned up easily. Doing normal curative actions such as the wash, wince, dab, wince, dry, helped to ground her back into the present and restored her appetite.

After devouring muesli, wholemeal buns and fresh coffee, all in matching tones of beige, string and brown to blend with the dining-room decor, she dashed out to an artisan workshop tucked away behind the hotel for a final browse round. She pushed through the narrow door and fumbled her way into the dark interior. At the back of the shop the owner was cleaning silver pieces in a bowl of vile-smelling cleaning solution. He was blowing them dry with a hair-drier. Music played and the melody reminded Kate of a song she'd heard somewhere this morning. She rummaged along the murky shelves and tables where sat the small pictures and ornaments. She wasn't after anything specific and consequently no symbolic gong struck a warning. But as she went deeper into the dark recesses of the shop, she could smell the smoke again. It was a signal, telling her she was on the path.

A large old box crammed with tarnished silverware crouched in a corner. She plunged her hands into it, pushing aside irrelevant pieces. Searching with increasing excitement, she reached her target, the one that called to her.

From the bottom of the box she pulled out an object and sank back on her heels, looking at it. It was a single silver candlestick, delicately made with a slim curved stem, tapering down and opening up to the solid round base. She held the beautiful object reverently, turning it over carefully.

Into her head drifted the image of a dark cellar, a woman moving her hands, making a blessing … The stem glowed warm, sighing please take me home with you.

A faint smell of smoke hung over it. Looking closely, Kate could make out old markings on the stem and along the base but she couldn't read them. She had to keep hold of this candlestick. It was hers before she ever saw it. She ran back to the silversmith, clasping it to her chest.

"Can you tell me where this came from?"

He stopped polishing. "Who knows? I think somewhere in Cordoba. Is very old, it needs a good clean up. It has been hanging around the shop for years. You interested in it?"

"Yes, I am."

"Is a very fine piece of work probably done by a Cordoba silversmith. Is only one of two matching."

"How old do you think it is?"

"Is hard to tell. Maybe two, three hundred years. It could be more."

"Do you know where the other one is?"

"I'm sorry, *señora*, we have only the one. But a single candlestick like this, you get for a cheaper price. Most customers want the two."

Kate didn't care, didn't ask how much it was. She went for it. The silversmith cleaned it up in the bowl and dried it with the hair-drier. It sparkled at her.

As the bus drove south, an English woman behind her went on and on about Cordoba. "It's got such amazing vibrations, so spiritual, and so good to be away from the Coast. We must move up to the mountains. On our next trip out here we have to look at properties outside town. This has really got us moving ..." And dum de dum de dum de dum. Kate lay back and let the cheerfulness lull her away from the events of the morning. She should buy some antiseptic cream for the bruised face. And have the second anti-tetanus jab for the scratched hand. She wouldn't think about Rosie and Steve cosily sharing drinks and mobile phone calls. She thought instead about her silver candlestick, wrapped in thick paper, resting on her knee. Why had it been hidden away like that? Was it waiting for her? She'd buy some silver cleaning fluid to keep it gleaming and beautiful. And come to terms with Cordoba and the whole weird experience. That dream of a young girl in the market; her pain and her connection, if any, to Kate.

All the way back to the Costa in the rocking bus, Kate dozed and thought back to her own youth. She'd known some Jewish girls at school and had been good friends with a few. Through her teenage years they'd played tennis in the local park and gone to clubs in town at weekends. She'd even gone out with a boy at college who came from an orthodox Jewish family. They'd met at a seaside party and swam nude in the sea on their first date. He became a TV producer specialising in wildlife documentaries.

Kate's family wasn't religious in any way. Her mother had gone to church occasionally and she used to accompany her at Christmas and Easter. Her father never went near a place of worship. Consequently, she grew up more or less religion-less. This lack of spiritual roots might be an indirect reason for her inability to settle down in one place and with one man. She'd been out with plenty of lads from the age of twelve onwards,

171

but she was the one to finish with each one. She couldn't commit. Now there was Steve and the desire to be with him was strong – Kate thought of the insolent stare from those blue eyes and she was hooked. But in her heart she knew that Steve was one more in a long line of unsuitable men. Her true passion came not from organised religion or men but from nature; from the mountains, the sea and walking the *paseo*. That was when she felt most at peace. Coming to Spain had brought this knowledge to her.

The woman behind fell asleep and snored gently as the coach whizzed down to the Costa. Kate hummed a sad song and the candlestick sang it back. What was its story? Where had she heard it before? Was this why she'd had to come to Cordoba, to find the link between past and present?

CORDOBA – 1470 ANA'S BEDROOM

The house is hushed on a quiet Sunday afternoon. In his bedroom Felipe picks out a minor key softly on the strings of his *vihuela*. The sounds filter into Ana's hot attic room where she is sitting by the open window. Grandmother climbs the narrow stairs and joins her. She stands for a moment patting her chest and getting her breath back.

"I've come to tell you a family story." She pulls up the small rocking chair close to the window and sinks heavily into it. It is a little tight for her. "I sincerely hope I can get out of this chair, I do not wish to spend the rest of my life stuck in it." She fans her face, to cool down.

"So, Ana, it is time. This is your family history, as it has been told to me." Ana curls onto the window seat, happily anticipating a lively childhood memory. Grandmother rocks to and fro for a few moments.

"You know before your family name was changed to Ramírez, our Jewish name was ben Alaman. The family moved to Cordoba from Lucena about a hundred years ago, that would be around the year 1370. So they have lived here for generations. The family trade was begun by Juda and carried on by his son Emanuel, followed by Isaac, then by his son Rafael who was my dear husband, and your father, Antonio, continues as a *platero*, a silversmith, to this day." Grandmother's voice

173

is steady, but her eyes are sad as she stares through the window. "It was in March 1391, after Ash Wednesday that it started. Isaac was then about twelve years old. He was the oldest of the four children born to Sara and Emanuel. Then there were the two girls, Sulanita and Dona, and Avram was the little boy. Just five years old."

"So Isaac was my great-grandfather?"

"Yes. It is less complicated than it sounds. One day, if Mama allows, I will draw you a family tree that shows it clearly. Isaac died well before you were born. His mother was Sara."

"Married to Emanuel?"

"Exactly, she was your great-great-grandmother. They used to say that Sara was the liveliest young girl in the community when she was growing up. But she was not at all like that when I married into the family." Grandmother speaks slowly. Her intensity and stillness indicate that this will not be one of her happy stories of when she was a child. Ana waits as Grandmother sits in silence for a few moments. Then she sighs.

"I am ready now, Analita." Automatically, she puts her arms up to her hair, checking that the pins are firm, holding her bun in place. "I will tell you how it happened, what has been passed down to me."

Silversmith Emanuel ben Alaman lived with his wife Sara and their four children in the Jewish Quarter in the heart of Cordoba. Most weekends the whole family gathered at the grandparents' house, a smallholding in the countryside outside the western wall of Cordoba.

On a warm Sunday in early spring, little Avram sat under a tree, watching the girls as they picked up their long skirts and danced in the long grass with their cousins. His big brother Isaac ran after them over the fields and orchards, darting among the vines, olives and fruit trees.

"Wait for me," Isaac yelled. They laughed and shouted as they pulled down oranges and collected the battered ones, rolling them along the ground. In the country Isaac enjoyed behaving like a kid again. A gangly twelve year old, Isaac had begun training as an apprentice silversmith in his father's workshop and his *bar mitzvah* was less than twelve months away.

It was after midday when a rider came clattering up the cobbled pathway to the house. Solomon, Isaac's favourite uncle dismounted rapidly. He tethered the horse to a nearby post and ran inside, his face flushed and anxious.

"Children, stop your playing and come inside," called Sara from the doorway a few moments later. They clattered in, rosy and excited from their games until the

175

silence in the room stopped them. They shifted enquiring glances to each other. What was happening? Isaac could sense trouble by the serious look on his Grandfather's face.

"The news is all over the Quarter, I had to ride out to tell you," Uncle Solomon announced when they were seated round the table. "It is what we have been fearing. The uprising against the Jews has begun in Sevilla." Two days' hard ride from their home in Cordoba.

"Oh God, no!" cried Sara.

"When did this happen?" asked Grandfather.

"On Ash Wednesday, Archdeacon Martínez incited the people to riot. They stormed into the Jewish Quarter. The police caught some Jews and publicly flogged and beat them."

The family sat in stunned silence, digesting the news. Finally Grandfather spoke. "We have been expecting this for a long time."

Cordoba was no longer the city it used to be, the vibrant centre that had produced Maimonides, a place of culture with philosophers, poets and musicians on every corner. Where Jews, Christians and Moors lived together in harmony and Jews were allowed to own and farm the land. But back in 1378, shortly before Isaac was born, the Archdeacon of Sevilla had launched an anti-Jewish campaign. He tried to incite the people to purge themselves of their 'dirty Jewish citizens.' In recent times, hostility and violence against the Jews had been spreading all over Andalucía. The Jewish community heard stories from the travelling pedlars who came to the bazaar, and it was the same also in the

176

north. Everyone in the *Judería* knew what was happening.

"The terror is starting," whispered Sara. Sulanita clutched Isaac's hand hard, her eyes filling with tears. Little Avram ran to his mother and pushed himself onto her knee.

"Please, let us try to remain composed." Grandfather looked round the table at his family. "The strongest things we have to sustain us are our religion, the synagogue and our family life. And most important, our sense of who we are and what we have been. As a race, we are used to persecution but we should not despair. Even now, not all the Christians hate us. I have good customers and Christian friends living nearby who respect me, and the ben Alaman family. They are as concerned as we are about the growing anti-Jewish attitudes. But we must try not to live in fear."

"It will not come here, will it?" squeaked little Avram. His mother bent down and hugged him.

Grandfather chose his words carefully. "We must extend sympathy to our Jewish brethren in Sevilla, and hope and pray that the troubles will not spread to Cordoba."

Two months later the mob in Sevilla attacked again. They set fire to the gates and stormed into the *Judería* where they attacked Jews on the streets and in their homes. All of Sevilla's twenty-three synagogues were destroyed and the community was in ruins; most of the Jewish inhabitants were massacred. Surviving Jews were removed from all positions of influence and power and given the same ultimatum: you must convert to Christianity or you die.

What Grandfather ben Alaman feared, came to pass. Riots against the Jews spread throughout Andalucía and they soon reached nearby Cordoba. When the beating of drums and the shouting was heard outside the gates of the *Judería* everyone fled home or out into the countryside to hide.

Emanuel and his son Isaac closed and bolted the workshop. Mother Sara stood by the door checking her family in: husband Emanuel, son Isaac, the girls, they were all there except for little Avram, the family favourite. Avram had been outside in the street and he did not come home.

"Avram, Avram, where are you?" Sara was screaming for him, the girls ran up and down the narrow alleys calling his name but nobody could find him. And all the time the mob was coming closer to the street where they lived, near the synagogue. Their neighbours had already disappeared, barricaded into their houses with the doors locked and bolted. "We have to go into hiding," Emanuel insisted. Ignoring Sarah's anguished protests, he got his family inside the house and opened the cellar hatch. They squeezed, tumbled and fell down into the cellar and Emanuel locked the door behind them. They were all there, safe and hidden. All except for Avram. They crouched in the dark. The air was heavy, making them cough. Isaac could smell the sweat of fear on their bodies.

The riots in the *Judería* went on for two days, with fighting, stealing and killing. The family stayed down in the cellar with no food except for some crusts of bread, dates and figs. From upstairs in the house came the intermittent sounds of the rioters, the shouting, crashing and shattering of furniture – and then the silence. And all the time they were praying for Avram. When Emanuel thought the noise had died down, he allowed them to creep up the cellar stairs. Most of the furniture had been smashed, chairs were broken into pieces and all the silverware was gone. The cat lay dead by the hearth. Smoke from burning houses hung in the air. And Avram had not come home.

Stunned men and women were emerging slowly out from their houses and surveying the devastation. The word on the street was that the attack on the Jews was more to do with theft than assault, so the family went on hoping and praying. But at the end of that week, their good friend and neighbour, Chaim the tanner, came to tell them. Avram's body had been found down in a ditch by the river, covered in mud, blood and stab wounds. He must have run down there to try and hide and he had been attacked. Sarah's screams could be heard up and down the street.

Sara never recovered from the loss of her beloved youngest son. The once lively woman descended into a deep depression where she did not wash or change her clothes for days and would sit staring at the wall, and speaking not a word, a sad, silent woman. At other times she shrieked, broke plates and tore at her face with her nails until the blood dripped down her face. And from the moment of Avram's death, she was pushing Emanuel to convert to Christianity.

"So many Jewish families are converting – all our friends are converting, why should we not do it also?" she cried to her husband every night. It would not bring Avram back but at least they would be safe.

The Alamans came from simple artisan stock, with a tradition of devout Jewish faith. Emanuel was stubborn and, like many of his brethren, he did not want to change his religious beliefs. But in the years after 1391, the pressure to convert was strong. Jews were continually being attacked, both physically and mentally. The Church would send Catholic preachers into the Quarters, surrounded by their fanatic Christian followers. These preachers would surge into the synagogues in order to convert the terrified congregations, and mass conversions inevitably followed. Some Jews fled the country, but the Alaman family stayed. The arguments between Emanuel and Sara grew; they were souring their marriage and weakening Emanuel's shaky health. In the end he had to

180

agree for the sake of Sara's sanity. In 1394 the family converted to Catholicism.

They were baptized on a June morning. The ben Alaman family went out as Jews, the holy water was poured upon them and they returned as Catholics or *conversos* as the Old Christians called them. They became known as the Ramírez family. Emanuel wiped the baptism water off his brow as soon as he was home. And although Sara always grieved for the death of her beloved son, she managed to live a life again.

Along with other *converso* families in Cordoba, they were moved out of the *Judería* northwards, but not too far away. Emanuel wanted to retain his links with the old community even if he was no longer part of it and their old synagogue was now a church. Their new home was near the market plaza, in a district where Christians and fellow *conversos* lived together.

Life in so many ways became simpler and easier for them all. They were safe from persecution. Emanuel was well-known as a good silversmith, his son Isaac was his apprentice and carried on the trade. Their business flourished, with an increase in Christian customers willing to trade with the New Christians. But there was the emotional question. How could the family cut their Jewish roots? Every family drew the line in a different place. Like many other new *conversos*, they slipped back to the Quarter, into the remaining synagogue on the Jewish Holidays. They secretly kept in touch with uncles, aunts and cousins who had not yet converted. They bought their meat from the kosher butcher in the Quarter and kept the Friday night Sabbath and the Fast

Days. Secretly they celebrated Passover. They tried to keep the law of Moses. They could not help it.

Ana kneels at Grandmother's feet, wrapping her arms round her waist. They hug and rock together.

"What became of the rest of the children when they grew up?"

"A moment, please, Analita." Grandmother retrieves the handkerchief tucked in her sleeve. "I was thinking also of my Rafael, my dear husband, may his soul rest in peace." She wipes her eyes and continues. "Sulanita, she married a Jewish man and went away to live near Almeria – your Uncle José is descended from this branch of the family. And when Isaac married, in the church, they also had a secret Jewish ceremony. Although we are forgetting, we try to remember. A little of the Hebrew learning has been passed down through the generations. Isaac taught his son Rafael the blessings and his *bar mitzvah* portion. When I was seventeen, Rafael married me in the church and we too had a secret Jewish wedding. Your dear grandfather taught Antonio, our son, your Papa, to read the Hebrew blessings from the Hebrew Bible as he is teaching Felipe now. And so it must go on. How can you ignore over four thousand years of religion?"

"What about Dona?"

Grandmother takes Ana's face in her hands. "What I am going to say now, Ana, is important for you, yes?"

"Yes," breathes Ana, her eyes fixed on Grandmother's face.

"Isaac's younger sister, Dona, she changed her name to Madelena. She took to Catholicism with a fervour, attending the church for every service. Like Sara she could be unbalanced in her emotions. After a quarrel with her father, it must have been about religion, she pulled off her fine Saturday clothes, tore them into shreds and threw them out of the window. She did not even look Jewish. She refused to marry within the faith, resisting her father's pressure. I used to hear them talk about her. How she was so beautiful, with the big blue eyes and long fair hair, who knows where she got it all from, and with such a temper. They would see her on street corners preaching against the Jews and *conversos*. She would not acknowledge her family at all, it broke her father's heart. Then one day she was not there. They heard that she had entered a convent up in the north and become a nun, lost to our religion and to the family. She became like a blank space that nobody saw again. But by then it was a relief to everyone. Such a relief."

Grandmother stops speaking. Her hands droop onto her lap, her pink cheeks are stained with tears. Felipe's music floats up the stairs. The melody has changed to a cheerful lilting rhythm and they can hear the stamp stamp of his feet accompanying the beat of the music. María is singing along, laughing and arguing with him. How innocent they both sound.

"Does María know any of this?" Ana asks. Grandmother shakes her head.

"Such hidden tragedy in our past," sighs Ana.

184

"There are secrets and sadness in all families. But there has been a worry with the Ramírez family connected to the women. You could describe it as an extremism, an imbalance and as I have told you, it goes back generations. It is important for you to know this. Sadly, it is present now." Ana knows who Grandmother is referring to: her sister and best friend.

"Of course María is fully aware that we practise some Jewish customs and rituals," continues Grandmother in a low voice. "She could denounce us if she wanted to. You never know what she might do. I am warning you yet again, Ana. Be very vigilant."

This is what Grandmother wants her to understand.

CHAPTER SIXTEEN

ESTEPONA – PRESENT DAY

Why did Kate feel such a sense of doom hanging over everything? She tried to be rational.

<u>List of Bad Things to Dampen the Spirit</u>:
Non-stop rain for two days – although technically not such a bad thing. Andalucía had been longing for rain for months. It poured down, and rivulets of brown mud tipped into the already greasy water of the harbour. At the rental agency, pipes burst and raw sewage swilled out with the water. In town, waterfalls gushed onto the pavements, the roads, the building sites, the motionless cranes. Clusters of locals huddled under overhanging shop fronts looking bemused. They didn't expect this on the Costa del Sol.

The Chuck Berry busker in Calle Real had gone.

Mango, Gertrude's little blind cat, had got an eye infection.

<u>Good things</u>
The silver candlestick.

She sat on the balcony, the roar of the waves below. The candlestick perched in front of her, freshly cleaned with silver fluid and sparkling. She ran her hands over its shiny curved surface and willed it to reveal its secrets. The engraved markings on the base, now seen more clearly, could be ancient writing and the squiggles might represent entwined initials but it was impossible for her to make them out. She stuck a long candle into the holder and placed the precious object on the sideboard next to the silver teapot. All that was missing was its partner, the other candlestick.

Apart from the joy of her new possession, there was little pleasure in returning to the apartment. The days went by and she was restless, in and out of the kitchen, on and off the windy balcony. She slept fitfully, four hours a night if she was lucky. She wanted Steve and she didn't. She unwound with some light *sevillana* music, stamping on the marble floor to give the lot below a taste of their own medicine. Even Gertrude and the latest cat episodes failed to get her going. She spent a lot of time on the bed, staring at the familiar mosquito blobs and counting the cars as they bumped over the road humps below. She mooched around the port, looking out for Steve, and up to the beacon at the end. The rocking fishing boats slowed down to enter the harbour, escorted by their posses of crying seagulls. The surfers in their black wet suits rode the waves.

Kate hadn't done her homework, yet her Spanish had improved. Because all the information was stored in the back of the head, it came out in more of a flow when she wasn't tense. The butcher must have noticed a difference. She asked for the chicken wings, *alas de pollo*, with a cool shrug, no longer bothered to get it out perfectly.

She felt caught between two lives. One level was there, in the apartment, Estepona life, Sexy Steve, even the butcher. Yet the other life grew stronger in her head, almost taking her over. She was semi-sleepwalking through the days. In the mirror her eyes were different: bigger, browner. She looked younger, like that girl in the market. She bought some colour solution to darken her hair. Kate wanted to look like her.

Rosie had left urgent phone messages: 'How about meeting up for a coffee ... haven't seen you for ages ... the new film at Banús? ... we do need to talk about that house.' She didn't reply.

Nothing from Steve.

What she was interested in was – the past. And that other life glimpsed in Cordoba, the dream that kept intruding, keeping her awake at night, trying to take her over and yes, she wanted to let it. Get back to that memory of a young man making boots and the beseeching eyes of a sad girl who was Kate or looked like her, but younger and more beautiful. Her imagination was getting out of hand.

If she had been in Manchester she'd have been off in a second to the old doctor who'd known her for years, asking him to refer her to a good psychologist – but out here? Kate didn't know an English doctor and her Spanish wouldn't stretch to explaining what she was experiencing. Which a goodly part of her didn't want to get rid of, it was like a drug or the daily crossword. She had to have it. It was like a novel she couldn't put down, two hundred pages to go, and she was in there, part of the central character.

She'd forgotten *The Book of Help*. Kate studied the cover and meditated hard on the deserted beach, the blue sky and the lone cloud.

Then she asked the question: "What did happen to me in Cordoba?" and opened the book.

'IT COULD BE SOMETHING QUITE SPECIAL' came back the regular tetchy response which didn't help in the circumstances. Action of some sort was required.

The doorbell rang as she was doing nothing on the balcony but watch the sunset streak pink orange tails and bubbles across the western sky. Gertrude was at the door.

"I've had a thought, Kate," she said, her head bobbing in conspiratorial sympathy. She was swathed in a dressing gown with a busy floral pattern that looked like curtain material.

"You know what, you should be doing more social things outside." She thrust out her hand. "And you try these sachets, they will help you sleep. I hear you at night, I think you're over-tired with all your travelling and the noise below, that's what it is."

"There's nothing going on below at the moment." They'd had a few days and nights of peace and empty lifts.

"I tell you, it'll come back." Kate took the creased packet with many thanks. Good old Gertrude.

The Spanish infusion guaranteed to get her to sleep with no side effects. And it worked. No noise, no smoky dreams, no fantasy lives, at least not for tonight.

Calle Real was bustling with late morning life. The rain had gone. Spring was coming and bronze pots of flowers squatted next to the shiny wooden and silver metal benches. Children scootered up and down the pedestrian walkway. New musicians had replaced Chuck Berry and were playing the tango on an assortment of ethnic instruments. Kate sat on her favourite bench after the Spanish class drinking in the good energy until she saw a familiar figure appear down the street. It was Rosie. Had she been following her?

"Kate!" she called, running towards the bench, her face lit up. "At last we meet. It seems like ages." Rosie swooped forward for the kiss-kiss. "Have you been in hibernation or what? My turn for coffee." She led Kate firmly towards the café terrace on the corner.

It was pleasant sitting on comfy wicker seats in the sun. The toast, with marmalade and butter, was crunchy and hot. The newspaper kiosk dangled the daily paper across the road where the policemen stood keeping a bored eye on the illegally parked cars.

"You been avoiding me or what?" Rosie asked as soon as they were served and settled. She looked thinner than usual, her large popping eyes standing out like stalks in her face.

"Of course not."

"It's just that, well, I wanted to explain." Rosie was curiously hesitant for her. "It's about that phone-call."

"Which one?"

"You know, when you called me from Cordoba and Steve answered. We were at a business meeting, I'd gone to the loo and left him with the phone, we were expecting Juan to call, that was all."

"No problem," Kate replied. And it wasn't. Her body missed Steve and the pleasure he'd given her, but the passion and jealousy over him seemed to be unimportant now, along with the rest of her present life.

Rosie continued. "I expect you've been wondering if we've any news from Juan, about the house."

"Not really. Has he changed his mind yet?" Although he was technically the enemy, Kate admired Juan for his stance against them and she wondered again whose side she was on.

"Not yet. I've raised the price a bit and he's thinking about it. He'll let us know soon. But we'll find another place if we have to." She sipped and smiled. "I've had a virus while you were away. I could have done with you around to get me some lemons."

"Poor you." Rosie possessed a special talent apart from her mania for house selling. It was called Trying to Make Kate Feel Guilty. Like, if she'd stayed at home none of this would have happened. "Do you need any help?" she enquired dutifully.

"Not to worry. I'm much better now." Rosie started to suggest goodies for next week and Kate rejected them with a polite, but firm, no thanks. She was no longer frantic about the Saturday market at the Bullring. She was sad to miss the Wednesday jazz and the

Thursday night salsa possibilities at the beach bar at the eastern end of the beach.

"You could at least come for a walk with me tomorrow. You and me. The migrations should be starting soon, we might see anything, like common cranes, which aren't that common, and the bee eaters, though it's too early for them."

"Where's the regular group?"

"Finished." Rosie had a spasm of coughing. She blew her nose, blotted her pink smeared lips with a paper napkin and rattled off an explanation. "Steve's gone off for two weeks with the boat again. Barcelona and Mallorca. Val n' Pete had to return to Aberdeen – some business crisis. And Christina's fallen down the stairs of her apartment block. Pat my back will you."

"The whole eleven flights?" Kate patted vaguely until Rosie had finished coughing. So Steve wasn't around. That was why she hadn't heard from him.

Rosie put the tissue away. She had a smear of lipstick on the protruding teeth. "Phew, that's better. No, not the lot but enough to put her out of action for a while. She is pushing seventy after all, and she'd found a better walking lot down her end in Fuengirola."

"She didn't look it."

"Had work done on her face. They all have down here."

Kate mused on the flightiness of the ex-pat life. The local Spanish had continuity and stability, but not them. There was so much materialism, so many activities starting and finishing, dinners out, golf and tennis, new people coming, new groups, ideas, businesses, projects, don't mention the cultural centre – and then they were gone. Until the next lot started up.

"So are you going to live life properly or continue to treat it as a dress rehearsal?" Rosie had more than a tinge of impatience in her tone.

"You've got lipstick on your teeth." She wouldn't be intimidated by Rosie anymore. She could stand up to her.

"I'll let you know." Kate marched off home along the *paseo*. Perhaps she should go walking with her. The puma might be roaming the mountains with a wife and three children. Maybe the puma would attack Rosie or she would. 'I could even push her down the side of a ravine …' what a dreadful thought! Guilt flooded her and she apologised silently, resolving to go with Rosie as a penance.

But she didn't need to. Next morning it was pouring with rain again and all was cancelled. Kate struggled the sixteen minutes' trek into town against the wind and a capsized umbrella to get the paper and a light bulb. The rain-driven *paseo* was deserted. The red terrace chairs with their Cruzcampo emblems were stacked in heaps outside the bars. Inside her favourite corner café swirled a mass of laughing, shouting and smoking humanity. She looked round for a vacant table in the crowd. A man was sitting nearby and the smoke from his cigarette thickened the air. Two women at the bar were deep in conversation, waving their cigarettes as they talked. A panicky need to get out of the place, swept over her. Smoke from every cigarette in the café headed straight for her and she couldn't stand it. She shouldn't have come to Spain if she wanted to avoid smoking, so said Spanish teacher Lali, said Steve, said Estepona. But since Cordoba, the aversion had been getting worse. When she was near to smoke she had to escape. She pushed the door open and gasped into the smoke-free rain. Kate was safe.

The Casa de Cultura was empty and dry, smelling of nothing stronger than lemon detergent. An exhibition of paintings by local artists filled the walls. There were simple watercolours of mountain *pueblos*, sea views and dancing women with red-fringed shawls and fans to match. Kate arrived at the end of the row of paintings and halted abruptly at a picture of children playing in a small plaza.

She held on to the wall for support, jamming her fist against her mouth, trying not to retch as recollection hit her. The picture was painted in predominantly brown and ochre colours to create an old-fashioned, medieval quality, with touches of light from the sky and flowers. The young girl sitting by the fountain in the foreground had dark hair. She wore a long brown garment, with a cream linen apron over it. A young man stood next to her, resting his hand on her shoulder. He was dressed in a corn-coloured tunic with a plaited leather belt at the waist and brown open sandals. A slim, fair-haired girl leant over the fountain edge watching her reflection in the water. Behind the group, an elderly woman in a long grey robe and shawl drew water from a stone well.

Kate could hear the creak of the chain. The high, thin houses bent inwards, helping to create a setting of claustrophobia and menace. In contrast the dark-haired girl looked ecstatic. She smiled straight at Kate.

She knows those dark eyes; they are her seventeen-year-old eyes, her brown curly hair and her joy ...

And Kate was collapsed on the floor, back in the exhibition hall with an aching head. She struggled onto to the bench and stared at the picture again. It depicted a traditional plaza with a small fountain. The plaza was empty. There was nobody in the foreground, nobody smiling with joy.

Who had painted this? Kate found the signature, a bottom right-hand corner squiggle, but couldn't read it properly. But she knew it. She'd seen this place with a fountain before. It was her plaza in Cordoba, the home of her silver candlestick.

CHAPTER SEVENTEEN

ESTEPONA – PRESENT DAY

The crowd was back in the apartment below, celebrating with an all-night party. Deep into the bang-boom-yap-yap-clip-clop, pound-shout, smoke, noise, crash-bang-boom, plus the loud pound-pound beat-beat music. No, Kate wasn't getting used to it. Even with Gertrude's special sachets she couldn't sleep through it. She had to slam down at least ten good things in her life. She had to find a t'ai chi teacher to help her stay sane, especially on a Saturday night/Sunday morning. The din went on. So she thumped back on the kitchen floor with the mop and put the radio on loud for three minutes until she thought of the disturbance she might be causing the gentle French couple above who made not a sound except when their grandchild visited and ran across the floor. She cursed the bloody self-help books which told her prissily to Live in the Now and Accept.

Deep in despair in the middle of the night Kate pulled on her tracksuit and paced the deserted *paseo*. It was empty except for an elderly man out with his dog.

She speed walked past them and up to the roundabout at Avenida Juan Carlos. The stone angels and cherubs stood in carved splendour in the night air. The serenity of these statues reinforced the instability of her present state. What was she doing out there?

196

Kate turned round to face the lighthouse. The lights were dim, the wind pulled at her and she wanted to be in the safety of her own surroundings, noisy or not.

At the sheltered corner of the building, the wind dropped. The sounds of distant shouting rang out, coming from above, or from drunken gangs at the port … or were the men getting closer to their house? The cats were poised and alert, pacing round, tails upright. A man went past on the footpath. He threw away the end of his cigarette and in the brief flame Kate saw her young face, lit up on the ground.

"*Ayúdame*, help me," the voice begs through the smoke. The sound of distant drums is getting closer, louder. Who will rescue her – and me?

"Kate, what are you doing down there?" It was Gertrude calling from her balcony. She was leaning over the edge and Kate twisted her head dizzily back to look up at her. The cats copied her. Nineteen faces, thirty-eight eyes squinted upwards.

"You know what time it is, the middle of the night, four o'clock in the morning," she shouted with a resonance that echoed round the port, bounced up to the mountains guarding the clashing energy and back. But Kate had left the apartment at around two, which meant she'd been out for two hours. This couldn't be possible.

"Come up to me now," Gertrude commanded from above. "You don't want to frighten the cats."

She fell into Gertrude's waiting arms. Cat toys littered the floor of her apartment, Blind Mango threw Kate a dirty look and scampered under the couch. She was one of Gertrude's rescued cats and therefore a threat to the one in possession. Kate was the competition.

"I tell you, he's better now, but he is not used to anyone here but me." Gertrude pattered to and from the kitchen in her woollen slippers, preparing the herbal tea. Kate gulped it down and waited for calm to descend, and the memory of that young face twisted with pain and sorrow to drift away. Gertrude had to help, that was her role. But she forestalled Kate with her own angst.

"You know what, the cat that was attacked by that big dog, now she is not there anymore. I'm so worried about her." The music from the party pounded on below.

"I'm deeply sorry about the cat, but what can we do about this?" she cried, jabbing her hand downwards. "I can't stand it any longer."

Gertrude swooped and pushed Kate's head against her chest. The closest thing to safety was Gertrude.

"Please help me," cried Kate, muffled in the cushion of her ample bosom. She needed to talk to somebody and Gertrude had to be Wise Woman because that's how she'd been cast. "What would you do if you were having what seemed like black-outs and imagining things that aren't there?"

Gertrude drew back. "You say that again?" She didn't understand and Kate didn't blame her. It was incomprehensible. She struggled to explain further.

"Okay. When I was in Cordoba and before – and after – like tonight – I kept seeing things, people that appeared I think from other times, and I was missing present time while I was seeing them and in the time that I'm – not here – I think that I'm there … in the past and then I come back and find I've missed two hours … and I know I've got a vivid imagination, but it's doing my head in …" She trailed off. Yes. It sounded like nonsense. Gertrude made a hissing sigh of loving semi-impatience that translated clearly into what is this girl talking about?

But Kate could stand in a class in front of forty teenagers and communicate coherently. She tried again. "Okay. This is it. I'm experiencing abnormal things. Hallucinations or flashes of another life and time are – taking me over. And yet I can't understand what they're trying to say to me."

Gertrude regarded her for a while and then delivered her solemn verdict. "You know what I think, I give you some more of the special tea. You can take up to four sachets a day. And I think you should go to the hairdresser. You could do with it and there is a very good girl, Janna, at the port."

"Thank you, I'm letting it grow. Have you any more meaningful suggestions?

"It could be something quite special," insisted Gertrude enigmatically, refusing to be drawn. But she wasn't a guru, merely a Gertrude who wanted her to do what she advised. Which included taking Mango to the vet to see about the blind eyes. Kate got out of that one.

Not again. Goodnight and good morning, sweet
Gertrude.

Ana is careful. She has heeded Grandmother's advice and said nothing to María about their family history. A little knot in her handkerchief and a scratch on the palm of her hand reminds her to watch her tongue at all times and keep the secrets. In hidden corners, she picks up the old Jewish ways from Mama and Grandmother. She has practised the Sabbath blessing until she can do it without thinking. She learns to cook always with oil, not lard. When María is out of the house, she sits with Grandmother in her bedroom and memorises Judaic prayers for the special festivals such as Sukkot and Passover. She knows when the special Holy Days take place, even though the family do not celebrate them except down in the cellar. Grandmother has taught her the rituals of how to fast and wash and when to wear clean clothing. She will know them for when she has her own household.

They have to be even more careful all the time, inside the house and out. There is a growing danger for the *converso* community. The Cordoban authorities are becoming less tolerant, more suspicious of the activities of the New Christians. Now Grandmother only prepares fish on Friday nights and Mama ensures that there is a fire going through Friday and Saturday. They are good Catholics like their Christian neighbours, who they visit for tea and to share gossip. They attend Mass with them every Sunday.

And Ana is distracted by – growing up. Pedro is often at her side, either in the streets or at his family booth next to theirs in the bazaar. As Ana weighs the spices, she is happy that he is close by, working with the soft leather shoes and slippers that he and his father make. Pedro sits at the back of the booth in his long apron, behind the rows of dangling pouches, purses and belts. He sings softly as he hammers in nails and sews the fine leather slippers. He is a skilled artisan, talented at his trade, and the ladies of Cordoba love his designs and his handsome smile. Ana sneaks glances at him when she thinks he isn't looking. Then he will glance up at her and wink and sigh, putting his hand on his heart in a mock gesture of admiration.

Pedro is so handsome. At eighteen, he is of medium height, slim, with sturdy legs, brown eyes and thick upward curls that frame his round olive-skinned face like a halo. A short beard lends a wisp of authority to his youthfulness. He has now perfected his conjuring art and can do incredible tricks that he performs for his friends. Pebbles vanish from his hand and appear in the deep pocket of a garment. Particularly in Ana's apron. It is impossible to watch his mock-solemn face without laughing. But he can be serious and contemplative like her. They enjoy lingering quietly by the river at eventide watching the birds chasing insects, unlike María who is too restless to stay longer than five minutes in one place.

Ana approaches her seventeenth year knowing that she loves Pedro. She watches as her sister chatters non-stop to him, her cheeks prettily pink, her eyes wide. Maria looks at him sideways, twirling her fine long hair, while Ana sits and tries not to care. Pedro is so correct with both of them, she does not know which one he favours most.

On the morning of her seventeenth birthday, Ana is working at the spice stall. It is a cool February day, the morning bright and sharp with clear skies. She has just finished serving one of her gentleman customers with two ounces of peppercorns and a packet of ginger when Pedro approaches her mother at the back of the booth. As Ana tidies the trays, she strains her head backwards to try and hear them talking.

"May Ana leave a little early today and might I accompany her?" Pedro asks. Mama stops her spooning and ladling, wipes her hands on a cloth and gives him a quizzical look. Ana waits for her refusal. How lovely it would be to have Pedro on her own, but Mama will not allow it. Elvira is away sick, and María has stayed home today to help Grandmother with the household chores. Ana is needed at the stall.

"Well, I do not see why not," says Mama. "Ana, do stop fiddling, please lay those packets out properly and then you may go."

This is so unlike Mama and how wonderful. It must be because today is her birthday. Ana hides her delight with a demure look and swiftly finishes putting away the spices she has been serving. She takes her apron off and folds it neatly, and as she does so, Mama gives her a squeeze and a farewell kiss. She has never done that before.

"Now do go along, Ana," chides Mama, returning to her spice weighing at the back of the booth.

Pedro and Ana thread their way through the crowds and debris of the mid-morning bazaar; past the prancing horses, the caged chickens, the shouting vendors, the stalls selling Persian carpets, silks from Damascus, shawls from Kashmir and beyond to the fruit and vegetables.

"Hola, buenas!" They wave and exchange cheerful greetings with stallholders they both know. Ana is alive and vitally in the moment, walking with Pedro down the long street. She is smiling as they reach the quiet alley leading to her home where Pedro stops and catches hold of her hand. Ana blushes. They have often touched before in games and childish horseplay but even when Pedro produced pebbles from behind her ear, he did not overstep the rules of decency that their culture demanded. This contact feels different, more urgent. Ana is not aware of the passers-by, the overhanging houses and rows of brightly coloured plants and greenery. She sees only Pedro as he fumbles to produce a package from his bag.

"Ana, I have a present for you."

She unwraps the parcel and gasps with delight. There lies the most exquisite pair of scarlet slippers. The material is a deep velvet, sewn with hearts and stars in blue and silver thread. Pedro has embroidered her name on the front of each one.

"They are so beautiful."

"I made them for you, for your birthday."

"Thank you, it is so kind of you." Ana turns them over, stroking their softness. She holds them against her cheek until Pedro takes them off her and lays them on the ground by her feet.

"Why don't you try them. I want to see if I got the size correct." She pulls off her dusty black shoes and eases them on. They fit perfectly and look dainty below her long skirt and cape.

"Today I am a princess," she sings, pirouetting in a circle in front of him.

"And you dance like one." He raises Ana's hand to his lips and kisses her fingers one by one. She quivers with delight and fear. To kiss in the street, even on her fingers, is not correct behaviour. Thank heavens Mama is far away at the bazaar.

"Ana." Pedro stops, looks at the ground and his black boots and starts again. "Ana, I have spoken to your father."

"What about?"

"Don't you know, can't you guess?"

"How can I know if you do not tell me?"

"I have asked him if you could be my bride." Ana's mouth falls open in amazement. Her heart is pounding.

"Your parents have discussed it with my parents and they have all agreed. They are delighted, it is what they wanted." He holds her hands tightly between his own. "Now it is up to you. Will you do me the honour of marrying me?"

Would she! Ana is so joyous that Pedro loves her, wants her for his wife, she longs to fling her arms around him and kiss him hard on his mouth, smooth the curls in his hair, stroke his body right there in the street. But she simply nods and whispers, "Yes."

Pedro clasps Ana's hand for a moment longer.

"Why did you choose me?" she asks him.

"Because I adore your cooking. I will grow old and fat on your saffron flavoured chicken."

"Silly boy, Chicken doesn't make you fat."

"And I love you."

"I have loved you since I was seven, my dearest Jacobiquo."

"Jacobiquo!"

Ana giggles. She picks up her old shoes, stuffs them in her bag and they walk on through the plaza with wide grins. An old family friend, the apothecary in his black coat and spectacles, hurries past, coughing. He gives them a quick greeting as he goes by. And there is one other person at the far corner of the plaza, intense as a stalking cat, who moves away as Ana approaches. María has no smile upon her face.

In the evening the two girls sit on the edge of the fountain with Rosita curled between them. María hangs forward and looks into the water, her rosary beads falling forward. Ana joins her and they gaze at their rippling reflections.

"Remember when I held you down?" whispers María. Ana pulls away from her.

"Please don't spoil it with nasty thoughts when I'm so happy. Will you not share our happiness?"

"Dearest Ana, I am thrilled for you both. I have admired Pedro as a good friend and I think you are perfect together." A perfect couple, that's what everybody was saying.

"You do not mind my getting married before you?"

"No. Why should I? I am glad you're happy, I've said so."

"And we would like you to be our attendant."

"Wonderful! I was waiting for you to ask me." The moment of uncertainty is past. Ana leans forward and hugs her sister.

María stands up and sings loudly and clearly. "I declare that Ana and Pedro are going to be married." She performs three cartwheels round the plaza and her skirts tumbles over her head.

"You are too indecent!" Ana runs to her and pulls her skirts down. She is appalled at her sudden, wild behaviour and she recalls again the horror of María pushing her in the fountain water.

María bounces back on her heels and performs a deep curtsey.

"To show how happy I am for you," she says, beaming. But her eyes are cold.

CHAPTER EIGHTEEN

CORDOBA – FEBRUARY 1473

Ana wears her new slippers as she dashes up and down the stairs a dozen times a day. She spills food on her apron and does not even notice. She misses what people are saying to her, skips to the stall at the bazaar and back, runs over to Pedro's house, dances to Papa's workroom, and blushes at Pedro whenever he looks at her for longer than a moment. Her excitement fills every room and for once she is at the bustling centre of family activity.

The betrothal is official and Mama has started planning for the wedding which is to be held in mid-March, a few short weeks away. There is nothing to wait for and the young couple's passion is so evident, it is deemed prudent by both sets of parents to wed them without delay. The nuptial agreement between the two families is drawn up, and Ana's dowry agreed. They will start married life at Ana's home until Pedro has saved up enough money to buy them a small house. There is room for the two of them in her large attic bedroom with the double bed that she and María shared. María has already moved down to the floor below, into a small closet with a tiny window and a large cupboard which Mama had been using for storing clothes and materials. Ana helped transfer her belongings and Papa has bought her a new bed. María has placed her small image of Jesus by the window and declared that she is content.

"And as soon as Ana and Pedro have their own home – it will not be too long – you can have the big attic bedroom back for yourself," Mama promises.

The wedding service will be at the Iglesia San Francisco and will be followed, at Papa's insistence, by a short Jewish marriage ceremony in the cellar. He has already asked the Rabbi from the old Jewish Quarter if he will kindly officiate and he has agreed. Felipe is to be the troubadour at the wedding party and play music for the dancing. He rehearses melodies every moment he is away from the workshop and is forever asking approval for this or that song to be included.

Mama is deep into clothes – she has decided that wool and silk dresses would be suitable because of the changeable spring temperatures. At supper every night the sole topic of discussion is the forthcoming wedding. Grandmother promises to make a traditional banquet with Ana's favourite saffron pastries and a honey cake for a sweet future. Mama insists on sewing new linen tablecloths and napkins and re-polishing all the silver. She has made Papa and Felipe whitewash the outside walls of the house. Ana prepares her trousseau chest. She is sewing pale white cotton nightgowns with fine lace trimming while Grandmother has started work upon the wedding dress she has designed with a square neckline and long fluted sleeves embroidered with gold thread. And in the workshop Papa has embarked upon a secret wedding gift that is to be a surprise.

Meanwhile María drums her fingers, sings loudly and does nothing. She can afford to wait.

Cordoba is changing. There have been more frightening displays against the New Christians in cities throughout Andalucía and Cordoba is no longer the friendly and familiar place where Ana grew up. Every day Ana senses the anger seething in their local streets. Old Christian neighbours who used to be their friends, look the other way when they meet. She knows what they are saying to each other:

"Those *marranos* are growing more wealthy and insolent, look at them in their grand houses, they want to control everything. They are not ashamed to practise their Jewish rituals in public ... see how they have no fires on Fridays. They refuse to eat pork, they sneak into the old synagogues when they think we are not looking, they get their meat from the Jewish butcher in the *Judería*, they parade their good clothes on Saturdays, they pretend to be good Christians ..."

Cordoba is a simmering pot of anti-*converso* insinuations, with accusations flying between Christians and *conversos*. Their apothecary neighbour is a sick man terrified of his own shadow but he has good cause to be. He was attacked last week inside his house and his windows broken. Houses belonging to other *converso* neighbours have been burnt down at night. Friends have been assaulted on the street. Two young men threw stones at Felipe and kicked him on his way to the workshop. His legs are covered in cuts and bruises.

Pedro wants them to leave Cordoba. One Sunday afternoon, he and Ana walk by the river with

Grandmother at a tactful distance behind. The path is lined with yellow blossoms and prickly overgrown briars. Men are fishing and Ana and Pedro stand by a bend in the river, watching them. Ana envies the fishermen their stability in contrast to the turmoil of their lives.

"We should think about change. It is not impossible," urges Pedro. "We must get away from here before things get worse, because they will."

"But how can we?"

"There are other *conversos* who are leaving to start a better life in a new country where they can revert to their Judaism, free from all this." Pedro's voice rises in excitement. Ana shushes him with a quick look at Grandmother who is picking the wild flowers behind and batting away burgeoning insects. Pedro presses her hand tight.

"At first I considered us travelling to Valencia and taking a ship heading for the Orient. There are many *conversos* who have done this. But there is a better way for us. I have a friend who has been gone a couple of months and I've already received news about him. He is now safely in Portugal. He could help us."

Portugal. Ana breathes in the word. A new country, a new life.

"It is nearer for us. I am familiar with the route he took westwards through the countryside to Sevilla and on to Huelva and the border. It is a trek of about four or five days. I know the safe houses where we could stop on the way. There is another good friend, a Christian, Diego, who could help us."

"Can you trust him?"

"As much as I do myself. We have been friends since childhood. We used to come fishing down here when we were young lads. Seeing these fishermen made me think of him."

"How would we travel?"

"That is simple. I can secure us a couple of horses for a good price. I have some money. Diego would advance me the rest."

Ana is torn. How she longs to go with Pedro to a new life of freedom. "But I could not bear to hurt my family, and I would miss them so much. And there is another thing," she adds. "I am sure my father would never allow me to leave Cordoba."

"I know that. I am afraid we cannot tell our parents." He skims stones into a quiet stretch of the river and they bounce two, three times across the water. Grandmother calls for them to turn round. The dragonflies hover, the birds fly over the water towards the hills and the late afternoon sun. Why can they not fly away also?

As they climb away from the river, Pedro carries on his argument.

"We have the constraints of our families to consider, it is true. But the times we are living in are extraordinary; this should encourage us to make our own decisions about our safety. We are the next generation and we should try to live it as we wish, if we can." Grandmother bounds up the steep path ahead of them. What energy she has for an old woman in her sixties. Ana wishes she could ask her advice.

Pedro is insistent. "I intend nothing dishonourable."

"How would we carry this out? What would your plan be?"

"Listen: we would get married in the Church as arranged, and then yes, we would have the Jewish wedding ceremony for your father's sake. For him and for us. My parents are in agreement over that. It will be performed in moments down in the cellar, with our two families present. It's not such a safety hazard. Who is to know?"

"And after that?"

"Then we would leave almost immediately: the next evening when everyone has retired for the night."

Ana looks at him, alarmed. "But that is so soon."

"You must heed me. I believe that we are no longer safe in Cordoba. You can see, the disturbances are growing, it's like a tinderbox." Ana shivers with fear at his words ... now stop it, Ana, be brave. One life to live and I want to live it with Pedro.

They walk on without speaking, both intent on their own thoughts. By the time they reach the top of the path Ana has made up her mind.

"I will do it." She is by nature impulsive and, despite her apprehension, she would agreed to anything he wanted. He clasps her hands.

"You will not regret it, I promise you."

Ana waits until the house is quiet, when Mama and María are out working at the spice stall and Grandmother is busy with her cooking. She is supposedly preparing her trousseau. Up in her bedroom,

213

she begins to gather the clothes, blankets and dried food necessary for their flight. She sets them out and stores them in her bedroom chest with her trousseau clothing. Pedro has advised her to take only the essentials, they must travel light with one pannier to each horse. Although she tries to make preparations without anyone noticing, sharp-eyed María is growing suspicious and follows her around. Ana has to make up continual excuses – she is tidying for the wedding or counting her trousseau – until the inevitable happens. As she re-checks items in the chest, María opens the bedroom door and stands in the entrance.

"And what is going on here?" she demands, hands on hips.

Ana slams down the lid of the chest. "Nothing out of the ordinary, I assure you. I am merely preparing for my wedding."

"I do not believe you."

"It is true, I swear." Ana's face is flushed with the effort of pretence. Unlike her sister, she is not a good liar. María pushes Ana aside and thrusts her hands into the chest. She pulls out a package of dried fruits and waves them triumphantly in Ana's face.

"Are these for the wedding night?" Ana stands with her head down, biting her lip. "Fine. If you don't tell me, I'm going straight to Mama."

"No you will not. Wait. Let me speak to Pedro first."

If Ana is honest with herself, she hopes that Pedro will not agree to María's involvement in their departure. She speaks to him that evening by the fountain. "She can be unreliable at times, you know." Ana hunts for the words to express her disquiet.

But Pedro thinks it is a splendid idea to include Maria. "Her strength of will can be a support to you and make you feel more confident."

"You do not know her as well as I do."

"Don't worry. Think how useful she will be in helping to get our belongings together."

"Very well." Ana is still not convinced, but she bows to Pedro's will. She can resist him nothing. The next evening she reveals their plans to María when they are sitting by the fountain edge.

"Tell me more!" María huddles close, drinking in the information.

"Will you help us?"

María flings her arms round Ana's neck. "How could I not! I would give anything to help my dear sister and her lover to be free. I adore the idea, escaping from here. What an adventure!"

"No, it is not an escape," Ana tries again to explain. Although she supposes it is.

"Please – can I come too?" breathes María. How she longs for excitement, adventure, change – a life where she can put her energies and capabilities to use, where she does not feel trapped.

Ana is shocked. Can her sister be serious? She speaks slowly. "I am sorry. But Pedro and I are going together, alone. Just the two of us."

There is a moment when María's disappointment and displeasure hang in the air. Her eyes narrow, her face shuts down into the familiar blank wall that Ana knows so well. Then she shrugs and the loving sister returns. "Don't worry, I'm only teasing you! It is so exciting and I really do want to help." María stands up and salutes Ana. "Now then, what are my duties, dearest sister?" She makes it sound like a game, Ana thinks, deliberately to annoy her.

"You could stop making a joke about it all!" Ana snaps and then feels guilty. She knows she's being irrational, and that Pedro is right. María's light-hearted approach will help to alleviate her fear. And she is running out of space. Clothes and gifts are piling up, making the bedroom resemble a bazaar stall. She now has a fine selection of clogs, shoes, scarves and towels and very little room to put them. There are no more hiding-places and Mama is constantly in and out, throwing instructions over her shoulder regarding tablecloths, nightgowns, sheets and linen. She is bound to notice the chaos soon. María's little room has the spacious cupboard with a lock and nobody goes near it now except María. Items for the journey, already falling out of Ana's chest, can be stored in there, where Mama is less likely to notice them. It makes sense.

In the weeks leading up to the wedding the preparations become like a secret game between them which Ana begins to enjoy. She is no longer frightened as they smuggle the necessary items down to María's room because her sister is sharing the activity with her, as she used to do when they were children.

María revels in arranging and stacking away all that is needed, including Ana's warm dark cloak with the big

216

hood that she folds neatly on top of the pile. Ana will wear that on the night they leave.

"It's all safe and in order, trust me," María says and Ana believes her. She forgets Grandmother's words of warning.

CHAPTER NINETEEN

Merriment from within the bowels of the building went on into the early hours. The sounds echoed, multiplied, bounced, skidded up and down the hollow channels between the inside walls. But it was eve of Easter. Spring and *Semana Santa*, Easter Week, was early this year. Estepona heaved with traffic and holidaymakers, so noise was inevitable and had to be tolerated.

A family from Madrid were in the apartment next door, the other side to Gertrude. The doors banged, their dog barked the minute Kate moved onto the adjacent balcony, but their Spanish energy helped to dispel her lethargy. She'd even managed to get back to the doctor and have the second anti-tetanus jab.

Andalusian spring was intoxicating. The heavy smell of orange blossom filled the plazas in town. Even the waste ground below the building was aglow with wild flowers sprouting up in pink and blue clumps between the dog poo and empty beer cans.

Kate needed to go down and clean the mess up for Easter. And buy some more colour rinse to re-do her hair an even darker brown.

Teacher Lali insisted her students should see the processions at least once and soon, because Spain had been officially declared a non-religious country. The

Spanish were divided on the issue, the young not as religiously fervent as the older generation. But in Andalucía everyone was flapping their hands and saying no no, we must stick to our traditions. Although, according to some reports, there were more foreign residents on the Costa del Sol than there were the local Spanish.

Kate ventured a statement in Spanish. "But surely it's not that traditional here, with such an influx of foreigners on the Costa, diluting the indigenous passion?"

"*Ah, sí. Muy bien.*" Well done, Kate. A difficult question to ask in any language and Lali acknowledged her attempt at progress. Lali loved a good debate and it was good practice for them all.

She told them in rapid Spanish that the Costa was a tiny part of Andalucía which was after all the largest region in Spain, and bigger than Portugal. There were so many native Spanish who didn't live down on the Costa. The rest of the class nodded in agreement, *sí sí,* and Kate shut up.

The Good Friday – *Viernes Santo* procession was coming up tonight, a serious business, more important to the Spanish than Christmas. The heavy religious floats sway dramatically as they are borne along by rows of men, arms across each other's shoulders. They carry valuable sculptures of the Virgin Mother and of Christ with a large golden cross. In Sevilla it takes one hundred men to bear the magnificent float and the spectators sigh in reverence as the edifice sways from side to side and all the jewelled lights wobble. Kate had to see this.

219

A smiling *señorita* handed her an information leaflet in Calle Real. This gave the locations, durations and routes of the Processions that passed through the heart of Estepona. Kate consulted the map and identified the *Nuestra Señora de los Remedios* church not far from her building. Tonight's procession started there at eight-thirty and ended at around twelve-thirty. How could it take them so long to get round town and back?

Kate was excited. This was an adventure in the Easter night air and she didn't need to consult *The Book of Help* for advice. She pulled on her jeans, black jacket and flat black shoes. She was going.

She followed the stream of people making their way up the back streets towards a large plaza where a salmon-pink, modern church stood with its flat roof and massive brown double doors. Brand-new apartment blocks surrounded the space. Elderly couples waited on the black wrought iron benches. A man dressed formally in a dark suit and carrying a trumpet hurried past and joined the waiting musicians.

The plaza filled up with an orderly crowd of what seemed like one hundred per cent Spanish except for Kate. Toddlers straddled their fathers' shoulders, spectators gathered on balconies. Estepona Television was there. A technician balanced on a platform high up a ladder, his camera trained on the church entrance.

At eight-thirty the church doors opened. The crowd went still and hushed as rows of penitents filed down the steps in their long hooded gowns, high-pointed hats covering their faces. Their eyes showed, glinting through the slits. They carried candles and the swaying lights

220

mingled with the smell of incense in the air. More penitents filed out and a magnificent float appeared in the doorway, bearing the effigy of Jesus with his cross. The float was supported by the brotherhood of men concealed beneath its curtained sides. The crowd applauded respectfully as the float made its lurching way down the steps. The bugles and drums accompanied its progress with solemn, harsh music. Glimpses of shuffling trainers peeped out incongruously from underneath its hollow base as it wavered past. And then the float sank down as the bearers halted, to ease temporarily the strain of its weight. A woman sang a mournful prayer in a soprano voice that resounded round the plaza, and the crowd applauded again. Their passion was palpable, a centuries' old passion, a shared brotherhood passion.

Kate's response was mixed. She was drawn in by the drama, reverence and spectacle, and yet alienated and even a little envious. She wasn't part of the communal religious occasion but a mere onlooker, emotionally removed from these powerful symbols of tradition merged with Christianity.

Bang-bang-bang. An official rapped on a bell at the front of the wooden structure supporting the Jesus effigy, the resting men heaved the float up, and the procession started again. More penitents emerged from the church, carrying crosses. A clutch of local women followed, sombre and elegant in black high heels and formal Spanish dress. Lace mantillas covered their heads.

Another float appeared at the church door to be greeted by another patter of applause. Another piercing lament filled the silence and then the bugles and drums started up again as the effigy of the Virgin Mother was borne past, weeping her tears of jewels, surrounded by a host of waving silver candelabra. Scented flowers and the richly embroidered robe swayed heavily as the float inched along its ritual path. Rows of elderly women followed, carrying lighted candles. At regular intervals the procession stopped, the float was lowered and remained stationary until the next bang-bang-bang when it was hoisted up into the air again. Slow stop slow motion, and this was why the procession took over four hours to get round town.

The woman standing next to Kate crossed herself and moved forward to touch the Virgin Mother's float as it swayed past. Kate edged in behind her to watch more closely. The tail end of the penitents, swathed in their gowns and high pointed hats followed the float. One of the penitents stopped and turned towards her. The two blobs of his eyes surrounded by the blank hood, looked straight into hers. Time fell away as their eyes interlocked and the space between them evaporated.

The smell of incense, saffron and smoke hung around her. Bang-bang-bang hit the night air, and down again went the Virgin Mother's float. In that moment, the whole procession turned towards her. Buglers and drummers frozen in time, their batons poised in the air, tentacle extensions of their arms. Men and women muttered in Spanish but she heard it in English.

'Jewish *marrana* pig, get out of here!' They repeat it louder, the menace creeping across the pavement, their hostility closing in. A man kicks out at her with his boot.

'*Marrana* pig, what are you doing here, pretending to worship. You shouldn't be here. Get out. Go!

My God! It was that man with the dirty jeans and wild hair again – the man who'd pushed past Kate in the street and in the lift. He spat in her face. A dog closed in on her, growling and snarling as she shrank away, cowering, covering her head with her hands.

"Let me pass," she shrieks, "let me run, hair flying, down this terrifying, long corridor of a street and out of here. She feels the heaviness of her thick skirt pushing against her legs. Somebody is trying to catch her, a hand reaches out and grabs her long cloak … no, it's my jacket, my jeans … and the procession sways round her as Kate spirals down into another black-out …

"Kate, are you there?"

"No!" She pressed her hands over her ears, she didn't want to hear what they were saying.

"You know what," called a voice from far away. "It's going to rain. The forecast is bad. We must hurry, we have no umbrella, you don't want to catch a cold." Kate knew that voice. Gertrude was here.

She squatted down, grabbed Kate's hand and heaved her up with surprising strength. "It isn't safe, there's going to be a thunderstorm."

223

"I thought I saw somebody I knew." Kate looked round in bewilderment to find that there was no wild man to be seen. The row of penitents had moved on. The threatening crowd had followed the procession and all was normal. She could still see them marching at the next corner. The crowd applauded. The procession had stopped again, the men lowered the float. Nobody was crowding her, staring at her.

They got back to Gertrude's apartment before the rain reached them. Gertrude pushed a protesting Blind Mango off the sofa and Kate sank onto the cushions and tried to make sense of this latest inexplicable event.

"What happened to me? And those awful sounding words … *marrana* pig." Didn't that guide in Cordoba talk about *marranos*?

"I don't know what you mean." Gertrude set her mouth in that stubborn line Kate recognised, but she ploughed on.

"How do you know when things are changing? You're always there to pick up the pieces."

"Hush now. You must not get excited." Gertrude studied Kate, her head bobbing. "You know what, are you drinking the tea I gave you?"

"Yes, I finished it ages ago."

"And did you have the next tetanus shot?"

"Yes, of course I did."

"Then I think maybe you should have one of the cats in your apartment with you."

"No no!" As Kate glared at her, Gertrude's face appeared to change. She became the woman at the well in the picture at the art gallery and Kate was a petulant young girl. But who is Gertrude and who or what is she – a *marrana* pig, a beautiful seventeen-year-old girl with flowing brown hair?

The expected rain poured down and lightning flashed across the sea piercing the sky from Africa to the apartment.

Gertrude prepared her Spanish brew and the mystery was resolved. "I went to the procession a few minutes after you. I saw you ahead of me in the crowd. I called to you but you were so engrossed in it, you didn't hear me. I thought it was going to rain and I came over to you so that we could walk back together." End of story. Home to bed, or was it?

Another flash of lightning illuminated the sideboard in Kate's apartment. The candlestick pulsated with jagged flashes of light that dazzled Kate's eyes like the edge of a migraine. She picked it up and found it hot to the touch, as if it were on fire. Deep in the round base, the reflection of a face with huge eyes stared back at her. It was warning her that danger was coming. She could smell the smoke and feel the crack in the universe over centuries.

At around midnight María shrugs into Ana's cloak and pulls the hood over her head. She takes the key from a nail near the front door and leaves the house. She is not nervous and does not even bother looking behind her. She knows that nobody has heard her go. They are all asleep and unaware of her regular nocturnal activities. And she doesn't care. María takes a delight in becoming another person and fooling the people around her. It helps to relieve her daily frustration. She can hide her face and adapt Ana's walk and her manner of speaking. It is so simple and she gets away with it. She can walk through the whole of Cordoba if she wishes.

María makes her way down the street, tugging the hood tight to cover her hair. Putting on Ana's clothes is fun and a good way of getting back at her. By rights, Pedro should be hers. She is the oldest daughter of the family and ought to be married first and going away. She had chosen Pedro long before Ana had even thought of him.

The alley with its row of houses is silent. She whistles softly as she slips through the streets and across the main *calle* towards Pedro's house. His window on the first floor is shuttered but she sings his name softly, finds some gravel and tosses it upwards until it grazes the wooden ledge. After a moment the shutter is raised. Pedro opens his window and peers out into the night.

226

"Pedro, my love," María calls, making her voice sound sweet and silky-soft like silly Ana's.

"Ana, is that you? What are you doing out there?"

"Ssh! I wanted to see you."

"But it is dangerous to be on the streets alone at night."

" I know, but I miss you so much when we're not together."

"I love you too, dearest Ana, but you must go now. Wait a moment, I will come down and take you home."

"No, I'm going, it is but five minutes to our house. I'll see you tomorrow. I cannot wait for our wedding."

María blows a kiss up at Pedro and he watches, worried, as she skips away into the dark night. Outside the church she stops to make a swift prayer and crosses herself. God is with her. From out of the shadows steps a tall heavily-built young man with fair hair. He pulls the hood off her head and clasps María in his arms.

Kate tried to rationalise. She thought again of what the doctor said when she was a little girl. There was nothing wrong with her. Her imagination had gone a bit wild, over the top, that was all.

She got onto the Internet and looked up *marranos*. They translated as filthy pigs in the Spanish language and referred to the name given to Spanish Jews forced to adopt Christian identities. She thought of all this on Easter Sunday morning as she showered, determined to go out again. She needed to get beyond the fear and prove it was her old tendency to fantasise that was causing all these images, hallucinations, dreams, to appear. Overwise she'd go mad.

At the appointed hour, the drums started up their distant beat. The Resurrection Procession with the effigy of Jesus progressed down the main avenue. But this time the atmosphere was different. The float carriers were no longer concealed. There were eighteen men on each side, about six men across the front and back, making around forty-eight in all. And they were strapping and youngish. They needed to be to tote this giant Jesus through town, naked except for his drapes, stone ribs and thin torso. The men sweated, wore sunglasses and chewed gum.

She scooted through the side streets and doubled back to meet the Virgin Mary. Surrounded by fresh flowers, the effigy made her stately way down Calle Real, supported by sturdy Spanish ladies in sensible suits, stockings and flat dark shoes. It was daylight, sunny, and there wasn't a hint of the sinister menace of Good Friday. The musicians put their trumpets to one side and popped off for a quick smoke or mobile phone-call, or to greet acquaintances in the crowd. Kate walked home slowly along the *paseo*, trying to make sense of it all.

Gertrude was in the foyer of the block and they waited for the lift to arrive. The glass door swung open and a man entered. He wore sombre dark trousers, polished shoes and a cream suede jacket. The sight of him jolted Kate and she shrank away in fear. It was the wild man again, the one who pushed her in the street and in the lift, the man who had kicked and spat in her face at the Good Friday procession. He stood quietly next to her and she could hear his breathing, his fingers tapping on his briefcase.

He looked completely different. His tie was neatly fastened, his untamed hair combed flat and pulled back into a tight, plaited ponytail; the expression on his face was cool and correct, and his eyes black and courteous. He looked gently at his expensive gold watch.

"*Buenas tardes*," he said politely, and Gertrude bobbed her head to him. Kate couldn't speak. The lift arrived and they travelled up together, a silent, civilised trio. He got out at the third floor, dropped a courteous '*adios*' to them both and turned gently to the left, towards the apartment beneath hers. The door closed and the lift continued up to their floor.

229

Kate grabbed Gertrude. "Who *is* that man?"

"You know what, I tell you, I am so excited, he is a very nice man. He has had a lot of problems, poor fellow. You know his wife died so recently and he was broken-hearted. He didn't know what to do with himself, he went to pieces a little. Now I believe he's found a girlfriend. And you know what I heard? He owns the apartment under you. Maybe he now gets rid of those people."

"How do you find out all this?"

Gertrude did the shrug. "I hear these things."

Kate was left utterly confused at her front door. She didn't know what reality was anymore. Had she seen him at the procession, did he ever attack her, or was he a part of what she was imagining? If he was an ordinary charming Spaniard in an elegant outfit, then the events between them must have been conjured up by her unhinged mind. A hallucination, connected to the after-effects of the antibiotic and the second anti-tetanus shot plus Gertrude's special sachets? How else to explain the inexplicable violence; the sickening jerks from one time to another, pulling her back and forwards – into another time, another life, another nightmare?

CHAPTER TWENTY

ESTEPONA – PRESENT DAY

Gertrude crooned to her cats. She had rescued yet another kitten, a white one with a squashed face, and planned to keep her along with Blind Mango in the apartment. The concierge, Miguel, tended the pool. Cleaning ladies mopped up and down the floors and exchanged good morning *'buenas'* greetings as Kate wandered by. She bought a baguette in the mornings and bit into its warmth and crispness. If she timed it right, the bread was piping hot from the oven. At least that was not a figment of her imagination.

Easter was over and all was supposed to go quiet again until the next Public Holiday. There were tourists about, but it wasn't the frenetic scene of last week. The *paseo* had been returned to Kate, the dogs and the old men. But Gertrude's optimism was misplaced because the gang below had not gone. Tonight the din was worse than ever. Anguish pushed Kate to the limit of desperation. She went down the stairs at three in the morning when the music was at its height and knocked on the door. No response. She knocked again, much harder, and waited. A young woman opened the door. Kate prayed that she existed in real time and she wasn't imagining her. She was dressed in Eastern clothes; long flimsy trousers were gathered at the ankles, jewelled moccasin slippers covered her feet and she wore a skimpy top above her bare jewelled midriff. The woman stepped back, obviously stunned at the sight of Kate, a candlewick dressing-gowned woman with tousled hair and wild eyes. And in that moment Kate realised the strangeness of all their different lives and cultures touching and not touching in this huge apartment block. They were partitioned off into separate packages in the same building, but in their own different worlds.

"*Por favor*," she started. "*La música es demasiado alta. Por favor más baja, más silencio, son las horas de descansar.*" Kate managed all that – 'the music is very loud, please lower, more silence, they are the hours of rest.' She looked dramatically dire and finished off with a good punch line.

"*Mi marido está muy mal, no puede dormir.*" My husband is very sick, and he can't sleep. Why not throw one in, for emphasis?

The woman's silvery hard eyes softened in reluctant compassion. She dipped her head briefly in what Kate presumed was a form of agreement and closed the door. And silence descended. She crept back upstairs. That was so easy. Why could she not have done this before?

It worked for two nights and then it was back to bang-crash-clack-smoke-pounding-music-normal. Gertrude was no help; she continued to bleat on about the cats and more of the special tea.

Kate phoned Steve but his mobile was switched off. She tried Rosie who was delighted to hear from her. They arranged a swift drink at the port, in a slot between her many viewing appointments.

232

"You look a bit rough," said Rosie. "And what's happened to your hair?"

"Nothing much. What's happening with Casa Sueños?"

"Nothing much, we're still waiting for him to get back to us. It's good to see you, Kate."

"And you." Surprisingly, Kate found that she'd missed Rosie and her rough down-to-earth energy. Unlike Kate, she looked tanned and healthy again. Long and slim in a lightweight top and summer skirt, dressed for Spanish balmy spring in this gorgeous April to June slot before the serious heat of summer got going. She must be sleeping at night.

"So what's new?" she asked, sipping her red wine.

"The worst!" Kate launched into her latest tale of woe and Rosie seized on it with triumph.

"It's such a shame we can't secure Casa Sueños yet, because you'd be out of all this mess by now."

"You always say that."

"Don't snap – I'm on your side. And don't think you've got the monopoly for moans and headaches." It was tit for tat as Rosie outdid her in disasters. She had a leaky sewage pipe that had been distributing raw stuff all over her block and she was being denounced by various neighbours. The builders had turned up once and hadn't come back and on it went.

"How do I avoid getting bogged down in all this mess?" Kate meant it metaphorically but she didn't elaborate; too complicated for Rosie.

"For a start, you shouldn't stop being sociable, don't cut yourself off." Rosie was right. That was exactly what Gertrude had said and it was good advice.

"You're right," Kate conceded.

"So how about Friday night?"

"Let's do it, whatever it is." They drank to it.

"Steve may be coming too," remarked Rosie. "I've not seen him for ages."

"I wondered where he was now."

"He's due back with the boat from Palma tomorrow."

"I can't wait."

On a cloudy day in early March, Pedro and Ana walk home from the bazaar together. As they approach the end of the plaza, a young man steps forward and blocks their path.

"*Hombre!*" He clasps Pedro on the shoulders and the two men embrace.

Pedro introduces him. "This is Diego my friend. He is a soldier from the fortress. Diego, this is Ana, my future bride."

"May I wish you every happiness for your forthcoming marriage."

"Thank you." Ana smiles at him.

"I'm so glad to have seen you, my friend." Diego is nervous, his eyes shifting from left to right. "I must not stay long, I should not be seen talking to you, but I have some news. Not good, I fear." He edges them into a corner. "You know the Bishop of Cordoba is aiming to stop all Judaising activities by *conversos?*"

"He is a fanatic and our enemy, I have heard." Pedro nodded.

"I believe they are planning to hold a procession very soon to honour the dedication of a society that he is forming. All *conversos* are excluded from this society." Diego comes closer, his voice low. "Have you also heard that the Old Christians are organising themselves into fighting bands against the *conversos*. They are led by a blacksmith by the name of Rodríguez."

"Yes, I know of that blacksmith." They have all heard of him. He is kind to the Christian poor of Cordoba and he hates the *conversos*.

"Bad times are coming, my friend," says Diego. "You must be careful."

After Elvira has departed, Papa closes the front door and bolts it firmly. The family, including Pedro, gather in the living room. Mama and Grandmother bring their wedding sewing in with them. María taps her fingers on the table in a monotonous rhythm until Ana wants to scream at her to stop.

Papa clears his throat. "As you know, Pedro has told us worrying news about recent events in our home town and we must take extra care. I have been thinking hard, what is the best action to take? I have even been considering for a few days whether we should postpone the wedding altogether for the moment."

"No!" cries Ana, shooting an imploring look at Pedro. This is what she has been dreading. María stops her tapping and leans forward, her body now taut with attention, her eyes glittering with intense interest.

Pedro's voice is firm. "We must marry now, sir." He speaks as forcibly as he can without being disrespectful. "I know my parents would wish it."

"I agree," replies Papa. "We will proceed with the church service, but on a much smaller scale with fewer guests present. People will understand." He chooses his words with care. "And I am wondering whether it is

236

prudent to continue with the Jewish ceremony." His pale, lined face shows the torment of his indecision. "I want it with all my heart, to me it is the Jewish ceremony that truly marries you, but is it not too dangerous? With the situation as it is?"

Mama bursts in, interrupting Papa's flow. "I know that when I was in the street yesterday, I passed Constanza Córtez and she turned her head away. My own neighbour from how many years, our children played together, we attend church together and now she will not speak to me. They suspect us of everything. We are so vulnerable, they will be watching us like hawks."

Papa raises his hands outwards. "You should remind her that we are Catholic, like she is."

"Constanza Córtez resents us. They all do," adds Grandmother.

"For why?" Papa's tone is sharp. "We are not extravagant and greedy like some. We work hard and live a simple life, like they do."

"You know what, Antonio? I speak the truth when I say many of us do not." Mama returns to her sewing. They remain silent until Grandmother speaks again.

"Look at José García Gómes."

"Mother, please!" Papa's irritation is evident. "Why do you always have to mention José García?"

Gómes is a prominent *converso* in Cordoba who works as a financial advisor in royal circles. He lives with his family in a mansion in the best district of town. His children have intermarried with aristocratic Catholic families, he is worth a fortune and he is not alone. Many *conversos* have prospered as they had done in the earlier

237

days when they were Jews, and they are prominent in their affluence. But although Gómes has been a Christian for a long time, he has been seen slipping into the synagogue in the Jewish Quarter. It is no surprise that they are all hated for being hypocrites.

"When I was young, it was easier," mutters Papa.

"Don't be sentimental," snaps back Mama. "Tell me when it has been easy."

Ana recalls those boys shouting at them by the fountain in the small plaza. And now? Although she craves the Jewish wedding ceremony for her own sake as well as her father's, is it not foolhardy to risk it?

"So what shall we do, Papa?" Ana asks.

"Never mind your father, the old Rabbi will not come anyway if there is trouble on the streets." Mama's voice is shrill with warning.

"Very well, I submit to common sense. We will cancel the Rabbi who, as Mama rightly says, will not leave the Quarter while the disturbances are continuing. We will have to cancel the Jewish ceremony, for the moment at least. And we get on with preparing for the church service. And our daily work."

"Thank God!" Mama hugs her husband. "I am so relieved."

Papa pats her arm. "Maybe we can have it later, when it is peaceful again."

"Again! When was it ever peaceful?"

"Beatriz, I am giving up what I want for the sake of our safety. Let us leave it at that. Agreed?"

"Yes, Antonio." Mama sits down and once again resumes her sewing.

238

Papa looks enquiringly at Pedro.

"I accept."

"Ana?"

"I accept also." She is sad but relieved. They have to be sensible. What is important is to be married in church and then they will be able to get away.

"I accept also."

"I'm glad we are doing it like this, Papa," squeaks Felipe, who everybody has forgotten. "I can still play a little music perhaps?"

Papa ruffles the boy's hair. Grandmother looks long at Papa, her son, and says nothing.

CHAPTER TWENTY-ONE

CORDOBA – 1473

"Do keep still while I get this hem level," scolds Grandmother, her hands full of pins. "My! How you have gone thinner these last weeks."

Ana stands up straight as Grandmother takes in the seams of the wedding dress at her final fitting. Grandmother finishes her pinning and Ana slips out of the gown, free now to go to the bazaar in her everyday clothes and work on the spice stall. She is getting married this very week. The bans were announced in church on Sunday and the wedding ceremony is set for three o'clock on Thursday afternoon. Papa has paid a swift visit to the Rabbi in the Jewish Quarter to confirm that he will not be coming.

The horses are ready at the stables belonging to Diego's family at the edge of the city. Pedro is impatient to get away. As arranged, they are leaving the night after the wedding. Diego knows about their departure but he is ignorant of their exact plans. It is better that way, says Pedro. María will explain to their parents after they have gone. When they are safely in Portugal, they will send word home.

"It is so romantic and exciting!" María sings as she tidies and straightens Ana's pile of clothing in her cupboard for the third, fourth time. Ana doesn't find it exciting at all. She cannot explain the reasons logically, but she fears that anything can go wrong at any time. Is it unease over what is going on in Cordoba? Or a deeper fear, an intuition that she is caught up in something more, that she does not understand.

Only last week Mama had asked Ana where her cloak was and why she was going to the bazaar without it. Ana couldn't say that it was folded away and locked in her sister's cupboard. She had to think of an excuse.

"I've lent it to María."

"What for?"

"She had a slight cold coming on and asked if she could borrow it."

Mama appeared satisfied with the explanation, but not Grandmother. She stopped her in the kitchen passage, blocking her way.

"You do not look good, Ana. Is anything wrong?" she demanded, her little hands firmly on her hips. Fortunately at that moment Elvira brought through the fresh laundry and Ana could be excused without answering. On the pretext of getting a clean handkerchief, she ran back up the stairs and stood at the mirror in her bedroom. It was true, she was not glowing like a bride-to-be should. As she gazed at her reflection, the image appeared to waver and she thought she saw the vision of another woman, the face of another Ana with a black hood covering her dark hair, looking back at her with sadness and compassion. Who was this woman in black who looked older than her, but so familiar? Who seemed to understand Ana's turbulent emotional state.

241

* * * *

At the spice stall Ana barely knows what she is doing. Her hands are trembling so much, she spills open a package of the precious ground ginger which scatters orange powdery puddles over the cobblestones and onto her apron.

"You are useless, daughter, it must be pre-wedding nerves," Mama pushes Ana out of the way. She brushes up the spilt spice and returns to the back of the stall to continue her weighing and packaging.

As Ana wraps up a packet of saffron strands for an elderly Moorish gentleman, she notices a woman waiting behind him. She is wearing black trousers gathered at the ankle and a hooded jacket in a soft material and style very different to what the local women wear. Most of their customers are regular clients who have been buying from them for years, but although this woman is a stranger, she seems familiar to Ana. She stands in front of the booth gazing at the saffron, and then she looks at Ana.

Wasn't this the same face that had stared out from her mirror yesterday? Someone who knows what she is feeling as nobody else can, not even Pedro. Ana gulps, her mouth dry. On impulse, she stretches out her hand.

"*Ayúdame*, help me," Ana implores her. The woman's eyes meet hers and there is the same expression of sadness and sympathy that speaks to Ana. She knows this stranger, wants to help her. She is on her side. But as her arm reaches out, the vision standing in

242

front of her starts to fade. "No, please do not go!" Ana cries. But the outline of the woman's body fades and merges into the crowd. Ana can no longer see her.

Perhaps she has drifted away to another stall. Ana twists her head round and scours the nearby booths, trying to find the woman. But she has gone, leaving Ana feeling even more insecure. When the day's trading is finished, she walks home in silence, her head down. María puts an arm round her waist and tries to cheer her up.

"Come, let's go over the luggage once more." She drags Ana to her tiny bedroom and closes the door. Ana sinks onto the floor, her back slumped against the mattress.

"You do it."

"It is your adventure. You're getting married this week, you should be happy." María heaves Ana up, and once again they check the garments and the goods they have stored. Ana tries to forget and be as light and cheerful as María who tosses her head and sings love songs as they work. She smoothes Ana's cloak as she folds it neatly again and again.

'Tap tap'. The family are at supper, when there is a light knock on the front door. María goes to answer it. They hear her scream and slam the door shut. She runs into the living room, her face ashen with fear.

"Mama! There is such a strange person out there, she frightened me," she gasps, and for once her agitation appears genuine. "She was staring at me and wearing these odd black clothes. Please come and see for yourself!"

"I will go." Ana knows immediately who it is. This has to be the same woman who stood before her in the bazaar. She has arrived at their house, but how did she find it?

"Come with me quick!" María runs back, followed by Ana and a more reluctant Mama. Ana opens the door but there is nobody outside.

"She probably came to the wrong house, looking for the apothecary." Mama shrugs and returns to the kitchen to serve the pudding. She is well used to her daughter's melodramatic ways and pays little attention to them.

"No! Will somebody listen to me!" shrieks María, two spots of red staining her cheeks. She stalks after Mama. "I am telling you, she was at our house, she looked like an old hag and now she has gone! It's witchcraft!"

"Hush girl, you are talking nonsense," says Grandmother.

"But she was there, I saw her. Oh why doesn't anyone ever believe me!" María storms out of the kitchen. She stomps loudly up to her room and slams the door closed.

"You come back down here now!" calls Mama. But she does not appear.

Grandmother sighs heavily. "That girl…" She believes that María has fabricated the whole story as a cry for attention because she is jealous of Ana's marriage. Only Ana knows that she has been telling the truth, there had been somebody outside their door. Except that the visitor, whoever she was, was a youngish woman, a little older than her. Not an old hag.

At bedtime that night Grandmother climbs up to Ana's room. Two candles stand on the wooden chest of drawers, lighting up the bedroom.

"Shall I?" Grandmother asks her.

"Yes please." Ana hands her the brush and comb.

"Come and sit down then, Analita." When Ana was a little girl and upset – frequently with María – Grandmother used to sing to her as she brushed her hair. The simple, intimate act would help to soothe her.

"*Hija mía, querida ...*" Grandmother sings a romantic ballad, the traditional Sephardic melody that women of the family sing to brides before their wedding day. Ana sits before the mirror as Grandmother brushes her wavy long hair. She weeps as she listens to the ballad.

The front door creaks open. Deep in the night, a young girl creeps out of the sleeping house again, wearing Ana's black hooded cloak. The moon is out and a light breeze whispers round the corners of the plaza, ruffling the waters of the fountain. The streets are shadowy and silent but María strides the cobbles with confidence. How she enjoys these night-time escapades. Sometimes she wishes she had been born a man and could sail the seas all the way to the Orient and back.

The moonlight shows the way and she has company. Beneath her cloak she is holding a white object, soft and squirming. But she grasps her bundle

245

even tighter, not caring about the pain she is causing. Even when the bundle reaches out and claws at her hand.

She climbs down to the river and stands a few moments on the bank, watching the water. A man comes towards her along the path and she eases back into the shadows. She had planned to perform her task in the river but now she prefers to stay closer to home, more interesting that way.

Returning home, she believes she is being watched from an upstairs window of one of the houses nearby. She stops and peers upwards, thinking she sees a figure staring down at her … no, she is mistaken. There is nothing but darkness, the silent houses silhouetted against the night sky. The water is inky black as she kneels over the fountain in the small plaza and thrusts the white object deep into the ripples. She keeps it pressed well down until it wriggles and claws no longer. She leave it there, hidden at the bottom of the fountain under two large stones.

Back in her bedroom, María removes Ana's cloak and puts it back on top of the pannier in the cupboard. She smoothes it out, straightening the folds with pleasure and brushing off the cat hairs. Then she locks the cupboard door and washes her scratched hand. Singing softly, she undresses and gets into bed.

CHAPTER TWENTY-TWO

CORDOBA – MARCH 1473

They are getting married in two days. Grandmother sends Ana on a quick errand to buy more of the fine gold thread so she can complete the trimming on her wedding dress. On her way home, Ana hears the beat of the drums starting up a few streets away. Men are gathering in noisy groups as the rhythmic sounds grow steadily louder. Crowds are blocking the narrow streets.

"*Perdón*, may I pass?" Ana has to push through the people, weaving and tripping her way in and out in order to cross the main thoroughfare. Please let me reach home safely!

A procession makes its way slowly along the wide street and Ana has to stop. She stands amongst the crowds, bowing her head and acknowledging its passing. The gold thread is thrust deep into her skirt pocket, her fingers clenched tight and clammy in tension as the drums beat, trumpets ring out and the solemn marchers move steadily towards her. The swarthy blacksmith leads the procession, carrying a statue of the Virgin.

A young woman is standing at the upstairs window of a grand house across the street. She pulls the half-open shutters up until they are fully open. Ana knows this girl, Elena. The family are wealthy *conversos* who worship regularly at their church.

Elena seems to be busy and preoccupied at the window, unaware of the procession below. She upturns a vessel that looks like a slop pail, and pours water from it onto the street, as many people do all the time, Old and New Christians alike. It is not a sin. But accidentally, some of the water splashes onto the image of the Virgin and the blacksmith witnesses this action. He stretches out his hand, feels the drops of water and he is furious. He glares up at the window, his face twisted with rage.

"Halt the procession!" he commands loudly. The shuffling walkers behind him stop and the instruments blare to a discordant shriek. The blacksmith points to the young girl framed in the window and the whole procession goggle up at her.

"That girl up there poured urine on the procession," he yells. "And this is religious blasphemy of the worst kind." One of his fellow leaders steps forward and curses her loudly and others join in the shouting. Elena looks down at them in open-mouthed horror and slams down the window shutters.

"Listen to me!" The crowd fall silent as the blacksmith faces his followers.

"I declare war on all the heretics and detractors of Catholics," he announces.

"Hurrah!" The crowd goes wild, cheering and stamping in support of him. A heavy middle-aged man standing too close to Ana nudges her insolently. His small, wrinkly eyes bore into hers. She knows this man with his bushy black hair and beard; she has bought trinkets from his shop.

248

"*Marrana* pig!" he snarls in Ana's ear and spits into her face. The chant is taken up by other men in the crowd. A dog growls and goes for her as she puts her head down, forces her way through the hostile gathering and runs for home. The sleeves of her dress tear as a man tries to grab hold of her, her skirt hem is in ribbons where she has tripped upon it. She gets away from the crowds, runs down the narrow streets, on and on, down the alley, down down, until she reaches home and hammers on the closed door.

"Ana, dearest, what has happened?" Grandmother finds her, collapsed and sobbing, against the step. She helps her into the living room where Ana throws down the gold thread and faces Mama, tears streaming down her face.

"That blacksmith is leading a religious procession, they attacked me on the street! Our own neighbours! We cannot go out again, it is not safe. How can we be married? Our wedding will be ruined. What shall we do?"

For once Mama is speechless. It is María who persuades Ana to wipe her face, straighten her bodice, sit down and stay with the arrangements.

"We will be safe," she repeats. "We should not let them frighten us, we have done nothing wrong. It will all be over soon."

Papa and Felipe get home early from the workshop. Papa locks and bolts the door and barricades it with heavy chairs. They secure all the windows and close down the shutters as Papa strides round the house, issuing orders.

"Stop! Where is Rosita?" cries Ana. "I must find her, she shouldn't be outside, she's not a young cat anymore."

"No, Ana." Papa pulls Ana away from the door. "It is not safe to go out, we stay indoors for the rest of the day."

The noise filters in from the streets beyond their alley. They can hear men shouting, the sound of running footsteps and the clattering of horses' hooves. Voices are raised in terror and panic followed by even more frightening moments of silence. Even inside the house the air is contaminated, foul with smoke and the smell of burning houses. The simmering violence against *conversos* in the city has finally erupted into full-scale riots.

"I hope to God the apothecary is safe," mutters Grandmother. She has known him for over fifty years.

"But what about Pedro!" Ana paces back and forth in the living room. María strokes her hair and the women cling together as they wait and listen. Rosita does not appear for her supper.

Her parents argue that night. This is a rare occurrence, because although Papa can be stubborn, he generally gives in and ends up doing what Mama wants. It is past midnight and Ana is unable to sleep. As she goes downstairs to re-fill her water pitcher she can hear them in their bedroom below.

"You are one misguided man!" Mama shouts. Ana halts outside their door and listens.

"Will you hush for once! I have done what I believe is right."

"If they come here to the house they will see what you've done!"

"I have managed to shorten the script. The words are barely noticeable."

"You are the biggest of fools!"

Before mid-day there is a heavy hammering at the front door.

"Antonio, what shall we do?" Mama cries. The banging grows louder.

"Open up, quick!" A voice shouts from outside.

"It's Pedro!" Ana shrieks, rushing to push aside the chairs and unlock the front door.

"Ana, no." Papa tries to stop her but she has already opened the door and dragged Pedro inside. He is panting, sweating, his clothes torn at the elbow, and he has a large bruise on his forehead.

"I've ... managed to get from our house to yours," gasps Pedro. "One of our neighbours, José the carpenter, used to be my friend. He went for me with a wooden pole."

They lead him to a chair. Mama pours him a tumbler of water as Ana dabs his forehead with a damp rag. They cluster around him as he relates the latest news.

"It is very bad out there. Cordoba is in chaos – the streets are crammed full with religious demonstrations against us. They're burning *converso* houses down. Alonso de Aguilar, one of the commanders at the

251

fortress, you know he is married into a *converso* family, he at least is on our side. He has allowed us to hire about three hundred soldiers in order to help defend ourselves. Both sides are well-armed." Pedro stops to catch his breath. "The word on the street is that a Christian knight was protecting us against the rioters who were led by the blacksmith. The blacksmith was wounded, they are saying he fled for his life to the Church of San Francisco."

"Ah!" whispers Grandmother. The San Francisco is their own church where the wedding will take place. She presses her hands to her forehead.

"It is so confusing, difficult to make out exactly what is happening – but I gather that our man, the good Christian Alonso de Aguilar then called to the blacksmith to come out of the church for a parley. When he appeared, Alonso requested him to retire his mob, but the blacksmith insulted him and Alonso flung a spear at him. Now I believe the blacksmith has been carried back to his home mortally wounded." Pedro gulps at his water and continues. "The situation is treacherous, there are fanatics abroad who are calling the blacksmith a martyr. They have seized weapons and are attacking us anywhere and everywhere. The peasants and labourers are pouring in from the countryside and joining in. Some *conversos* have carried their possessions to the fortress and taken refuge there, while others have managed to escape from the city and are wandering about in the fields trying to find a safe shelter."

"Our family converted to escape persecution," moans Mama. "And now we have this!"

"This is what I have heard. But it is all moving so fast, there are so many rumours." Pedro is breathing heavily. Ana puts her hand on his arm and he grasps it tightly. María's face is blank. Felipe, a young man now, stands firmly by Papa's shoulder. Grandmother is hunched into her seat, her sewing forgotten upon her lap. Rosita is still missing.

Papa speaks slowly, thinking his thoughts aloud. "I do not know what to say or do. We have to decide whether we should stay here or try to escape outside the walls."

"I for one am not moving," says Mama. "We dare not go out until the disturbances have ceased and you children cannot go through these streets to get married in the church. The very church that sheltered the blacksmith! We have to postpone it. Nobody will come, not even our close families. Nobody will leave their houses. We have to stay indoors."

Pedro scrambles to his feet, almost knocking over his chair. "But we must marry tomorrow, it is our wedding day. We should not change it. All is agreed, the marriage contract has been witnessed and signed by both our families."

"You think you can walk through those streets with your bride in her wedding gown! You will be killed, we all will."

"Perhaps the priest could come here and perform the wedding ceremony?" suggests Grandmother from her corner.

"No, he must not." Mama is adamant. "It would be wrong to ask him to put his life at risk. And again, there is the connection with the blacksmith in our church. Whose side would the priest be on?"

"But I am not waiting." Pedro is determined.

It is stalemate until Papa speaks. "There is one other possible way that you could get married tomorrow."

"There you go, talking nonsense again!" snaps Mama.

"Beatriz, one moment," Grandmother breaks in. She turned to Papa, her eyes full of an unspoken knowledge. "What were you going to say?"

Papa faces his wife. His words are clear and deliberate but the tremor in his voice gives away his tension. "Tomorrow we do not go out of the house. We stay here, we bolt the doors and nobody comes. We go down to the cellar and we have a wedding service."

"What are you suggesting?" asks Mama.

"What I am saying is that I am perfectly able to perform the Jewish wedding service. It will be a shortened version but I can do it. I will marry my daughter to Pedro."

"You! You know two bits of Hebrew that your father passed on to you. How can you do it?"

"I am used to it." Papa brings a folded piece of paper from his pocket and carefully smoothes it out. "The Rabbi gave me this a few days ago when I went to see him. He wrote the Hebrew out for me clearly so I could say it and he went through it with me in translation. These are the necessary blessings for a basic Jewish wedding service. A Rabbi should officiate but in extreme cases a layman can do it. I would say this is an extreme case, wouldn't you?" Mama for once is

254

speechless. "So you see, there is enough here for me to marry them tomorrow quite legally and legitimately."

"Hurray! So we can get married!" cries Pedro.

Grandmother claps her hands in delight. "Yes Antonio. And later, when all this is over, they can go to church and have the Christian ceremony which everybody can attend."

"It is not a bad idea, eh Beatriz?" Papa turns to his wife.

"But is it safe?"

"It will only take a few moments. And who is to know?"

"But we have all this food ready. If nobody comes, what will we do with it?"

"We can have the party, we'll eat it all," cries María, her eyes sparkling.

At supper time, the noise outside appears to be dying down and Pedro runs a circular route home to tell his parents and other relatives of the new arrangements. They will have to miss the secret wedding ceremony. His mother grieves but realises that it is not safe to leave their house.

He dodges back through the eerie and deserted plaza near Ana's home. Smoke is heavy in the air from houses that have been set alight. Broken, half-burnt doors hang open on shattered hinges, stones litter the ground and rotting fruit and vegetables splatter the cobbles. Wooden stakes lie in harsh, broken piles. A woman's gown is discarded on the ground, stained with blood. A dead cat has become detached from the stones

255

holding her down and her body floats in the dirty water of the fountain. Pedro recognises the cat and lifts Rosita gently out He removes his jacket, wraps her in it and carries the bundle into the house.

Ana digs a hole in the soft earth of the patio and with María's help, she buries Rosita under the orange tree. Pedro holds her as she cries softly against his shoulder. María stands beside Ana, her arms tightly round them both. She sings a gentle song of mourning in her beautiful pure voice, tears glistening in her eyes. Pedro squeezes Ana's hand.

"A change of plan," he whispers to them both. "We must not stay a moment longer than is necessary."

Ana pulls away from his grasp. "But Pedro both our families expect us to have a church wedding later. How can we do this to them?"

"We cannot help the circumstances, we have to leave tomorrow night. We go as soon as we can. Agreed?" It is agreed between the three of them.

When María hears Papa's steady snoring from behind his bedroom door, she slips out of the house again. Picking her way carefully through the debris littering the alley, she knocks on the door of the house opposite, belonging to the apothecary. There is no reply and she is not surprised. The door is not bolted, it falls open at her touch. Even in the dark, she can see that the interior has been ransacked. Chairs are lying on their sides, the table tipped over and its contents strewn in broken pieces on the floor. There is no sign of the apothecary but María

256

knows where to look for what she wants. Feeling her way round the chairs and the litter, she goes straight to the long bench at the back of the room. The bottom drawer is half-open and there is the small parcel she ordered two days ago. She thrusts it into her pocket.

CHAPTER TWENTY-THREE

This was one crazy evening and it was doing her good to get out of the house. Kate was with Steve and Rosie at a beach bar in the warm balmy air. She'd made a deliberate effort to make an effort and was encased in tight jeans, a large hip-level belt and a sleeveless cut-away white top with bra straps, brown shoulders and a fair bit of bosom showing. She'd already had two large glasses of wine. Steve and Kate were on track again and could hardly keep their eyes and hands off each other. Nearby, the mega hotel sat watching benignly in its landscaped palm-tree garden in the twilight. Another Dream Development rose to the right of them with its attendant cranes and bulldozers, now silent for the night.

The perky English girl in cut-off jeans and bare midriff took their orders for grilled prawns in garlic sauce, more red wine and salad. On Friday nights the entertainment included live music which would be starting any minute. Drinks flowed, every table on the wooden floor was taken, and the smaller circular tables on the sand were filling up fast. Uncle Roger's wife, Aunt Susan, who marked the success of a restaurant by the number of its occupied covers, would have approved.

Down near the lapping water's edge, holidaymakers lay out on deckchairs. A bronzed middle-aged woman with a massive brown stomach, sprawled, unashamedly topless. A couple of riders from the equestrian school up the valley pranced their horses along the beach. Dusk fell and the first stars shone clear in the sky.

The entertainer arrived, turned on and adjusted his equipment. He played guitar, clarinet and saxophone, and sang along with his music centre. His repertoire included rock and roll and rhythm and blues, all Kate's old-fashioned sixties' favourites.

She was hyper with the beat, couldn't stop her body from moving. When *Mustang Sally* started, she dragged Steve onto the wooden springy floor. Although there was nobody else dancing Kate threw herself around and so did he.

"Mustang Sally now baby, think we better slow that Mustang down ..." They sang, danced wildly and ground hips in unison. Other couples joined them on the floor and clapped when they'd finished. Kate was sweaty, hot, and Steve grabbed her, led her onto the sand and held her tight. Their bodies shuddered together and they kissed under the stars. Oh boy, did she want Steve.

Amidst this joyous abandon, Kate caught sight of Rosie. Her face was thunderous, her eyes met Kate's and her presence struck a hideous chord of memory.

She'd danced this wedding dance before, wearing a long dress trimmed with gold thread. She had seen that look of cold hatred in another time.

259

The front door remains closed and locked all day. They pray that their *converso* relatives and neighbours are safe.

'We are marrying today, we're leaving tonight, we have to continue, we are leaving tonight and will be safe,' is an unsung thread that runs round Ana's head. She tries to reassure herself that all will go as planned. 'The arrangements have been made. After we retire, Pedro leaves to fetch and saddle the horses. I change into my travelling clothes, María and I carry the loaded panniers to the corner of the main plaza where we will meet Pedro. She helps us to depart, if all goes well, please God. Pedro says again and again do not worry. In the continuing turbulence outside he is sure they will not be noticed.'

Grandmother eases Ana into her heavy, flowing wedding dress with its gold embroidered square neckline and long muslin sleeves. Mama and María have made an effort to be festive. Coloured lamps adorn the living room. The air is heavy with perfume from the flowers that Mama has picked from the patio and placed in vases on the table. Grandmother and Mama sprinkle a few drops of rose water on Ana's head and bridal veil. This is an old tradition performed at a Jewish marriage – the water symbolising a joyful and sweet life to come.

The time has come. Papa and Pedro move the table and they all climb down into the cellar, Mama helping

Ana, holding up her dress behind her. In the dim light below, Mama, Grandmother, María and Felipe hold a fine sheet over the bridal couple as a makeshift canopy.

Papa draws the prayer shawl round his shoulders and, with the light shining on him, he carefully recites the blessing that the Rabbi has written out for him, first in a stumbling Hebrew and then in a translation they can all understand.

"Behold thou art consecrated to me with this ring in accordance with the law of Moses and Israel." At Papa's request, Pedro produces the wedding ring and slips it onto Ana's finger. Papa continues with his blessing: "Blessed art Thou, O Lord our God, who has hallowed us with Thy commandments and who makest the bridegroom to rejoice with the bride." He passes a glass of wine first to Pedro and he drinks from it. Mama holds up Ana's veil so she can drink also.

"Now you should throw the glass against the wall." And Pedro does so. The traditional breaking of the glass represents the destruction of the old temple in Jerusalem. The service is short and takes only a few moments but Papa is satisfied. In Jewish law, his daughter is married, Ana and Pedro are husband and wife. Pedro takes his bride in his arms and kisses her. The family crowd round the bridal couple, crying "*mazel tov*" and hugging them. And it is over.

Mama and Grandmother swiftly remove the sheet and Papa folds away his beloved shawl. María brushes up the broken glass and they scurry up out of the cellar. The men push the table back into position and they all stand there, breathing heavily. The tension eases a little

261

now the ceremony is over and they are safe in the house with the door locked. Now they can try to celebrate a little.

Grandmother's saffron-flavoured chicken stew is delicious, as are the sweet baked saffron pastries, the lemonade and the splendid iced honey cake decorated with almonds and dried fruit. This is a joyous occasion and they are safe. As they wait.

Felipe plays lively wedding music on his vihuela and Pedro and Ana dance in the space cleared of furniture. Their arms encircle each other as they smile and try to be joyful. The family watch and applaud them and María claps the loudest. Her bright blue eyes match her dress trimmed with ivory lace. She sings as she sways to the rhythm.

"Please Felipe, could you stop the music a moment?" Papa asks. Ignoring Mama's sigh of exasperation, he turns to the small group.

"I would like to give these to my dear daughter Ana and her husband Pedro on the occasion of their marriage. May they use them in good health." Papa takes a parcel from a dark corner, unwraps it and hands the bridal couple his present. It is a pair of fine silver candlesticks to represent their marriage union. He has fashioned them secretly in his workshop and even Felipe who works alongside him has not known of their creation. Papa has carved out entwined initials at the bottom of each curved stem and on the round base he has included the traditional words for welcoming the Sabbath. Papa reads out the blessing in Hebrew.

262

"I have shortened it to 'Shabbat shalom umevorach.' This means a peaceful and blessed Sabbath."

"Thank you so much, dearest Papa." Ana kisses her father and lifts up one of the candlesticks reverently. She repeats the words softly. "Shabbat shalom umevorach."

Pedro does not look as thrilled as Ana. The candlesticks are beautiful works of art no doubt, but the open, obvious link with Judaism is there for anyone to see. This is what has so enraged Mama. She does not want to spoil the pleasure of Papa's gift, but she is deeply upset. She scoops up the candlesticks and takes Ana to one side.

"You must hide them away at once and not use them until you have your own house with its secret hiding-place."

"Yes, Mama." But Ana loves the gift from her father, seeing the candlesticks as a link with their Jewish past and a beautiful testament to their love. Papa raises his hand for silence again, and with a flourish, he brings out a little silver bowl that he has tucked behind the honey cake on the table.

"And this little ornament I have made for Mama, my wonderful wife, for being so patient with me." The family laugh and cheer as Mama takes the bowl.

"You are a naughty boy, Antonio," she whispers, reaching up to kiss him. Papa signals for Felipe to start the music again. He plays a lively melody and Ana and Pedro dance together with Mama and Papa beside them and Grandmother taps her hands and feet to the rhythm.

'We are leaving soon, we are leaving tonight.' Ana should be joyous but she is too frightened ... as it starts up. The rhythm grows louder, the drums are beating ...

"Listen!" María shouts from the door. Ana and Pedro freeze in their movement and Felipe stops playing.

"Antonio, they are back!" cries Mama.

"Ssh," hisses Papa. The steady beating of drums starts up not far away. They can hear the men shouting and distant screams. In the hushed room the family stand motionless, as if in a frozen tableau. This is what they have been fearing all the time. The sounds grow louder. Is the mob already in the plaza? Mama is whimpering with terror and Papa holds her tight, his hand covering her mouth to stifle her screams.

"Clear the room!" commands Papa. The tableau breaks. Pedro runs to the door, already locked and bolted, and stacks chairs against it. He blows out the celebratory lamps and pulls the furniture back into place. Mama and Papa lift the tablecloth of food between them and carry it, squashed and dripping into the kitchen. Felipe runs to hide his vihuela at the back of the spice storeroom. Ana grabs the precious silver candlesticks and hurtles up the two flights of stairs to the bedroom. She pushes them deep under the bedclothes and tears off her bridal gown. She pulls on a plain shift and runs back downstairs. And all this time Grandmother is rooted in her seat, mumbling and praying as the sound of the drums comes closer. But they will not come to their house and why should they? They are doing nothing wrong. All appears normal, although the tell-tale rose water perfume lingers in the air. The drumbeat and the shouting grow louder and nearer; the mob must now be in the little plaza. Getting closer to the alley and their home.

"I knew we shouldn't have done it," Mama wails.

"Beatriz, hush!" Papa slaps her face and she stops immediately. Grandmother stays motionless. Across the room, María's eyes meet Ana's. She cannot read her sister's blank expression. Is it anger or shock? Could it even be hatred?

They are in time. Sitting heavy and steady as stones they are wearing their crucifixes clearly displayed on the outside of their clothing and apart from the flushed faces and heavy breathing, they appear calm.

Now the noise pours down their alley. Men's voices are yelling right outside the house and then comes a loud banging and hammering on their own door. María is steely stiff with attention as the wooden door heaves, splinters and breaks open. The mob surge into the house, knocking aside the furniture. They are holding burning torches and shouting curses at the *marrano* pigs. Ana instantly recognises one of the men, a big fellow, pushing in behind the leader. It is Luis, the boy who attacked them years ago by the fountain. María's friend.

"You lot! Out of the way!" Luis charges across the room and pushes them heavily against the walls. Ana crumples to the floor, clinging to Pedro, as the gang throw chairs across the room, and slash at the sideboard with long knives and sticks.

"Move this table!" shouts Luis. The men push it over and kick and pull at the heavy carpet covering the cellar entrance. As they lift the carpet, more shouting comes from the alley. A team of armed soldiers stream through the broken door, led by Pedro's friend, Diego. Their swords are unsheathed and in a few moments the mob is surrounded and subdued. Luis' gang have not found what they are looking for. The soldiers kick them outside and send them on their way, to do what? Presumably attack another *converso* dwelling in the neighbourhood. The soldiers are red-faced, sweating, breathing heavily as they survey the room, put their swords away and depart. Diego looks back for a moment at the door and exchanges the tiniest of nods with Pedro. Then he is gone.

The double invasion of the mob and the soldiers who saved them has happened in what seems like seconds. And they are all huddled on the floor against the wall. María stays close to Ana, her face a mask of non-emotion.

"Who has betrayed us?" whispers Papa to nobody. He gets up and hobbles over to the broken front door. Pedro runs forward and they manage to lever up what is left of it and half-close it. Papa slumps against the wall, looking at the ruin of his home in front of him.

"Come, Beatriz." He helps her to her feet and puts his arm round her shoulder. They stand silent for a moment and then make their way upstairs to their bedroom, moving slowly and heavily, bent over like an old couple. Felipe follows them, sobbing. Grandmother remains shrunken, against the wall. Her hair escapes in wild thin wisps from the soft bun. No longer does she resemble a sprightly woman.

María alone appears unaffected by the attacks. Her cheeks are flushed with excitement. As Pedro takes the weeping Ana in his arms, she stops them.

"Please," María begs. "We are safe and alive, that is the important thing. Try and put aside what has happened and celebrate. Let me be allowed to join the bridal couple in a glass of wine."

But Pedro shakes his head. "No," he says with great weariness.

"At least allow me to bid you a joyous night." She nips Ana's waist with a saucy pinch. Ana is stunned at María's light-heartedness. How can she be so unmoved at this invasion into their lives? And why did the men choose to come to their house – it was if they knew what was going on.

"We have not yet taken a drink to the bride and groom," Marìa reminds them with a smirk.

"It does not matter now," Pedro says.

"But we must, to make up for missing the party. Let us go to the bedroom and drink to your future."

"It is not a good idea," he persists but Ana stops him.

"What is the harm in drinking a final toast?" It is, after all, their wedding night.

"Ana, we both need a clear head."

"I'll take only a little, enough to settle me down."

"But you must have your wits about you for what is to come. It will be dangerous on the streets."

A shot of panic runs through her body. "Do you think we should not go then?"

"Come upstairs. We leave tonight. Now it is even more necessary."

María runs up the stairs after them with a bottle of wine, glasses and a saffron pastry especially for Ana. "Because you didn't have one and you love them so much."

Pedro refuses a drink, but María pours full glasses for both her and Ana. Ana drinks the wine and devours half the pastry. She desperately needs the release of tension that alcohol and saffron will bring her. Humming softly, María gathers the glasses. Hers is mostly untouched.

"So, I meet you with the panniers as arranged?" she enquires briskly.

"Let us make it in an hour from now," says Pedro.

"Enjoy yourselves until then." And with a broad wink, María picks up the tray. She stands for a moment watching them, the shadow of her long skirt by the door. Then she clatters down the stairs and away.

The night sky is red with fire and smoke. Ana and Pedro stand together, looking out of the window. She tilts her head up at him, and twines her arms round his neck.

"We would be safer if we stayed here."

"Maybe, but another mob could come by at any time."

Ana grips his arm. "I implore you. Do not say that."

Pedro presses her cheek lightly. "All this will be good for us. We will go carefully but with confidence, heads up, as if the city belongs to us and we know what we are doing. We do not meet anybody's eyes and they will not look at us. They do not expect us to be out, they are far too intent on burning houses. And do not forget, we have Diego and his troops on our side."

"Yes." Ana holds him close and he kisses her lips. Arms entwined, they sit on the bed and go through the plan once more. Pedro will stay upstairs to allow time for the family to settle. Then he will slip out and go for the horses. Ana will give him time to get them and then follow in her hooded cloak accompanied by María, carrying the stored belongings between them. They meet at the pre-arranged point and from there they will gallop west, straight out of the city and beyond. To freedom.

"For safety's sake, bring as little as you can," he reminds her. "Stick to the essentials. We don't want to burden the horses more than we have to."

"I know." Ana roots under the bed and brings out the candlesticks. "But we have to take these with us."

"No! We should not take further risks."

"I will not leave without them."

"But Ana …"

"Hush. There is no argument."

Pedro sighs in resignation at Ana's stubbornness. "Very well, but let us separate them, it makes them less bulky, less of a hazard."

Ana finds a piece of linen from her trousseau chest and wraps up Pedro's candlestick. "I will take mine in my baggage, and you bring yours."

"I love you," he says, his face close to hers.

"You are not going yet," she whispers. She reaches for her glass and drinks the remainder of the wine. There is a bitter taste of sediment at the bottom.

"My darling wife." He buries his head in her neck and kisses her again. They lie back and make love on her bed. She clings to him, dizziness sweeping over her.

"We will be together again in but a short time," says Pedro, reassuring her. It will happen as arranged. They embrace again and he is at the door when she stops him. He has forgotten his candlestick.

"Ana, we really should not take them."

"We have to, it is our heritage." She pushes the candlestick into his hands. "Go, now, I will see you soon." He closes the door softly behind him and is gone.

Ana almost loses her balance as she turns round. She stumbles to the bed and collapses onto it. For the last few minutes she has been feeling drowsy and now weariness overtakes her. Her eyelids are heavy, her eyes closing. She fights to keep them open, tries to sit up again, but she is falling back again onto the rumpled covers. No, this is not right. Come on Ana, wake up, get ready and go away. Her husband, love and freedom are waiting. But her body will not stir. Her head lolls, her tongue is heavy as she slips into a slurred sleep.

The rancid smell of smoke wakes her. The taste of smoke and saffron is in her mouth, her nostrils. The house is crackling with fire and burning. She screams and the smoke billows into her nostrils, filling her lungs. She rolls over, falls heavily out of bed and lurches to the door, heaving and retching. She wrenches open the door and smoke from the landing pours in. She forces it closed again. The window is barred, with the spaces between the black grilles too close to get through. Down below in the street she hears shouting, the terror spilling up three burning flights to her bedroom. Then she hears a voice she knows.

"*Venga!*" She hears the call again. The heat is growing. She can barely speak, the smoke, the saffron smoke curls under the door, choking her lungs, she is trapped in the house of smoke and fire …

"Help me!" she cries. Somebody is shouting "*Venga, Venga*" – but she is stuck in the bedroom, unable to get out.

"*Ayúdame* … help me!" She is hoarse and getting weaker. She's coughing, struggling to breathe, tears of soot and smoke are running down her face. Somebody's hand reaches out for her, and she grabs it, she is dragged through the door and onto the burning landing, somebody is with her as she stumbles, gasping, choking, towards the burning stairs. The wooden beams above are alight. The flames are flickering round her. No! Stop! She has forgotten her precious candlestick. It has to survive.

"Ana no!" Somebody is urging her on, not back.

"No, I must get it!" Fighting against the pulling arm, she claws her way back into the bedroom.

CHAPTER TWENTY-FOUR

ESTEPONA – PRESENT DAY

Kate gulped, heaved and brought up onto the sand whatever was clogged within her. She lay huddled beyond the wooden platform of the beach bar, The music had stopped, the musician long gone. The shutters were drawn down, the bar closed, with not a plate, beer can or person in sight. And Rosie and Steve had gone also. There was nothing there but the damp sand, the sea and stillness. The moon was up, its light reflected in a beam along the waves. The stars glimmered in a navy sky. Despair overwhelmed her.

How long had she been like this? On the plus side, she hadn't crashed to the ground and she wasn't in pain. Nothing was broken. Her watch hung on her wrist, showing one in the morning. Last time she'd noticed, the time was around eleven.

Kate struggled to her feet and the twenty-first century hit her. Where was her bag? And her house keys, her purse, credit, debit cards, tampons, mobile phone, makeup, brush, throat pastilles, Rescue Remedy, her life, and how was she going to get home? Hunting through the back pockets of her jeans, she found a folded ten euro note and her house keys. Yes, she remembered now. For security reasons, she put her bag on the floor under her chair and the keys into her

272

pocket when she got up to dance with Pedro – no – not Pedro. Steve.

The large hotel was five minutes' walk away. Kate trudged across the beach, pushed open the heavy glass doors and found Reception.

"Please could you phone for a taxi," she demanded in straight English. No more messing about in Spanish. This was an emergency.

"Certainly, madam."

The taxi arrived within minutes and whisked her through town along the brightly lit avenue. She had enough to pay the driver plus the tip.

Kate must have had an escape-mechanism tuned into her psyche otherwise how could she live through these things and not go mad? When she was deep in them, they were real, but when they stopped, it was like a dream ending, and her other world vanished. But they were lingering longer and stronger each time.

'I wonder what will happen today,' she kept repeating in the morning as she didn't rub medium beige spot remover over the dark circles under her eyes. It was in the missing bag. Good things please, and quickly.

Although her purse was gone, her credit cards were by the kettle. She didn't take them when she went out in case they were stolen. And for this reason – that she might be abandoned in a wedding dress in a different existence on a deserted starry beach?

So what was missing was the purse with the cash plus make-up and the odd bit of stuff, as well as the bag

273

itself. The bag was on its last legs. She'd miss the hairbrush and the money. Already her memory of last night had been transferred into the deleted dream file. Was that a good or bad thing?

She did know she'd got a red-hot rage for Rosie. This was not a good thing.

She confronted Rosie at her first floor office in a large new block halfway up Avenida de Andalucía. But Rosie started in before her, full of righteous bluster.

"Where did you get to last night then?" she demanded from behind her computer, working glasses quivering in indignation on the end of her nose.

"I could ask you that."

"*You* were the one that went off," she retorted.

"What are you talking about? I find myself alone on the beach and you say I went off. I've had enough of it, Rosie!" They continued to ding-dong back and forth until the plump girl at the second desk heaved her head up from her computer and butted in.

"Will you sort this out you two, or I'm going. I can't get on with my work."

Rosie dragged Kate into an empty storeroom next to the office, closed the door and blazed at her.

"Let me tell you, I was disgusted with you last night."

"*You* were disgusted with me!"

"The way you were carrying on with Steve. Throwing yourself at him like that, you were all over him, rubbing up against him, in front of everyone at the bar. I was ashamed for us all!" Rosie's eyes popped.

274

Even her bobbed hair was stiff with outrage. "Disgusting!" she repeated with vehemence.

Kate was furious at this unwarranted attack. "What I do with Steve is entirely my own business and his. It's nothing to do with you."

"It is when you behave like a tart and you're with me. I've got my reputation, you know. And you were not being loyal to me," came back the baffling Rosie response, designed to defeat her.

Yet Kate was regaining a feisty strength to match the opponent snarling in front of her, a strength that had stood her in good stead when dealing with stroppy students in the old Manchester teaching days, but which had been semi-submerged since she got to Spain. It was as if she had someone else in there with her now, encouraging her to stand up against Rosie's attack.

"You hear this," she hissed. "Steve is a free agent and so am I. If I choose to get drunk and enjoy myself, it's my business. What we do or don't do is nothing to do with you. Or is it?"

Rosie wouldn't look at her. She fiddled with a filing cabinet and caught her fingers in the drawer. "Damn," she muttered.

"To get to the important thing," Kate carried on, looming over her. "I found myself outside the bar that you took me to, alone, in the dark, and abandoned."

"It wasn't like that," stammered Rosie, backing away.

"No? What was it like then?" Good job she couldn't hear Kate's heart thumping, protesting at the audacity to

275

yell her mind. She couldn't suspect the secret desire Kate had to throttle her. "You tell me!"

"We thought you'd gone to the toilet. I went to see where you were, Steve looked all round, so did I, and we couldn't find you."

"I could have been abducted for all you knew."

"Now you're being silly." Rosie breathed out, visibly relaxing. But Kate wasn't finished yet.

"How could you go off, not knowing where I was?"

"Not true. We got the whole bar looking for you. God knows where you were. I rang your apartment again and again, left messages for you on the landline. Have you checked it?" Kate hadn't thought of that. Rosie opened the cabinet she'd been fiddling with and produced her bag.

"You see how I'm looking after you. You left your bag on the floor by your seat. I took it for safe keeping." She threw it across and the mobile jiggled inside.

"Thanks." Kate clasped the bag and could say no more. They were locked in fruitless deadlock. Rosie didn't help her but at least Kate knew where Rosie was or had been – dancing at her wedding.

"You were there, standing at the door, you were supposed to be on guard, you let them in, you betrayed me!" she shouted.

"What!" Rosie stared at Kate. "Now you've completely lost me."

Kate had lost herself. She didn't know who she was or where she belonged. She backed away, out of the room, the office and Rosie's life. She and Rosie were finished. Goodbye looking for cute houses and cultural

276

centres. She was hurtling towards something much more tragic.

CHAPTER TWENTY-FIVE

ESTEPONA PRESENT DAY – SHE HOPED

Morning was here. No noise in the night. The port din had also ceased. The garbage lorry had arrived, the dog in the hut began howling as Kate fell back into restless sleep. A voice battled in her head, shouting in an *español* she didn't comprehend. She shouted back at it, "for God's sake shout in English if you have to shout at all."

The reflection in the mirror continued to show a different Kate. Her body was thinner and, with the aid of colour rinse, her hair was growing browner and longer. Her eyes were bigger, darker, her expression more desperate. She ate her cereal with saffron powder sprinkled on top. Gertrude's missing cat returned with another bloody ear and scratched nose, mewing pitifully. She identified with it.

She was aware of the beauty of late spring, the colourful rows of flowers ordained by the mayor of Estepona. But through the purples, yellows and pinks, the smell of smoke dominated her senses. Was it from the apartment below, or from the past?

On a warm windy night she woke to find she was hanging over the balcony.

"Jump, jump, go on do it," a voice sighs. Part of her wants to lose her balance and plummet.

"Who are you?" she cries, gripping the rusting railings.

"Ana," whispers back the wind, through the smoke. She is awake and again in other-time, in the burning house. She can't get out except through the open window, which is blocked by the black grille. She hears a hammering on the door and screams a mouth full of smoke. The hammering sound continues.

"Kate," shouted Gertrude, knocking on the wall between their bedrooms. "I can hear you. Shall I come round?"

"No!" she shouted back.

She was continuing to lose touch with reality, while a young woman was out and about, radiating evil.

"What shall I do about all this?" Kate begged *The Book of Help*.

'IT COULD BE SOMETHING QUITE SPECIAL.' She'd had that one so often, it fell open automatically at the page.

It was on Avenida Juan Carlos that life changed. Gertrude's tea had given her violent stomach cramps and she was down at the healthfood shop hunting for a potion that would make her sleep solidly and dreamlessly through the night with no side effects and no nightmares.

"*Sí*, I assure you with these you have no harmful effects," said the shop-owner, caressing a packet from the second shelf. "You must take one sachet and if no good, take two." The package was expensive. "All

279

products that come to Spain from outside are more expensive because we have to pay duty and tax on it." Valerian was prominent in the list of contents and she didn't care, she wanted it there.

Kate stumbled out of the shop, pale-faced and wild haired because she refused to tame the growing bush on her head, and halted at the nearest café. The bright plastic awning shielded against the heat of the sun and the constant noise of workmen digging up another roundabout, another pavement, another street.

Classical violin music was playing over the café sound system and it reminded her of the man from the artisan shop in the mountains who was no longer her friend. She couldn't help weeping soundlessly into her decaff coffee and toast. The Spanish businessmen at their solitary tables rustled their newspapers and hunched themselves away. The babies gawped with big eyes and open mouths over their mothers' shoulders. The mamas exchanged sideways glances and moved their babies' heads away. The coffee was ruined and she'd no hanky. A kindly waiter came over and handed her a container of paper napkins from the next table.

Kate blew her nose and wiped her face. An enormous lorry proclaiming 'Construcciones Córdoba' along its side pulled up at the roundabout, its lights flashing. Cordoba twinged her memory. When did all this start? Was it before or after she got back from Cordoba … her mind raced. Cordoba had to be the key. Where it started good and proper with the medieval market, the smell of saffron, the sad familiar brown-eyed girl and fair-haired girl – and she knew what she'd forgotten about Cordoba.

Slamming down two euros plus twenty cents tip, she ran away. Up Avenida de España, past the road works, building works, flowers, roundabouts, fountains, cherubs, unicorns, more pansies and the pedestrian crossing opposite the chemist. An oncoming car screeched to a halt as she crossd the road without looking or acknowledgement – Spanish *señora* style – and arrived home to a silent apartment. The gang below were out doing their who-knows-what shady work and yapetty-yap must have been taking a nap.

Now where was it? That scrap of lined paper. His name was Josef Gómez. He came from Toledo and she'd met him in the synagogue in Cordoba. He had given Kate his address, but where had she put it? It wasn't in her diary where it should be. Nor in the purse which was burgeoning with useless old supermarket bills. Could it be in the suitcase? She dragged it out from under the bed – no, that was empty. She hunted through pockets in the wardrobe and found rows of lists of good and bad things and a plumber's phone number, but not his.

Then she had a hunch. Got out the diary again and opened the black leather pouch flap. The small, folded piece of lined paper was there, tucked inside. She read Josef's address, his landline telephone number, mobile number and email address. This man was making it so easy for her to contact him and she'd done nothing about it.

Re: Meeting in Cordoba

Hi Josef. We met in the synagogue in Cordoba a couple of months ago. Could we talk sometime, if you have time?

Kate.

This was a rather formal, even terse email. Kate bit her nails for forty-eight hours, got no reply and sent it to him again. Checked her on-line horoscope, bank statement and the current price of houses in Manchester and Andalusian white villages. No reply. No sound from below.

She rang Josef's mobile number and got the unavailable signal. Nothing from his landline either. The man no longer existed, she was in despair again but she wouldn't give up. She tried his mobile one more time, left a message and her number, and waited on as the cats watched the dogs who watched the cats below.

Five minutes later, he rang back.

"*Hola?* "

"Hi. *Hola,*" she replied.

"This is Josef, who are you? Who is Kate? You rang me."

"Yes, it's Kate. I sent you a couple of emails."

"My computer has been not functioning for a few days. Another virus."

"You were with some American women in the synagogue at Cordoba a while ago. I came up and spoke to you there."

"I'm sorry, I don't know you."

"I had a scratch on my cheek. You told me to get it cleaned."

"A scratch … ah yes, now I remember. And what can I do for you?"

Kate hadn't thought beyond contacting him but now she knew clearly what she wanted and he was the person who could help. "I would like to visit Toledo and meet up with you. Is that convenient?"

"When do you want to come?"

She was doing nothing with nobody for the rest of her life but mustn't look too needy. "How about next Monday?" Four long days away.

"Please hold on a moment I'll have a look, it's my mother's birthday that week." She waited through the rustling of distant pages.

"That is fine. Why do you want to come?"

She gave it to him straight. "I'm having some trouble with the past and you said I shouldn't ignore it."

"I said that?"

"You did."

He spelled out what he called straightforward directions to a gift shop in the heart of the old town. It wouldn't be simple finding it, it never was, but she would get there.

Kate put the mobile down and did a tiny *sevillana* twirl round the room. She was off to Toledo on Sunday. Impulsive Kate was back, vibrating with possibility. When things flowed as smoothly as that, she was convinced they were meant to be. Josef might at least be a key, a doorway to a history, if one existed for her. This man was going to lead her to her buried past. She'd drive up to Toledo, southwest of Madrid. She rushed to the map of Spain and then *The Book of Help*.

"Do you approve of Toledo?" she asked, staring furiously at the cloud. She opened the book at random praying hard that 'IT COULD BE SOMETHING QUITE SPECIAL' wouldn't come up again. The answer sent shock waves through her body.

'YOU ARE ON THE RIGHT PATH.' What a wonderful book!

The silver candlestick with its lone candle gleamed and glittered from the sideboard. The heat was rising, the hot hazy Saturday morning heavy with brilliant sun.

As she was packing, Steve rang, demanding attention.

"Hello Steve." Kate blushed over the phone. She'd forgotten all about him.

"How are you Kate, girl? Recovered from the other night?" he asked. His voice was low, charming, intimate and her blush deepened. What should she do about Steve now? They'd had so much going last week at the beach bar but okay, maybe Rosie was right, maybe she did lead him on just a little. Then everything else happened and he got pushed to the back of her head.

"Steve, I'm fine, how are you?" she forced out.

"I've been really worried about you." His voice was buttery soft with concern. "Can we get together very soon? I've got a meeting tonight but how about tomorrow?"

"Sorry, I'd love to Steve, but I'm off to Toledo in the morning."

"What on earth for?"

"Just a trip."

284

"For how long?"

"A few days, I can see you later in the week?"

"You're always rushing off somewhere." His tone suggested that real people down here didn't go gallivanting. They got on with real work and waited for him to call.

"It's only a little adventure."

"And how are you getting up there?"

"I'm driving myself."

"Well, I'll miss you."

"Me too," Kate replied. Maybe she would.

"If you have to go, look out for the azure magpies on the way up, they're at the Desfiladero de Despenaperros."

"What? Where?"

"By the roadside in between La Carolina and Valdepeñas. They're spectacular."

"I'll do that."

"And Kate, be careful. Come back soon."

"Yes I will," she promised. "See you later."

The fact that she was relieved to put the phone down told her a lot about her current feelings towards him. But right now, there were better things to do than worry about Steve.

The doorbell rang continually and she was inundated with more of Gertrude's herbal tea and non-stop advice.

"You must be careful, Kate." Why was everybody telling her to be careful? Did they know something she didn't?

"I promise I will drive very carefully." Gertrude was on her way to a Flower Arranging Club function and looked divine in black cut-off trousers, fitted jacket and the red hat.

"No, Kate," said Gertrude. She shook her head and the hat wobbled with her. "I don't mean with the driving." What she did mean, Gertrude wouldn't or couldn't say. She heaved her round frame out of the settee and teetered to the door on precipitously high canvas mules with long linen straps tied criss-cross up her plump legs.

"You know what, I think I come with you."

"What?"

And so it went on. She comes to Toledo, she doesn't, she brings the cats, she brings their food, she doesn't bring the cats, that nice German woman on the first floor will feed them … and Kate kept saying no no no, the assertive cracked record. It wouldn't be feasible to go to Toledo with Gertrude. And eighteen feral cats on the back seat? She didn't think so. She couldn't wait to get to Toledo where she believed some of her questions would be answered.

"Where I'll find," Kate declared to the waiting candlestick, "what I've been searching for." Whatever the outcome, she was imbued with a new optimism. She didn't need confirmation from *The Book of Help*. Toledo and Josef would be Something Quite Special.

She was backing and twisting the car out of its slot past the columns in the labyrinth of the basement car park, when she remembered it. Leaving the car standing there with the door open, she dashed back to the lift and up to the apartment. Removing the candle, she grabbed hold of the candlestick and stuffed it in her bag. It was coming with her. As a protection.

CHAPTER TWENTY-SIX

TOLEDO – PRESENT DAY

The drive up the hot spine of Spain was slow and steady, along mostly empty roads. Kate took a comfort stop at a wayside hostal by the mountain pass with a mouthful of a name – Desfiladero de Despeñaperros, between La Carolina and Valdepeñas, and saw beautiful blue-winged birds everywhere, swooping and diving round the hillside. These must be Steve's azure magpies and they were spectacular.

At the first sign for Toledo she followed the arrow right and swerved over to the left. She was deep in burnt-brown country, the ground dead dry and dusty. Numerous windmills stood gaunt on the high bare rocks to the left. It was very Don Quixote.

The historic mound of Toledo rose from the flat countryside surrounding it. She bumbled through various roundabouts and came to rest in a side street in what she believed was Toledo. But the bar across the road said no. The whole bar including a little boy in his Real Madrid football shirt, directed her further on. She was not yet in Toledo, hadn't even crossed the river Tajo. This was merely an outlying district. Armed with diagrams of roundabouts, fountains and left turns, she managed to retrieve the big roundabout, circle it and take off again.

It was extremely difficult finding the hotel. Toledo was piled onto a hill of narrow one-way streets and blind alleys and it was clogged with traffic. Kate arrived for the third time at the ruins of an important-looking building swathed in scaffolding and asked a passing helpful Spaniard what it was. All this Toledo aggravation was excellent for the Spanish. "Is the Alcázar, one of the most important historical buildings in Spain. You see, there is the sign for it in front of you: Alcázar." *Sí?* She saw.

She got stuck on a tight corner leading to a blind alley. As she was reversing up, another helpful man came forward shaking his finger and his head.

"*Estoy perdida y busco Hotel Santa María,*" she bleated – I'm lost and seek the hotel. He gave her instructions. Is down, down, down, as far as you can and then right and up up up. And she achieved the hotel in the centre of the old town. It was a miracle and not even a minor one. A lad on the desk directed the car through a garage door into the basement car park. It was bizarre to find this cavernous space under the crush and density of Toledo above.

Kate had asked for a quiet room and this was it, across the entrance hall in an annexe behind a huge wooden door. The room overlooked a side street down which surged a constant stream of cars and revving motorbikes. The candlestick lurked at the bottom of her case, like a nervous cat wary of its new surroundings.

It was Sunday evening, Kate was exhausted, but she had to go out and explore. She crept along the streets enclosed by tall dark houses until she reached the main thoroughfare – and she was in a new setting of strolling jollity, plazas of playing children and closed shops, most of which appeared to be selling men's clothes or swords. If ever she wanted a sword she'd come to Toledo.

With the help of the hotel map, it was easy to find the main square. It was all so simple, as much of life was, if Kate could let it be. Toledo was compact. It was straight down, left, right – and there was Plaza Zocodovar, alive with bars and youth scoffing drinks and *tapas*. But on the route back the close proximity of the narrow back streets hovered and a sinister atmosphere lurked in the cobbles. A cheerful restaurant beckoned where she stuffed herself with a large onion and mushroom pizza and two glasses of red wine. It was hard to find her way back to the hotel.

Kate was due to meet Josef at midday and had time to spare. Reception suggested taking a tourist trip on the little train round town. It trundled and bounced up and down the alleys and out over the river. From the other side, Toledo was hazy against the morning heat, an ancient silhouette, bright and bristling with life, but brooding. Up and down, freezing in winter, boiling hot in summer. It must be a difficult place to live in. On the return journey, the train got jammed going round a tight corner between overhanging buildings in the old town. All the tourists started to get out.

"No no," pleaded the driver, "It is fix in a minute." But they all scarpered. Reception did the Spanish shrug when Kate told him. The little train he is always

290

crashing into the walls. Toledo was not making it easy for her.

She packed the candlestick into her bag. In the midday air, hot with no breeze, she located the shop, two minutes' walk from the hotel going down the hill the other way. It sold books, gifts and jewellery.

"*Hola,*" smiled a friendly woman sitting behind a cluttered desk.

"*Hola.*" Kate smiled back. "I'm meeting Josef here. Do you know him?"

"*Sí sí.* Josef is not here yet, he rang to say that he is a little late, looking to park. Please to wait."

Kate browsed the books until the doorbell pinged and Josef charged in, dipping his head to get through the door. She recognised him immediately, with his mass of black hair and beard shot through with silver. His long body crackled with energy.

"Good morning, *shalom,*" he said briskly, bending down to kiss her without looking. He handed some paperwork over to the woman at the desk. Did he know who she was?

"Hello, I'm Kate," she reminded him.

"Yes, yes, you are the lady from Brazil."

"No no, I'm from England." This was not an anti-climax. She wouldn't let it be. "We met in the Cordoba synagogue a couple of months ago." Josef continued to look blank. "I was the one with the scratch on my cheek."

"Ah yes. You were the one with the problem. So did you do the research on *converso* Jews as I suggested?"

"I've made a start. I've looked up *marranos.*"

Josef tut-tutted like a teacher with a lazy pupil and checked the time on his large bronze watch. "So – you are ready?"

Kate was flustered. She didn't know what to expect from meeting him except some form of deliverance. Obviously he'd planned to show her Toledo. So off they went. She rushed to keep up with fast, non-stop-talking Josef, his long legs taking enormous seven-league strides down the streets. They cantered past the impressive cathedral with Josef in full guide mode.

"You see, this is one of the largest cathedrals in the Christian world, it has five naves, it measure one twenty metres long, fifty-nine metres wide … we cannot see it so well from the outside because the streets are so tight but please look at the statues on it … Napoleon tried to destroy the cathedral, you know, he cut off the stone hands of all the statues …"

This was Toledo history rapid style, and it was bouncier than the little train. Josef moved on to the synagogues. In the Jewish medieval era there used to be at least seven and now two remained. The grand *sinagoga* was now a great church – the Santa María la Blanca. All the Toledo churches faced East – indication that once they were all synagogues because that is how they were built.

"Come now, please," directed Josef. "We move on to the other." They speed-walked into the *sinagoga* El Tránsito where Josef skidded to a long-legged stop and Kate caught her panting breath. He pulled out a round cap from his pocket and clipped it onto his head.

"What is that cap called?"

"In Hebrew, is a *yarmulke*. Also it's called a *kippa*. Now please look up, and you can see the Star of David up there." The columns and the small carved hexagram were visible high up in the ornate decoration on the great walls. "That proves this was once a synagogue."

They stood with other tourists, gazing upwards. Josef, being Josef, took over from their guide who smilingly gestured, stood back and let him. Josef launched into his Jewish Medieval Spain spiel and the group watched and listened, entranced, while Kate waited. Until Josef remembered who he'd come to the ball with.

"Now, we move on to see the shop with the cellars." He couldn't resist asking the group: "You want come along with us, it is very interesting?" But they were stopping for lunch, their guide was waiting and Kate was tempted to go with them. Informative as it was, this was not what she'd come for. And she was starving.

But as Josef strode along Calle Ángel, what he was now saying and pointing out became so fascinating that she did want to know it all. She ran hard to keep up with him.

"You see that – a brown cross on a building in the streets means that it was once an Inquisition office. It is like a sword upside down. And this building was the Inquisition office. From here the penitents used to have to march in procession dressed in *sambenitos*, they are like a long vest or tunic of sackcloth or thick cotton, worn over their clothes, indicating them to be condemned heretics … and here is where the Edict of

293

the Expulsion was issued, it is now used as a School of Art …"

The past was so close, she could almost smell the smoke, taste it in her mouth again as they went through a large arch in the street. Josef continued to talk and explain.

"Here is the Arch of the Jew – that separates the Christian and Jewish Quarters. And right here where we walk was the actual Jewish Quarter." They were running around in thirty degrees of heat and the sweat was pouring off her, but the dense streets and thick houses helped to cool the air and dispel the painful memories. Kate focused on Josef and his non-stop flow of information.

"You see, the old houses in Toledo and other cities like Cordoba are restored now to how they used to be. They had the big front door, the wooden framed windows and the balconies. And inside they had the wooden beams, the inner patios – half of the *mezuzzahs* they moved indoors, so nobody passing would know it was a Jewish house."

"Please stop a moment, Josef. What is a *mezuzzah*?"

Josef suppressed a tiny sigh of irritation. "It is a small ornamental replica of the scrolls in the synagogue that contain the Torah – those are the Jewish laws. They bring good luck to the Jewish house. But they also indicate that it was a Jewish home, that's why they removed them. But you know, if a house had blue paint – that was also a sign that a Jew lived there."

They reached a shop selling gifts, silverware and swords, and Josef halted his walking tour.

"We go in here." He exchanged greetings with the shop owner who smilingly allowed them to pass through. Everyone smiled at Josef.

She followed him to the back of the shop and down steep old stairs to the large basement level.

"Please note the wooden balcony and the tiled cellar floor. These cellars used to house the secret *mikvahs*, or bathhouses, where the Jews performed their ritual bathing. Look, you can see the original steps leading to the bottom. And there you can see the stone chimney in the cellar, which warmed the water for the *mikvah*. All the houses in Toledo had underground cellars." It was dank and hushed down here, holding in its concealed past. A dark tunnel led away from the cellar.

"Where does that go to?" Kate asked.

"You see, this was a passage, all these houses had tunnels in their cellars and people used them. Through all the Toledo hill, layer on layer, they were leading to the cathedral, to the synagogues, and going to the river."

It was impressive and she was glad Josef was here, showing her this side of hidden Toledo. He was the right person to do it. His fervour and knowledge imbued present time with such strong emotional links to the past.

"You will please take a present from my wife, what would you like?" Upstairs in the gift shop, Kate accepted a terracotta tile. It was painted dark blue with a golden candelabra of seven branches carved onto it. Josef told her that this ornament was a Menorah, one of Judaism's oldest symbols, representing the continuously lit candles used in the old temple times.

"You know those shop owners are Jewish," he informed her when they were on the street again. "But they won't admit it." He stopped to acknowledge a man passing by. "He is Jewish also, but he doesn't know it." Josef knew the hidden past of everyone in Toledo.

"You want we stop for a drink?"

"Yes please." She was hyperventilating from heat, thirst and information. In a simple café where the owners were Jewish but didn't know it, Josef bought coffee and cheese baguettes. They sat at a table under a large striped umbrella on the small terrace. At last they had stopped running.

"It's good we take the break, yes? And then you want to see the Alcázar?"

"No no." Kate said and then felt guilty. 'Please yourself' reminded the inner self, a technique acquired from the Overcoming Low Self-Esteem book.

"You are tired?" queried Josef. "We could take the little train?"

"I've done the little train. And what you've shown me is fascinating and I thank you so much for giving me your time."

"It's nothing."

"But, I'd like to ask you something."

"Yes. What you want? You tell me."

Kate bit into the hard fresh crust of the baguette and reflected as they munched companionably, staring out towards the street. Some crumbs made their way into Josef's wild beard and ever tidy-minded, Kate longed to remove them, but it was too intimate a gesture. He had a wife to do those things. She laid the baguette onto its nest of folded serviette and dared to put a hand on his arm.

"Josef, I want to know about you."

"So?"

"You are Jewish?"

"Yes, of course." What a ridiculous question was implied by his tone.

"How did you discover that you were a Jew?"

"Why do you wish to know?"

She replied softly. "Because it may help with my search for my own identity."

"Sorry, I am a little deaf, from a recent operation." Kate repeated her question and louder. Josef struggled anyway with the listening, he was more used to talking at punters. But she'd got through to him. He took his glasses off, wiped his eyes, put them on again and surveyed the passers-by on the street, no doubt searching for more Jews who didn't know it. His eyes were moist. The Josef that now faced her was not the tourist guide giving the history lesson.

"I am a fifty-five year old man," he said, at half his speed and volume. "You know, my great-great-grandmother she died more than one hundred years ago and the family had to go to Mass. It was the same when my great-great-grandfather died – it's like you have to buy your own salvation in heaven – with church, with confession, the priests are never satisfied." His voice was bitter.

"My great-grandparents, they stopped going to church. They had no images in the house, they didn't join in the processions. They cleaned the house on a

Friday and they didn't light any fires. So there was no smoke coming through the chimney on Friday nights, all day Saturday. The neighbours knew. As a child, I slept in the cellar, close to the fire that warmed the water. Friday nights, my grandmother salted and hung the meat in kosher fashion. My grandpa bathed himself, put on a clean shirt, nobody knew why he did it. It was a family tradition. It wasn't easy to keep clean where we lived, but on Friday nights, he was fastidious." Josef stopped talking and watched as a couple arrived at the café and chose a table away from them. When he continued, his bitterness had intensified.

"The Toledans were poor, they learnt what the Catholic Church told them. You had to kiss the priest's hand. They kicked my mother out of the church for not being baptized. They called me the son of a prostitute because my mother didn't marry in the Catholic Church. I wasn't baptized either, and I had a Jewish name." Josef broke off again from his story and jabbed a finger at Kate.

"If you know anyone with a surname ending in '-ez', they don't know it but their surnames show that they could have converted from Judaism. Look at me, my name as you know is *Gómez*. And you look at all the lawyers in Spain now, nearly all of them have a surname ending in '-ez'! Many of the Spanish are Catholic from Jewish roots – even if they don't know it." Josef took off his glasses, produced a handkerchief from his trouser pocket and dabbed at his eyes.

"And then, you know they kicked me out of school at about nine years, again because my mother had not

298

been baptized. After that, an Englishman we knew, he came here many years ago as a missionary, he paid for my studies at a private college. But it was not an easy life." He stopped again, overcome by emotion. Josef's story had churned up his past, and it was causing him pain.

"It's okay if you'd rather not tell me."

"Don't worry. I don't mind. It was good, the education. This was where I learnt to play violin and read all the time. I used to open a book and start reading the Bible. You know reading the Christian Bible was forbidden until not long ago. Most of the books were burnt in the Civil War. My family, we wanted to read the Bible. If you want to read the Bible, it's an indication."

"An indication of what?"

"Anyone who has a thirst for God's words, it shows the thirst of the Jew for God in the word. It shows that they must have been Jewish at one time. Eighteen years ago, I knew for certain I was Jewish."

"How did you know?"

"From what I have told you. I was descended from Crypto-Jewish ancestors from around the fifteenth century. They stayed here and lived as Spanish Christians but kept their secret Jewish ways as best they could. That is all I know, nothing more. I am not converted yet but I have one hundred per cent commitment to my Judaism."

"It must have been a crucial change in your life."

"Yes, it was a tough decision to decide to be openly Jewish. Most of them who think they are, or were, they change names, they want to stay unseen, invisible. For me also, I have this from my background. There are many psychological hang-ups in my generation. For my kids, there's no problem. I did the circumcision myself to my son."

Josef had opened up his life and his heart and Kate appreciated his honesty and candour. She got to the question she'd been wanting to ask.

"What is it like, living this open Jewish life here? You have to be brave, even now? What is the percentage of Jews in Toledo today?"

He shrugged and she was already disappointed. Josef was not what she'd expected and the story had to change. She had hoped that Josef would give her the answers she'd been seeking. Real life wasn't like that. But Josef had opened other doors.

"Things could change of course, but at this moment there are no other practising Jews here except me and my family and maybe one other. They accept me for what I am, but we don't feel that much at ease in Toledo." Kate could identify with this. Last night she'd been nervous in the dark side streets.

Josef continued. "Toledo has so much past, many tourist Jews from America, England, say, we have to come here. They do a quick visit and they go. And many come to stay, but they keep quiet, they won't say they are Jewish."

"The ones that stay, where do they come from?"

"For example, from Argentina. They wait, they blend in. Many are now emerging. Since the 1978 Constitution, the Catholic church has no longer been Spain's official faith which means other religions are free to worship. And you know near you, in Marbella, is the first new synagogue to be established in Andalucía since 1492. There are re-discovered Jews in Madrid, Barcelona, Malaga, with their own synagogues. Small communities are springing up. But the situation with Israel is not good – some are thinking of going back to Israel but orthodoxy is hard and these people have not been brought up as Jews. So they stay here."

"What work do you do here?"

"I trained as a teacher but at first I couldn't teach because I was Jewish. It was only in 1880, you know, that the Inquisition was abolished. Not that long ago considering the four hundred years it had been operating since the fifteenth century. And there has been a long tradition of anti-Semitism that lasted through from 1939 to 1975 with Franco's dictatorship. Franco, for his own reasons, was quite good to European Jews in the war. He kept the Spanish border with France open to help the entry of Jews into Spain and through to the west."

"And now?"

"Now, as I said, it's different. There have been over twenty-five years of democracy since Franco. But what I want to do above all is to work as a bridge between the Christians and the Jews in Spain, uniting two worlds."

And that was Josef. He was not an open sesame to the past but what he'd told Kate made her tingle with recognition. Could she also come from Jewish roots without realising it? In her own family, her grandfather on her mother's side used to wear a clean shirt on Friday nights and so did Uncle Roger. And her grandmother always cleaned her terraced house on Fridays. But a fresh shirt and a clean house on Fridays was not enough to say she was descended from Spanish Jews in the fifteenth century. Kate wished that she knew more.

Josef had finished his story and his coffee. "So, young woman. Are you satisfied? Have you got from me what you came for?

"There is one more thing." She dug into her bag and brought out the candlestick. It gleamed in the bright sunlight. Josef's reaction was unexpected. He sucked in his breath and snatched the candlestick from her.

"Where did you get this?"

"I found it in a silverware shop in Cordoba."

"You only have the one?"

"Sadly, yes."

"You know what it is?"

"Well, yes. It's a candlestick."

"No no." Josef brushed aside her naivety. "But this is very old. You can tell from the markings."

"I've seen them. Do you recognise them?"

"Yes. It is Hebrew writing." He turned the candlestick over in his hand and stroked it as if it was a well-loved object.

"What does it say?"

Josef scrutinised the base. "I can read Hebrew, but it is difficult to see the script properly. It could refer to a traditional Jewish marriage. It was a custom that parents give their children candlesticks when they get married." He rubbed his glasses and squinted further at the writing on the base. "You know even though it may be

302

hundreds of years old, it's the same language, the same letters and words. Wait a moment, I think I can make out, maybe '*Shabbat*' and two initials carved perhaps ... no." He shook his head. "I am sorry, but it is too dull to be able to read it properly." He handed the candlestick back to Kate. "You must not sell this on. You should be careful with it, please."

"I wouldn't sell it ever. Why is it so special?"

"Well, to find an antique Jewish candlestick which this is, and probably made before the Inquisition, because after that they would be forbidden, is very very special."

She senses a soft breath of air on the back of her neck and a whisper in her ear. 'My name is Ana ...' and then it is gone. A mere fancy, leaving a pair of initials and the hint of a blessing, perhaps referring to a wedding.

"I wish I could find the other one," Kate sighed.

Josef would say no more except to repeat warnings of care and caution regarding her precious candlestick.

"Don't let anybody else see it, even today. Keep it safe." He called the waiter over and settled the bill. "And now *shalom* and goodbye." He stood up, ready for off.

"Please wait." She leapt to her feet to stop him.

"I'm sorry but I have to go. I have a meeting at my son's school."

"Can I contact you if I need to?"

"Any time. You have all my numbers and addresses." He bent down awkwardly to embrace her

303

and she lifted her head right up, to hug him back. He planted two wet, smacking kisses on her cheeks and he was gone. Kate was alone with her candlestick at the table of a café terrace in the old Jewish Quarter of Toledo. The waiter cleared the table as she sat on. He looked curiously at the candlestick and she packed it away. Josef's story was starting to sink in.

She walked slowly back to where Josef's tour had begun, near Calle Angel. There was the brown cross on the building, signifying that it had once been an Inquisition office.

Her lips twist into words without thinking. "Our family converted to escape persecution. And now we have this!"

She had to hold onto the wall to straighten her dizzy head as a passer-by eyed her curiously. She wasn't due to leave until tomorrow. She would dream of the smoke tonight.

The drumbeat grows closer and the smell of burning houses pollutes the air. I can taste smoke and sadness in my throat, hear the furniture smashing and cracking, motorbikes zooming down the street. Then I hear no more …

Kate sat straight up in bed. A large moon shone through the window lighting up the candlestick on the bedside table. A young girl wearing a full-length dark skirt and hooded cloak was perched on the edge of the bed. Kate knew this girl with the long gold hair hanging below the hood. She recognised her large blue eyes, the carefully arranged expression of deep sadness. Her dirty hands, smeared with grime and smoke, were staining the hotel bedspread. The last time Kate had seen her she was hurrying down the path below the balcony at home.

The girl looked back at her steadily. She reached forward to push the candlestick away. Kate made an effort to grab it, protect it but the girl waved her off.

"You don't want this silly thing anymore. Why don't you leave him alone? You'll be sorry, he preferred me, always."

"No that's not so," Kate said as she fell back into sleep. The other voice was in her head, fighting her corner.

"Bring it back. Help me, please help me. There will be no peace until they are together again." The smoke continues to swirl.

CHAPTER TWENTY-SEVEN

ESTEPONA – PRESENT DAY

Kate was desperate to get out of Toledo. On the motorway, a camper van overtook her, increasing the sense of anxiety until she was speeding, careering away from some three quarters-imagined threat. The sun beat down on parched beige coloured fields spread out on both sides of the road. She shot past avenues of olive groves and burgeoning baby vines with rags flapping to deter the birds. A crooked peasant working the land looked up as she passed. She was back on the Costa in an unbelievable six and a half hours.

Kate still didn't feel safe. The apartment was choking with dryness and dust. After two days away, grey candyfloss balls had gathered under the bed. The sun lit up the particles of grime on the stained marble floor. The country needed rain while the golf courses of the Costa remained glossy and green and the flowers and fountains continued to blossom and spurt. Why so waspish? Because this wasn't the Real Spain? This wasn't the market in Cordoba or Toledo or wherever it was she'd been to and rushed away from.

Kate stuck the candle back into the candlestick and put it in its spot on the sideboard, next to the silver teapot. The waves rolled in seaweed and debris from

Africa and thousands of starlings came to roost, chattering into the two large eucalyptus trees near the fishing harbour.

Around midnight a crowd of youths surged along the narrow pathway by the building. Their raucous calling triggered a flashback memory of shouting, terror and breaking down of doors. She wept for her non-existent husband, her lover.

Early in the morning Gertrude came in to welcome her back and complain.

"Kate, I tell you, I have had the most ghastly night."

"Me too. Those lads outside?" Kate was relieved that Gertrude had also heard them, proving they were real-time, not part of that other nightmare world. "Or was it the gang in the apartment underneath?" There had been no sound from them since she got back.

"No. They have gone at the end of the month. Good riddance."

From the edge of her balcony Kate peeked down to see the one below swept clean and cleared of stuff. There were no plants, no cushions, no washing line, no dogs. And no shouting men.

"I have been sick and more," continued Gertrude. "Both ends you know, going to the toilet all night."

"I'm so sorry." But Kate found it hard to sympathise with Gertrude and her bowels at this moment.

"Are you going to the shop this morning?" she asked plaintively, breaking into her reverie. Kate wasn't but she would.

"Do you think you could get me some full cream milk?"

"Should you have full cream on an upset tummy?"

"It's not for me, it's for the cats. And a bottle of water, Lanjarón,"

"Do the cats like still water or with gas?"

"Still. They won't take anything else. Thank you so much."

"Shall I feed them for you this evening?"

"You are a darling, would you?"

The heat of the day died away and she headed off to the beacon at the end of the harbour, looking out for Steve. His boat wasn't there. A medium-sized yacht was stationary in the centre of the harbour, its sails half furled. No sign of anyone on board. A young policeman, divine in tight trousers over a cute little bottom, stood poised on the paving stones. He was scrutinising the yacht's unorthodox position and reporting back on his crackling mobile as Kate stomped past and up to the harbour mouth where the birds deposited their poo on the edge of the yellow beacon.

From this angle, the building cranes were obscured. The view of the sea, boats, and pretty blue and yellow buildings circling the harbour, typified a picturesque Mediterranean resort. That's all she wanted it to be – harmless, pretty and safe. The Sierra Bermeja mountain range was half wreathed in heat haze. A scrawny ginger cat not living under Gertrude's protection, prowled by, stalking an unwary seagull. She'd forgotten the cats! Kate rushed back, past the policeman, past children playing at the harbour's edge where skittish fish tumbled and dived for crumbs. All the cats were hanging round the blue back door. They glowered at her accusingly.

She mixed the water (*sin* gas) with the carton of milk (full cream) into a plastic dish and got down there. As she spooned the meat mixture out, she stepped back and trod onto a soft brown lump of dung fresh on the ground. It squashed down deep into the ridges on the soles of her shoes. The cats, tails in the air, ignored the milk/water mixture because it wasn't done precisely to their liking. How could scrawny feral cats be so cat-like choosy?

Kate threw away the shoes and tidied up the waste ground early next morning. It took a satisfying one hour and five extra-large plastic bags and it would all be a tip again in under a week.

Gertrude leant over her balcony and watched.

"Come to me when you finish," she shouted hoarsely.

"I'll see you later."

The dressing-table mirror assured Kate that she was still losing weight, her hair growing darker and longer, eyes getting larger with every blink. Apart from Gertrude, there was nobody she could turn to down here. Tightness gripped her chest in panic. But tomorrow could be different. She'd get out and go to a place where she felt safe.

* * * *

It was good up here in the *pueblo*, her favourite part of the mountains, beyond the river. Good to breathe deeply in the pure air, feel the nothingness and stop thinking. The mountains in the morning air caressed and enfolded her, rather like Gertrude wanted to do and Kate was pushing her away.

Normal life was stretching itself into another day. Elderly women pattered through the streets in their black slippers to the crammed supermarkets that contained all one would wish to buy except the daily British paper. Motorbikes ridden by swarthy young men zoomed loudly up and down the alleys. The old men stood at the corner by the bank, surveying the dusty four-by-four vehicles squeezing through the narrow spaces. Bright-eyed British tourists clutching their converted-house-for-sale details talked loudly as they strode along. The indoor market was open and the butcher in his striped apron chatted at the top of the steps with a fellow stallholder.

Kate's mind was the clearest it had been for days. She climbed slowly up through the *pueblo* towards the castle on the top of the hill and stopped at the viewpoint halfway up. Fragrant lavender bushes and mountains surrounded her, with Gibraltar a distant haze. As she walked back down, a funeral procession was making its stately progress to the church in the plaza. Men stood at the side of the street as it passed, their hats clasped to their chests. She stopped and shared the reverent moment with them.

The owner of the little café by the fountain served her strong decaff coffee from the machine and a flat piece of local bread. A silver jug with a long spout joined the feast. She tipped up the jug and olive oil poured onto her toast in a golden stream, so she ate it like the Spanish did. The jug reminded her of the silver teapot and helped to give her the answer she'd been subconsciously seeking. But the artisan shop was closed.

As she was driving off, Juan emerged from a small bar on the Ronda road. Kate saw him in the rear-view mirror at the same as he caught sight of her. She hooted and waved and he ran after the car, gesturing for her to stop. He pointed up the alley in the direction of his shop. She reversed the car, parked and followed him.

Juan was flustered. He unlocked his shop door and deposited a pile of shopping bags on the desk. His mobile phone was ringing and he waved Kate to a chair while he dealt with the business of his day. She crossed her legs and had another good look at him. Liked what she saw – the roundish tanned face, the neatly-parted, thickish longish hair; the wide mouth, dark eyes, and strong lines deep on his forehead. He wore a short-sleeved cream shirt and tan trousers. She glanced round the shop but there was no sign of the flamenco dress.

"Ah! Now I am ready," said Juan, putting down his mobile. He began in a business-like tone. "I am glad to see you. I have been trying to contact your colleagues."

"Please!" She clutched her hair, immediately frustrated and angry. "Can we get one thing straight. They're not my colleagues."

"But you are with them in their desire to buy the house, no?"

"No. It wasn't like that, Juan."

311

"I don't understand."

"Yes, it looks as if I'm in business with them. But I'm not. I didn't know anything about your house being for sale until the day before you came to meet with us. I didn't know it was yours and I had not decided to go in with them. I'm not as yet, and never have been in business with them." Nor ever will be, Kate thought.

There was a longish pause as Juan digested what she'd said. He pulled out a small notepad from a drawer in the desk and leafed through the pages. "You are Kate Mason, no?"

"Yes, that's right."

"Then your name is down here as the chief investor, the main prospective buyer of the property."

"No! How can that be? That's not right."

"You look." Juan pushed the paper towards her. At the top of the page, Kate saw her name as the main buyer, with her full address and telephone number.

"Who gave you that information?" Although it was obvious. Steve had asked for all her details on the first walk. What a sucker she'd been. She was slowly getting very angry with Steve and Rosie.

"But it was your colleagues – unless, forgive me, they are not your colleagues."

Kate hit the table hard with her clenched fists and her fingers hurt. She didn't care.

"Look, I'm telling you the truth. If you choose to believe them and not me, then that's your prerogative."

"Please – I don't understand your word?"

"It means I don't want to see you again!" No. She didn't mean to say that. She had to explain the truth to him. Slowly she spelt it out to him: "I didn't even know Casa Sueños was for sale, or that the place existed until the day before we saw you. I'm not a speculator, do I look like one? I'm an English teacher on a break, and believe me, I'm as angry with them as you are."

"*Vale.*" He shrugged. "Okay."

"No, it's not just okay. You've got to believe me."

"I know what they are. I do believe you." With his eyes fixed on hers, he tore out the piece of paper from the pad, crumpled it into a ball and, without looking, tossed it into a wastepaper basket behind him. It landed right on target. Kate had been holding her breath, watching him.

"You want a drink?"

"Yes."

He reached down for two glasses from the cabinet behind him. From a deep drawer below his desk, he produced a bottle of brandy. He poured out two generous portions and passed Kate's glass over to her.

"Let us have no more misunderstanding between ourselves," he said softly, the crinkled smile back again. They clinked glasses and drank. He had an important message for Steve. "I want you to tell him to stop contacting me all the time. I don't want to hear from him or that woman again."

"I'll do that." The brandy warmed her throat and chest. It felt good.

"And make it clear please, that my mind is made up, the deal is most definitely off. Because they take no notice of what I'm saying." Juan pushed a sealed envelope across the table. "I don't like the way they do

313

business. I have said all this in a letter to them. Please, Kate, I'm trusting you now. I don't want to hear from them again."

"Leave it with me." She put the letter in her bag. "And what has happened to Casa Sueños?"

"For the moment I have let it out again to a charming couple from New Zealand. It is up for sale, but with a different agent."

Their meeting was concluded. But she did have one more question.

"Juan, can you say now what is so special about that old ruined house?"

"Kate, I ask that you don't mention this any more."

"And the red flamenco dress?"

"Fiesta time is here and it is sold. I am sorry."

CHAPTER TWENTY-EIGHT

ESTEPONA – PRESENT DAY

Kate stamped round the apartment, slamming doors and banging kitchen cupboards closed in frustration. She was furious with Rosie and Steve but mostly with Steve. He wasn't answering his phone, and she hadn't managed to discover where he lived. But she could see his boat was back in the harbour and there was a man working on it. She ran down to the port towards him. It wasn't Steve, just an ordinary fair-haired lad stripped to the slim waist, spraying and washing the paintwork.

"*Hola*," she called up from the side, praying that he wasn't local Spanish and thus incomprehensible to her limited listening skills.

"Hello my love and what can I do for you?" he responded in a blithe Irish accent.

"I was wondering – do you happen to know where Steve is?"

"Steve? Now who might that be?"

"You must know him. He looks after this boat."

"Okay, that Steve. Haven't seen him for days. Might have gone back to the UK for all I know. They called me in to get it cleaned up for next week. Sorry I can't be any more help."

"That's fine. See you around."

"Yeah. See you."

Kate swung away from the harbour, looking and sounding like the got-together crisp Costa lady she certainly wasn't. She greeted a couple of happy, normal, residential tourists sitting in a port bar who she'd met at some social evening between here and Malaga.

"See you at the Thursday lunch next week," they cried.

"Yes, great!" What lunch and where? As if she cared. She had to find Steve. She had a message for him.

She had to drive somewhere to look for him and Gertrude wanted more food for the cats. The supermarket would do.

A miracle occurred near Carrefour. As she approached the roundabout, Kate caught sight of him in his old blue Saab leaving it. She changed direction and indicators, infuriating the driver behind, and continued on the roundabout towards the main N340 road. His car was in the distance.

"Steve! Steve!" She yelled to the windscreen and beyond. Steve was a blue dot cruising along ahead of her. She was about six cars behind, in and out of the fast lane, five, four cars and edging up behind him. The Kempinski Hotel flashed by, the building cranes dipped and nodded. Slowly she was catching up with him. He was driving east, towards San Pedro, Marbella, Fuengirola, Malaga. They could be in Barcelona tomorrow, Beijing by next Friday. And then he signalled right, darted out of the fast lane, and whizzed off at the next exit.

With an orchestra of discordant horns tooting at her, Kate cut across two lanes and another three cars to achieve Steve's roundabout with a good inch to spare. The slip road swung left under the main N340 road and out the other side. Where there was no sign of his Saab.

She stopped in the car park of a pink-painted restaurant to consider. She could continue on up the hill but an instinct told her not to. He had to be somewhere close. She could sniff his presence. Beyond the restaurant stood a fenced off woodyard and at the corner was the discreet entrance to a campsite. A frothy array of thick greenery concealed the banners and flags from the screaming traffic on the road.

A young Spanish man in the office looked up from his magazine as Kate approached.

"May I look round?" He waved her into this new world of caravans and camper vans, dotted with middle-aged men and women standing, chatting and sitting outside their vans. They were reading and sunbathing on their green plastic patches of grass, under attached awnings. She wandered up and down the slanting avenues, in and out of the toilet block and the showers, and noted a splendid indoor swimming pool beyond. It was empty, steaming softly, surrounded by acres of tile and foliage. This campsite was an alternative non-Costa-glitz universe with its down-to-earth residents, twittering birds, palm trees, bushes, orange flowers, sky and sun slanting through the gaps in the greenery.

An old caravan, rust staining its brown and cream bodywork, stood in a tucked-away corner pitch on the bottom avenue. It was next to a wire fence with sloping fields beyond. Beside the van she found Steve's car.

317

Was he inside? Was he visiting or was this where he really lived? How could big-shot Cock-Of-The-Costa Steve be here in this run-down caravan by a wire fence? But that was his car, so what should she do? Now that Steve was within her reach and grasp, Kate was hesitant. Did she barge straight up to the door, knock on and tell him the deal was off and how dare he use her in his treacherous dealings? As she was making frantic Pros and Cons in her head, an elderly man approached from the main avenue. His thin red legs protruded from baggy khaki shorts and he was holding a toilet roll.

"Looking for Steve then?" he said.

"Well, I may be."

"Better catch him quick, he's due for the bowls match at four-thirty."

"Right."

"You his latest?"

"I – er no. Sorry. Don't think so."

"Oo-er, put my foot in it again. Freddie's the name."

"Well, see you, Freddie."

"Do you play bowls? Smashing game."

"Not as yet."

"Shame on you," he said. "See you then."

"Yeah, see you."

Freddie hobbled away towards a neighbouring neat van snuggled into an awning with a row of garden gnomes adorning the plastic lawn. So Steve did exist here. Kate approached the caravan door. Some self-preservation instinct warned her to take it carefully. Instead of knocking, she edged towards the window,

318

squatted down and peeped her head cautiously upwards to look inside.

In the caravan kitchen, Steve sat at a banquette table lighting a cigar. Opposite him was Rosie. She had papers strewn over the table and her head was down. She was talking hard, as if discussing some vital piece of business and they were deeply together and engrossed. She reached out a hand and touched his. What was going on between these two? Kate couldn't bear to see them and she couldn't break into this.

She wheeled away, up the avenue, back to the campsite entrance. To the left was Rosie's parked car and how could she have missed it when she arrived? It took a lot of willpower not to kick the tyres as she went past. If she'd had a knife on her, she'd have slashed them.

Kate drove to the supermarket, bought the cat food, deposited it with Gertrude and fell out onto the *paseo*, all on the one stupefied breath. What an idiot she'd been. She needed an antidote to Steve and Rosie.

The ice-cream café was in a small plaza in the centre of town. Family groups sat at every table. The café was perfect for distraction, deep in the late afternoon life of Estepona. A little girl chased a ball that rolled beneath Kate's chair. She wore a checked red and green pinafore dress over a blouse with flowers embroidered on the sleeves. Kate retrieved the ball and handed it back to her with a smile. If only her own life were as uncomplicated.

She chose an obscenely piled-up scoop of vanilla topped with chocolate and whipped cream. Two rolled wafers stuck out, a jaunty paper parasol between. She guzzled the lot and leant back with a tight stomach.

As she walked home along the *paseo*, Kate was conscious of the children playing on the swings and slides, the families stopping to greet each other and exclaim over new babies in prams. On the beach below, artists worked on the swirls and water sprays of their sand sculptures and passers-by leant over the rail watching them. This stroll was an interlude of interweaving humanity. Kate wished she could exist on a peaceful, stable *paseo* with people she trusted. Where she wasn't conned and used by a best friend and a lover – where she didn't live more than half her life in the past.

CHAPTER TWENTY-NINE

ESTEPONA – PRESENT DAY

"Kate," shouted a male voice that she recognised. It was four in the afternoon and deep into siesta time. Not the hour for anyone to come calling except Gertrude and this was not her. This was a clear ring from the automatic phone hailing from the main front door.

"Is that you? Are you there?"

"Yes it's me and I'm here," Kate answered.

"It's Steve."

"Yes I know. Hi, Steve."

"Can I come up then?" She pressed the button to let him in.

"What a view! You can't get tired of this!" Steve gazed seawards beyond the lighthouse. He was carrying a bunch of exotic flowers wrapped in cellophane, straight from the nearest garage. "Welcome back from Toledo. I believe you paid me a visit yesterday." He threw the flowers on the patio table and pulled up a chair. Steve as usual was one step ahead of her and she'd been so determined to be cool and in charge. He sat down, blue eyes, tanned face, legs wide apart, deep macho-style.

"How do you know I visited you?" Kate took the wobbly seat opposite him.

"Can't hide anything from old Freddie. He told me a luscious young piece was asking for me yesterday. Had to be you, didn't it? Why didn't you stay?"

"What was Rosie doing in your caravan with you?"

"Pardon?"

"I saw her there. You looked very close, the two of you."

"I don't like being checked up on." His sigh was a mixture of weariness and impatience. "It's nothing Kate, girl. We've worked together for years. It was a business meeting."

"It didn't look like nothing."

"You're over-reacting as usual. You know how I feel about you."

"Do I?"

"Course you do."

"So what are you doing in that place?"

"I'm only on site temporarily," he said airily. "I know the owner. I'm waiting for the new apartment to be ready."

"And where's that?"

"New Golden Mile way. Brand-new duplex penthouse. Should have been ready in the spring, but you know what it's like. And if it falls through, there's a boat at Gib I know of. They're looking for a new skipper."

"Why aren't you working on the usual boat?"

"Hey – what is this? I'm getting a lot of stick here. Who says I'm not?"

"You were not around."

"I can take a break whenever I want." He shrugged and so did Kate. The crisp dialogue was over.

"I've a message for you from Juan," she said. "He couldn't get hold of you."

"Right. The deal's off. Did you know?"

Damn Steve. He always had to be top dog. "Who told you?"

Steve sprawled back, hands crossed behind his head. "I know everything and everybody down here. You should know that by now."

The moment was here. She addressed him directly, close up.

"Why did you tell him that I was the chief buyer of the property? When you knew very well I hadn't even decided to invest in it."

Steve turned defensive. "What are you getting at? You do leap to conclusions."

"No, this was not a leap, Steve. It was in your writing. This was what Juan showed me and told me."

"What is this, the bloody Inquisition? Who do you believe, Kate? Somebody you hardly know? Or me?"

"You!" spluttered out of her. It was said and meant with deep sarcasm but Steve took her literally.

"Well I'm glad you said me. Look what we have between us."

"For God's sake, stop twisting my words, can't you! I'm not going to invest in this or any other property with you."

"Well you don't have to make speeches about it, because, as we said, the deal is off." Steve brought his chair close to hers. "Kate, I'm here to help you. And it's time to move on."

"Why are you so anxious about my needs so suddenly?"

"Because there is a new house that came on the market just last week. Rosie told me to tell you about it."

"Not another fantastic property!"

"It's perfect for you."

"I've told you Steve, I don't want to go into business with you. Or with Rosie."

"And I'm telling you, this is not business, Kate, it's a home. Outside the village of Pueblo Nuevo de Guadiaro, a ten-minute walk away from the centre." Steve voice grew silky smooth. "It's a pretty house, at the side of a little plaza, by the river, in a very old Spanish neighbourhood."

"Mmm, near the village, in a little plaza," Kate repeated and mused. Of course she wouldn't in a million years contemplate anything more to do with these two, but Kate and cute village houses did go together. And Steve knew it. He seized the opportunity.

"At least take a look at it and if you like it, then let Rosie handle the sale for you. But you need to snap it up. You should trust Rosie. If she says it's a bargain, you should go for it."

Arguing with him was clearly a waste of time but she couldn't resist it. "What is the rush, Steve? The market is saturated, prices are collapsing. The Brits coming down to buy can pick and choose." How did she know all this? Because it was the talk on the *calles*, streets, in the clubs, in the free papers that she still devoured.

"Will you listen to me for once and be sensible," he hectored in the old Steve manner, thinking he'd got her again. "A good house at a good price is hard to find. If you see what you want, you don't mess around – you go for it. Makes bloody good common sense." Steve stood up by the balcony railings, watching the waves kiss the shore and the fishermen settle onto the rocks with their rods. Kate stood next to him and stared out past the lighthouse. There was more than a little part of her that longed for a dear little town house in a real *pueblo*.

"Kate – you paying attention? You're different somehow."

"In what way?"

"Hard to say." He studied her intently. "Your hair looks different, eyes look bigger. And you're more, I don't know."

"Ethereal?"

"Whatever that means. Desirable is the word I'd use." He pulled her towards him and kissed her softly. She moved her head slightly and the kiss landed on her cheek.

"You win, Steve." She forced a smile at him. "I'll contact Rosie and make an appointment. Satisfied?"

"No need to. I'll drive you there now. She's at the house taking measurements, waiting for your phone call."

"Well, if you insist."

"Good girl. And don't forget to put those flowers in water."

"Please don't call me a good girl."

"Sorry, sweetheart." He rang Rosie as Kate ran about plonking the flowers in the sink, finding keys, sunglasses, yanking down the blind in the kitchen, closing the patio door.

Gertrude was getting out of the lift as they were getting in. They all wove round the landing to avoid collision and ended up bumping into each other. Gertrude's bag of lemons tumbled onto the floor, the lemons fell out and started their bumping descent down the stairs towards freedom and the swimming pool. Steve chased after them and brought them back to Gertrude.

"I think they're all here, safe and well," he gasped charmingly, out of breath. "A bit bruised, but edible." Gertrude snatched the bag from him, opened the swing glass door between the main lobby of the landing and her section and kicked it closed. She entered her apartment and slammed the door behind her hard. A stray lemon rolled across the floor. Steve picked it up and stuffed it in his jacket pocket.

"She's an old lady, what do you expect. Let's get going." But as they were getting into the lift, Gertrude's door opened and she stuck her head out.

"Kate, could I speak to you for a moment."

"Keep your finger on that pause button," Kate instructed Steve. Gertrude drew her into the apartment, like a spy on an urgent mission and closed the door again.

"You should steer clear of that man," she hissed.

"I'm being extremely careful."

"I tell you, Kate, you are not yourself." Grabbing her arm, she pushed her face close up to Kate's. "Tragedy and danger are all around you, I can see them."

"Gertrude, this is ridiculous." Kate shrugged her off.

"Very well, if you are stubborn I can help you no further. Now go." She pushed her out of the apartment and Kate was left with an empty space in her psyche. Gertrude is/was my mate. 'Gertrude, stay with me, I need you Gertrude, I want your protection …'

Steve was waiting by the lift, finger obediently on the button. They sailed down together. There was some unfinished urgent business connected with this house that had to take precedence over any Gertrude angst.

They crossed the river that flowed deep and wide, and drove towards one of the Guadiaros of which there were so many: Torreguadiaro, Guadiaro Alto, Bajo, Pueblo Nuevo de Guadiaro, known as PNG, and other permutations all situated on a bewildering array of roundabouts. The softer range of hills down this end of the coast was reminiscent of a rolling English country scene. The area had a lighter energy than the harsh pink glow of the Sierra Bermeja mountain, sending out its mixed messages with the tossing sea. Perhaps she could live down here.

Steve stopped the car and Kate looked round before going in. This time Rosie had come up with the goods. Such a pretty little village house it was and just a tree-lined avenue walk away to the nearest Guadiaro with its little shops, where the daily paper could be bought and a large new supermarket had been built across the road. The neighbourhood was very Real Spanish and she liked it. The house was two hundred and thirty-five thousand euros which roughly translated to an affordable one hundred and sixty thousand pounds, more or less. But she couldn't hesitate for long, there'd already been a lot of interest. She knew what had to be done.

CHAPTER THIRTY

That afternoon, Kate tried to kill her.

Rosie was waiting inside the pretty house above the deep flowing Guadiaro river. She looked neat and businesslike in her tight black trousers, cream shirt, leather jacket and glossy lipstick. The two women were hesitant with each other after the screaming match of their last meeting.

"Kate! It's so good to see you." They kissed warily on both cheeks and Rosie drew back to look at her. "I've been really worried about you. How are you?"

"I'm fine."

"I'd love you to come round for supper very soon and we'll sort it all out. Will you?"

"Sure."

"Great!" She pressed Kate's hand. "Now follow me, you are so going to love this." Steve went outside for a quick cigar while they did the tour of the house, with its two bedrooms on the ground floor, open-plan first floor living area, and two small roof terraces, one shaded and one in the sun. Rosie popped a Werther's Original into her mouth, happy she'd got Kate onside again.

"And just bear in mind that it's been converted but it's retained all the charm of the original. With the charming indoor patio and the rustic tiles, new, but again, so characteristic of the traditional style … do look at this wood burning stove," she added with a proud flourish. "So authentic and picturesque."

Kate flinched away from stoves and burning and plodded after Rosie up the broad stone staircase to the top floor and onto the roof. She duly admired the open roof terrace for sunbathing and drying the washing, the shaded area for evening cocktail parties – as if – and the obligatory fantastic view of Gibraltar. She followed her down to the main bedroom where Rosie drew back the curtains and pulled up the drawn shutters. Light filled the room.

"You can see the river from here," she declared with pride, as if it were her river. "And there are these black railings outside, you've got these against all the main windows. They serve as added security, especially living on your own and sleeping on the ground floor. You must have heard about these gangs who break in and gas the residents – and even the dogs – while they're asleep and take everything? But you'll be absolutely safe with these. They're such an attractive feature, and so like the … did I say 'railings'? I meant 'black grilles' on the traditional Spanish houses, going back centuries I should think." On and on she droned.

'Grille', that was the word. Kate felt she'd walked into a glass wall she didn't know was there. The crash of impact went through her whole body, like the firework flaring into her face, terrifying her as a child. She had done 'black grilles' before. She'd been trapped behind one, overwhelmed by flames and smoke. It was a black

330

grille that had blocked her escape and it was a woman like this who took away what was hers.

And now she'd been click-switched to another time and the anger of centuries came pouring from her. She couldn't control it. She didn't want to. She knew it was this wicked, jealous bitch who had done it – and now *she* must die.

"And you can't be too safety conscious in the rural areas these days" continued Rosie.

Kate glared at her. "Shut up!" she shouted.

"Sorry?"

"You heard."

Rosie stopped her talking and selling; studying Kate's face and body language she was frightened. As she should be.

Kate's arms were raised and her hands arched ready to attack. She inched towards her, breathing heavily. Her mouth was pulled back into an ugly, involuntary grimace.

"You took my husband away from me – he was mine, not yours!" she screamed.

Rosie fell back, banging her shoulder hard against the window. The sweet she'd been sucking fell from her mouth. Good! How Kate hated those sweets and those lips.

"And you left me to die in the burning house," she screamed on.

Rosie staggered against the window, her hands trying to grip the sill behind her. She finally got her balance and attempted to edge past Kate and out through the door.

But Kate was ready for her. "I'll kill you! I hate you." She lunged at Rosie, her hands finding her neck. "*ERES UNA PUTA ASQUEROSA!*" she yelled in a Spanish she didn't know she knew. "YOU ARE A DISGUSTING PROSTITUE!"

Panting and breathless, she dragged her onto the floor. Rosie tried to struggle free but Kate had become unnaturally strong. She climbed over her like a crab over the lobsters in the Chinese restaurant aquarium. Locking her hands round Rosie's throat, she smacked her head against the floor, over and over again; shrieking as she tried to squeeze the life out of her.

Steve heard the din and bolted into the house. "What the hell!" Flicking his cigar onto the floor, he rushed at the struggling pair. In one movement, he gripped Kate round the shoulders, dragged her off Rosie, and threw her across the room like a doll.

Rosie crawled off into a corner, whimpering and clutching her neck. In a daze she began re-buttoning her torn shirt. Steve crossed and kneeled beside her, closely inspecting the light bleeding on one side of her throat.

"What am I doing," Kate mumbled to herself, sobbing where she lay – on the new yet *rustico* floor of the little town house they wanted her to buy. "What have I done?" She tried to raise her head, she'd landed heavily, and it was throbbing. She was only too aware now of what she'd done but as Steve approached her, she could sense the burning again. The room smelt of burnt linen and smoke. "Please no, God no!" she whimpered.

Steve rushed to the front of the room. "We're on fire," he shouted stamping out the cigar which had rolled under the curtains. They were smouldering so he folded them where they hung, rubbing them together vigorously.

Kate began to raise her shoulders and sit up. But no! She let her body fall back to the floor. And gazing at the beamed ceiling, the conflict within her raged on. 'I'm glad I tried to kill her ... and him next. Am I mad? What were you doing Ana? ... ah, but she did it to me and so did he ...' and her eyes glazed over.

CHAPTER THIRTY-ONE

ESTEPONA – PRESENT DAY

The avenue led straight to nearby Guadiaro village. In the central plaza Kate found a taxi to take her home.

She stumbled through the lobby of the building and out to the enclosed communal area, where children were diving and splashing in the swimming pool and brown bodies lay on the marble tile surround, brown fingers turning the pages of holiday paperbacks. She went up in the lift and knocked on Gertrude's door. Kate looked at her, dazed, and couldn't speak.

"Oh my dear, it has happened." Gertrude grabbed her hand. "You come into my apartment right now. And you know what, I give you supper and you stay with me tonight. You will sleep in here. I move the cats to one side and I make up the couch."

"*Ayúdame, por favor.* Help me please!"

"What do you want from me?"

"She destroyed my life."

"And you're destroying mine."

"Help me …"

"Leave me alone …"

"Grandmother!"

Where am I, who am I, Gertrude, help me. I have done a terrible thing.

The voice played ping-pong with her mind all night long, in sleep, in dreams, out of dreams. Through the haze Kate saw a young girl throwing back her fair hair. An old woman was drawing water from a well and boys were shouting, a man snarling. She saw a little girl playing with stones on painted tiles and Mama calling her in for supper. Two candlesticks standing together. A woman was wearing her cloak and holding a man, her husband. Kate moaned and her head fell back onto the pillow as the smoke, voices and shadows continued to swirl around her … 'Help me …'

"Kate! Wake up now, you are dreaming, you should wake up." Kate felt herself being shaken and opened her eyes. Gertrude was crouching by the couch, her hair sticking out in thin red spikes round her creased forehead.

"What time is it?"

"Don't ask. The middle of the night."

"Where am I? Are we in the cellar?"

"You are here, safe in my apartment. You were shouting in your sleep, frightening the cats." Kate looked round the living room. She was on the converted lumpy couch where the sleepy cats had made resentful room for her. Gertrude handed her a mug containing her special brew and she gulped it down gratefully.

"I must get back to my apartment now." Kate heaved herself up, her head swimming. Gertrude pushed her down again.

335

"It's best you stay with me for the rest of the night here."

"I should go." But Kate did want to stay. She wanted Gertrude's goodness, her bosomy nurturing. She slumped back onto the couch, her body cushioned by a thick pillow and Blind Mango. And the guilt flooded in again. "I have done such a dreadful thing." Gertrude shushed and stroked her arms, head, shoulders. She stayed near, crooning softly until Kate was asleep.

The chugging of the fishing boats setting off at dawn woke her again. Mango was on her shoulder, the white one tucked behind her arm, as she drifted back into non-dreaming sleep.

"The thing is, Gertrude, I can't go around attacking people."

"Hush now." They were at Gertrude's crumb-laden table in her kitchen; Kate was drinking green tea and trying to eat muesli with a tiny little spoon.

"But I could have killed Rosie. I've never been a violent person. I even wanted to attack Steve. What is going on with me?"

"No, you don't look at it like that."

"There's no other way to look at it. Should I see a doctor?"

"Not yet, no."

"Gertrude, you have to help me. What am I doing? I'm mixing up everything in my head, from the past to here and back again." Had she made it all up? This was way beyond creative imagination. Was she going mad? Suffering a form of schizophrenia?

"I must get some treatment, medicine. Do something."

The little white cat rubbed against her legs. Gertrude folded her arms and regarded Kate steadily.

"I guess now I need to tell you, for your own peace of mind."

"Please tell me anything if you think it'll help."

"You know that Steve, he is not a good man."

"Gertrude, you've said that a million times. It doesn't help."

"Okay, I am telling you straight. You know what, he is in a partnership with Rosie as well as plenty of other things. They have been doing it for years. They make the bee-line for all the new ex-pats who come down here to live, especially the women who don't know from nothing and they fleece them for all they can. And then they move on to the next one."

"I've realised this already, Gertrude. Tell me something new!"

"This latest house they wanted you to buy – you know who it belongs to? Him! It's his house. He's been trying to sell that house for years. Nobody goes near it."

Kate pushed away the muesli and gaped at her. "How could it be his?"

"You were Target Number One. The current Number One."

"But they said it had just gone on the market."

"That's what they always say. And you know why he can't sell it?" Gertrude slammed her hand down on the table and her fingers sharply emphasised each word she was saying. "Because everything is wrong with that

337

house. It is full of termites. They had to clear them all out first and then they come back. That house, it's been on the market for as long as I've been living here. Nobody wants to buy it. The ceilings and the walls have got cracks you can see through to the sky. They paint over them, one two, bing bang and it's done, and then they present it all to the next sucker."

"Why didn't you tell me this before?"

"Because I am careful, that is why. I don't want to cause no danger, no tittle-tattle. What you say down here, you know how it is, it goes round the whole place and gets twisted. And he is a powerful man. He knows everyone, people owe him favours. They are frightened of him."

Kate sank her head into her hands. "What a fool I've been."

"And there is plenty more. You know some people have had their car tyres slashed, an elderly man who threatened to denounce him, he was killed, knocked off his balcony on the fourteenth floor – we all knew who to point the finger at. He got one woman to pay over twenty thousand euros deposit to build a house. Then he goes off – with his boat again. He waits a bit, then he comes back. He has the money and there's no house."

"But that's illegal. She could have sued him, why didn't she denounce him?"

"I tell you why not, because he'd be gone again. Or she gets her legs broken, she can't live like that. So I am prudent, I protect myself. If I had told you anything of this, you would have been different with them and they would know for sure it came from me. You know I tried to warn you."

"You certainly did."

"And there is more between those two."

"You're not going to tell me that they're married?"

"They are not brother and sister, I can say that."

Kate thought of all the clues and evidence she'd disregarded: Rosie's face looking at Steve in the caravan; her reaction to Kate dancing with him at that beach bar. And much more.

"It goes back years. He wants to keep it quiet but everyone knows. If he starts something with you, she has to bite her tongue and not care because it is bad for business."

It was all so obvious, now she knew. Kate's head was spinning, she could barely digest all this information, but there was something she had to understand. "What about this blur between past and present, my belief that Rosie and Steve are connected with what's been going on in my head?"

"You give me a few moments and then we get down to that." Gertrude cleared the bowls, wiped the table clean and poured more tea. Then she sat down and faced Kate. She was very intense in a most un-Gertrude-like manner.

"Now you tell me. Do you have any idea why you attacked Rosie?"

She knew the answer, no problem with that one. "Yes!" She shouted out the word. "It was an utter hatred and desire to get even with her for what she did to me."

"Which was?"

339

"She took him away and left me to die! She wanted to destroy me. And I couldn't get out, the fire was stopping me."

Gertrude raised her right hand with authority. "One moment, please."

"Sorry?" Kate was bewildered, halted in full flow.

"I think you are mixing up different times and persons. Rosie has not tried to destroy you."

"Does that matter?"

"Yes, my dear, it does." Gertrude's voice was strong and firm. "You tried to kill that girl."

A cliché of a shiver unfurled. It started at the back of Kate's neck and travelled down her arms until every hair was as taut and upright as the tight bristles on a new hairbrush. Gertrude was right. She had to work out why she attacked Rosie and whether she'd do it again. She needed to find this link between Rosie and the past, and where she fitted into it all.

"Please help me, Gertrude."

"I cannot help you, until you are ready to help yourself. You have to open up to me and be truthful, then I can."

"I am being."

"Good. So now we can get down to business."

"Meaning?" Gertude's enigmatic manner was starting to annoy her.

"Meaning you. We forget the others for the moment. What we have to do is get to the root of your being."

"And how can we do that?"

"From general observation, my diagnosis would be that you are not yourself. You are in the grip of some form of mental delusion that makes you believe that on specific occasions of varying length, you're in another time and place. Is that right?"

Kate was stunned by the clarity of Gertrude's perception, but uncertain at first if these words had actually issued from Gertrude's mouth. She sounded more like a psychiatrist than head-bobbing cat-lady Gertrude.

"I am referring," Gertrude continued smoothly as if she talked like this every day, "to the evidence which shows you are doing things that are increasingly out of character, as if you have somebody else in there, directing you, as it were. I think this is what the whole Steve and Rosie business is about."

Gertrude had come so close to verbalising what Kate was hardly able to contemplate. Look at it all: the time-slip visions, the aggression and enmity towards Rosie. Even the perception that her eyes were changing and the growing curly hair with its deepening colour – none of it was her.

"And I believe the condition has been accelerating. You have not been yourself since Cordoba."

"Has it been so obvious?"

"For a start you've lost weight."

"I was quite pleased about that."

"You don't want to go too thin. And your sleeping has been bad." No question about that. Gertrude could hear it through the wall.

341

"So Kate, to sum up." Gertrude sat upright in her chair and put her hands together like a wise headmistress handing down the school rules. An effect spoilt somewhat by her short legs dangling off the ground. "As you have suggested, you are experiencing forms of hallucination. Also, at these times you appear to take on another persona doing things that are not in your nature. And sometimes they trigger memories from a life that is not yours. Am I correct?"

Kate nodded, speechless, unable to take her eyes off her.

"Yes my dear, this seems unexpected, I know," Gertrude continued. "I will explain in a moment. I know you have been desperate to tell me these things, believe me, I know. Now I need you to confirm my observations. It's very important."

What a relief it was to open up to a listening, receptive Gertrude at last. It poured out of Kate, like a river being allowed to burst its banks.

"I've had bad dreams and been frightened of fire since I was little, but the nightmares started properly when I came to Spain. They're always the same, about being in a burning house and unable to get out. And then I've been getting these hallucinations which must be connected; some of them are so real that I semi-recognise them, as if I've lived through them before and I'm doing so again. And some of the things I find myself saying and doing, they're not me and yet they're part of me. I have such anguish that can't be mine. I'm normally a reasonably balanced person, well more or less, that's what I can't understand. The one single thing on my side is my candlestick. I keep feeling it's linking the whole thing." There was that voice in her head again. The voice was intermittent, reminding her, wanting, demanding, clamouring for attention and then stopping.

Smoke filling her throat and soul, choking her life … stop!

Breathe deeply. Choose at this moment to ignore it. And breathe again, hold it, and in and out. That was better. The Self-Help books would be proud of her. "I feel as if I'm going mad," Kate said slowly. "That I've got a split personality."

"No, my dear, you are not going mad," affirmed Gertrude. "And you have not got the split personality. Believe me, I know. I have had the experience of it."

"You?"

"No not me, it was my big brother, Hans. When he was about sixteen he was diagnosed as being schizophrenic. He was himself and then at other times he believed he was Jesus. He would dress in a shroud and make us kneel before him, and he would bless us. It was so sad. He was deluded."

"What happened to him?"

Gertrude shook her head. "Don't ask me, Kate. It was not good. You are not like that, thank the heavens, I can tell you."

"Then what do you suggest I do?"

"Well you know, I think you should see a hypnotherapist. You've had so much stress, what with the losing weight, and not sleeping, probably not eating properly, all of which could contribute to your present condition."

"Yes." Kate tried to reply with dignity to mask the raging tumult within, not easy with a single-syllable word.

"You do need to get help and I am the one who can do it."

"You?"

"And why not?" Gertrude rummaged in the mess of her stained leather purse lying on the shelf, and pulled out about twenty creased business cards. Sighing to herself, she searched through until she came to the one she wanted and handed it to Kate. She read that Gertrude was a professional therapist with rows of qualifications after her name, stretching back for years.

"It's true. I studied in Vienna. You know my grandfather was a well-known psychiatrist. He went to Freud's lectures in the nineteen hundreds. I take after him."

"But I thought you were a secretary?"

"I used to see my patients after work finished. I would have preferred to do the therapy the whole time but we needed the money."

"Gertrude, you've kept this very quiet."

"Like I said, I keep my mouth shut, you don't know what might come back to you. And I don't really want to get involved anymore, it is very exhausting, you know. I am retired now. It's just the cats to look after, eh?"

"And me."

"Well you know, I was not too convinced if I could help you or if I was the right person. I guess I was hoping it would resolve itself naturally. You don't go into these things lightly. But now I have to intervene. Kate, for you, I would recommend a form of regression therapy. We start there."

"Regression? I've heard of that. What is it exactly?"

"You see, by using a form of hypnosis it can lead you into the subconscious and a past life. This is what we call regression, or past-life therapy. You might then get the total picture of what you're catching the glimpses of."

Kate shook her head in disbelief. "I can't believe this is you talking. You've actually done all this?"

"Yes, I know that you are surprised." Gertrude pushed the cards back into her purse. "But please let me explain. By using a form of hypnosis we tap into the subconscious. If you are in a state of deep relaxation, you can, with the proper guidance, produce vivid and detailed memories of past lives. We regression therapists believe that we have all lived before and many times, so you can resolve issues in this life by understanding what you lived through in another. And if you have the faith in it, you get the better results." Gertrude paused to give Kate time to assimilate all this. "So now do you follow me?"

"I think so."

"Good. I will continue. When you're hypnotised very deep, you are open to whatever comes up. And you know, it can be a very intense process. Sometimes we have to travel back and back again through many lives

345

before we can sort out the problem with the past life personality."

"And you can do it?"

"Of course, but I do need time to prepare. Perhaps I don't go to Flower Arranging this week. We are having a talk about carnations and right now I am more interested in re-incarnations." She suppressed a titter at her irreverent pun.

Although Kate did trust Gertrude – she had to – past-life therapy sounded incredibly scary. And did she want to be regressed? In a weird way, she didn't want to lose whatever had got hold of her. And it definitely didn't want to let go of Kate. That was the nub of her dilemma.

"Now let me see." Gertrude thumbed through a black leather diary, even older than the purse. "I could do tomorrow afternoon? Around six o'clock. I can feed the cats early. Or maybe later."

"Tomorrow!" And the voice was off again, yammering in Kate's head.

'I'm not ready for this. Help – Gertrude, Grandmother!' – No! Stop. Breathe deeply again. And still comes the yammering.

"Can't we wait a few days," she pleaded.

"I don't want to worry you Kate, but you shouldn't waste more time."

"I'm bloody terrified. I don't know what to do."

"Life is so hard. You have to fight every inch of the way. It has been such a year, Kate. Believe me, I know.

346

Tomorrow you come to me at six o'clock."

"Let me think about it first."

Kate made lists. She paced the living room, the balcony, inside and out. Miguel cleaned the pool. The dogs barked, the cats prowled. The fishing boats pulled out in a steady line. The lighthouse beam would be snapping on at any moment. The silver candlestick waited patiently on the sideboard.

The Book of Help. It had to help! Where was it? Dropping bits of papers en route, she searched the drawers, wardrobes, sideboard and discovered it skulking at the back of the pantry wrapped in a Carrefour plastic bag. She sat on the bed, stared at the cloud in the blue sky on the cover and asked the question:

"Please could you tell me what I should do?" She opened a page at random.

'THIS NEEDS CAREFUL CONSIDERATION.'

"Please, please help me. Should I do what Gertrude suggests?" She opened another page.

'THINK HARD AND LONG. THEN THINK AGAIN.'

Pause.

"Or should I not?" And another page.

'THIS NEEDS CAREFUL CONSIDERATION.'

"Then what should I do? I'm desperate." And another.

'SENSE THE MOOD OF THE UNIVERSE.'

"You're not being helpful. One clear un-enigmatic un-obscure word of advice might help." She refrained

347

with difficulty from throwing the book over the balcony.

Kate stomped back into the living-room and stopped when she saw it. The candle she'd put back in the silver candlestick was alight, its flame flickering gently towards the ceiling. She had not lit it, she knew she hadn't. But its message was clear.

CHAPTER THIRTY-TWO

ESTEPONA – PRESENT DAY

"Kate, my dear, do come in and please wait here a moment." Gertrude greeted her with a formal hug. She was wearing a long brown skirt and loose blouse with embroidered sleeves, and her wispy hair seemed thicker, neatly braided round her head. She looked younger and more efficient as she bustled down the corridor. The balcony door was closed, the living room clean and tidy. The cats were out of sight, their yo-yos, toy ducks and bits of fluffy string stacked neatly on a small table by the couch. A door banged in the distance. Kate could hear the occasional echoing tapping footstep as a Spanish *señora* clicked round her apartment somewhere in the block, in another universe.

"I am ready for you now," Gertrude called, sounding like a dentist's assistant ushering in the next appointment. Kate entered Gertrude's second bedroom, where she'd never been before. It was a simple room furnished with a single bed, a white chair and a small bedside table. The fine net curtains were drawn. A crystal ball balanced on a wide shelf, next to a small statue of Jesus.

"Now Kate, you can lie down on the bed, and pull the quilt over you. And please will you keep your right hand out, it should be on top." Kate settled back and Gertrude sat beside her.

"I need to tell you that when I hypnotise you and you hear outside noises, you may be aware of them, but they don't bother you, you will remain hypnotised. It doesn't mean you are not responding. Do you understand?"

Kate followed Gertrude's spray of double negatives with difficulty. "Yes, I think so."

"And I must remind you again, it doesn't always work. So let us see, shall we? How are you with planes?"

"I don't want anything to do with planes."

"What about lifts, doors, corridors?"

"No lifts, thank you."

"That is fine, we will use an alternative." Gertrude produced a worn piece of typed paper from her pocket and unfolded it. "Now, because I am a little rusty, my memory is not quite what it was. So I'm going to read this to you from the script if you don't mind. Please keep your eyes open and fix your focus on a point on the ceiling. Your eyes should roll back towards it, if you can concentrate on this."

Kate stared at the ceiling and waited. Her mouth felt dry.

"You can count yourself slowly downwards from three hundred whilst I'm talking."

She started to murmur slowly. "Two hundred and ninety-nine, two hundred and ninety-eight …" as Gertrude intoned softly, monotonously in a gentle, sing-song voice.

"Settle down and concentrate very hard on the sound of my voice. Now breathe slowly and very deeply. Let each breath out be very smooth. You are feeling very safe and at peace. Your eyelids should be flickering slowly, and when they do, you will feel the urge to close your eyes ... and you can close them. And when you want to, you can stop counting."

Kate relaxed, let her eyes close and breathed deeply as Gertrude proceeded in a soft, even tone. She felt herself slipping into sleep. Gertrude took her through the relaxation, concentrating on all parts of her body from the feet upwards, relaxing her further and deeper. This was so easy. She wasn't thinking, she was simply sinking into a deep repose but then she'd got a lot of catching up to do. Kate hadn't felt this relaxed for more than thirty years.

Gertrude continued in a voice that was soft, slow and hypnotic. "Now, keeping your eyes closed, I would like you to let come into your mind a spot where you are happy and at peace; it can be the first place you think of."

"Yes." The same image came to her straightaway. She was performing t'ai chi in a glade in the pinewoods.

She breathed slowly. "I'm in the woods."

"That is good, Kate. Now you can see and feel them all round you, yes? The smells, the colours, what the ground is like."

"Yes."

"And now please imagine there is a guide beside you, keeping you safe. A path leads through the wood, do you see it?"

351

"Yes." Kate could visualise it clearly. She was there on it – a straight narrow path, bordered by long grass, wild lavender and camellias, white petals with black-eyed dots.

"Now take that path. Walk along it, feel the sun on the back of your neck. You are warm, safe and relaxed. Then it goes darker as you go deeper into the woods where there is no sun. Keep walking as the path leads you to a cave. Round the mouth of the cave there are sparkling lights of all the colours of the rainbow. Do you see them?

"Yes."

"Can you choose a colour?"

There was no hesitation. "I choose green."

"Good. Now let that colour become stronger and the others fade away. Follow that green light into the cave and down a corridor of doors. Walk down this corridor until you come to the green door with a green handle." Kate saw herself walking down the long narrow corridor of cream walls and silent closed doors. She arrived at the green door, halfway down on the left.

"Yes, I've done that."

"You can turn the handle and the door will open, and then you can step inside."

"I'm doing it." She felt a prickling sensation through her body as she stepped over the threshold into another life, another world. Where fountain water sparkled, the air was warm, and the kitten played close to her.

"Now, you answer my questions with the first image you think of."

"Right."

"Are you a man or a woman?"

"I'm a little girl," Kate said immediately.

"What is your name?"

"I'm Ana."

"And how old are you?"

"I'm seven years old."

"What country do you live in?"

"Spain."

"Where are you in Spain?"

"In Cordoba. By the fountain.

"What year is it?"

"I think it is around fourteen hundred and sixty-two or three. I am not sure."

"And what are you doing."

"We're in the plaza."

"Who are you with?"

"María and Pedro. We're playing with the stones."

"Who are they?"

"She is my older sister, Pedro is our friend. He's so funny, he makes me laugh."

"And how do you feel about María?"

"I wish I was like her. I'm a round dumpling."

"Who says so?"

"María does and I know it to be true, although Grandmother says not – oh no! Stop them!"

"What is the matter, Ana?"

"I don't like those boys."

"What are they doing?"

"The big one is shouting horrid words. They're pulling faces at me. I don't want to stay here. My head hurts."

"That's all right then," said Gertrude. "Now I would like to take you forward. One … two … three … four … five … and it is some years later. How old are you now?"

Again Kate had no hesitation. "I'm fourteen years old."

"And where are you?"

"We're down in the cellar."

"And what are you wearing?"

"I'm in a long dress, my favourite, it's red, with little red buttons down the front. I've got a cream petticoat on underneath and black boots and a cream shawl is covering my shoulders. It has been quite cold today."

"What are you doing, Ana?"

"It's Friday night and I am wearing a white handkerchief covering my head …. and I'm lighting the Sabbath lamps and doing the blessing over them, with my two palms towards the lamps and then turned towards my face, and I'm kissing my hands three times while I'm doing the blessing as Mama has taught me, like this, you see. And Papa is praying. He is wearing a shawl round his shoulder. Felipe is standing beside him."

"Who is Felipe?"

"He is my younger brother. He's so pleased that he is learning the blessing from Papa, it is the one that the boys do."

"And what religion is your father praying in, Ana?"

"Well, we are Christian but I know what Papa is doing is dangerous."

"And what is that?"

354

"No. We must not speak of it."

"Have you always been Christian?"

"Yes. Except that we are New Christians, they call us *conversos*. And other names I do not like."

"And what does that mean?"

"Our family converted to Catholicism many years ago."

"What religion was your family before that?"

"We were Jewish. But we're not now, we mustn't talk about it any more. We are good Christians."

"I see. And who else is with you down in the cellar?"

"I'm standing with Grandmother. María is not with us."

"Why is that?"

"She says it's stupid what we do."

"And how do you feel about her now?"

"I don't quite know. She is like my best friend and then she is not. You don't know with Maria. I hope she doesn't tell anyone."

"Why should she do that?"

"I don't want to talk about her now."

"That is fine. I'm now going to take you forward again. One ... two ... three ... four ... and where are you now, Ana?"

Kate's face broke into a wide smile. "I'm standing in the street with Pedro. We are looking at each other. I'm so happy I want to hug him."

"Why is that?"

"It's my seventeenth birthday and he has asked me to marry him."

355

"Have you accepted?"

"I have. Our families are agreed. Our wedding will be soon."

"What year are you in now?"

"It is fourteen hundred and seventy-three and nearly March. I am so happy!" Kate couldn't stop smiling even with her eyes closed.

"I am going to take you forward to your wedding, Ana. One ... two ... three ... four ... five ... and where are you now, Ana?"

"In the living room, it's after the wedding ceremony in the cellar. The silver candlesticks are on the table, Papa has made them, they are so beautiful, with their carved initials. I love them very much, but Mama is angry because they have also some forbidden words engraved upon them. We are trying hard to celebrate but they shout and march against us *conversos* in the streets, they hate us ... Stop! María is calling to us. The men are coming! They are here. And I know that big man at the front, it's María's friend, Luis. Why did they come to our house ... let me go ..."

"Where are you now, Ana? Speak to me."

"... I am in my bedroom. It is our wedding night. María has given me a drink and a saffron pastry and she has gone to gather the things, ready for our departure. It is a secret – we are leaving for Portugal very soon. Pedro and I make love, it is beautiful."

"And now?"

"He has left me to go and prepare the horses. I will meet him at the corner. But I am so sleepy, I mustn't fall asleep ... why am I so sleepy? What was in the drink

356

María gave me? It tastes bitter … and my throat is hurting. I can smell the smoke."

"Tell me what is happening now."

"I don't know. My eyes won't open, I can hardly move. I want to sleep …"

"What can you feel around you now. You must stay awake, please, Ana."

"It is so hot. The smoke is here, making me choke. I feel sick. I should have gone by now … to Pedro … I cannot get out of the bedroom … too much smoke outside the door. I grab the black grille but it is barring the window … I cannot get out that way either. Somebody is shouting … forcing open the door, a hand is there, stretching out for me ..."

"Who is it?"

"I think … it is Grandmother. She is grabbing me, pulling me out but I have to go back."

"Why, Ana?"

"Stumbling through the flames, so hot, frightening, but I have to get it. Take it with me."

"Take what?"

"The candlestick of course. Now I have it."

"What is happening now, Ana?"

"Grandmother has my arm, she's pulling me down through the fire. I follow her, stumble down the stairs. She collapses by the door … I try to help her and fall over also – try to crawl …"

"Where are you now? Speak to me!"

"On the ground outside. I'm coughing so much, my chest hurts."

"Are you alone?"

"There are two bodies lying in the street near the house. I think they are Mama and Papa ..."

"Is María there?"

"I don't know where she is. The candlestick is on the ground rolling away – tell Felipe to take it, find the other one, they must be together ..."

"Felipe is with you? Ana, answer me: Is Felipe there?"

"Gone now. He is hiding from the men ..."

"What men?"

"They must have come back ..." Ana's voice is fading. "I cannot see, cannot breathe, leave me now ..."

Gertrude spoke loudly and clearly. "Don't worry, I'm going to take you back down the corridor with the doors, to the entrance of the cave now, Kate.

Ten ... nine ...eight ... here you can see, all those coloured lights round the entrance. You can come back anytime you want, and all these lights can lead you to other lives. Seven ... six ... five ... I'm going to wake you up now ... four ... three ... two ... one ... and when I snap my fingers you will be awake."

CHAPTER THIRTY-THREE

ESTEPONA – PRESENT DAY

Kate lay cocooned under the blanket. When she opened her eyes she could see her everyday hands, the nails that needed trimming, the creased cuffs of her denim jacket. Normal things that helped ground her back into the present century. Gertrude went into the kitchen and brought back two glasses of water.

She sat beside the bed, her head gently nodding. "How do you feel now?"

Kate drank some water and tried to compose herself. How did she feel? This was a hard question. What had happened in there was so powerful, emotional and bizarre. It was imprinted in her mind, just as if it were her own story.

"I grieve for Ana and her tragic life. It was so clear, as if I was actually living in it like a waking dream. I could see the colour of Ana's clothes, the texture of her gown, that creepy dark cellar. I can even see her now, doing those arm movements over the oil lamps; Felipe's smile, even the bubbles in the fountain when she was a little girl. And those awful boys. It all seemed so painful and real."

"From my work with many clients, it was real. Believe me, Kate."

"And that ending in the fire. She died, didn't she? It

was horrible but I had to do it."

"Yes, you were very brave."

"If it was real, that means that my family were once Jewish and lived in Cordoba in the fifteenth century. Or rather, that family then." Again she was mixing up Ana's life and her own. Another thought struck her. "If this previous life was in Spain, why wasn't I speaking in Spanish?"

"Other clients have asked me that question about the language. There is a simple answer. It's because she, Ana, was speaking through you with your voice."

"But perhaps I made it all up? Couldn't I have created these memories myself?"

Gertrude shook her head. "That is a very common response."

"But why not? I'm very good at imagining things."

"The experts can rationalise it and say that your subconscious mind was acting out a life. But I can assure you, it is not a false memory."

Kate didn't think it was. It explained the nightmares, the memories and experiences; it made sense of the other half-life that had been with her maybe all her life.

"Are there any particular moments you can recall that bring you happiness?" asked Gertrude, breaking into her reverie.

Kate looked straight back into the past and smiled. "Pedro asking me to marry him."

"Do you recognise Pedro from anyone you know now?"

"No. Well – I'm not sure."

"Does anyone from the past seem familiar to you in

the present? Think hard."

Kate sat bolt upright, gripping the pillow hard. "María of course. I don't know how but she's all mixed up with that bitch Rosie and me.!" The words howled out of her.

"Kate? What is going on in your head? Tell me." Gertrude's voice was urgent.

"Help me, Grandmother!" Kate stared wildly round the room. For a moment she'd mixed herself and Gertrude up with the past. Gertrude said nothing but waited and watched until Kate calmed down. The sound of their breathing filled the space, Kate's hoarse and racing, Gertrude's steady.

"What are you thinking now?" insisted Gertrude.

"Of Ana and María and how they're somehow linked with me and Rosie. They hated and loved each other and so do we." Kate fanned her cheek to cool it. It was hot from where the flames had reached her. "Why is it all happening now, since I came to Spain?" She paused to think. "And more so, after I found the candlestick. 'They must be together,' that's what Ana said."

Gertrude heaved a very big sigh. "As you are beginning to realise, Ana is you in another life. You and she are one. You are her reincarnation. Coming to Spain has brought it all out. And the candlestick has served to accelerate the journey."

So Kate did exist before as Ana. A life of Ana growing up, holding the family secrets, falling in love. And dying in the fire. Ana's joy and tragedy had always been within her.

Gertrude continued. "As a therapist trained in regression therapy, I do believe in the soul's immortality, in life after death. We have lived before and we will live again. The soul is reborn into another body."

"Why have I been so aware of this past life taking over mine?"

"Because she is trying to use you to find peace. Ana has so much sorrow she is unable to let go. And the events and people are in a way repeating themselves."

"You asked me if I recognised anybody from the past."

"We do meet the same people over and over again and as I said earlier, the same love and hate, the same unresolved issues can be related to another life. Until there is resolution."

"Then Rosie and María could …"

"Could indeed be the same person. But you know, the antagonism you feel was Ana's anger towards María, not yours with Rosie. It is a long-ago issue, not to do with Rosie and you and what is going on now."

"Even if she is the reincarnation of María?"

"Whatever she did in the past, you have to forgive her. Only by doing that, will you bring peace to Ana and yourself."

"No I can't." Kate felt again the biting fury over that evil María and the desire to punish Rosie. Gertrude took Kate's hand and pressed it between her two palms. She was very intent.

"Now listen and good, Kate, this is very important. Obviously part of the therapy is to discover the root of the problem and relating it to a previous life usually

362

releases and resolves the suffering. But to make the therapy work, you need to forgive. You hear me? It is up to you. Only you can do it. You have to get rid of this anger towards María which is destroying you."

"But it's here inside me. I can't let it go. And Ana won't let me."

Gertrude passed Kate the glass of water. "Here, you should drink more. You need it." Kate gulped down the rest of the water as Gertrude watched her intently. She sat on the bed close to her. "Now speak to me," she urged. "As if I were María and you wanted to get it off your chest."

"What do you mean?"

"Kate, grow up! You are a good drama teacher, you do role-play, yes? You know how to act it out. Simple! You become Ana and talk to me as if I were María."

Kate thought of that girl on her bed in Toledo. With the long fair hair, face streaked with dirt, the blue eyes and intensity. She had seen her before – at the door of the Cordoba house and scurrying down the path below her apartment. That had to be María, flirting with Ana's lover, taking him away, destroying her life. She could talk to her all right, tell her what she thought of her.

Kate exploded. "I know you! Always telling me what to do! What was in that drink you gave me? Did you betray me and leave me to die? And you took Pedro away, didn't you? How could you do all that!"

"Yes," whispered Gertrude. "Go on."

"We were best friends as well as sisters. We shared everything – but not my husband! Grandmother was right, I should never ever have trusted you."

"But will you forgive her?" Gertrude asked.

"No, never!" she shrieked. "No I won't – until I find the other one. And punish her. Leave me alone, go away."

"Stop right now!" Gertrude rose and faced Kate. "I am speaking to you now. Only you can do it. You must not let Ana's anguish and her soul possess you. To bring peace to yourself and to Ana, you have to repent and forgive. And you *must* do it or this will never end. Do you hear me?"

"But Ana won't let me," Kate cried.

Gertrude looked steadily at her. "She is possessing you. This root of terror got a hold in the fifteenth century and this weakness has been in the family line ever since. You have been a captive of this spirit of fear through years of your ancestors. The fear is in your spiritual genes and something has to be broken. She has to be told to leave. Do you understand?"

Kate clenched her teeth, squeezed her hands together. What should she do? Ana wanted to stay with her, take over her mind and body, she realised that. But the Kate that was a good teacher, loved walking and dancing, loved life – *she* wanted freedom from that voice. And from Ana.

"Yes, I do understand," she cried.

"So do it. Gertrude faced the small statue of Jesus on the shelf. "Please stand up also." Trembling, Kate stood by the bed.

Then Gertrude spoke in clear loud tones. "Ana you must go. I cast you out by commanding you to leave Kate. I command you to go in the name of Jesus."

Gertrude repeated the command twice more. "I cast you out by commanding you to leave Kate. I command you to go in the name of Jesus."

There was silence in the room. A bird flew past the window. Gertrude turned to Kate. "It is done." She raised her hands upwards. "Oh Lord, fill Kate up with Your Love and Your Spirit."

The silence continued. Kate felt nothing. She couldn't believe that any change had come about in that short time. There were no bells ringing, no lights flashing, just a silence. She looked round the room, as if searching for what had gone.

"How do you feel now?" Gertrude asked.

"Sort of ... as if I'm on my own, at last. Nothing yammering at me. It's so quiet."

"That is good. She has gone and you have been set free. Now you can repent on behalf of the poor soul that was within you. On behalf of your ancestors you have to forgive. Can you do that now?"

"Yes I can." The realisation came to her along with a perceptible lifting of the spirit.

"Then it is up to you to forgive María, it is that simple. Then you will both be cleansed."

"Wait." Kate held her head down again, concentrating, listening. No, there was nothing there, no voice begging, crying 'help me.' She sat up straight and her voice was strong. "I forgive you, María."

Gertrude seized her hands and kissed them. "That is good. You are cleansed now. Bless you, Kate."

She had done it, managed it. She was free. It had not been that difficult. She could do more. "And I'm

365

sorry Rosie, for what I tried to do to you." The anger and pain drained from her and she was filled with a deep sense of something that might resemble peace. She almost felt sorry for Rosie, shackled to Steve.

"Thank you Gertrude."

Gertrude sighed. "Thank God. It is over. You are cleansed now," she repeated. "Now you will be protected."

Gertrude led Kate into the living room and opened the balcony door. Mango glared at her accusingly with his blind eyes. The two cats stalked in and sat on the couch. Kate pushed in between them and sank her head back against the cushions.

"It has been one tough afternoon for both of us." Gertrude stood at the window, exercising her shoulder muscles, heaving them up and down again.

"Kate, you should relax now and live a serene life, it will help the cleansing and keep you safe. I tell you, now that summer is coming, it is easier. You swim in the sea, the minerals are very good for you, but you keep a look-out for the jellyfish. And in the heat, life is slower, you take a long siesta every afternoon, just enjoy it. I can give you simple exercises for relaxation and breathing. They will all help to heal you." Gertrude moved away from the window and came close to Kate. She stretched again. "And now I go to feed the cats."

PART THREE

CHAPTER THIRTY-FOUR

A large block had been cleared away. Thanks to Gertrude's intervention, the turmoil had ceased. Although the images she'd experienced remained as memories, Ana had left her and the suffering come to an end. No more nightmares, no more time-slip jolts. She moved slowly through the days.

Gertrude heard on the grapevine that Rosie had moved to the Nerja office on the other side of Malaga, so Kate was safe from her. No more bumping into her at the port, in Estepona or at social functions which she no longer attended. And it was too hot to go walking. As for Steve, he'd disappeared in his usual Steve fashion, he could be anywhere. She'd let them both go and was proud of her ability to do so. A lot of good stuff had come out of that session, now who else could she forgive and ask forgiveness from? Uncle Roger?

"No," said Gertrude. "Don't overdo it, Kate."

Summer was here and, as Gertrude said, it was easier. Kate was indeed calmer, with relaxation, reading and swimming in the sea. She walked the *paseo* in the early morning, before the heat of the day got going, along with a multitude of fellow walkers, cyclists, joggers and dogs. It was summer, a healing time. She slept well, with no bad

369

dreams.

Gertrude was late tonight feeding the cats. Kate watched over the balcony as she crooned softly to them and spooned out the lumpy brown stew with an added mix of herbal remedy to fortify them all. Two of the cats snarled as they faced up to each other with feral concentration, and Kate was reminded momentarily of the two battling sisters, Ana and María. They were like long-gone feuding relatives, mercifully no longer a fighting part of her.

As summer drifted to an end, her energy returned and she was back at Spanish class. And she saw no harm in doing some research into the past, to explore and corroborate what had happened in the regression. Although she was taking Gertrude's good advice to let the therapy heal, she did want to find out more about life in Cordoba in the fifteenth century, for her own peace of mind and interest. Was there unrest connected to the Jewish community and *conversos* in that specific period? Were there riots and burnings of their houses? If she could establish that some of these tragic incidents did occur, it would be tangible proof, and her precise teacher's mind would appreciate that.

Via the Internet she ordered a host of books. An official note with a tick in the 'Parcel Awaiting' section arrived regularly in her mailbox and she speed-walked down to the Post Office to pick up yet another tome on the history of Spain, Jewish life in the Middle Ages, *conversos*, Crypto-Jews, Mediterranean cooking with saffron etc. History had been a favourite subject at school and she couldn't put the books down. They were not easy reading, with their dates, battles and kings, and the complicated Spanish rigmarole of the Visigoths, Conquests and Re-conquests by Moors and Christians. But Spanish history was part of her history and she wanted to know it. Consequently she devoured information on Cordoba and its tenth to twelfth century Golden Age of poets, philosophers, courtiers, where Jews, Christians and Moslems co-existed in harmony. It was a pleasure to meet up with Maimonides again. She read avidly of the Sevilla uprising against the Sephardic Jews at the end of the fourteenth century and the subsequent pogroms and mass conversions to Christianity. Those were the *conversos*, the *marranos*, also known as Crypto-Jews, descendants of Sephardic Judaism. Many of them embraced Catholicism but secretly retained some of their Jewish traditions. Maybe they were her kinsmen?

And Kate learnt that racial and religious hatred did indeed break out in 1473 in Cordoba and other cities of Andalucía. Houses were ransacked and burnt, and many *conversos* slain. The disturbances reached their peak in the middle of March of that year after sixteen days. Following this occurrence, it was decreed that no *converso* should live in Cordoba or its vicinity, nor should hold public office.

This covered the period of her recollection. This was vindication. The past life she'd known in the therapy session could have occurred. But the line stopped many generations ago. There was no way to trace from there to here unless through more past-life

371

regression and she wouldn't go there again. Was she descended from Ana through a chain of family links stretching five hundred years? Was she Jewish or did she come from Jewish stock? Past life did *not* automatically make her of Jewish descent, or Ana her ancestor. So she didn't know. She had one thing though to hold onto – the candlestick. Kate would love to believe that the solid silver object transcended time and linked her with Ana, but in a safe, non-threatening way. Ana had no power over her now.

Uncle Roger and his Cordoba connection was unresolved. Kate kept phoning him, but he was currently unavailable. He and Aunt Susan were on a round-the-world cruise. She couldn't tie all the ends up neatly.

'*La Herencia de Sefarad*' – 'The Sephardi Inheritance' – was being performed at the Cultural Centre this Friday by a visiting soprano and guitarist/singer. Admission was free, courtesy of the Town Hall.

The late October streets of Estepona were empty. It had rained at last, and green was returning to the dry lighthouse land. The approach of winter was an optimistic time here, a renewal and rebirth, instead of the closing down of nature as it was in England. The evening air was cool and Kate wrapped up warm in the thick creamy coloured quilt that passed for an anorak. However hot it was during the day, it could get chilly at night.

This was the quietest time of the year. The port might be lit up with weekend youth raving until dawn, but the good citizens of Estepona were prudently tucked up in their thick walled village houses with their Repsol gas heaters and Spanish television.

Plaza de Las Flores was deserted except for a few late-night lads kicking a ball around. Inside the chilly Cultural Centre an official, muffled in a thick grey sweater and scarf, hovered around … Yes, she'd come to the right place; no, the artists had not arrived yet.

The audience drifted in. The women wore shawls, jackets and boots, like Kate. To the locals, this was cold but they didn't know what real cold was. They didn't know about British howling gales, four degrees under, and thick encrusted ice on morning windscreens.

A fellow student from the Spanish class was there with his wife. Kate waved to the girls who ran the English bookshop and the man from the computer shop gave her a nod. As the crowd thickened and they surged towards the stairs, she semi-recognised the back of somebody's head. It was a pleasant male head, dark hair mingled with silver. The man turned the corner of the stairs and she didn't see him again.

The performance space was not ideal – a long, bare room with a long bleak set of lights set in the ditto ceiling. Rows of chairs stretched in a long block and Kate was stuck at the back. But this was a free recital so she shouldn't complain. Whatever they got was a bonus.

They waited. The official came forward, minus his scarf but full of melting brown-eyed concern. The performers had taken the wrong road and were at the moment at Elviria, on the other side of Marbella. The audience waited on. Some left, some came back. Kate

373

studied the programme and read the notes. The artists had a great passion and interest for folk music, hence the Sephardic connection. The guitarist was born in Sevilla, the woman in Orense and they had been performing as a duo for the last twelve years if her translation was correct. No it wasn't. Kate tried again. The woman had started music training when she was twelve years old. They'd been performing as a duo for twenty years. She must work harder at the *español*. The artists were forty-five minutes late.

A bearded man hurried into the room, carrying his guitar and an apologetic demeanour. He settled onto a small platform and the depleted spectators clapped politely and with relief. The female singer joined him. They had a recital and Kate could see it.

The guitarist introduced each Sephardi song and explained that many were sung on joyous occasions. Much of the music was related to love and marriage, with a mother serenading her daughter before the wedding. Traditionally, it was the women who sang and carried the music through to the next generation. One of the melodies caught her attention and she hummed along with it, almost as if she knew it.

The recital was short, an hour in length, and when it was over the artists announced that their CD was for sale outside. The music enriched Kate and she was content. As they filed out, she overheard a brightly dressed woman tackling the guitarist.

"Would you come and play for our association in Marbella? We could guarantee you an audience."

The guitarist was politely non-committal. "We do have a filled-in tour schedule."

"Excuse me but I have to ask you," continued the woman, elbowing the line waiting to buy the CD out of the way. "Are you Jewish?" Kate hovered as close as she could in order to catch his answer. It was what she wanted to know also. The guitarist did the Spanish shrug. He was the master of non-committedness.

"I am Spanish. I may be Jewish but I don't know. We could all be."

As Kate left the hall, a man approached her in the foyer. It was the man she thought she'd recognised. He was warmly dressed in a thick padded jacket and tartan scarf.

"*Hola* Kate," he said, tentatively, bobbing forward to kiss her on both cheeks.

"*Hola* Juan." She kissed him back, tentatively.

"I was not sure if it was you," he continued.

"Me neither."

"It's been quite a time."

"What are you doing down here in Estepona?" she asked.

"You mean, I should be on the hillside tending my goats?"

"Well, no." Kate laughed. "Obviously you like Sephardi music."

"I like all music. I thought this recital was worth coming to. The artists, Miguel and Sofía, I have known them since they were students. They are extremely talented." They stood and gawped at each other like teenagers as the audience swam past and out. No

375

wife/girlfriend was coming up and claiming him. Should she speak again, before he walked out of her life?

But he spoke first. "Are you on your own tonight?"

"Yes. As you can see."

"Would you like to share some *tapas* with me before I return to my shack up in the distant mountains?"

"I'd be delighted."

She walked with Juan along deserted streets lit by intermittent street lamps. He led her into a bar in the oldest part of town, an area she hadn't visited before. Inside it was warm and cosy and they were the only customers. The bench seats were comfy, padded with gold-tasselled red cushions, and the large rectangular tables were of dark knotted wood.

"Shall I order for us?" Juan asked.

"Please do."

Kate opted for a warming brandy and the waiter brought a jumbo-sized goblet and proceeded to pour, pour, pour from the bottle. Juan settled for red wine. A platter of cold meats, cheese, fresh stubbly bread and olives arrived. They devoured the food, picking at the slices of meat with their fingers as they talked.

"Is the music authentic Sephardi?" Kate asked.

"Most of it originates from Salonica, from around the fifteenth century, but it has its roots in Sepharad. We don't know exactly what they sang here in Spain. Why are you so interested?"

She hesitated. She couldn't share her intense experiences with this man. It wasn't fair to load such a

376

story onto someone she hardly knew. She decided on a sideways route in.

"Do you think the musicians are Jewish?"

His reply was guarded, similar in style to the guitarist's response. "Well, they could be. But we could all be Jewish in Andalucía." He looked as if he wanted to say more, but didn't. The moment passed and Kate let it go. Her face was flushed, eyes bright, due to the gallons of brandy she was consuming. And a little of Juan.

"You like walking in the country?" he enquired.

"Love it. I don't get enough of it though."

"If you want, we could go for a ramble sometime?"

Kate whipped out her diary. "You say when."

Juan laughed at her eagerness. "My free day is Sunday."

"Next Sunday then?" she said, pencil hovering over the page. "Where shall we meet?"

"In the *pueblo* where my shop is. There is a petrol station at the entrance to the main street, on the right."

"I know it. What time?"

"Eleven o'clock?"

"Right." She marked it all down. "I'll bring sandwiches. Cheese and ham?"

"*Perfecto*," said Juan. "You like turtles?"

"To look at or to eat?"

Juan laughed again. "I will show you Turtle Valley," he said.

CHAPTER THIRTY-FIVE

ESTEPONA – PRESENT DAY

That Sunday they climbed down the stony path to Turtle Valley and walked along a rocky path beside the river as far as the old bridge. Then they headed back to where the green plateau of land sloped into the river, and sat on flat stones as birds sang in the sharp clear air. Juan put her cheap binoculars back in the bag and lent her his. Looking through them, she could see a couple of turtles sunbathing on the slabs of rock upstream. Two young boys rode past on great horses and a group of lively Spanish teenagers chattered by.

Kate liked Juan's brown arms and the line of his firm body as he moved. She liked his short-sleeved blue checked shirt tucked into his thick beige trousers. She liked his silver and dark hair, his kindly round face, his sad eyes. She liked the way he looked at her, as if he knew and liked her as she was. As if she could start a song and he could finish it. Juan and Kate were on the same wavelength, where they should be. She was completely at ease with this man as they ate their ham and cheese sandwiches. She lifted her face towards the sun.

"It is different to the coast, no?" he said.

"In every way. Want a grape?" He took one and they spat out pips in a companionable silence.

"How long have you lived up here?" Kate asked when they'd finished spitting.

"About three years. I used to be a lawyer in Malaga. Then I decided I wanted a new, quieter life away from the city. And you? What did you do before coming to Spain?"

"I was a teacher in Manchester. It's another big city. So different to this." She stretched her arms up to the sky. "I love it all."

"So why do you not come and live here?"

Kate laughed. "It's not as simple as that."

"What is stopping you? Do you have a job on the coast?"

"Not yet. Work will have to be found soon, probably teaching. I promised myself a few months off to see and it's stretched already to a year. But that's not it. All my life I've been impulsive and rushed into things. I don't want to make another mistake."

"Are you saying it was a mistake to come to Spain?"

"No. It was not a mistake." At last she realised this. They finished lunch and Juan skimmed stones into the water. She watched his concentration and made her decision. It was a quick one, as usual.

They sat on the terrace of a bar facing the *pueblo* across the road. The little white houses with terracotta roofs spread up the hill opposite, with the grey craggy castle on the top.

"I've decided. I want to move up here," she declared, drinking strong coffee. To hell with the decaff.

Juan put his cup down and laid his hand on her arm.

379

"Kate, I am happy for you, it is a good decision. But whatever you do, you don't come here."

"But you said it was a good idea."

"Sure, come to the mountains, and I can help you to find some work. But not to this *pueblo*."

"Don't you live here?"

"My shop is here, but I live in another *pueblo* not far away."

"What's wrong with here?"

"Look, I explain. This is not a particularly harmonious place. The priests, they try to make peace but the locals have been feuding with each other for generations, since well before Franco. The *pueblo* was divided then, and that was before the foreigners came in. Now it is losing its heart. Every time an old person dies, the house becomes vacant, the family bring in the builders and convert it and it is snapped up as a second home. 'Residential tourism', how I loathe that term. It is good income and employment for everybody, a better standard of living, but tourism has shot the prices up. If you want a *pueblo* life, we can find you cheaper, more authentic and more hospitable, a little further from the coast. I will advise you the one to look in."

"All I want is some stability. And I'd like to learn t'ai chi."

"You will have it Kate. There is a class on Tuesday evenings near where I live." Juan cleared his throat. No, he was not asking her to marry him, but it was a significant question.

"Would you like to meet my family?"

"I would love to."

"We are having a big luncheon in a few weeks, after I come back. We do the same every year at this time, and we invite friends. It is our tradition."

"Where are you going?" She was panicked. She didn't want him going anywhere, now she'd found him.

"I take regular buying trips, every three months or so. This time it is to Extramadura, Caceres and Merida, north-west of Cordoba. They are very beautiful old towns, with ancient buildings. Perhaps you will come with me some time. In my camper van?"

"Yes please." Kate beamed at him and he beamed back.

"I would like to bring you to the meal as my guest," Juan said. "You must meet Teresa. You will like her. She is my favourite sister." Relief poured through her body and soul. For one hideous moment Kate thought he was going to say she must meet his wife.

CHAPTER THIRTY-SIX

ESTEPONA – PRESENT DAY

Kate wasn't knocking Estepona, it had been good to her, gateway to a new life and all that but she'd be glad to get away. In the blink of a twinkling, she found a furnished house in the mountains to rent, situated in the *pueblo* recommended by Juan. The house was waiting for her, tucked away down a white-washed alley with little passing noise except the odd motorbike and nowhere was perfect. The little roof terrace faced the mountains – not Gibraltar – and the interior was spaciously open-plan with a central fireplace for the fires that she now had no problem with, and thick stone alcoves for books. In the middle of the inner patio an orange tree blossomed and Kate cried when she saw it. She'd move in at the beginning of the next month.

Gertrude was delighted with her decision. "You know what, I could have told you it was the right thing to do." She was encased in thick woollen purple leggings and a matching top she'd knitted herself. As Gertrude waded through the cats' toys on the floor Mango rubbed against her legs and she scooped him up into her arms. He'd grown almost bigger than her. That little scrap of thin fluff was now rounded, purring and contented, but unseeing.

"He is so sweet, you know what, he climbs into bed

each morning and licks my ear to wake me up." Mango slithered from Gertrude's arms, threw Kate a withering look although he couldn't see her and stalked out of the room.

"Come, I make you some tea."

"But not that special brew, thanks. I don't need it now."

"It's okay, I have the ordinary green stuff." Kate followed Gertrude into the kitchen and watched her fill the kettle and get out the mugs. "I tell you," said Gertrude, "we take our chances when they come to us. Life is so hard. You know what, back in the summer I waited weeks for them to come and fix the washing machine. And they find behind it so many *cucarachas*, cockroaches, you know. It cost me two hundred and twenty euros to have them removed. You have to be strong. I told you so at the beginning."

"Yes Gertrude, you did."

"You know what, I have so many two cent and five cent pieces they drive me mad. I can't see them properly and they fill up my purse."

"Pass them over to me, I'll give you change for them." Kate was glad Gertrude had returned to mundane Gertrude-sounding things. She reached for her purse, poured out a brown river of *céntimos* and they counted them and put them in piles. They amounted to five euros and a bit, and Kate handed over a note to her and scooped up the brown coins. She'd give them to the nearest tango musician playing his accordion heart out in Calle Real.

Mango walked the six-inch ledge of Gertrude's

383

balcony with precision and disdain. The white cat sat on Kate's lap, alongside the mug of Gertrude's tea and permitted Kate to stroke her.

"I'll miss you so much, Gertrude."

Gertrude patted Kate's hand. "You don't waste no time being nostalgic. I tell you, you have done the right thing." She nodded her head in the old safe Gertrude way. The cat jumped off Kate's lap.

"You know what, she's so funny, she sits with me and watches Eurosport every night on the television. She loves the skating." Gertrude nodded towards the cat. "You must have her when you go. A goodbye present." There was the suspicion of a tear in her hard-boiled eyes.

"How wonderful! Thank you so much, Gertrude." They hugged tightly, bosom to bosom. "What will I do without you?"

"Don't you worry, Kate, I have a German friend in your *pueblo*, she goes to my Flower Arranging class. You will be seeing me often enough up there."

Back at home, Kate shiftily asked *The Book of Help* one final question:

"What should I do with you now?"

'JUST DO WHATEVER FEELS RIGHT AT THE TIME' was its wearied, eye-rolling response. The book had had enough of her and she of it. Kate popped down to the port and gave it to Vicky, the rental agency secretary, who was thrilled with it. She was staring at the cloud, flicking the pages and asking it questions before Kate was out of the door.

Steve was standing at the corner of the port by the Chinese restaurant. He was with a woman, smiling down at her. She looked about Kate's age and as she clutched her bag and smiled back, she seemed new and vulnerable. He hadn't seen her! Kate raced away, past the big supermarket, along the dark shady side of the street, past the Karaoke bar, ran until she was safely back inside the building, heart racing. Something was tugging at her memory. Back in the apartment she reached into her bag, rooted into the back of her purse and pulled out the photograph that Val had taken of the group on that first walk in the mountains, centuries ago. She studied Steve again in close-up. Then it hit her right between the eyes, middle of the forehead. She had known him before: that thick body, the aggressive stance, the sharp blue eyes and the continual friction between them. She'd seen him in the regression therapy and now she recognised him from a past life. Steve and Luis were one and the same person. Steve was Luis, the boy who threw the stones, and who led the men into the house. Luis was her enemy and so was Steve. She tore the photograph into shreds.

"Luis came back. The mob finished what it had started."
Diego puts his arm round Pedro's shoulder.

They stand in the dark Cordoban alley, in front of
the ruins of the Ramírez family home. The wooden roof
has caved in and the remains of the fire are still
smouldering there, the smell of smoke lingering in the
air. The broken door and upper windows are burnt
black.

Pedro is filthy, his face a mass of bruises. His eyes
look dead."What have they done with Ana?"

"I am deeply sorry, my friend. They all perished in
the fire except the boy, he has gone into hiding. They
have taken the bodies away."

"I have to see her."

"You must not. Luis is out looking for you. He
believes that you betrayed him with María."

"How did Luis and his men know to come to the
house? Did she tell him about our wedding service?"

"According to Luis, she was planning to inform on
the family and then escape with you."

"That woman is evil! I would never have left Ana
behind."

"She intended to drug her sister and present herself
as Ana. She has done this pretence before."

"I know." Pedro falls to his knees and weeps
uncontrollably.

Diego crouches beside his friend. "Where is she now?"

"Somewhere to the west, in the countryside. She has kept the horse and gone for good."

"How did it happen."

Pedro controls himself. "It was all confusion. We met as arranged and rode through the night. She was wearing Ana's cloak and hood and I did not realise it was her until it was light, next morning. My God, Diego, in the dark I lay with her. Then she told me that Ana had a terrible accident and could not come. She gave me a fake message from Ana, saying that she, María, should take her place. I wanted to turn back immediately but I could not. She had me drugged."

"As I suspected."

Pedro cries out again. "She got rid of Ana and used me to get away. That had been her intention all the time. Then she begged for forgiveness, saying no harm was meant, it was only a small draught and everybody had always loved Ana more than her! The woman is a monster, maybe even mad, Diego. It could well have been her who started the fire."

"I think not; spare her that sin. Luis has confessed to the burning. Come my friend, you have to go. It is not safe here."

"Is there news of my parents?"

"I believe they are safe but are planning to leave Cordoba soon. Go to their house as fast as you can. Carry nothing extra with you."

"I have the candlestick."

"Best to leave it with me, I can dispose of it."

387

"No Diego, I cannot. It is all I have of Ana now."

Then keep it hidden well. Now you must make haste to leave Cordoba as soon as possible." They clasp each other in a silent embrace. "Go," repeats Diego.

Pedro mounts his horse and clatters down the alley. He rides south out of the city.

CHAPTER THIRTY-SEVEN

THE PUEBLO – PRESENT DAY

Kate made a list of Good Things in Her Life. She'd applied to become a resident of Spain. She now read a Spanish paper daily and did the crosswords in Spanish. In the local market, an elderly lady in slippers, black from head to toe and with contrasting grey hair and grey teeth, advised her on the best fruits to buy. She blew a kiss at the grapes that were ripe. The fruit-man gave her free parsley along with the bananas and potatoes because she was a beautiful woman. Kate was overjoyed until she discovered that he did the same with all the women.

On the first Sunday of her new life, Kate went out for lunch. Many members of Juan's family had returned for this reunion, and taken over the whole place. There were at least forty people gathered at a long table in the popular fish restaurant beside the Algeciras/Ronda railway line. The owner had a brother who lived in Algeciras and sent the fish up daily on the train.

Kate was introduced to a multitude of aunts, uncles, brothers, cousins, babies and friends; some with glasses, some with nappies, some chubby, some stooped and thin as rakes, some round as oven-ready turkeys, some with moustaches and that included the women. They were all so welcoming to her.

Juan's sister and Kate sat next to each other and they got on instantly. Teresa taught at a primary school in Malaga and was married with a handsome husband and three polite little boys. She was slim, with a pale, oval-shaped face, and dark-rimmed glasses that shielded her gentle brown eyes.

The party began in a formal manner but as the courses followed each other, the noise level slowly rose. The drink flowed, little stringy things in shells were passed round and Kate didn't know what anything was except the tuna, sweet corn and beetroot salad. Juan leant over with advice.

"Now a Spanish *señora* would sprinkle oil and vinegar over the salad for her end of the table." She did so and handed the salad round to her neighbours. The row of faces beamed at her approvingly. Glasses of wine were clinked. More little crispy, fried fish dishes arrived which she picked at with her fork until Juan advised her to eat them with her fingers as the Spanish did. They drank more wine and consumed red peppers, tomatoes, onions and prawns followed by monstrous grey things in a stew. Was it fish? It was gorgeous whatever it was.

Teresa teased her. "Kate you know you're eating eel."

"Ugh." She pushed it away. "I can't eat eel."

"Don't worry," chortled an aunty two seats away. "The Spanish only eat eel up in the north."

"So what is it?

"It's oyster mushrooms."

And they ate and laughed with good drunken merriment. Gradually the noise settled down to a steady mellow level and Teresa and Kate sat back in their chairs. Teresa told of the change in her brother's life when he moved back to the mountains.

"Juan was so tired of his work, he was a lawyer in Malaga, no time for relaxation. Then he and his wife split up, fortunately there were no children. He wanted a fresh start. Because our family came from this area, this is where he wanted to be."

Juan was on his feet, tapping his glass to attract attention. He made a speech to the two rows of shiny faces.

"… and a special welcome to our special guest, Kate." Juan produced a guitar to serenade them and the whole party joined in. It was the music and tempo from her *sevillana* class. Everybody clapped and stamped and shouted '*olé*.' Kate was twitching to jump up and dance.

"I'm longing to do this," she whispered to Teresa.

"You know *sevillana*?"

"*Sí, sí.*"

She pulled Kate up and they faced each other. They waited for the next section to start, hands on hips and then they were off. Arms up, fingers curling, dancing, swaying round each other, stamping and *olé*-ing as if they'd been doing it together since childhood. The group cheered and clapped on to the rhythm. And when it was over, Juan presented Kate with a parcel he'd kept hidden under his seat. It was a new polka-dotted red flamenco dress, identical to the one she'd fallen in love with. As she thanked him with a kiss on the cheek, the golden glow of the restaurant held the eternal moment. Past and present merged. And then time moved on.

They finished the feast with strong coffee, chocolate mints and a final liqueur on the house.

"This is good, yes?" Juan said. He picked up a chocolate and threw it lightly into the air. With his head raised upwards, he caught and balanced it on the tip of his nose. Kate laughed at him as the chocolate rolled off and he tossed it into his mouth and ate it.

"Why did you do that?"

"Why not?" he said. "Can I drive you home?"

"Thank you Juan, but I've got my own car."

"Let me go in front and you follow. I want to know that you get there safely. And it is time I saw your beautiful house."

She followed him up and down the deserted bends of mountain road and invited him in for a non-alcoholic nightcap.

"Yes!" Juan clapped his hands. "But this is so right for you!" He loved the house the moment he stepped in the door. The white cat Kate had named Blanca, curled round his ankles.

"I'll show you round after a cup of tea. Camomile?"

"Sure." He crouched down to make up the fire with firelighters, kindling and logs while she went into the kitchen to fill the little silver teapot with hot water. She heard him exclaim and splutter behind her.

"Anything wrong?" she called. Juan didn't answer. He was standing at the small table where she kept the silver candlestick. He was trembling from the top of his head to the pointed tip of his tan lace-up shoes.

"Juan, what's up?" He didn't speak. Kate put the

teapot down and ran to him. Was he having a seizure?

"Please, Kate," he gasped. "Where did you get this candlestick?"

"I bought it in a shop in Cordoba."

"Cordoba! Where in Cordoba?"

"In an artisan's workshop, near my hotel in the Old Quarter. It was right at the bottom of a box. Nobody would have found it but me. And I had to have it, I felt that it had always belonged to me."

Juan picked it up and studied it closely. Especially the engraved script on the base.

"I believe these are Hebrew words," he whispered. She didn't understand. Perhaps he wanted it for his shop? The significance didn't register with her until he flung his arms up to the ceiling, his fists clenched in triumph.

"Yes! *Gracias a Dios!*" he shouted. Kate felt the thud of both their hearts beating as he pulled her close to him.

"I was always knowing this is important to me meet you," he said in appallingly ungrammatical mixed-tense English but then he was tremendously flustered. "From the moment I see you at my shop."

"So did I, *yo también*, I do too," she babbled.

They were so close, their breath was intermingling.

CHAPTER THIRTY-EIGHT

THE PUEBLO – PRESENT DAY

Juan had been busy all week and it was not until Friday afternoon that they made their way back to the green land of the valley. They sat by the river and talked. Further downstream the turtles sunbathed on their rock slab in the crisp wintry sunshine.

"The candlestick from Cordoba," he asked her, "I have to know what is its meaning for you?"

Juan deserved a version of the truth if anybody did.

"I felt very drawn to Spain. But when I got here, I started having these strong nightmares that I felt connected me to the past. And then I found the candlestick in Cordoba with its Hebrew writing. I believed that was part of it all, part of my heritage. It was buried away at the back of the shop, as if the man was ashamed of it and didn't want anybody to see it."

"Kate, I too would have hesitated to put an object like this in the front of my shop. I know the climate has changed, you see the Star of David T-shirts, the Jewish bookshops in Cordoba and other places, but it's not so different at heart, especially in the rural areas. Even today there is a great ignorance about Jews. Most of the Spanish don't even know one, but the prejudice persists. I have a friend who wanted to marry a Jewish woman from London, he had a bad time with the church. But it is changing, slowly. Things once hidden are now in the open again."

"That's what my friend in Toledo said."

"And the candlestick, did it help you with these bad dreams of the past?"

"Yes. They've stopped now. I had them removed. But I'm still convinced there must be a Jewish connection somewhere, going right back for centuries."

"I thought so. You need to come with me." He stood up and pointed to the right of the river, way past the turtles.

"Can you see the roof of that old house over there? On the other side of the river, high up on the bend, yes, can you make out the chimneys? The grounds go down to the riverbank. That is where we are going. Come, Kate, let's pack up."

It was easy crossing the river by the large stepping-stones, even though the water level was now high, full with autumn rainfall. With Juan's help Kate clambered over the boulders and followed him along the narrow path. They approached the corner where the river meandered left. A new vista opened up to reveal the other side of the valley with its cork forests and distant mountains, dotted with white villages. After about ten minutes' walk, a rusty old gate bristling with barbed wire blocked their path. The whole area in front of them was fenced off and impassable. Juan unwrapped the wire, produced a huge set of keys from his rucksack, selected one and unlocked the padlock. The gate creaked open and they entered the grounds of the property. The old house was half-hidden, rising above an overgrown garden with the hillside behind. Kate helped Juan push back the gate and and he locked it behind them.

"Follow me. We go in this way."

"Is there anybody living here?"

"Not now. Everyone has moved away." They climbed steadily upwards through grounds overgrown and thick with weeds. As they approached the house along a rough pebbled path, she stopped. Everything was starting to look familiar. Three Alsatian dogs bounded out, barking. They ran up to Juan and he fondled them and slapped them gently. As they leapt up round his legs, they turned from vicious animals into tail-wagging *amigos*. She'd seen these dogs before. And when they reached the tumbledown, derelict house she was positive. Because they'd approached it from a different angle, she hadn't recognised it at first. This was the hideous old ruin that Juan wouldn't sell to them and these were the dogs that guarded the place. Now she recalled the broken roof with trailing weeds growing between the tiles, the stained, cracked walls, the scrubby patch of rough land in front.

"Please stop a moment." Kate was breathing heavily from the climb and mixed emotions. Why had he brought her here? Not to start the old argument again? But Juan was smiling. He wiped the sweat off his face and took her hands in his.

"You see where we are, no?"

"Yes I do. But I thought that was over."

"You wait. Trust me." The dogs settled down as Juan opened the front door and they stepped inside to a musty-smelling room with a high, wooden beamed ceiling. A strong animal smell exuded from a corner of the stone floor. The house was dilapidated, thick with dust and cobwebs, empty of furniture and household objects, but it was not a complete hovel of a ruin. It was in better condition inside than out: spacious, with high ceilings, thick stone walls, and an old black range standing in the kitchen. Up the stairs were five large bedrooms.

"Let us continue." Juan led her through the house to the back door and out again and round the far side of the building. They stepped over dry blades of prickly grass, giant weeds and suspiciously large lumps of dung, denoting animals she didn't care to meet. She didn't even think of pumas. Juan pointed to a small collapsed building standing directly behind the house, abutting the hillside.

"There was once a river up here and a stream that went down to the main river. This outbuilding used to be a small mill. Look, if you bend down here you can see where the old wheel was. And there was an oven, I think at one time they baked the bread here." Kate crouched down at the edge of the broken wall, and by sticking her head well down, she could make out a large sturdy iron wheel embedded firmly at the base of the building.

"All this land used to be cultivated with fruit and vegetables. Olive trees, lemon, avocadoes, they grew everything."

"Why has it been left to go so wild?"

"Well you see, it's a complicated story. We are a big family and when the older generation died, many of the

397

young ones didn't want to stay here. Some moved away during the Civil War anyway. Some of them went abroad and have not returned. The cousins, brothers, sisters, they live all over – Madrid, Germany, even the United States. A few stayed on in Andalucia. Only I came back from Malaga to live here. So who is going to see to the land now? Nobody, and I don't have the time. That is why we decided to sell the stuff inside."

Kate dared to ask him, risk his displeasure once more. "But why have you held onto this land, this old house? You've not even developed it, and it would make a perfect rural hotel. What is the point of leaving it like this?"

"Yes Kate, it may seem we are foolish, it is falling down and sure, we could make a lot of money from the house and the land, alongside Casa Sueños. We all know that. Casa Sueños is different, we are agreed to sell that when we can, but legally we must not sell this particular property. And it is divided between so many of us, it is too complicated. It stays as it is. I have to keep an eye on it, look after the dogs. A farmer down the valley feeds them for me. And I could not leave it anyway."

"It was your family who lived here?"

"My great-grandfather, he made the wheel. Come, we go this way now." She followed him to the back of the ruined mill house.

"Please be careful here, the land is very rough." She scrambled after him up a hilly mound to face the back wall of the building which was standing intact on a higher level. Juan unlocked a concealed hatch door and they squeezed through. With the door open, the natural

398

light showed up a small room with a long work bench in the far corner and an assortment of spades and shovels lying against the wall. Juan produced a torch from his rucksack, switched it on and locked the door. He crossed over to the workbench, heaved at it hard with both arms and it swung smoothly away from its base to reveal yet another low door inside, set into the wall. He got down, poked his head forward to unlock this door and beckoned Kate to follow him. She crawled through and Juan closed the aperture behind them and locked it firmly.

"Here please, you hold this." He handed her the torch while he rolled an old wine barrel in front of the door to block it. She shone the torch round and saw that they were in yet another dark space, a windowless room. The torch lit up an old wooden desk in the corner.

From the top drawer of the desk Juan produced a little cap similar to the one that Josef had worn in the synagogue. He put it on his head and then took out a thin length of material, a fragile yellow-grey piece of silk with blue markings and fringes. This he arranged carefully like a shawl over his shoulder.

"It is a prayer shawl, known as a *tallis*." Tenderly he bunched the tassels in his hands. "And as it is Friday afternoon and we are nearing the Sabbath ..." He muttered a prayer and kissed the fringes. And then he draped the shawl over his shoulders and faced the wall. He bowed and rocked back and forth slowly and proceeded to chant softly in the Hebrew that Kate had heard before. She caught some of the sounds of the words … "*Boruch atah Adonai Alohiynu melech haaolom …*"

The words were familiar. Was it from Josef in Toledo she'd heard them or had she learnt them in a cellar long ago, somewhere else? When he'd finished, Juan removed the shawl and handed it to her.

She placed the torch on top of the desk and took it from him. She stroked the silk between her fingers, pressing it against her cheek. The torchlight revealed the thinning, intense fragility of the material.

"Juan, what were you reciting?"

"I was praying to God who commended us to wear fringes. And I also prayed for a peaceful and blessed Sabbath."

"Why do you do this?"

"When I am anxious about a particular thing, I pray to Dios and Our Saviour Jesus Christ in my church in the *pueblo*. And if things are going tough, not getting better, then I come up here to be on my own."

"And you can speak Hebrew."

"As you see, a little. I can pray in the old Jewish way. When I put the shawl round me, I feel different, as if I'm in a different place. All the earthly problems are left behind me."

"Juan, that's so beautiful." Her eyes filled with tears and she touched his arm gently.

"My father taught me and his father before him, and so on back into the past. It has to be very secret, that is why it is hidden so carefully."

"So you do have Jewish blood in you."

"Hush." Even in their cave within a cave by a crumbling house, Juan was nervous. "As I said to you

400

before, with many in Andalucìa, it's the same. Each generation grew further away from the original, but part of that genetic strain is there, within the descendants. How many thousands of the Spanish do you think have Jewish or Moorish blood? I can meet somebody and I know straightaway if we are on the same wave-length. And probably come from the same background."

"Like you and me?"

"Yes Kate, exactly. The link cannot be proved except perhaps by genetic testing, but the instinct tells you it is so. We will never know the truth except what we have here. Here the past has kept itself alive."

"Would you ever consider converting to Judaism?"

"I don't think so. I have been brought up as a Catholic, we leave it as it is." Juan took the shawl from her. With great care he folded it and replaced it in the drawer with the yarmulke. Kate watched as he closed the drawer firmly and locked it.

"Why did you react so strongly when I talked about Cordoba?" she asked.

"It's impossible to trace exactly back and back. My family has lived here in these mountains for centuries. My uncle tried to do the research but he came to a stop about five, six generations ago. We do know from what our grandparents said and their grandparents told them, that the family originally came from Cordoba a long time ago. There was trouble and they had to leave. We would have been assimilated New Christians by then."

"The *conversos* were ordered to leave Cordoba in the fifteenth century," she murmured.

"It is remarkable that you should know so much

401

about this."

"I've read the history recently. I want to believe that my family also came from Cordoba. But there is no way of finding out."

"Correct. But it is possible. The *conversos* and the Jews who left Spain after the Inquisition spread all over Europe. In later centuries, they went also to England."

"They might even have ended up in Manchester, my home town."

"That is also possible."

"So I may be Jewish even if I don't know it," she said, quoting Josef from Toledo. Juan had amazed her today and she had a surprise for him. She opened up her rucksack and produced the silver candlestick.

"Kate, that is so good." Juan beamed with delight. "I thought you might bring it. May I see it again please?" He took a pair of eye-glasses out of his pocket and put them on. She passed the candlestick over to him and he held it up to the torchlight. She hung over his shoulder as he peered closely at the markings.

"Yes, I can recognise the writing as Hebrew but I am not able to make it out. I know how to say a few prayers in Hebrew, that is all. I could not learn to read, we had no books, and who was to teach me?"

"I've been told that the words could relate to a wedding blessing."

Juan nodded his head. "*Sí*, it could be so."

"Look." She pointed to the interwoven initials at the bottom of the stem. "I think they are initials."

Juan took a closer look. "I believe you are right."

"Can you make out what they are?"

"It is difficult, they are so old."

"The initials could possibly be an 'A' and a 'P'? What do you think?"

"Let me see." He examined the engravings again. "Why yes, it is so. How clever of you, Kate." He stroked the candlestick lovingly and placed it on the desktop. "And now I show you." Juan put his glasses away and stooped down. "Something else was brought from Cordoba when the family fled." He unlocked and opened the bottom door of the desk and brought out an object wrapped in old cloth. He removed the cloth to reveal a silver candlestick with its slim delicate stem and round base. For a full minute they remained still and silent in the presence of the two of them.

"Well, Kate?"

She picked up his candlestick with immense care. Juan trained the light on it as she studied the markings. They were identical to the markings on hers. He put his head close and together they traced the same entwined initials, 'A' and 'P' on the stem.

"I wonder what their names were."

"Ana and Pedro," she told him.

He looked at her questioningly. "You think so?"

"I know so."

Juan placed his candlestick next to Kate's on top of the desk. They seemed to shine brightly, lighting up the room.

"This is what I've been looking for in your shop since I first came to the *pueblo*," whispered Kate.

"I think they should be together now," he whispered back.

403

"That is what Ana wanted. And did you know, the two candlesticks are used by the woman of the house to make a blessing on Sabbath nights. Like this!" Kate jumped up and spontaneously made the hand movements over them that she'd performed in the regression therapy – as Ana had learnt, hidden in the family cellar centuries ago.

"But you must have Jewish blood if you know how to do that. And let me correct you a little, this is how I saw my mother and grandmother do it." He stood beside her and moved her palms towards the candlesticks and back, in the flowing gestures that had been performed for centuries.

"That is right," he said. "*Shabbat shalom*. It is Friday evening, a little early, I know. A peaceful and blessed Sabbath."

Ana's face shone out of the base of her candlestick with her joy and thanks. Kate stretched out her hands and her fingers touched Ana's against the cold silver. There was peace now. The spirit of happy Ana faded. Kate wouldn't see her again. Juan smiled at her with Pedro's smile as he took her in his arms. It was like the first and the last time.

CHAPTER THIRTY-NINE

Uncle Roger and Aunt Susan came to Marbella for three weeks to escape the Manchester winter and drove up to the *pueblo* to visit. As Auntie rested after the twists and turns of mountain roads, Kate settled Uncle down with a large whiskey and hot water.

"So did you get yourself to Cordoba, Kate?"

"Yes I did. And please may I ask you a little about the past?"

"Fire away."

"I was wondering, was there anything about your childhood that had any links with any unusual practices?"

Uncle Roger regarded Kate with amusement. "We weren't cannibals if that's what you mean, my dear. You'll have to be more specific."

"I know it sounds silly, but when you were young, did you ever put a clean shirt on for Friday nights?"

"Well yes, I suppose I must have done, like my father and grandfather did before me. I still do, in fact." But then Uncle went and spoilt the link. "And so did most of the men in our street."

"Do you know how long our family have lived in Manchester?"

"Stop, Kate, you're going too fast." She waited. Tiny beads of perspiration gathered on Uncle's forehead. It could have been the effort of concentration or the alcohol. "Now that's a tricky one. The family were in the census of nineteen hundred and one, I do know that. Johnny did me a copy from the Internet. But before that, who knows? Anything else?"

"Were there any special ornaments about your Grandma's house that had any religious or Spanish feel to them?"

"Not a thing out of the ordinary. There were the usual family photographs and chinaware, mostly little china dogs and ladies with frilled pantaloons. My grandmother loved Victorian ornaments."

"Talking of ornaments, do you like my candlesticks?" She pointed to them, standing together on a wooden table. Under a little gentle pressure, Juan had agreed that it was safe for her to display them there.

"Very interesting," murmured Uncle Roger, downing his drink.

"And see what I can do!" Kate danced over to the candlesticks and carefully performed the hand and arm movements of the Sabbath blessing over the candlesticks. Juan had helped her perfect the ritual and it was now part of her. Concentrating, she turned her hands out towards the candles and then in towards her face and kissed them three times.

Uncle Roger was watching her intently. At last she'd got his full attention.

"Do you know, Kate, when I was a little boy, I saw my grandmother doing that after she'd lit the candles."

"What!"

"Another whiskey my dear, and then we must go."

EPILOGUE

Juan drove the camper van in through the wide entrance. It was a couple of weeks before Easter and the campsite, up in the hills above Cordoba, was practically empty. They pitched amidst pine trees. Juan let down the steps and plugged in the hook-up for electricity while Kate got out the folding chairs and opened them up in a warm patch of sunshine. Blanca sat impassively on the step. This was their weekend off. Kate worked in Juan's shop part-time and taught English at the primary school in her *pueblo*.

It was crunchy underfoot with nests of pine needles and cones. The smell of pine filled the clear air. The toilets were miles away, it would be scary to visit them at night even with a torch. They might meet wolves. Or a puma.

They took the signposted walk round the hills and were in a mist of flowers, wild lavender, camellia, white petals with black-eyed dots. She performed t'ai chi in a sunny evening glade while Juan sat outside reading his book and listening to classical music. Kate was home now.